EXILE'S VALOR

A NOVEL OF VALDEMAR

MERCEDES LACKEY

DAW BOOKS, INC.

DONALD A. WOLLHEIM, FOUNDER

375 Hudson Street, New York, NY 10014

**ELIZABETH R. WOLLHEIM
SHEILA E. GILBERT
PUBLISHERS**

http://www.dawbooks.com

First Printing, October 2003
1   2   3   4   5   6   7   8   9

DAW TRADEMARK REGISTERED
U.S. PAT. OFF. AND FOREIGN COUNTRIES
—MARCA REGISTRADA
HECHO EN U.S.A.

PRINTED IN THE U.S.A.

Dedicated to the members of the FDNY, lost 9/11/01

Engine 1: Andrew Desperito; Michael Weinberg

Engine 4: Calixto Anaya Jr.; James Riches; Thomas Schoales; Paul Tegtmeier

Engine 5: Manuel Delvalle

Engine 6: Paul Beyer; Thomas Holohan; William Johnston

Engine 8: Robert Parro

Engine 10: Gregg Atlas; Jeffrey Olsen; Paul Pansini

Engine 21: William Burke, Jr.

Engine 22: Thomas Casoria: Michael Elferis; Vincent Kane; Martin McWilliams

Engine 23: Robert McPadden; James Pappageorge; Hector Tirado, Jr.; Mark Whitford

Engine 26: Thomas Farino; Dana Hannon

Engine 33: Kevin Pfeifer; David Arce; Michael Boyle; Robert Evans; Robert King, Jr.; Keithroy Maynard

Engine 37: John Giordano

Engine 40: John Ginley; Kevin Bracken; Michael Dauria; Bruce Gary; Michael Dauria; Michael Lynch; Steve Mercado

Engine 50: Robert Spear, Jr.

Engine 54: Paul Gill; Jose Guadalupe; Leonard Ragaglia; Christopher Santora

Engine 55: Peter Freund; Robert Lane; Christopher Mozzillo; Stephen Russell

Engine 58: Robert Nagel

Engine 74: Ruben Correa

Engine 201: Paul Martini; Greg Buck; Christopher Pickford; John Schardt

Engine 205; Robert Wallace

Engine 207: Karl Joseph; Shawn Powell; Kevin Reilly

Engine 214: Carl Bedigian; John Florio; Michael Roberts; Kenneth Watson

Engine 216: Daniel Suhr

Engine 217: Kenneth Phelan; Steven Coakley; Philip T. Hayes (Retired); Neil Leavy

Engine 219: John Chipura

Engine 226: David DeRubbio; Brian McAleese; Stanley Smagala, Jr.

Engine 230: Brian Ahearn; Frank Bonomo; Michael Carlo; Jeffrey Stark; Eugene Whelan; Edward White

Engine 235: Steven Bates; Nicholas Chiofalo; Francis Esposito; Lee Fehling; Lawrence Veling

Engine 238: Glenn Wilkinson

Engine 279: Ronnie Henderson; Michael Ragusa; Anthony Rodriguez

Engine 285: Raymond York

Engine 320: James J. Corrigan (Retired)

OFFICIAL TIMELINE FOR THE

by Mercedes Lackey

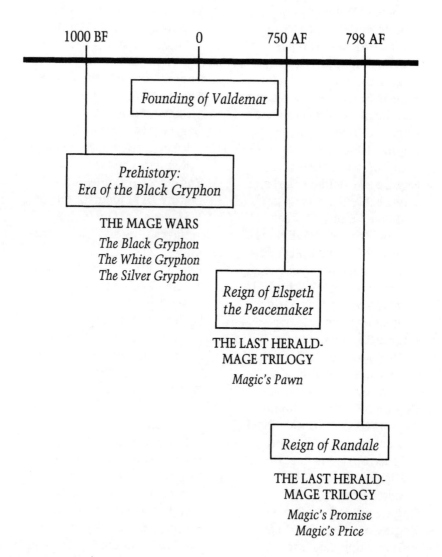

1000 BF   0   750 AF   798 AF

Founding of Valdemar

Prehistory:
Era of the Black Gryphon

THE MAGE WARS

The Black Gryphon
The White Gryphon
The Silver Gryphon

Reign of Elspeth
the Peacemaker

**THE LAST HERALD-
MAGE TRILOGY**

Magic's Pawn

Reign of Randale

**THE LAST HERALD-
MAGE TRILOGY**

Magic's Promise
Magic's Price

BF   *Before the Founding*
AF   *After the Founding*

HERALDS OF VALDEMAR SERIES

Sequence of events by Valdemar reckoning

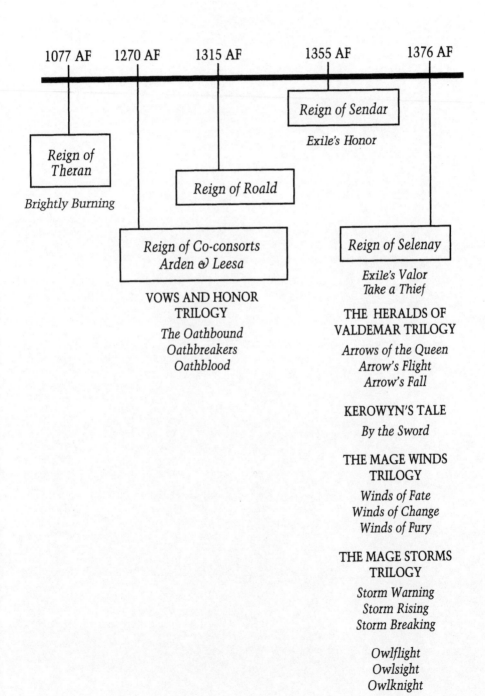

1077 AF   1270 AF   1315 AF   1355 AF   1376 AF

Reign of Sendar

Exile's Honor

Reign of Theran

Brightly Burning

Reign of Roald

Reign of Co-consorts Arden & Leesa

VOWS AND HONOR TRILOGY

The Oathbound
Oathbreakers
Oathblood

Reign of Selenay

Exile's Valor
Take a Thief

THE HERALDS OF VALDEMAR TRILOGY

Arrows of the Queen
Arrow's Flight
Arrow's Fall

KEROWYN'S TALE

By the Sword

THE MAGE WINDS TRILOGY

Winds of Fate
Winds of Change
Winds of Fury

THE MAGE STORMS TRILOGY

Storm Warning
Storm Rising
Storm Breaking

Owlflight
Owlsight
Owlknight

EXILE'S VALOR

MUTED light, richly colored, poured gold and sapphire into the sparsely-furnished sitting room in Herald Alberich's private quarters behind the training salle.

Now that the colored window was installed, and the protective blanket taken off, it made that little room look entirely different. Alberich hardly recognized it.

The four Journeymen glass workers who had helped their Master install the piece were gone now, leaving Alberich alone with the artist himself.

Both of them gazed on the finished product in silence, while behind them a warm fire crackled on the hearth. It was a staggeringly beautiful piece of stained-glass work; in fact, Alberich thought, it would not be exaggerating to say it was a masterpiece. Not that he had expected less than a fine piece from the Master of the Glassworkers Guild, but this was over and above those expectations.

The artisan responsible for its creation stepped forward and gave the top right-hand corner a final polish with a soft cloth,

1

removing some smudge not visible to ordinary eyes. He flicked off an equally invisible dust mote as well, and stepped back to view the expanse of blues and golds with a critical eye. A man gone gray in his profession, he was tall, but not powerful, with wiry, knotty muscles rather than bulging ones. His expression was unreadable, a square-jawed, hook-nosed fellow whose face might have been stone rather than flesh.

"It'll do," he grunted finally, his long face betraying nothing but a flicker of content.

"A work of power and beauty, it is," Alberich replied, unusual warmth of feeling in his voice. "It is exceeding my expectations, which were high already. Your skill is formidable, Master Cuelin."

"It'll do," the artisan repeated, but with just a touch more satisfaction in his own voice. "I'll not praise myself, but it'll do."

This was such understatement that Alberich shook his head. In so many ways, this was a piece of artwork that went far, far beyond even the monumental works that only the great and wealthy could afford, be they individuals or organizations. It was the care to every detail, as much as the design, that showed that expertise. For instance, to protect the fragile leaded glass, made up of pieces no larger than a coin, the panel had been installed against the existing window. Now, the bars holding those old panes in place *could* have cast distracting lines across the new pattern—except that Master Cuelin had taken that into account in his design, and the shadows had been integrated in such a way that unless you looked for them, you did not notice them.

Yet Master Cuelin seemed no more than mildly pleased that everything had worked out as he had planned. Alberich knew that tone; not only from working with Master Cuelin on this window, but from working with others who shared the same obsessive drive to excellence that marked the man's work. No point in heaping him with effusive praise, for it would only make him uncomfortable, and he would begin to point out "flaws" in the work not visible to anyone but him.

"Very happy, you have made me," he said instead. "Never shall I weary of this piece." And although he had paid Master Cuelin already, when he shook the man's hands in thanks, a heavy little purse that had been in his hand slipped quietly into the Master's. That was the way of doing business, in Karse, when one was pleased with special work. Some things, Alberich felt, were probably universal—an extra "consideration" for work that exceeded expectation being one of them.

Evidently the custom held true in Valdemar, because Master Cuelin did not seem in the least surprised; he said nothing, only pocketed the purse with a nod of thanks. He dusted off his hands on the side of his brown leather tunic—all of his clothing, tunic, breeches, even his shirt, was leather, because leather wasn't likely to catch fire.

"Well, if you're that satisfied, Herald Alberich, I'll be off," the Glassmaster said. "I've that lazy lot of 'prentices to beat back at my studio, for no doubt they'll have ruined the cobalt plate I laid out for them to cut for the new 'Pothecary Guild window, aye, and muddled the designs I set them to copy, and complain I've assigned them too much work."

Alberich shook his head, in mock sadness. "It is ever so," he agreed, and sighed. "The younger generation—"

"We were never like that, eh?" Master Cuelin barked a laugh and slapped Alberich's back. The Weaponsmaster allowed a hint of a smile to show, and the Glassmaster winked. "Well, 'tis heavy work we have before us—you know what the old saw is, 'A boy's ears are on his backside, he heeds better when he's beaten!'"

Since there was nearly the identical saying in Karse, Alberich nodded, and with another exchange of pleasantries, he escorted the Glassmaster out. Indeed, some things were universal.

But since it was not yet time for the next class of Heraldic

Trainees to arrive for their weapons' training, he returned to his sitting room in the back of the training salle to admire his newly installed possession once more.

This was more than mere ornament; while there was a Temple of Vkandis Sunlord down in Haven proper—though for obvious reasons, it was referred to even by Karsite exiles as "the Temple of the Lord of Light"—Alberich seldom was able to get there for the daylight ceremonies. Certainly he was never able to arrive for the all-important SunRising rite.

Contrary to what the current Karsite priesthood wished their followers to think, it was very clear in the Writ—now that Alberich had seen copies of the old, original versions—that any follower of the Sunlord could perform the rites, with or without a sunpriest. It was what was in the heart, not the words, that mattered, and prayerful meditation at any time was appropriate. And now Alberich had an image here, a proper image, that would put him in the proper frame of mind.

There had been a plain glass window here, but the presence of such an expanse of clear glass had made Alberich, on reflection, rather uneasy. It was fine for the former Weapons-master, Herald Dethor, to have such a thing, but Dethor didn't have to think about potential Karsite assassins peering through it—or the far more common, but equally annoying habits of the young, idle, and foolish offspring of Valdemaran nobles daring each other to spy on the dreaded Weaponsmas-ter from Karse. Not that they'd see anything except Alberich reading, pacing, or staring at the fire, or occasionally enter-taining a visitor, but it made him irritated to think of them watching him. It wasted their time, annoyed the Companions, and made the back of his neck prickle for no good reason. If he sensed someone watching him, he wanted to know there was danger, not adolescent curiosity behind it.

But he hadn't wanted to block off the window either. Very useful light came in there by day, although the view was noth-ing spectacular, just one of the groves of Companion's Field. It had been Herald Elcarth who had suggested the stained-glass panel when he had mentioned the annoyance of looking up to see lurkers in the bushes one night.

It had nearly been *former* lurkers in the bushes, and it was a good thing for them that he had Kantor out there to warn him it was only some Unaffiliates and a Bardic Trainee, because his hand had been on the one-handed crossbow he kept under the table, and he had no problem with shooting out a window. Especially not his own window. A bit of broken glass was a small price to pay for your life.

He hadn't mentioned that to Elcarth, however, though he *thought* he saw some understanding in the other's nod. Perhaps that was why the Herald had suggested the stained-glass panel. And at that moment, Alberich had realized how he could bring a kind of Vkandis chapel into his own home, make this place truly *his* home, and solve that problem of the huge window in a single stroke.

Elcarth hadn't known where to obtain such a thing, but Herald Jadus had. In fact, Jadus had pointed him to the particular glassworks involved in creating most of the stained- and etched-glass windows for the various Temples in and around Haven, whenever a generous patron was moved to donate such a thing.

Until he went to the workshop and saw some of the designs, Alberich hadn't been entirely certain of the exact shape and image of the design, only that it should have some link, somehow, to the Temples that he had felt most comfortable in. As soon as he realized what Cuelin specialized in, heraldic (rather than Heraldic) designs, he had realized what his window surely must show.

The Sun-In-Glory of the God of Karse, of course; Vkandis Sunlord in a form that few in Valdemar would recognize as such, and no one who mattered would likely take offense to. Particularly as *this* Sun-In-Glory would be laid out, not on the usual field of reds as in a similar window in Karse, but on a field of Heraldic blue.

If Master Cuelin realized just what the pattern was, he hadn't said anything. Alberich would not have wagered on his being ignorant, though. He had been doing religious glass-work for far too long not to have learned virtually every symbol of every deity worshiped in Haven, and every possible variation and nuance of each symbol. Vkandis *was* worshiped here, and by Karsite exiles—just not under that name. The "Lord of Light" was what He was called here; all things considered, a title and a name less likely to evoke hostility from the good neighbors of those exiles.

Alberich would not have taken it much amiss had Master Cuelin delegated the work to his apprentices either—but he hadn't. He'd attended to it all himself. And the result was glorious, well worth the cost of the one indulgence that Alberich had permitted himself since he'd been made Weaponsmaster.

:*Very nice for us, too,*: his Companion Kantor commented, as Alberich sat down and allowed himself to drink in the color and composition. :*We get the best view of it at night, when the light is coming from inside. Clever of you to station lanterns with reflectors shining outward at the bottom corners. Gives us a lovely piece to look at.*:

:*And prevents any shadows falling upon it and telling people what goes on in my sitting room,*: he pointed out. :*After paying no small fortune for such a piece, I've no mind to have it shattered by an ill-considered crossbow bolt from outside, because I was foolish enough to show a target.*:

Since there was no graceful reply to that, Kantor wisely declined to make one.

The leaded glass was thicker and heavier than the window it had been mounted against, and Alberich realized after a moment of sitting there that the drafts he'd become accustomed to were gone. Well! An unforeseen advantage!

And a third—as he bathed in the golden light from the Sun-

In-Glory, despite the fact that on the other side of the glass, there was a bleak winter landscape under overcast skies, he understood *why* Master Cuelin had insisted that the Sun dominate the panel. No matter what the weather outside, the light coming in would be warm and welcoming. Already Alberich felt his spirits become a little lighter.

:*For which my gratitude to Master Cuelin knows no bounds,*: Kantor observed dryly. :*Anything that sweetens your temper makes me grateful.*:

:*Indeed?*: Alberich countered. :*Alas, that he cannot do me the return favor of creating such a thing for you, since you spend your days out of doors. Perhaps I should query Bardic Collegium about the possibility of serenading you on a thrice-weekly basis to sweeten* your *temper?*:

:*Then who would chastise the greenlings properly?*: Kantor asked airily. :*Disciplining the youngsters requires a certain acidity of temper to deliver correction with the appropriate degree of sting.*:

Alberich shook his head. He should learn never to try and exchange barbs with his Companion; Kantor would always win. Kantor was at least as old as his Chosen, probably a few years Alberich's senior, and twice as witty.

Not that there wasn't some truth in what Kantor said; Kantor was to the young Companions what Alberich was to the Heraldic Trainees, in a way. Not so much the trainer in fighting technique, for a great deal of *that* was in the hands of the riding instructors, but as the disciplinarian of the Companion herd. Normally that would be in the hands—or rather, authority, backed by speech, and occasionally hooves and teeth—of the Companion to the Queen's Own Herald, the Grove-Born Rolan. But Rolan's Herald was Queen's Own Talamir, who had very nearly died in the last battle with the Tedrels on the Border with Karse; Talamir's original Companion Taver *had* died, and one never spent much time in Talamir's presence without realizing that in many ways it had been no great service to

Talamir that he had been brought back to life again. Though Kantor had never said as much in so many words, Alberich got the distinct impression that most of Rolan's time was taken up in making sure that Talamir remained—well—*sane.* So a good portion of Rolan's duties to the herd had been delegated to those best suited to the task.

Not all of those duties had gone to Kantor either. Some were the provenance of some very wise old Companion mares, thus ironically echoing the hierarchy in a real horse herd, where the leaders were the oldest mares, not the stallion, as Alberich very well knew.

:Hmm. And human herds, though ye know it not.:

:Your point being—?: Alberich replied. *:Though you'd best not let Queen Selenay discover you think of her as an old mare, wise or not.:*

He sensed Kantor's snort of derision. *:Selenay should be perfectly happy to be compared to a Companion mare.:*

Alberich let that one go. There was no use trying to explain to Kantor that no nubile young woman was going to appreciate being compared to a mare, ever, under any circumstances.

Particularly not when her Councilors—some of them, anyway—were very diligently trying to make her into one. Of the brood-stock variety. . . .

Which was one reason why he had welcomed Master Cuelin's arrival this afternoon to install the window, as the perfect excuse to avoid the afternoon Council meeting. *That* particular item was on the table for discussion, and it was a subject that Alberich was particularly anxious not to get embroiled in. For one thing, no matter how publicly he'd been lauded and laden with honors after the Tedrel Wars, no matter how trusted he was by most—by no means all—Valdemarans of note, he was still the outsider. He was, and always would be so. It could not be otherwise. And for another, well—

—well, it was a subject where nothing he said or did was "safe." Someone would take exception, whether he urged that

Selenay remain single, or weighed in on the side of those who wanted her to wed, and at this point, he didn't need to add any enemies to a list that was already long enough.

The atmosphere of the Council Chamber this afternoon was unwontedly subdued. Usually there had been at least three arguments by this time, and the kinds of icy, polite catcalling that made people who were not used to Council debates blanch and wonder if a duel was about to break out. Today, however, was different. The atmosphere hadn't been so edgily cordial since the first, tentative sessions after Selenay's coronation. Around the horseshoe-shaped, heavy wooden table not a voice had been raised. The representatives of the Bardic, Heraldic, and Healer Circles, in their red, white, and green uniforms respectively, had been extremely quiet, as had the Lord Marshal's Herald and the Seneschal's Herald, and of course, her own, the Queen's Own Herald, Talamir.

As for the rest—well, they had been nervous. They didn't really know her, although she had been in their midst all of her life. They were her father's Council, really, not hers. They were his friends, advisers, and peers, and none of them had expected to serve her at all, much less so quickly. So they often argued and battled among themselves, as if she wasn't even there, or was no more than a token place holder.

Except on the rare occasions when what they wished to do was going to have to involve her. Then they generally acted as they did today; becoming very quiet, and rather nervous. These elder statesmen and women were apparently unaware that they gave themselves away, acting as they did.

Queen Selenay knew why they were nervous, of course. They didn't know she knew, which might have been funny under other circumstances. In the throne that had been her father's, with the chair at her right hand empty, Selenay watched her Councilors behaving as if they were good little schoolchildren debating beneath the strict disciplinarian eye of their teacher.

This was, of course, because they were shortly going to unite in a totally uncharacteristic burst of single-mindedness and do their level best to force their Queen to do something she had no intention of doing whatsoever.

Marry. Worse than that, to marry someone *they,* not she, had chosen. The potential candidates were as sad a collection as nightmare could have conjured. The youngest was ten, the oldest ninety. Among them were a number of young men, but even these were impossible. Some she had heartily detested from the moment she'd met them, others she didn't even know, and from their reputations, had no desire to know. A very few might be reasonable fellows, some were pleasant enough company on a casual basis, but that was no reason to marry any of them. Some were even Heralds, or at least, Trainees—but the Heralds all had lives of their own that she was not a part of, and as for Trainees—well, they seemed like mere infants to her now.

Her Councilors, however, did not see it that way.

It hadn't been like this when her father had sat in this throne, but Sendar had *ruled* as well as reigned. She reigned, but only the backing of the Heralds made it possible for her to command much of anything. She knew that; she had expected it from the moment she took the Crown. She was much too young to be a Queen, much too young to command the respect of men and women old enough to be her parents. Not even the white uniform proclaiming her a full Herald managed to gain her that respect.

Well, there were ways around that. But she was getting weary of the artful dodges, of setting her words in the mouths of others, and she had not even reigned a year. And these marriage plans were more than a mere inconvenience; they were an attack on her autonomy. Her good Councilors would not be happy with a mere Prince Consort. They wanted a King.

She tapped her index finger idly on the stack of papers just under her right hand, and smiled a grim little smile. Her Councilors—the non-Heraldic ones, anyway—were not aware that she had come prepared for this afternoon's meeting. She knew what every man and woman around the table was about to put forward, for not all of them had been close-mouthed about it, and Talamir had gotten wind of it and let her know what was planned. That had given her ample time to prepare for what they were about to unleash on her. They had no idea that she had come forewarned and forearmed.

For that matter, other than Talamir and Elcarth, she wasn't sure the other Heralds at the Council table were aware that she'd been engaged in laying the groundwork to defend her freedom.

It was nothing less that she had done, for her Councilors were determined that she should not reign alone—and each and every one of them had a particular candidate to place in the running, sometimes more than one. All of them, of course, with the best interests of the Kingdom foremost in their minds, or so, at least, they would tell themselves. Of course, every candidate would have blood ties or ties of obligation to the Councilor who put him forward, but never mind that. They would put such things out of their minds, telling themselves that they were doing this for Valdemar, and not for any selfish reasons. *There was no Heir! Selenay had been an only child, and the Crown now rested on her fragile head alone! She must marry, and produce children, quickly!*

Of course, if the chosen spouse happened to be helpful to friends and families, well. . . .

Every one of them had given over whatever disputes they had to settle on that list of potential Consorts, arguing and trading without any consideration for what *she* wanted, until they had mutually agreed on enough men that if they couldn't bully her into taking one, they could wear her down until she agreed out of exhaustion.

When Talamir told her what the plans were, Selenay had gone straight to Herald-Chronicler-Second Myste, who was surely the only person in Haven who had the esoteric knowledge to help her out of the trap. And although she had not really expected a great deal of sympathy from Myste, the Herald had amazed her by reacting with indignation to the plans.

"By Keronos!" Myste had exclaimed, her eyes behind the thick lenses of her spectacles going narrow with speculation. "That's obscene! You haven't been Queen a year, girl! Shouldn't they at least wait until you've settled, and gotten comfortable with your place?"

"Apparently not," Selenay had replied, seething with anger. "And apparently none of them want to see a foreigner brought in as Consort either—or at least, they don't seem to have taken much thought about that particular possibility. Insane, I'd call it. Not that I particularly *want* a foreign Consort, but Father used to have serious talks with me about the possibility of needing to cement a foreign alliance with a marriage."

"Idiots," Myste had muttered under her breath, pushing her lenses up on her nose. "The hand of a Queen's too damned valuable to waste. What if, as your father said, we need an alliance?"

"What if we just need to keep five or six princes dangling on promises?" Selenay had countered. "And besides—"

She didn't add the "besides," which was that she wanted to be able to love her husband, not merely tolerate being in the same room with him. Myste probably guessed it, for she'd given Selenay a shrewd look, but she hadn't said anything, except: "Well, if they haven't got the sense to see past their own interests, it's up to some of the rest of us to see to it that they can't meddle."

And Myste had outdone herself on the Queen's behalf, spending every spare moment locked away with dusty law and record books going back generations. The result was the pile of neatly-written papers under Selenay's hand.

Aside from the two exceptions of Talamir and Elcarth, there wasn't a single person around the Council table that had the slightest inkling that they were about to see what Selenay could do when she was *not* in a mood of sweet cooperation. In point of fact, no matter who was brought up, the various candidates for potential spouse were going to be mown down like so many stands of ripened grain. . . .

Myste had not even told Alberich; she had sworn herself to secrecy before Selenay had even asked. There was no tighter-lipped creature in Valdemar than Myste when she opted to take that particular path.

It's too bad Alberich isn't here, Selenay thought, still tapping. *He might enjoy watching me dispose of this idiocy.* She missed his craggy, scarred face at the table today; although he did not have an official position on the Council, as Talamir's right-hand man (and in no small part, hers as well), he could and did sit in on it whenever he chose. When he did, he usually took Elcarth's seat as the representative of the Heraldic Circle. The Weaponsmaster knew of the plans, of course, though not how she intended to counter them. And she thought that he would take great pleasure in how she was going to discomfit them all.

Or maybe not. In Selenay's limited experience, a confirmed bachelor like Alberich had a tendency to panic when confronted by the question of potential matrimony, regardless of whether it was his or someone else's.

Besides, he's probably concerned that if I flatten every other possible consort, someone will suggest him as an alternative. The mere thought made her stifle a smile. While the Heralds would welcome the idea, and possibly even the Bard and Healer would as well, the rest of her Councilors would have apoplexy. They'd suggest she take an illiterate fisherman from Lake Evendim before they suggested Alberich. Not that she'd mind an illiterate fisherman from Lake Evendim half so much as she disliked some of the so-called "candidates" for her hand her Councilors were going to suggest.

The Councilors had been well aware from the moment they started their plotting that this was a subject their Queen was *not* going to entertain gladly, which was why they were intending to surprise her with it, in hopes of taking her off guard.

As they disposed of some final trivial business, they kept glancing at her out of the corners of their eyes, and there was a certain nervous tone to their voices that would have been amusing if she had not been so very angry with them. Her father had not been dead a year, and already they were at her to marry! As if she could not rule by herself, or at the very least, rule with the true counsel of those who were loyal to her (and not merely devoted to their own interests), and rule well and wisely!

:You can rule with more wisdom than some of their choices,: her Companion Caryo said into her mind. *:Not that some of their choices would be allowed to rule at all. They wouldn't be Chosen by a Companion if every living male in Valdemar were to drop dead this moment.:*

A stinging indictment indeed, coming from Caryo.

And there was the real rub. What some of her Councilors seemed to keep forgetting was that any husband she took would be nothing more than Prince Consort unless he was also a Herald. Only *then* could he be a co-ruler.

Of course, they probably assumed that a young woman would be easily led by her husband to give him whatever he wanted, which would certainly make him the power behind the throne, if not an actual monarch. Some of them probably assumed that she could *make* a Companion Choose him, if she wanted it badly enough.

:The more fools they,: said Caryo.

:Well, they have a poor opinion of how strong a woman's

will can be.: Selenay reflected, as she gathered her nerve, that it was a very good thing that Caryo was of a mind with her. It would be great deal easier to resist both bullying and blandishment with Caryo behind her.

:And don't forget, you have Myste, too,: Caryo reminded her.

Yes, indeed. Myste, her secret weapon, who not only had supplied her with this vast and intricate report, but was currently mewed up in the library with every book of Valdemaran genealogy in Haven at her fingertips, and a page to bring her whatever she needed for as long as this meeting lasted. No, her Councilors surely could never have reckoned on Myste.

The last of the minor business was disposed of. The Councilors put up their papers, some of them poured themselves wine, and there was a great deal of coughing and shuffling of feet. Then, as she expected, really, it was Lord Gartheser, more portly now than he had been before the Tedrel Wars, and more florid of face, who cleared his throat awkwardly and put the subject on the table.

"About the matter of Your Majesty's marriage—" he said, and stopped.

Selenay smiled sweetly, a smile that went no farther than her lips, as she looked down each side of the horseshoe-shaped table before she allowed her eyes to rest on Gartheser.

He makes a poor conspirator, she thought. It was from him that Talamir had learned what was toward, though Gartheser himself was probably completely unaware that he had betrayed anything. But he gave himself away, according to Talamir, in a hundred ways, by little nervous tics, by being unable to meet a person's eyes, by dropping far too many hints when he was satisfied with himself. At that point, both Talamir and Alberich had gone to work, and no secret was secure when those two were ferreting it out.

Though it occurred to her that Talamir had probably not done nearly as much work as Alberich. Talamir's sympathy was probably at least in part with the Council. Well, give credit where it was due; he *had* told her in the first place.

"My marriage?" she asked, in feigned innocence. "I wasn't aware I had been betrothed, much less that there was a marriage in view. Certainly King Sendar never said anything of the sort to me."

"Ah, well, Your Majesty, that's the whole point," Gartheser managed. "You haven't one, you see. Betrothed, that is."

She took her time and looked carefully around the horseshoe-shaped table again, making sure to look each one of her Councilors steadily in the eyes. The silence was deafening. No one moved. "Indeed."

"And you—that is, we thought—that is—" Gartheser couldn't look her in the eyes anymore. He dropped his gaze and stared at his hands, and stumbled to a halt.

"We have some candidates in mind, Selenay," Lord Orthallen took up the thread smoothly. Orthallen looked the part of the senior statesman; he had retained a fine figure, and the silver streaking in his dark blond hair in no way detracted from his handsome appearance. Women younger than Selenay threw themselves at him on a regular basis, though she had never heard so much as a whisper to indicate that he was unfaithful to his wife. "You really must marry as soon as may be, of course. A young woman cannot rule alone."

"Indeed," she said levelly, hiding her rage with immense care. She wanted to scream at them, then burst into tears, and nothing could be more fatal at this moment.

But the others took that lack of objection on her part as the signal that she was going to be properly malleable, and took heart from it. Only Elcarth and Talamir understood that Selenay had her own plans. Elcarth winced a little at her tone; Talamir's lips quirked, just a trifle.

"The first, and indeed, the most eligible candidate is my nephew Rannulf," Gartheser said brightly, "who—"

"Is not eligible at all, I'm afraid," she interrupted smoothly, with feigned regret. "He's related to me within the second degree, on his mother's side, through the Lycaelis bloodline. You know well that no King or Queen of Valdemar can wed a subject who is within the third degree of blood-relationship. That is the law, my Lord, and nothing you nor I can do will change that." She raised her eyebrows at them. "The reason is a very good one, of course. I shall be indelicate here, for there is no delicate way to say this. As my father told me often, the monarchs of Valdemar cannot afford the kinds of—difficulties—that can arise when a bloodline becomes too inbred."

And with you and yours marrying cousins and cross-cousins with the gay abandon of people blind to consequences, that's the reason half of your so-called "candidates" are dough-faced mouth-breathers who couldn't count to ten without taking their shoes off, she thought viciously.

:Harsh. With justification, but harsh,: Caryo observed sardonically.

Gartheser blinked, his mouth still open, and stared at her. Finally he shut it. "Ah," he said at last. "Oh—are you quite sure of that?"

She opened Myste's report to the relevant page. "Rannulf's mother is Lady Elena of Penderkeep. Lady Elena's mother was my father's cousin through his mother. That is within the second degree."

"Oh—" Gartheser said weakly.

"Then there is my nephew, Kris—" said Orthallen quickly.

"Related to me within the third degree on *both* sides of his family, as his mother was a cousin-by-marriage of my father, and his father was a cousin-by-blood to my father," she said briskly, already prepared for that one. "Besides being so young that there is no question of consummation for *at least* eight years." She smiled dulcetly at Orthallen. "Which does rather negate the entire reason for marrying with such remarkable speed in the first place, before my year of mourning is over. Doesn't it?"

To her great pleasure, Orthallen was left so stunned by her riposte that his handsome face wore an uncharacteristic blank look. Not that she wanted to humiliate him—she was really awfully fond of him, after all—but it gave her no end of satisfaction to make him understand, in no uncertain terms, that just because she was fond of him, she was not going to allow him to manipulate her into something she did not want to do.

And blessings upon Myste; she suspected that not even Orthallen knew about the nearness of her blood relation to his nephew. He proved it in the next moment by saying, cautiously, "I assume you have the particulars of these degrees?"

She went to the second page of Myste's notes and gave him the genealogical details, chapter and verse, in a no-nonsense, matter-of-fact tone of voice.

"Ah," he said. And wisely said nothing more.

So it went. Every single candidate that any of them brought up, she cut off at the metaphorical knees. Including the ones that she had not given Myste to research; that was why Myste was shut up in the library. She would leaf through her thick sheaf of papers to give Myste the chance to trace pedigrees, then pretend to read what Myste Sent to her.

At last they ran out of names—or at least, of names that they could all agree on. Now the daggers were out, and the looks being traded across the tabletop were wary. Any new candidates would be men and boys that had already been rejected, because one or another of the Councilors objected to them for reasons of his or her own. She could sit back and let them play against each other, which was the better position to be in.

At least, that was true among the highborn Councilors; the Guildmasters were a different story entirely. None of them—and no candidate outside of the nobility—would be related to her, which eliminated that argument.

However, she thought she could count on the highborn Councilors to fight tooth and nail against any common-born man being put up as a potential Prince Consort. There was an advantage to snobbery.

Mind, if she did happen to fall in love with a commoner, she wasn't going to let snobbery stop her—

That would open up a whole new set of problems which she wasn't going to think about right now. The current set was more than enough to deal with.

It's too bad Alberich isn't here now, she thought, letting her anger begin to die. *This is the part he'd really enjoy—watching them cut the legs out from under each other.*

Ah well. She hoped the installation of his window had gone well. She was looking forward to seeing it. It would be the only part of her day she was able to look forward to.

Why would anyone want to be a Queen?

"Oo *wouldn't* want t'be a Queen?" demanded the rather drunken tart sitting at the table next to Alberich's. "Larking about, doin' whatever ye please, gettin' waited on 'and an' foot—"

Not from Haven, thought Alberich to himself. *Though you have the accent, it isn't quite good enough, my girl. And you aren't nearly as drunk as you seem. What's your game, and who put you up to it, I wonder.*

Now perhaps, at any other time, perhaps in another year or so, she might have gotten away with such an ill-considered remark. But not now. Not when barely six months had passed, and Selenay had been making herself very popular with little gestures like the "Queen's Bread." People down here had a lot of trouble keeping their children fed, and one guaranteed free meal a day, at the trifling cost of lessons in rudimentary literacy and numeracy, was a small price to pay. A youngling down here couldn't earn the price of that breakfast himself in the course of a morning. It was good economics to send your younglings to a temple until noon, *then* put 'em to work.

" 'ere now!" a man just near enough to have overheard the speech stood up, glaring at her. "Our Selenay ain't like that, ye owd drab, an' if you was a man, I'd'a thrashed ye fer that!"

The woman shrank back, and well she should have. He was big and broad, and looked as if he knew very well how to handle that cudgel at his belt. "No offense meant, I'm very sure," she said, hastily. "I didn' mean Queen Selenay! I just meant, *a* Queen, in a gen'ral sort of way."

The man glared at her. He *was* as drunk as the whore pretended to be, and he was at the very least going to say his peace. "*Our* Selenay ain't no layabout!" he insisted. "Why, I *seen* 'er, I even *talked* to 'er, couple'a nights afore the last battle. Come right to our fires, she did, 'avin' a word with our officers, seein' we 'ad good treatment!"

"Oh, yeah, an' she talked t' you, did she, ye old liar!" jeered someone else—

Ill-advisedly.

The drunk rounded on the skeptic with a roar, and grabbed the man's shirt in one hamlike fist. Only the intervention of the "peacekeeper" that the proprietor of the Broken Arms had seen fit to hire prevented mayhem from breaking out. But there was the start of a fight, and under cover of it, the woman slipped out.

Alberich followed.

She wasn't at all difficult to follow, the silly wench. She paid absolutely no attention to what was behind her. The man she accosted just outside, the alleyway next to the tavern was a little more careful, but not enough to spot Alberich. He was a darker shadow in the alley—people always thought that wearing black would make them blend in with shadows, but it didn't; it made them into man-shaped black blotches in an *almost* black place. Alberich was wearing several shades of very, very dark brown and gray. Each leg was a slightly different color. So was each arm. And his tunic was blotched. There was nothing about him that was man-shaped, when he stood in shadow.

"I'm not doin' that no more!" the woman shrilled at her contact, just as Alberich eased within listening range. "You go do your own dirty work from now on!"

There was a murmur, too low for Alberich to make out the words.

"I didn' get but a word out," she said sullenly, "an' up jumps this drunk bear and nearly thrashes me!"

More murmuring, and the clink of coins. The woman departed, muttering.

Alberich followed the man.

There had been a lot of money exchanged there for such simple services—a lot for this part of town, at any rate. Alberich hoped that his new quarry would try another quarter, one where such a payment would be the norm rather than the exception. And lo! As if his wish had flown straight to the ear of Vkandis, that was precisely what his quarry did.

It wasn't a *wealthy* part of town; working class was more like it, but working class that got work regularly, of the sort that came with weekly pay packets and a little something extra on the holidays. A place, in short, where there were City Guards and constables on patrol regularly.

A place where Alberich could manage to do something to get them both arrested.

Which, as soon as a constable hove into view, Alberich did.

He nipped back around the corner so as to be able to intercept his quarry coming, apparently, from the opposite direction. It wasn't hard; he knew this part of Haven better than the back of his hand. There were few yards with high fences and even fewer with dangerous dogs tied up in them. Once he came back around, he saw that the constable was strolling along at a leisurely pace that would take him past his quarry before Alberich reached the man. Good. He didn't want the constable to actually *see* what was going on between him and the stranger, only *hear* it and make some inferences that, as it happened would be entirely unwarranted.

:You're enjoying this,: Kantor accused.

:Hush. I'm busy.:

The fact was, he *was* enjoying this. It was the first hint of trouble, real trouble, *his* sort of trouble, that he'd had in moons.

As he approached the man, he stared at him—easy enough to do, since there were streetlamps here. Then he contorted his face into an expression of rage and roared.

"You! You bastard! *Thought you could ruin my sister and run away, did you?"*

And then he flung himself at the startled man.

As he had expected, the man was not startled for long, and he was armed. So what the surprised constable saw when he turned was a man with a knife attacking an unarmed man. Since he couldn't know which of the two of them the accusation had come from, he assumed—as any good constable would—that the man with the knife was the attacker, not the defender.

That Alberich was in no danger from a mere knife was something he couldn't know. So, to his immense credit, he waded in himself, wielding his truncheon and blowing a whistle for dear life to summon help. He was aiming most of his blows for the head of the knife wielder, and Alberich helpfully positioned the target so that, by the time the help arrived, his quarry was out cold and he was able to protest feebly that *he* didn't know what the madman was talking about, he'd just jumped for him with a knife, screaming about a sister. . . .

"We have to stop meeting like this, Herald," said Captain Lekar of the City Guard, with a feeble attempt at humor. "People are going to start talking."

"I fervently hope not," Alberich replied, rubbing his wrists where the conscientious constables had tied them—being too wise ever to take one potential miscreant's word over another's. He warmed his hands on his cup of tea, but did not drink from it. The herbal teas consumed by the night shift of the City Guard were not drinkable, even by the standards of a former Karsite Sunsguard. "If talk they do, my personae will in danger be."

"Yes, well, I wish you'd find some other way of catching your lads without getting the both of you thrown in jail," the Captain replied wearily.

Since this was only the third time that Alberich had used that particular desperation ploy, he held his peace. "Keep him safe," was all he said. "Speak with him under Truth Spell I wish to, when he awakens."

The Captain did not ask why. The Captain did not want to know why. The Captain was an old friend of Herald Dethor, Alberich's mentor in this business, and he knew very well that he did not want to know why. And Alberich knew that he knew, and both were content with the situation.

Now, if this had been Karse— he reflected soberly, as he left the City Jail by an inconspicuous exit, making certain that there was no one to see him leave.

:If this was Karse, and you were an agent of the Sunpriests, that man would be in extreme pain for a very long time, and at the end of it, he would be dead,: Kantor said.

:He may still be dead when this is over,: Alberich replied, grimly, making his way toward the stable of the Companion's Bell. *:But if he is, at least it won't be by my hands.:*

:If he's lucky, we'll find out he's just a troublemaker.: Kantor didn't sound as if he really believed that would be the case.

Yes, and if that happened to be true, well, there was no law against speaking out—or having someone else speak out— against the Monarch. Laws like that only made for more trouble; *some* people always had to have a grievance, and making grumbling illegal was a guaranteed way of ensuring that grumbling turned into resentment, and resentment into anger. If that was the case, he'd be let go, with the vague memory of having proved he didn't know anything about anyone's sister to the satisfaction of the City Guard.

If it was not the case—

Well, there was one Herald in the Circle who had no trouble with dirtying his hands with difficult jobs. Alberich would find out who had sent this fellow down into the dark parts of Haven to foment discontent. And he would follow that trail back as far as it would go.

And the man would *still* be let go—but this time with the very clear memory of having been questioned under Truth Spell by a Herald. Chances were, he would cut and run, and hope his employers never found him. That would be convenient, because it would take the problem off of his hands.

And if he didn't run—his employers would probably take the problem off Alberich's hands a little faster.

He collected Kantor and the two of them made their way up to the Collegium—Alberich feeling the effects of the truncheon blows that *had* connected with him, and Kantor brooding. Alberich didn't press him as to the subject of his brooding; whatever it was, Kantor would talk about it when the Companion was good and ready and not one moment before.

And in fact, as Alberich hung up his saddle, Kantor finally spoke. :*I hope this doesn't mean it's all starting again.*:

Alberich sighed. :*My good friend—I hope this doesn't mean it never finished.*:

"**W**HY is it always me?" Myste asked, as Alberich made his second trip of the night down into Haven, this time with her in tow. The scholarly Herald pushed her lenses up on her nose and shivered beneath her cloak.

"Because you have the strongest Truth-sensing ability in the Collegium," Alberich said. "And because the two of us can speak in Karsite. If our naughty boy doesn't understand Karsite, he won't know what we're talking about, and it will make him nervous, and if he does, you'll know it, and we'll have him where we want him."

"Bloody hell," she said with resignation, and pulled the cloak tighter around herself. She hated cold, she hated winter, and she hated being dragged out of her study, and he knew all of that. He also knew that unless someone dragged her out of her study periodically, she would hibernate there for as long as the cold lasted. Which was, so far as he was concerned, just as valid a reason for making her his assistant in this case.

The city jail was not bad as such places went. It was clean, insofar as you could keep any place clean considering the standards of hygiene of the inhabitants. It smelled of un-washed bodies, with a ghost of urine and vomit, for no matter how many times the cells were cleaned, *someone* was always fouling them again. It did *not* smell of blood. If anyone was so badly injured as all that, they went under guard to a separate set of cells that had a Healer in attendance. And it went with-out saying that no one here—at least, among the jailers—spilled the blood of the prisoners.

Of course, the conditions were spartan and crowded, and no prison was a good place. But compared with those jails that Alberich had seen in Karse—

—not to mention the ones that were rumored to exist—

Myste grimaced as they rode in at the stable, and grimaced again as they walked in through the front door. Alberich was wearing his Whites—no one looked at a Herald's face, they only saw his Whites. The prisoner would see the Whites and not even *think* that the man inside the white uniform might be the madman that had attacked him.

They were taken to a little room, windowless, lit by a single lantern, that held a single chair. The chair was for the pris-oner, whose legs would be tethered to it; Myste and Alberich would be free, so that they could evade any attacks he might try.

The prisoner was brought in and his legs shackled to the legs of the chair. He was as pale as a snowdrift when he saw who was there to speak with him.

Slowly, and carefully, Alberich outlined exactly what he had observed, while the man listened, jaw clenched, eyes star-ing straight ahead. "So," Alberich finished. "What have you to say for yourself?"

He half expected the man to flatly deny everything, but after a long, tense silence, he spoke.

"I cannot tell you what you want to know."

A candlemark later, Alberich and Myste left the jail. There was a frown of frustration on Herald Myste's round face.

Alberich didn't blame her. The man certainly *had* been paying people to try to foment discontent against the Queen—quite a few of them, in fact, but with, by his own admission, limited success. And he had been doing so on the orders, and with the money, of someone else.

The only problem was, he didn't know this "someone else." He had never even seen the man's face.

Myste had not even needed to cast the Truth Spell to force the truth out of the man; her own innate Truth-sensing Gift had told her he was telling them everything he knew. He himself had a grudge against the Crown in general, and Selenay in particular, for when she had served her internship in the City Courts of law with Herald Mirilin, she had made a ruling against him. So there was his personal motive—

But who had sought out this man with a grievance against Selenay? Who had supplied him with the money and the idea to foster rebellion?

And why?

Only one thing was absolutely certain; the trail came to a dead end now. It was unlikely that the man would ever be contacted again, for someone astute enough to find him in the first place would certainly be sharp enough to discover he had been arrested and know not to use him again.

"Now what will you do?" Myste asked, as they neared the Collegium.

"Keep looking," he said, and shrugged.

There seemed nothing more he could say. Or do.

The closing in of winter always brought one definite disadvantage to the weaponry classes; much of the time practices and lessons had to be held in the salle instead of out of doors. This limited the kinds of lessons that could be given and the way that practices could be held. Every season brought its difficulties for a Weaponsmaster; in spring and summer there were torrential, cold rains to deal with, it was difficult to muster enthusiasm for heavy exercise in high summer, and in the winter, of course, there was the cold and the snow. Well, if the job had been easy, anyone could have done it.

Alberich still held some outdoor archery classes in the winter, but when, as today, snow was falling thickly, with a wicked wind to blow it around, there wasn't much point in keeping the youngsters at the targets. Yes, they *would* find themselves having to fight for their lives under adverse conditions, but adverse conditions affected the enemy, too. And as for needing to hunt, well, no Herald was going to starve because he or she could not hunt in a blizzard; Waystations were stocked with sufficient supplies, and every Herald on circuit carried emergency rations. During their last year, each Trainee would get an intense course in survival hunting and disadvantaged combat, and there was no point in making the youngsters utterly and completely miserable for the sake of showing them what it was like to be utterly and completely miserable. Not even the Karsite Officers' Academy did that to its students, and having seen what life was like at the Collegia, Alberich knew that the lessoning he'd gotten at the Academy was harsh, and not at all conducive to training youngsters like these.

Besides, with the Tedrels gone, and Karse itself essentially neutralized for a while, the only enemies that Heralds were likely to encounter in the field were bandits and brigands.

Now, as Alberich well knew from long experience, bandits and brigands are humans; they are essentially lazy, or they wouldn't be trying to steal rather than earn an honest living, and they are just as attached to their own creature comforts as any other humans. Given a choice in the matter, *they* wouldn't attack under adverse conditions either. By night—certainly. In ambush, definitely. In a blizzard? A flood? A raging storm? Not likely. In fact, in all of the time that Alberich himself had led his men of the Sunsguard against the bandits on the Karsite border, never once had he encountered a band moving against a target when the weather was foul. That didn't mean it was impossible, just unlikely. That made the circumstance something to guard against, but not something that required extensive training.

So, when the snows began to fall in earnest just after the noon meal, Alberich herded the next class to arrive into the salle itself. Which occasioned the inevitable delay in the cleaning of boots at the door, and the taking off of cloaks and gloves and hanging them up to dry along the oven wall before anything could get started. And then, because this was a mixed class of Trainees from all three Collegia and some Blues as well, there was more delay as Alberich sorted them out into the limited space inside the salle.

Although there was no fire actually in the room—far, far too dangerous to have a fireplace in an area where someone could fall or be thrown into it—the salle was kept reasonably warm by a huge brick "oven" in one corner. A relatively small fire deep inside it was set alight in the first really cold days of autumn and never allowed to go out, night or day. That fire heated the great mass of bricks that made up the oven and chimney and the wall, and that mass, in turn, radiated heat into the room. It also wasted heat along the outside of the same wall as well, but unfortunately, that couldn't be helped . . . and anyway, that outside wall was a nice place for the Companions to come and warm themselves on a cold and sunless day. The salle wasn't cozy—but no one was going to freeze without his cloak.

You could—and Alberich occasionally had—actually bake meals in that oven, if said meals were the sorts of things that required slow baking. You could—and Alberich did, quite often during the winter—leave a pot of soup or stew in there as well, to stay warm during the day. It was off limits to the Trainees, however, not by virtue of any orders but by common sense. You couldn't open the cast-iron door without burning your hand unless you used a heavy leather blacksmith's gauntlet, and Alberich prudently never left any of those lying around outside; you had to go into his quarters to get one, or, like the servant who tended the fire now and again, you brought one with you.

Of course, on a day like today, every youngster in the class was doing his or her best to get close to the oven and the warmest part of the room, which meant that unless the Weaponsmaster took a hand in it—*and* remembered who had gotten that choice part of the room last—there were going to be difficulties right from the start of the lessons.

Especially today, when devilment seemed to have infected all of them. There was pushing and shoving, teasing and a few insults and counterinsults, and the general restlessness that showed he was going to have to be an autocratic brute today. He gave a purely internal sigh; what *was* it about adolescents that made them run wild at utterly unpredictable intervals? Maybe it was that all of the students in this class were boys. Girls were a steadying influence, at least in these classes. The boys in this age group didn't seem quite so willing to run about like idiots when there were girls around.

Well, run—that was a good idea. He ought to have them run first. It would warm their muscles up and might exhaust a little of that too-plentiful energy. It would give him a chance to make a mental partner-list and decide who to assign where.

"Run!" he ordered, barking out the single word. "Full speed. Around the salle, ten times."

Grumbling, and in a straggling line, they ran, while he tried to remember who of this lot had gotten the prime spot during the last indoor lesson, and who hadn't gotten it in a decent while. By the time they finished their warm-up run, he thought he had it sorted, and before they could get up to any immediate devilment, he separated the most likely troublemakers and paired them up with the more tractable for this practice session.

"Short swords, no shields," he ordered. "Single line for equipment, by pairs. No pushing." Those who had headed for the storage room, eager to be at their practice, got the best choice of equipment, while the stragglers got what they deserved. Not that any of it was bad—Alberich saw to that—but those who got first choice got the padded armor and helms that fit them best, and those who brought up the rear paid for being laggards by getting equipment that Alberich would make them add extra padding to, so there would be no slippage.

With his pairs of youngsters distributed across the salle and trading blows, Alberich began his slow walk up and down the lines, giving the call.

Every blow had a corresponding number, starting from "one" for a straight thrust to the center of the enemy's body, and the two students in a pair were designated "odd" and "even." Alberich called out sequences of blows, beginning with "odd" or "even" for the students to follow, rather like a dancing instructor calling out a sequence of dance steps. Beginning students, of course, were taught one blow at a time, and specific parries for each. At the level these students had reached, the active student was given a pattern to follow, and the defensive student could use any sequence of parries he or she chose. Alberich began slowly, but as muscles warmed up further, and reactions quickened, he slowly sped up the pace of the call. And, as the students concentrated on what they were doing, the clatter of wooden sword on sword, which had started out rather ragged, became a single beat, just a fraction off the rhythm of the call.

Meanwhile, Alberich circled the floor like a hunting cat, watching the students, alert for any weaknesses, any bad habits. He wasn't going to interrupt the call just yet to correct them—this was part of the business of making blow-counter sequences automatic and instinctive—but he watched for them and noted them for later.

Now that they were up to speed, he added the next variation to the call. They had been fighting toe-to-toe. Now he ordered them to move.

"Odd!   Five-seven-*advance*-four-two-*retreat*—five-seven-*step right*-one-eight. Even! Four-three-*step left*—" Now it really did look like a dance, and with movement added, some parries were not always working, some blows were getting through. Still, he was not going to make corrections just yet; this was the point in the practice where experience was the teacher, and there was nothing quite like the experience of a good bruise to drive the lesson home.

Again, he sped up the call, forcing them to move a little faster than they were used to. But now they were beginning to tire. The response was getting ragged again, and some of the students began dropping some of the sequence as weary muscles failed to keep up with the cadence. Time to stop, and go on to individual lessons.

"*Rest!*" he barked, and at that welcome command, the points of a dozen wooden practice blades dropped to the wooden floor with a loud *thwack.*

"Kiorten and Ledale, center! The rest, circle!" That order called the first of his pairs into the middle of the floor, with the rest around them to observe. It was not as unfair as it might have seemed, to order a pair straight into the next part of the lesson when the rest were getting a breather. Kiorten and Ledale were the strongest and had the most endurance; a Blue and a Heraldic Trainee, and as alike as brothers. They were still relatively fresh after the call. That endurance needed to be tested; they needed to learn what it was like to fight real combat while they were tired.

Now Alberich took up a wooden long sword, to separate them when he saw something that needed either correction or scoring. The two combatants squared off, standing warily, balancing on the balls of their feet. They'd fought often, of course. Though Alberich made a point of rotating partners in practice, he tended to put these two against each other more often than not, just to keep things even. They enjoyed the practices, too, and he had more than a suspicion that they practiced against each other recreationally.

He held his sword out between the two; they tensed, waiting. "One—" he counted, "Two—three—*heyla!*"

He pulled back the sword and jumped back in the same instant, and they both went on the offensive, which was what he expected from them. They were aggressive fighters, and neither one had learned yet that immediate offense wasn't necessarily the wisest course to take.

He didn't separate them, even though they immediately tangled up in the middle of the wooden floor, with Kiorten seizing his opponent's sword in his free hand and Ledale grabbing the front of Kiorten's padded jerkin with *his*. Neither could do anything against the other when they were bound up like that, and a moment later, they broke apart by themselves, circled for a moment, then began an exchange of blows.

Kiorten got a hit, and Alberich stopped the combat for a moment. "Na. Let me look—" He made a quick judgment of position and strength. "Ledale, you are losing the free hand; struck it truly, Kiorten has. Tuck it behind you. Heyla." Let Ledale judge for himself that he had left that hand out there as an easy target. With the wooden blade, the blow probably only stung a bit, but had it been a real short sword, even with an armored gauntlet, the hand would have been seriously injured.

But Ledale wasn't taking this lying down; he launched himself at his opponent with a flurry of blows that drove Kiorten back, and scored a hit himself, that made Alberich stop the combat again. "Na—a flesh wound, but you bleed. If this goes on, you weaken. Heyla."

It didn't go on for very much longer. Ledale was at a disadvantage with that hand tucked behind him; it made him turn a little too far to the right, leaving his body more open to attack. Kiorten saw that, and saw also that Ledale was going to go aggressive again. So this time, he wisely *let* it happen, and by the way he avoided the blows, led Ledale in the direction he wanted, until he got a good opening for a body shot. He had to commit everything to that, but he made the full commitment, and the sword *thwacked* home against Ledale's torso with an impact that made him grunt in pain.

"Enough!" Alberich called, although he hadn't really needed to. Ledale backed up immediately, saluted his opponent, and pulled off his helm in surrender.

"Curse you!" he said amiably, though his face was a little white. "I'm going to have a bruise the size of my head for a week, even assuming you haven't cracked my ribs!"

"See the Healers," Alberich directed brusquely, as Kiorten pulled off his helm and extended his hand for his defeated opponent to shake. "After lessons." He knew full well that no ribs were cracked; if they had been, the lad would not have been able to breathe, and what was more, the Trainee's Companion would immediately have told Kantor, who would have told Alberich. "Ledale, observe. Kiorten, you drop your point too often; go to practice lunges at the mirror. Aldo and Triana, center."

Two more students came out of the circle to face off against each other in the center, while Ledale took a vacant spot in the circle and his erstwhile partner obediently moved to the side of the room to face one of the full-length mirrors set into the back wall of the salle, and began lunging with his sword fully extended, watching his reflection the way he would watch an opponent.

Those mirrors had utterly shocked Alberich the first time he had seen them. Mirrors were expensive, appallingly expensive, and that much mirrored glass at that size represented a sum of money that had made his head swim. But when he'd gotten over the shock, he had to admit that putting those mirrors there was a brilliant idea, for nothing enabled a student learning *anything* involving body movement to correct himself like being able to see for himself as well as feel exactly what he was doing right or wrong.

Right now, however, he kept his attention on the two students before him; a pair of the children of the nobly born. Trainees, that is, not Blues, though a pair of Blues would have worked just as hard as these two. Things had certainly changed there—perhaps not in the attitude of those highborn toward him, but at least in the fact that they no longer expressed their contempt for him aloud. And no longer permitted their children to act on that contempt. The Blues for the most part now worked just as hard in his classes as any Heraldic Trainee, and there were no more sneers or other expressions of disrespect in his presence.

As for what happened outside his presence, he cared not at all. If they respected him, well and good. If they feared him, perhaps that was just as good. If neither, as long as they behaved themselves *in* his class, it mattered not what they thought, nor their parents. Let them revile him behind his back if it pleased them, so long as they maintained respect to his face. Discipline in the salle was what he demanded; so long as he got that, they might actually learn a thing or two from him.

These two, Grays both, were going at it with the same concentration and will—if not skill—as the previous pair. And with a touch less aggression; not so bad a thing, since he preferred to see caution over bravado. When one finally defeated the other, he sent them to observe, rather than to the mirrors.

The third pair, Healer and Heraldic Trainees, also bouted and retired; one went to the mirrors, the other to point practice on a ball suspended from the ceiling. The fourth pair, however—

Well, both of them were high-spirited most times, and today, truly full of bedevilment. One was a Heraldic Trainee,

the other a Bardic Trainee, and between them, the two were
responsible for half the pranks that were pulled at the two
Collegia. Both were slender and agile, both possessed of so
much energy that their teachers sometimes despaired over trying to get them to hold still long enough to learn something,
and envied their inexhaustible verve at one and the same time.

So Alberich knew he was going to have to be sharp to keep
these two within bounds today.

If he could. Adain, the young Bard, and Mical were harder
to keep control of than a bushel of ferrets today; he saw that
within moments of their bout.

The two went at each other with the same concentration
and will as the first two, and a great deal more energy and
enthusiasm. As a consequence, *they* didn't stay inside the circle of observers, and those who had been quietly practicing
found themselves scrambling out of the way as their combat
ran from one end of the salle to the other.

Alberich had heard some rumors that these two were in the
habit of experimenting with new moves—well, here was the
proof that the rumors were true. It looked less like a practice
bout and more like an acrobatic exhibition. Very few of their
blows actually connected with anything. They weren't actually
parrying each other; they were tumbling and spinning and
jumping about so much that they never even got near each
other with their wooden blades.

"*Stop!*" Alberich roared, just as Adain, by more luck than
anything else, bound Mical's blade in a complicated cork-
screwing parry—

—and with a wild flip of his arm, disarmed his opponent
and sent the wooden sword flying—

—straight at one of the precious panels of mirror.

Alberich opened his mouth to shout, and knew it was already too late.

It was one of those moments when time slows to a crawl,
and the coming disaster is observed in painful detail without

anyone being able to actually do anything about it. Adain's grin of triumph slowly turned to one of horror, Mical clawed the air in futility after his lost sword as it headed straight for the mirror, its own reflection seeming to fly to meet it in mid-air. As the heavy, weighted stick flipped over and over in mid-air, Alberich just braced himself for the inevitable.

And, with a terrible crash, it came. The weighted end hit with the sound of a hundred hand mirrors hitting a pavement; the mirror spiderwebbed—and shattered.

A profound and dreadful silence fell over the salle, broken only by a belated series of musical *chinks,* as a few of the shards that were left detached themselves and landed on the wreck of the rest of the mirror.

Chink. Chinker-chink. Chink.

"Uh-oh," said Adain, in a very small voice.

Chink.

Alberich stood behind the two miscreants with his arms crossed over his chest, as they faced the desk of the Acting Dean of Herald's Collegium. Elcarth was not alone; the Dean of Bardic Collegium, Bard Arissa, had joined him for this particular conference. While Elcarth, slight and birdlike, with an inquisitive face and mild manner, was not normally the sort of person who might inspire trepidation in a student, the look he wore today would have frozen the marrow of anyone's bones.

The two boys huddled unhappily in their chairs. It was the first time within his knowledge that Alberich had seen these two subdued. Their shoulders, under gray and rust-colored tunics respectively, were hunched with misery; their dark heads were both bowed, and two sets of hazel eyes were bent upon the floor.

"What, precisely, possessed you two to demonstrate your— new fighting techniques today?" That was Bard Arissa, a slim, autocratic woman, dark as a gypsy and resplendent in her full formal Scarlets, and you could have used the edge in her voice to cleave diamonds.

"It seemed like a good idea?" Adain suggested, in a whisper.

"And why did you not ask Herald Alberich if you could show him these things in private?" asked Elcarth, his voice like a wintry blast from the snowstorm outside.

"Um. He's very busy?" Adain seemed to be doing all the talking; Mical was sitting like a stone. Alberich knew why; Mical was from a family prosperous enough to possess one or two real glass mirrors and he knew just how expensive they were, although he probably had no idea that the price increased exponentially with the size. Adain was highborn; until he came to the Collegium, he had never had to pay for anything himself in his life, and he had no idea what even a hand mirror cost, much less one of the huge panels in the salle. Mical thought he knew, and he was scared, just thinking it would cost about the same as a good horse; Alberich knew better, knew that you could buy a nice house with a garden in a good part of Haven for less than one of those mirrors.

"Never, to my knowledge, did you inquire of me, these new moves to observe," Alberich said from behind them. "My duty it is, to make time for such things."

"You wanted an audience," Arissa said, in that same hard, sharp voice—which, given that she was a Master Bard, was certainly deliberate. And, given that she was a Bard, and so was one of the miscreants, her statement about their motive was probably correct. "You couldn't bear not to have an audience. You wanted to show off what you thought you could do."

Alberich's surmise that she had uncovered what had really driven the match today was borne out by the way that both the boys winced.

"Well," she continued, "you *got* an audience. I trust you're pleased. You've made fools out of yourselves in front of that audience, not to mention the damage you did in the salle."

Now it was Elcarth's turn. "Speaking of damages . . . are either of you aware of just how difficult—and expensive—it is to replace a mirror of that size?"

Identical head shakes.

Elcarth named a figure. Both of them went white as the snow falling outside. Even Alberich was impressed, hearing the exact cost; it made what he had paid for his stained-glass window look like pin money by comparison.

"Now," Elcarth continued. "Naturally, some of this is going to come from your stipends. We shan't take *all* of your stipends, but you're going to be down to less than half of what everyone else gets."

Mical finally said something. "But—we could never pay all that back, not even if we stayed Trainees for a hundred years!" He gulped audibly.

"Which is why you are *both* going to be spending all of your free time working for the Master of the Glassworker's Guild until he finishes the new mirror," Arissa said flatly. "We intend for you to see why, at first-hand, such things cost so dearly. We intend for you to have a very proprietary interest in the replacement. When the mirror is finished, I trust you will have an entirely new understanding of your folly."

"And a new set of muscles," Elcarth added enigmatically. "Now you may go, and reflect on the fact that you will not have any time to get up to any more clever ideas for the duration. This will be your last evening with any leisure in it, because you'll be spending your mornings, your afternoons, and half of your evenings down at the glassworks for a while. Enjoy it."

As if they could, with a sentence like that one hanging over their heads. The two rose, heads hanging, and shuffled out of the room, the very image of dejection.

Elcarth sighed once they were gone, and ruffled a hand

through his hair. "I wouldn't mind so much if they'd gone about their little project sensibly," he said. He motioned to Alberich to sit; Alberich did so. "Consulting with their instructors, for instance. Not that all of that gymkhana nonsense would have *worked,* mind you. I wonder where they got such a notion?"

"Out of their imaginations, I suppose," growled Arissa, sitting on the other chair. "Which are entirely too active if you ask me. Or perhaps out of some idiot play or other; the two of them are always running down into Haven to see some fool drama whenever there's one to be seen. I presume they're going to be put to working the bellows at the glassworks for the next moon or so? It could be worse; this could be summer."

"It will be summer before they see the end of their labor," Elcarth said. "I intend to leave them down there for more than a moon. Master Cuelin tells me his apprentice is ready to go on to more complicated work, and he doesn't have a junior apprentice to start on the bellows or do any of the other simple labor in and around the place. So our lads can serve until he gets one. It could have been worse. At least it was only one mirror panel, not two or more."

"How often does this occur?" Alberich asked curiously. "Assume, I must, that accidents do happen. Stupidity probably rather more often than accident."

Elcarth shrugged. "About once every hundred years or so. I mean, we designed the salle to minimize the possibility of an accident, and you Weaponsmasters rarely permit flying objects in the salle itself. It does happen, and it isn't always a Trainee's fault, though I must say that this time is probably going into Myste's Chronicles for sheer wrongheadedness. The panels are all a standard size, and the glassworks has the dimensions in their records from the last time, so Master Cuelin won't even have to come up here to take measurements. I can't tell you how long it's going to take to replace the mirror, though. The Master will have a lot of failures before he gets a success."

"I would interested be, to watch," Alberich admitted. "Or at least, to hear from the Master how such a thing is made."

"Then deliver the criminals yourself in the morning, after breakfast," Elcarth told him. "Someone will have to escort them the first time."

Alberich took quick account of his schedule, and smiled thinly. "So I shall," he decided.

Arissa laughed, her voice full of ironic humor. "Oh, they'll enjoy seeing *your* face tomorrow morning!"

The snow was still falling all that afternoon, into the night, and the next day, and Alberich had sent word up to the Collegia that the Trainees were to have a day-and-a-half holiday from their weaponry classes while the salle was cleaned. A small army of Collegium servants were scouring the salle floor for the tiniest slivers of glass, and would not leave until the floor had been swept several times over, then washed down, buffed and lightly sanded, so that it wasn't slippery. The one proviso to this "holiday" was that the Trainees were to spend the class time out of doors, but with this much snow, he doubted that would be much of a trial for them. The first lot was already building a snow fort when he and Kantor left to escort the two troublemakers to their appointed labors, while snow continued to fall from a sky that was the same color as a pigeon's breast, and looked just as soft.

When Alberich got to the grounds of Herald's Collegium, the two boys were waiting for him on the road that ran among the buildings, mounted, Adain on his Companion and Mical on a sorrel gelding from the Palace stables. There was a conspicuous absence of Trainees anywhere near them; they waited alone in their disgrace.

As Alberich and Kantor approached, he observed that Adain and Mical looked just as subdued as they had last night, and even Adain's Companion drooped a little. They kept the hoods of their cloaks well up, and aside from a soft, "Good morrow, Weaponsmaster Alberich," he got nothing more out of them. Not that he intended to try to get them to talk. It would do them good to contemplate their sins in silence.

Snow drifted down now as fat, slow flakes; there wasn't even a breath of wind, and the air smelled damp. Most of the trees bore burdens of snow along their black, bare branches, and large mounds bore testament to bushes hidden under heaps of the stuff. Nothing had spoiled the pure whiteness yet, except for where the road had been cleared by the Palace gardeners.

By midmorning, people would be out playing in it. And the two boys would be painfully aware of that. A good thing; better they should have to reflect on their sins in sorrow than congratulate themselves that today would have been a miserable one to be out in anyway.

Alberich led them away from the Palace and toward the wall that surrounded the entire complex. They left from the Herald's Gate, the guarded postern at the Collegium side of the Palace grounds. Outside the walls, the road hadn't been cleared as yet. Heavy as the snow on the road was, the Companions made easy going through it, and the horse was able to follow in Kantor's wake. By the time they got down through the manors of the highborn and the very wealthy, there were crews out starting to clear the road. Traffic was limited to a few riders and people on foot; except for a few main thoroughfares, the streets hadn't been shoveled out yet either. Fresh snow was nearly up to the knee, and drifts blocked many smaller side streets and alleys. But people were already out with shovels and teams of horses pulling scrapers, and work was going apace.

After all, it was in the interest of a shopkeeper to get the street in front of his place of business cleared quickly. So as they passed farther down into the commercial parts of Haven, there was more clean pavement, and more activity. And by the smoke coming from the chimney of the glassworks as they arrived, things were busy in there as well.

Alberich dismounted and gave a hard rap on the door to the glassworks courtyard with his fist. Two of the apprentices met them at the door; one took charge of their mounts, and with an evil grin, the other took charge of the miscreants. Alberich understood the reason for the grin perfectly; the apprentice would now be put to doing something far more interesting and less labor intensive than mere manual work, while Adain and Mical took his place at the bellows. The furnaces were always going in a glassworks; the fire needed to be quite hot indeed and at an even temperature. The least-skilled job was that of keeping the bellows pumping air into those furnaces, so that the molten glass was always ready to use, cane for decoration could be melted, and glass being blown into vessels could be reheated.

Alberich knew from his previous visits where to find Master Cuelin; in the Master Workshop. That was where he headed. The glassworks itself was a dangerous place, and he was extremely careful as he made his way through it.

Even now, in the dead of winter, it was very warm in here. Surrounding the furnaces were stations for molding glass, for those who decorated finished vessels, for beadmakers, for glassblowers. The floor was of pounded dirt, the benches and tables made of metal and stone. There was very little that could catch fire, logically enough. It was surprisingly dark here, too; Alberich supposed there was a reason for that. Perhaps it made the hot glass easier to see while it was being shaped.

Glass was both blown and molded here, and all manner of things were made. The most common pieces were molded disks and the thick "bullseye" glass for inferior windows, made by dropping hot glass into molds and pressing it. That was a job for an apprentice; it was relatively easy, relative being the proper word when you were talking about glass, a substance that ran like melted wax and would burn you to the bone if it got on you. Beadmakers formed their amazing little works of art on mandrels at their own little benches—or spun out long, thin tubes of colored glass to be chopped into bits and sand-polished in big drums when cool. Glassblowers formed the molten stuff into every shape imaginable, and decorators took the finished vessels and shapes and embellished them with ribbons of colored glass.

Alberich had been here once before, when he had commissioned his window, and then, as now, it had occurred to him how like a glassworker Vkandis Sunlord was. The glass had no notion of what it was going to be; it was melted in the heat of His regard, then molded or shaped, polished, turned into something that bore little or no resemblance to the grains of sand it had been.

Sometimes mistakes happened. And when they did, He gathered up the broken shards with infinite patience, put them back in His furnace, and began again.

The more conventional analogy—and the one that the Sunpriests favored—was to compare Him to a swordmaker. But it had come to Alberich that He was really nothing like a swordmaker; for one thing, the vast majority of the people He made were not creatures of war. And for another, few of them were tempered and honed. Most of them were simply made, humble creatures of common use, as perfectly suited to their lives as a thick pressed-glass window. Some were merely ornamental, like a bead. Some were honed and polished like the glass scalpels the Healers used for the most careful surgery. But they all came from the same hands, and the same place.

Better window glass was made in the same way as mirror glass, and required a glassblower as well. Alberich had been rather surprised by that when Master Cuelin told him; it had not occurred to him that one would use the same technique that created a goblet or a vase to make a flat pane of glass.

But, in fact, that was precisely how it was made. Glass was blown into a bubble of the right thickness, the bubble was then rolled against a flat and highly-polished metal plate to form a cylinder, the ends were swiftly cut off the cylinder and the cylinder slit up the middle while the glass was still soft enough to "relax," and the resulting pane unrolled itself onto the plate and cooled flat. A master of the craft created a flat, rectangular pane of even thickness with irregularities so few as to be trivial.

But of course, the larger the pane—or mirror—the more difficult the task of blowing and cutting. Something the size of the mirror in the salle was going to be extremely difficult to do.

And in fact, it was Master Cuelin himself who was taking the first tries at it. A pile of rejected shards to one side testified that he had already tried and failed a time or two this morning.

"Ah, I give over," he said, as Alberich arrived. "I thought I'd give it a try, but I've not the lungs anymore. I'll stick to my colored glasses and let young Elkin here do what he does best."

But "young" Elkin—who was older than Alberich—shook his head. "It won't come quick, Master Cuelin," he said honestly. "I've never done aught that big. I'll need to work up to it."

"I wouldn't expect anything else, my lad," Cuelin told him. "Give it time; you'll manage. Kernos knows so long as you don't make the mess of it that I just did, we can find buyers for the smaller panes and mirrors while you work your way up to the right size."

"Are you sure of that, Master?" the other craftsman asked, surprised.

Cuelin laughed, and pulled off his leather gauntlets. "Certain sure. You just wait; as soon as word gets out that we're replacing a salle mirror up there on the hill, there'll be a stream of highborn servants at the door. 'If you'd happen to have a spare window glass, so-by-so, Master Cuelin . . . if you're like to have a mirror for milady's dressing table . . .' *They* know we have to work our way up to a pane that big, and *they* know they'll get a bargain they wouldn't get if they'd commissioned those glass panes and mirrors special. Then it'll be the polishing, and then the silvering, and that'll be a bit tricky as well. Master Alberich, I want to show you something that'll catch your interest, aye, and you, too, Elkin—I had the Collegium servants bring me down the old glass, and when I got it, this is what I found."

He held up a shard of silvered glass. "This'll be from the top of your mirror—" and a second, "—and this'll be from the bottom. Now, what d'ye think of that?"

The top shard was clearly thinner than the bottom. Alberich scratched his head. "Glass not so good as you can make it?" he hazarded.

Cuelin laughed. "Oh, flattery! No, no, it was fine glass, and we'll be hard put to match it. But I'll reckon that mirror was over two hundred years old if it was a day, Master Alberich. Maybe more. And when it was made, top to bottom was the same thickness."

He wanted Alberich to look puzzled; with some amusement, Alberich obliged him. "Then, how?" he asked.

"Glass never quite *sets,* Master Alberich," Cuelin told him. "It's like slow water, my old Master told me. Believe it or not, it keeps flowing—oh, slow, too slow to notice, but over a century or two, or three, you look, you'll see that any glass has got thicker at the bottom than it is at the top. Mind, most of it doesn't stay unbroken long enough to find that out, 'specially with lads like your two troublemakers about, but there you have it. You can tell the age of a piece by how thick it's got on the bottom compared to the top."

Alberich examined the two shards, then passed them on to Elkin, and blinked at that, and tried to get his mind wrapped around the idea of something that flowed that slowly. "I am—astonished," he admitted after a moment. "Astonished."

"Wonderful stuff, is glass," Master Cuelin said with pride and pleasure. "And I'll see to it your lads get their heads stuffed full of more than they ever cared to learn about it. No point in exercising their arms and leaving their heads to come up with more mischief. I'll send them back up the hill on time for their classes, though, no worry. And—" he took a slip of paper out of a pocket in his tunic and consulted it, "—I see I'm to expect them back down here at fourth bell, and keep them until our suppertime. We eat late, mind."

"Correct," Alberich said. "Be here, they will be. Fed, they will be when they arrive, then they must study for the morrow, then bed."

Cuelin laughed. "If they've strength enough to hold up their heads without falling into their books, I'll be main surprised."

Alberich took his leave of the Master with better humor than he had arrived in; clearly Cuelin understood boys, and was quite prepared to handle them as they needed to be handled. Mical's horse and Adain's Companion were comfortably housed, as the Weaponsmaster saw when he went to fetch Kantor, so Alberich left them in peace. The horse was happy enough; the Companion still looked subdued.

:An interesting place. Have you ever thought of glasswork as a hobby?: Kantor asked, as Alberich mounted.

:I think I would not be good enough to satisfy myself,: Alberich replied truthfully. They rode out into the street; already, the industrious craftsmen here had gotten it cleared, and the snow had been piled up along the walls. *:Why was the boy's Companion so quiet?:*

:Because he is as much to blame as the children,: Kantor told him. *:Apparently, he was in league with them. He is very young.:*

Alberich snorted. *:He must be. I thought your kind had better sense.:*

Kantor sighed gustily. *:Those of us who are older, are. Some of us, like Eloran—are young.:*

:Have you got any plans for delivering some sort of chastisement to Eloran?: Alberich asked after a moment, while he tried to sort out the meaning behind his words and couldn't come up with anything.

:Oh, yes,: came the reply. *:Rolan and I have devised something quite—appropriate.:*

And since nothing else was forthcoming, Alberich's curiosity had to remain unassuaged.

3

SELENAY looked out of a window in the Long Gallery on the way to her Lesser Audience Chamber and sighed with regret. The garden was alive with color and movement against the snow—the brilliantly colored cloaks, coats, and hoods of the younger members of her Court as they chased one another, flung snowballs, and generally forgot any pretense of dignity. Young men who had lately fought the Tedrels had cast aside their adulthood for a few hours as they fired snowballs at pages safely ensconced behind the sturdy walls of a snow fort. Young ladies giggled and joined the pages in flinging missiles back at their suitors. Others were on the way to frozen ponds with skates slung over their shoulders, or moving toward the artificial hills in the "wild" garden with sleds. Selenay would have given a year of her life to be down there with them.

Alas. The Queen had an audience with the ambassador from Hardorn, and there was no time for frolicking in the snow, no time for skating, no time for a fast run on a sled.

Curse it.

She nodded to the guards on either side of the door of the Lesser Audience Chamber and went inside. She'd had the room repainted in softer colors than her father had favored, though she couldn't do much about the leather paneling, which had been there for decades and would probably be there for decades more. It was easy to keep clean and looked far more luxurious than anything she could install to replace it; she'd settled for painting the trim an ashen brown with silver-gilt touches here and there. The Ambassador and his entourage were already waiting, as was Talamir. Bless him. It was clear he had been keeping the Ambassador properly entertained; although such gentlemen were notable for being able to conceal any evidence of impatience, the smile Ambassador Werenton turned on her was quite genuine and warm, and his eyes were relaxed. He wore the fine shirt, tunic, trews, and floor-length, open vest in the current Valdemaran style, which was a little disappointing. She'd wanted to see what the Hardornan mode was, for the talk was that the new Queen was quite a fashion setter.

She gave him her hand; he bowed over it, and she was pleased to note that his hand was warm and dry, not cold or clammy. She took her place on the small, velvet-covered throne on the sketchy dais, and motioned to him to sit. This was a room meant to welcome rather than awe; the warm ocher of the leather-covered paneling and the aspect of it, situated so that it looked out into a sheltered courtyard, made it surprisingly comfortable for a formal room. The furnishings were all upholstered in leather that matched the paneling, and the floor carpeted; there was a fine fire in the fireplace, and servants with mulled, spiced wine to serve. Everything that could have been done to relax the Ambassador and his entourage had been—more of Talamir's work, no doubt.

"Ambassador Werenton, it is good to see you again," she said warmly. "And I am glad that you were able to reach our Court before this snow closed us in."

"As am I, Majesty," he replied. "And my King wishes me, first, to tender his sympathies for your loss, and second, offer his apologies that he was not able to send me sooner."

She smiled at him, and hoped that her weariness with all of the official expressions of condolence did not show. She knew very well that the King of Hardorn could have cared less about who was on the throne of Valdemar. He knew that Valdemar would *always* favor allies and peace over conquest. In fact, so long as that attitude prevailed, the King of Hardorn would not have cared if the Council had elected a horse to wear the crown. "Please, Werenton—the message of condolence arrived with the usual promptiness of our friends and allies, and I can certainly understand how your King would be otherwise too occupied with his own defensive preparations against Karse to think about sending you to our Court."

"If Valdemar had fallen—or even been pushed back—" Werenton said apologetically, and shrugged. "We share a border with Karse, as you know. The King was prepared, at need, to unite our force with yours if it had come to that. As it was, the defeated Tedrels spread into our land, and we were forced to deal with them as one would any other plague."

The King would not have bestirred himself unless his Border Lords forced him to, she translated to herself. *In fact, it probably wouldn't have been the King of Hardorn who united his forces with us at all; it would have been the local Hardornen border-levies.*

"And your King was right to concern himself first with them, and concern himself with other things second," Selenay agreed. "I am glad it never came to the point of asking our allies for help."

She knew, and probably the Ambassador did, too, that the reason her father hadn't asked Hardorn for troops was precisely because there was no telling what the Tedrels were going to do for certain. Yes, Karse had hired them to take Valdemar. But if Hardorn's border troops had been removed to bolster Valdemaran forces, leaving that border unguarded, the Tedrels would probably have taken southern Hardorn and come at Valdemar from the eastern flank. The King of Hardorn was a good man, and served his people well—but he was not a very good strategist, nor were any of his military advisers, sad to say. All of them were old men, and more accustomed to dealing with the odd bandit force than a real campaign. Karse's long-standing and increasingly hostile feud with Valdemar had ensured that Hardorn had been very little troubled over the past two reigns. Her father had deemed it wise not to distract Hardorn's king with—as he had put it—"conflicting needs."

She had better say something flattering, before her mouth let something unflattering escape. "And am I to understand that congratulations will shortly be in order?" Selenay continued, with a slight smile.

"We do expect the birth of an heir before spring, yes," Werenton admitted. He did not mention that the young Queen was only a little older than Selenay, nor that the King was older than Sendar had been. Nor did Selenay make anything of it. She was just grateful that the King of Hardorn had married *before* the death of her own father. Now at least there was one old man who was out of the running as a potential suitor. Had he still been single—his previous wife having died without producing a living heir—there soon would have been advisers on both sides of the Border clamoring for a match between them.

"I will have to rack my brain to find a unique birth gift, then," Selenay replied. "I'm sure that by now His Majesty has an entire room given over to silver rattles and ivory teething rings."

The Ambassador smiled politely, as if to suggest that a royal infant could not possibly have too many silver rattles and ivory teething rings.

Selenay spent the better part of two candlemarks with the

Ambassador, mostly taking her lead from Talamir or the Ambassador himself as to when subjects currently under negotiation needed to be mentioned. There were some, of course. Hardorn badly wanted to take back some land that Karse had overrun half a century ago, but if they did, the King wanted to be sure that Valdemar wouldn't take it amiss. Valdemar wanted warning if this was going to happen, so that when Karse reacted (though given how unsettled things were there at the moment, Karse might not even notice for a year or two) there would be extra guards on the Border again. Hardorn wanted to know what Valdemar was going to do with all those "Tedrel" children. Valdemar politely told Hardorn it was none of Hardorn's business, but that, in fact, the children were more than halfway to being Valdemaran by now. Hardorn suggested polite skepticism; Valdemar offered examples, and pointed out the general ages of the children. There were some matters of trade to discuss, some concessions that both of them wanted. No few of these would have to go before the Council, and, presumably, an equivalent body in Hardorn, but in a simple, convivial discussion like this one, it was possible to get a feel for how such overtures would be met when presented formally.

Finally—and none too soon, in Selenay's opinion—the Ambassador gave signs that he had said all he needed to, and she politely decreed the audience was at an end. He withdrew; she turned to Talamir as soon as the doors had closed behind him and his entourage.

Talamir shrugged wearily—he did everything wearily these days. He seemed to have aged twenty years since the end of the wars. His hair had gone entirely to silver-gray, and that lean, careworn face had lines of pain in it that had not been there a year ago. The eyes had changed the most, though; now they were an indeterminate, stormy color with the look in them of someone who has looked into places that mortal men are not supposed to see.

Still, most of the time he was the same Talamir she remembered, stubborn and difficult to move once he had decided on a thing.

"No hidden agendas, I think, Majesty," he said judiciously.

"Other than the obvious; that the King waited to see if I'd survive six months on the throne on my own before sending a formal envoy," she said, with a feeling of resignation. All of the envoys had been like this; it was disheartening to think that there were probably bets being placed on how long she would remain Queen *and* sole ruler of Valdemar.

"Well, you *could* have wedded immediately," Talamir pointed out. "From his point of view there was no harm in waiting to see if you did before sending the Ambassador."

"Or I could have been toppled by one of my own nobles, or assassinated by a leftover Tedrel." She did not add *after all, I'm only a woman,* but the unspoken words hung in the air between them.

"Well, you weren't," Talamir replied unexpectedly. "And those of us who knew you also knew you wouldn't be. And if some foreign monarch is foolish enough to think that your youth and sex means that you are weak or foolish, well, I pity him. He'll take a beating at the negotiation tables."

She flushed, feeling suddenly warm with pleasure. "Thank you for that, Talamir," she replied. So Talamir really *did* think she was capable! It was a welcome surprise; she would not have been at all surprised if he had still been thinking of her as "little" Selenay, who needed a firm hand on the rein and a great deal of looking after.

He gave a little bow, and smiled; he still had a charming smile. "Credit where credit is due," he said simply. "And by this point, I'm sure the Throne Room is filled with impatient petitioners—"

"So on to the next chore." She thought longingly of the fresh snow outside, and ruthlessly pushed away the longing. Queens did not desert their Court to frolic carelessly when there were duties to be done. Queens had responsibilities.

"Time to get to it; the sooner we clear the work out, the less likely it is I'll incur the wrath of the cooks by delaying luncheon." She rose, and shook out her skirts, still startled, even after all this time, to note the trimming of black on her Royal Whites where the silver of the Heir or the gold of the Monarch should be. "Speaking of wrath," she continued, as Talamir went to hold the doors of the chamber open for her, "What's the outcome of that little disaster down at the salle?"

Talamir coughed, to hide a smile, she thought. "Alberich escorted the two miscreants down to the glassworks just after breakfast," he told her. "They will be spending from now until—we're thinking—Vernal Equinox pumping the glassworks' bellows every free moment that they have. We're loath to keep them down there once the weather begins to get significantly warmer, because work switches to the nighttime once it becomes hellish to keep the furnaces going at full heat in the hottest part of the day. But we also want them to feel they're really being punished when the weather turns and all their friends are enjoying themselves outdoors again."

"Poor things!" she said, feeling rather sorry for them, seeing as she was in a similar situation with no hope for a reprieve.

Talamir coughed again; this time it sounded a bit disapproving. "Selenay, do you have any notion how much the Crown's treasury is going to have to pay the glassworkers for a new mirror? You could replace every horse in the Royal Guard with Ashkevron war stallions for less than the cost of that mirror. Personally, I think they're getting off lightly."

"If those mirrors cost so much, how on earth did the Crown manage to pay for all of them when they were first installed?" she asked, as the two of them, flanked by a couple of guards, made their way down the gallery that overlooked the snow-covered gardens.

"If the legends are correct, no one paid for them at all," Talamir replied. "The Herald-Mages made them, supposedly.

Just as whenever one was broken, the Herald-Mages fixed them."

"How very convenient," she said dryly. "Did the Herald-Mages fix plumbing, too? I've had an Artificer in my bathing room twice now, and that drip still isn't fixed. When I was trying to sleep last night, that was all I could hear."

"Sendar used to say he found it soothing," Talamir said quietly.

I am not my father, Selenay thought, and felt a surge of resentment as well as sadness. But she was not going to say it. "Just have someone send a different Artificer, please," she replied instead. "If I have to move into my old rooms for a few days until it's fixed, I've no objections. If I have to listen to that drip for many more nights, I'm going to go mad."

With classes canceled for the day, Alberich found himself with unexpected free time on his hands. In light of the frustration of pursuing inquiries to dead ends recently, he decided he had a good idea of how to fill some of it. At this point, all of his usual sources of information had run dry. It was time to find some new ones, but to do that, he would have to create new identities.

What I am looking for is not going to be found around Exile's Gate, he decided.

It was with a distinct feeling of pleasure that he noted that Kantor had followed his thought, and had altered his course, heading, not for the Collegia, but for the Companion's Bell. This was a prosperous tavern that played host to Heralds quite regularly—and to Alberich quite a bit more often than to most, although, if you had asked the staff, they would have said, truthfully, that they didn't see him there very often.

There was a secret room in the back of the stables where Herald Alberich would retire, and someone else would emerge, by way of a door that no more than a handful of people knew existed. In that room was a chest of disguises, which were apparently tended to by someone in the Bell, for no matter what state they were in when Alberich left them there, the next time he returned they would be clean—or at any rate, cleaner, since the apparent dirt and real stains were an integral and important part of some of them. Furthermore, any damage he'd done to them would be repaired, and the clothing neatly put away, back in the chest.

He'd inherited that room and that chest from Herald Dethor, his predecessor as Weaponsmaster, and he'd put quite a bit of wear on the disguises he'd found there. Enough that it was time to do something about the situation, before he found himself literally without anything to wear.

He'd have to do it in disguise, though. Even though he flatly refused to wear Herald's Whites, his own gray leathers were distinctive enough to mark him as the Collegium Weaponsmaster. If the Weaponsmaster was noted visiting the used-clothing merchants, it would be a short step for anyone keeping an eye on him to determine that he was purchasing disguises. Why else would he be making a great many purchases of used clothing?

So, after leaving Kantor tucked into an out-of-the-way stall in the section of the stables reserved for Companions, Herald Alberich retired into that room, and a persona he had never used until now emerged into the alley behind the inn.

His clothing was well-made, of good materials, but a little out of style, as befitting a prosperous merchant or craftsman from one of the farther or more rustic reaches of the kingdom. Good thick boots with a significant amount of scuffing and wear to the tops suggested that he was used to doing a great deal of walking in rough country. Leather breeches with little wear on the seat but a great deal to the legs and knees added to that impression. His heavy wool cape with an attached hood was significantly old-fashioned, though the material was very good, and it was lined with lambswool plush, which was quite a luxurious fabric. Beneath the cape was a knit woolen tunic that went down to his calves—also significantly out of fashion, for it should have been (but was not) worn with a sleeveless leather or cord-ware jerkin if he'd been living in Haven for any length of time. All of this gear looked home-made rather than tailor-made, and every bit of it made him look rustic.

If he spoke slowly and took care with his syntax, despite the odd accent he still had, he'd be taken for a farmer or craftsman—or, just possibly, a country squire—from some agrarian part of Valdemar with its own regional accent. It was a fine guise, and very useful for what he was about to do—which was to buy used clothing.

Such was easy enough to acquire, and it was easier to put mending and patching onto gently-used clothing than it was to repair clothing that was getting far past its useful lifespan. It was easier to put on stains than remove them. That so-helpful, completely invisible accomplice at the Companion's Bell was quite literate, as Alberich had proved to himself by leaving some instructions with one of those disguises, and returning to find that those instructions had been carried out to the letter. So he would buy appropriate outfits, and leave instructions on how the items were to be abused if they looked insufficiently used.

And finally he would have things that fit him, rather than Dethor. His predecessor had been slightly shorter and significantly broader in the waist than Alberich, with much shorter legs.

It will be good not to have to wear my breeches down around my hips to keep them from looking too short.

He spent a very profitable morning, going from shop to stall to barrow, examining items with all the care that any thrifty fellow from the hinterland would use, exhibiting all the suspicion that he was being cheated by a city sharper that any Haven merchant would expect from a shrewd bumpkin, eager to get his money's worth. He never bought more than one piece from any one place at the same time—though he *did* come back, later, if he'd seen more than one item that he wanted. In this persona, Alberich was not particularly notable. There were several men like him, engaged in similar errands, up and down the quarter where used clothing was sold. Most were alone, though a few had wives or older children with them. Whenever he had a collection of three or four items, he went back to the Bell, and left them, so that he was never observed carrying great piles of clothing.

By doing this, he was able to acquire disguises for a good dozen personae, including one or two that were just a touch above his current character; good, solid citizens who would be welcome in any decent house or tavern in the city. Anything else, he'd get from the Palace; he had a notion he'd like to have a set of Palace livery, perhaps a Guard uniform, and clothing appropriate for the lower ranks of the highborn.

And, under the guise of purchasing something for his wife, he bought some women's clothing as well. Not that he'd ever tried to impersonate a woman, but—well, he might need to.

:You'll never pull it off,: Kantor said critically as he stowed these last purchases away, hanging them up, rather than putting them in the chest, as even with all of the old guises taken out and left with a note to get rid of them, there was no more room in that chest. *:You'd need a wig. And how would you hide that face of yours?:*

:I've seen plenty of ugly women in this city,: he objected.

:I'm sure you have, but none that looked as if they'd been through a fire, then fought in a dozen bars and a war,: Kantor argued. *:And you don't act like a woman; you don't know how to act like a woman. If you need to find out something only a woman can, then get a woman to do it. Myste would probably fit those skirts.:*

:But—: he started to argue—then stopped. Myste *would* fit those skirts. And she was a native of Haven. And she'd come

into the Heraldic Circle as an adult, which meant that she was used to being a civilian, acting like a civilian, and she had all the knowledge that an ordinary citizen of Haven had. He wouldn't want to take her down into the area around Exile's Gate, but—

:But she'd go if you asked her to. Think about it anyway. There's Herald Keren, too. She'd go, and she'd fit in anywhere that was rough, including around Exile's Gate. Good gods, some of the clientele of those fishers' taverns in the ports of Evendim would frighten the whey out of the loungers in the Broken Arms!: Kantor sounded very sure of himself, but Alberich saw no reason to doubt that he was right. Keren was a tear-away of the first order, and back in the day, if the Sunsguard had permitted women to take up arms, he'd have had no objection to her in his cavalry unit. She made a fearless bodyguard for Selenay.

:I'd have to find a way to persuade Ylsa to stay away, though. The two of them together would be a dead giveaway to anyone who knows anything about the Heralds.:

:Pointing that out ought to be enough to persuade Ylsa,: Kantor replied with a hint of humor. *:Wild they might be, stupid, they aren't.:*

Well. Two excellent ideas in one morning, one from his own mind, and one from Kantor!

:And didn't I tell you, back when we first came here, that you and I were a good match?: Kantor asked smugly.

:So you did. And you were correct. So very correct that I don't even mind hearing you say 'I told you so.':

Kantor's only reply was a sort of mental snicker.

Alberich finished writing notes on what he wanted done—or not—to each of the new disguises, left them piled atop the chest or hung up on pegs around the room, went to the stable-side door, and blew out the lamp.

:Don't worry, you won't be seen. No one here but us Companions,: Kantor told him, and he slipped the catch, moved

out into the stable, and shut the door carefully behind himself. It locked itself with a soft *click*.

There were, indeed, two other Companions in stalls with Kantor. One was partnered with Herald Mirilin, who was one of the two Heralds assigned permanently to dispense justice within Haven. The other assigned to that duty was Jadus, who, since losing his leg, could not ride for very long or very far— but whose insight and understanding of human nature made him very suitable for this job. Jadus' Companion was not here, though; the third Companion was not one he recognized.

:Not a Herald you know either. Someone just in off circuit, and an old friend of Mirilin's.: And something about the tone of Kantor's mind-voice told Alberich that the "old friend" was female and that neither Mirilin nor the newcomer would be found in the common room. But that they *would* be found with each other.

Heh. So Mirilin was human, after all. Mirilin, with a woman! Now that was a thought to hold onto. From the way that Mirilin usually acted, Alberich had the idea that he'd be very embarrassed if he was caught playing truant with a woman—and no matter if the woman was another Herald.

:I believe,: he said, as Kantor turned his head to wink one blue eye at him, *:That I will have one of the Bell's delicious pigeon pies. And I believe I will linger over it.:*

It would do him no end of good to see the expression on Mirilin's face when the Herald finally did emerge. . . .

Kantor snickered. There was no other word for it. The sound wasn't even remotely horselike.

:I'll see to it that their Companions "forget" to mention you're here.:

Mirilin and the stranger strolled into the smaller common room—the one usually used by Heralds—with a careless and casual air, as of people who expect to find a room empty. And since Alberich had deliberately set himself in the most secluded corner of the room—which happened to be right beside the cheerful fire—Mirilin and his friend would not be able to see him until they were already well into the room.

"Heyla, Mirilin," he said calmly, and was rewarded when Mirilin actually jumped a little, startled. The other Herald, an attractive little redhead, didn't jump, but did look surprised.

The Herald peered at his corner. To Alberich's further pleasure, he flushed and looked extremely discomfited. Not that there was anything at all wrong with two Heralds having a quiet mark or two alone together, far from it! But being discovered by the enigmatic Alberich—

That same Alberich that Mirilin had openly and avowedly not trusted at all when he first became Selenay's bodyguard? And who was now one of the great heroes of the Wars? And if Mirilin was not acting as a Justiciar in the Heraldic Court, shouldn't he be up the hill at the Collegium at the moment?

Again, there was no reason why Mirilin should *not* take a mark or two out of the day to please himself—but someone like Mirilin would feel guilty that he had, and moreover, he probably wouldn't want anyone to know he had done so.

"Ah. Herald Alberich? What are you doing in Haven?"

"Delivering our miscreants to their place of punishment," he replied, "Heard of the incident in the salle, I presume you have?"

"A broken mirror, wasn't it?" Mirilin said, after a moment. "And a couple of Trainees with more enthusiasm than sense?" Mirilin was regaining his composure, which made Alberich smile a little. After all, he only wanted to discomfit the fellow a trifle, not humiliate him.

Alberich uttered a dry chuckle. "Well put. And no more free time, in which to devise more such mischief, will they have until well into spring. Pumping the bellows at the glassworks, Dean Elcarth has decreed, is to be their task."

Mirilin smiled and winced at the same time. "Well—at the least, they'll have stout muscles when spring comes."

"Make the punishment fit the crime—I like that," said the woman—not as young as Alberich had first thought. She wasn't as old as Mirilin, but she was older than Alberich. "Are you the new Weaponsmaster,' then?" She left Mirilin and approached Alberich, her hand extended, somewhat to Mirilin's consternation. "Sorry I haven't met you before this; I've been on one circuit or another for almost six years, and when I come in, I usually stay here rather than at the Collegium. When I'm off, I'm a bit of a carouser, and why disturb people's sleep when I can have all the fun I like and not upset anyone down here? I'm Ravinia. Mindspeech and Animal Mindspeech."

Alberich rose, took her hand, and bowed slightly over it. "And I am Alberich," he told her, releasing it. "ForeSight, for whatever good it does."

She smiled at him. Mirilin was very clearly discomfited again. Perhaps because the lady he had come here to meet was being so very friendly to someone he—used to—not trust very much? "So you are indeed the very famous Herald Alberich; it's a pleasure to meet you at last. Since I'm staying at least a moon this time, I expect you'll see me at the salle. I could use some sparring practice; can you find me partners at short notice?"

:Is she flirting with me?: he asked Kantor incredulously.

:No. She really does need sparring practice. Find some of the mid-level Guards from Selenay's bodyguard. Or Keren or Ylsa.: Kantor chuckled. *:She's not flirting; she's being direct. And she doesn't mistrust you. She hadn't met you at a time when you were under suspicion. You are not Alberich of Karse to her; you are Herald Alberich.:*

"You will welcome be, and partners can be found," he replied, and decided to end Mirilin's discomfort by taking himself off. "Rude I do not wish to seem, but my task and meal both being over, returning I must be."

"Certainly," Ravinia agreed. "I expect we'll meet again in the next day or two."

"Excellent." He nodded at Mirilin. "And fare you well, in your afternoon's tasks, Mirilin. Perhaps the heavy snow will thin the plaintiffs."

Mirilin shrugged. "I wouldn't count on it, but I wouldn't be upset if you were right." But there was a change in Mirilin. A subtle one, but there it was. Perhaps because, for the first time, he saw Alberich through the eyes of someone *he* trusted. And he saw the man before him as *Herald* Alberich.

Alberich took that as a dismissal, and took himself off, keeping his chuckle strictly internal. *Well, well, well.*

Of course, neither of them could know that *he* knew the two of them hadn't just accidentally arrived at the Bell at the same time—but Mirilin suspected Alberich knew. And Alberich was never going to let on one way or another.

:They let the stablehands take their Companions in,: Kantor told him. *:They had a great deal of—catching up to do.:*

:Indeed,: Alberich replied. It was interesting that Mirilin was clearly embarrassed, but Ravinia was not.

:Shelteny says that Ravinia isn't embarrassed by much,: Kantor observed dispassionately. *:A very cool one, she says.:*

:I can believe that.: Alberich paused at the door to swing his cloak over his shoulders, and pushed out into the stable yard. Snow was still falling, but at least it was not much more than token flakes, and a single stable boy with a broom was doing a reasonable job of keeping up with it. He crossed the yard and walked into the stables again, and a bay horse in the stall nearest the door peered over the side of the partition and snorted at him.

:I trust that the boys are already on their way back up to the Collegia?: he added.

:Halfway there, and just in time for their classes,: Kantor confirmed, as he picked up saddle and blanket from the side of the stall, and heaved them onto Kantor's back. *:Just about*

in the state of sore-muscled, worn-out wretchedness you'd hoped for. Not utterly miserable, certainly not feeling any desperation, but definitely feeling—chastised.:

:*Good.:* He didn't *want* them to be desperate, but he wanted them to *feel,* well and truly, that they were being punished for making not one, but several bad decisions. Not the least of which was that they made the choice to act recklessly in a place where mistakes would be magnified. Elcarth had made an excellent decision as to their punishment, and he and the Dean of Bardic had made it crystal clear that the boys were being punished by their respective *Collegia,* not by Alberich alone.

He finished putting on the last of the tack, and Kantor backed out into the aisle so that Alberich could mount. :*What had you planned for this afternoon?:*

:*I believe I'll have a talk with Keren about that suggestion of yours,:* he replied. :*And perhaps with Myste—though I had rather speak to Keren first.:*

:*Good. Mind you, I'd feel better if you had more than one set of hands and eyes helping you—:*

:*But the more people there are in on a secret, the harder it becomes to keep it.:* He felt Kantor's sigh of resignation beneath his legs as they trotted out into the stable yard, under the arched gate that led to the street, and onto the thoroughfare itself. Kantor didn't argue with him, though. The Companion knew just as well as anyone that if Alberich was going to do the covert part of his job effectively, it *had* to be kept secret. Heralds were humans—as witness Mirilin!—and humans talked, gossiped, let things slip by accident. That was one of the reasons why Alberich needed to do his job in the first place.

The ride up to the Collegium was uneventful, and now that substantial inroads had been made on clearing the snow, it was a bit faster than the ride down had been. And Alberich noted as they rode that it wasn't only the Trainees that had been infected by a spirit of play—there were snow fights and sliding, the building of snow sculptures and castles, and he saw no few people going by with skates over their shoulders. As they came into the region of private houses, larger and representing more wealth, the closer they came to the Palace, there was even more sign of merrymaking in the snow.

:Well, it isn't often that Haven sees a snowfall as heavy as this one has been.:

:Personally, I have never seen anything of the sort,: Alberich admitted. *:There are snows in my hills, but they are thin and dry.:*

:This is winter weather typical for the North of Valdemar, not so much here,: said Kantor. *:I wonder—:*

There was a long pause, as they wove their way among the houses of the highborn, and laughter and shrieks of pleasure and excitement echoed behind the walls and fences.

:You wonder—?: Alberich prompted his Companion.

:Well, it's dreadfully soon . . . and the Court is technically still in mourning . . . but a snowfall like this doesn't come very often, and there's going to be a hard cold spell coming behind it.: Kantor gave the impression to Alberich that he was musing aloud, though Alberich wondered for a moment where he was getting his weather information. *:The Terilee is going to freeze solid when that cold spell comes—that hasn't happened in fifty years. I just wonder if it's occurred to Selenay to decree a Snow Festival.:*

Although Alberich had never heard of a Snow Festival before, the name pretty much told him everything he needed to know. *:If the river freezes solid, isn't something like that bound to happen spontaneously anyway?:* The very novelty of the frozen river would bring skaters—the skaters would draw vendors of food and drink, and those would attract musicians, skate sharpeners, skate vendors, and probably more merchants than that. On the whole—well, it wouldn't be a bad thing for an official Festival to take place, official mourning be damned. The Wars had dragged on for years. Sendar's death had cast a pall over the entire country, but there was only so much grieving that you could do before you just wearied of it. Selenay's coronation had been a triumph, but it had been a shadowed triumph.

:Well, you can hear it beginning for yourself,: Kantor agreed, tossing his head in the direction of yet more laughter. *:And once the river freezes, people will come flocking down to the banks. If it were me, I'd go ahead and make the decree so that what is going to break out anyway gets some time limits to it. And while we're at it, something like this would create a number of excellent opportunities for* you *to nose about and listen.:* Kantor paused, perhaps to gather his thoughts. *:If any-one is going to try and foment discontent, oddly enough, a Festival is a good place to do so. You can say things then that people will dismiss as the drink talking—but the words will still stick in the memory, and should Selenay or her Council do something that people don't agree with—those words will be remembered.:*

:We really do think too much alike,: Alberich agreed, as they turned in at the gate, with a friendly nod to the Guards-man on duty. *:So, to whom should we drop hints, and when?:*

:Leave that to us Companions,: said Kantor. *:It's what we're good at.:*

The area around the salle was extremely quiet without streams of Trainees coming and going. When Dethor had moved out, Alberich had gotten the carpenters to put in a good, stout, one-Companion "stable" up against that oven wall for Kantor to stay in when he chose. It was immensely more con-venient not to have to go all the way up to the Companions' stable in order to tack him up—and this way, he and Kantor could come and go without any fuss or anyone noticing. Kan-tor himself always went up to the main stable to eat and drink, and Companions being Companions and not horses, the inte-rior of this secondary stable didn't need to be cleaned. Alberich being Alberich, he saw to Kantor's tack himself, except for the fancy "show" or "parade" tack, so it wasn't really any inconvenience to the stablehands, either, for Kantor to have his everyday kit down here. Alberich dismounted at the door of the little lean-to addition, and Kantor followed him inside. It was pleasantly warm, thanks to that brick wall.

:I'm going up to the stable,: the Companion said, as Alberich took off his halter and he shook his head and neck vigorously. *:I'm going to have some consultations.:*

Alberich bent to unbuckle the girth. *:I'll probably be here for the next mark or two. I want to think a few things over myself.:*

Kantor tossed his head, and when Alberich had a good grip on the saddle and blanket, walked out from underneath them. *:I'll let you know if anything gets started.:*

And with that, the Companion trotted back out into the snow, leaving Alberich to wipe down the tack and hang it up to dry.

It was less quiet in the salle than Alberich had thought it would be. He'd forgotten that there was going to be a crew of cleaners making sure that there was not the tiniest bit of glass left behind, then setting the floor to rights again. The soft murmur of voices was rather pleasant. He slipped in without disturbing them and went back into his own quarters.

The glory of his window took him by surprise—a blaze of gold and blue, color in a room that had been pale and faded in winter light before the window had been put in.

It was going to be a while before he got used to the change, but the shock was one of pleasure, and he found that he liked it. He sat down where he got the best possible view of the glass, and was bathed in the golden light coming from the Sun-In-Glory.

Ah. . . . It felt good. It felt right, to have the light of Vkandis about him. It felt like a blessing, and perhaps it was. If that was so, well, this was a good place for him to be when he was thinking about important decisions.

Now, the question about Keren and Myste was, should he take one or both women into his confidence concerning his covert work? Myste had the better knowledge of Haven; Keren would fit into rougher places. As he weighed the abilities of one against the other, it became clear that if he was going to do this, it *would,* eventually, have to be both. Neither had the ability or the skills to move in all the places that he could. But he thought that he would approach Keren about this first. It was, after all, the rougher places of Haven where most of his prowling was done.

That made him feel easier. Later, perhaps, he could ask Myste, if he thought he'd need her. She wasn't much good at anything physical, and he wasn't sure just how well she could conceal her feelings. He really didn't want to involve her if he didn't have to.

No matter how good a notion Kantor thought it was. Companions weren't *always* right.

"Bloody hell!" Herald Keren said, in sheer admiration. She shook her head. "All this time? You've been running around in Hell's own neighborhood all this time? By yourself? Bloody hell!" Keren had held Alberich in high esteem for his skill, but he sensed that this had not been anything she would have pictured him doing. "So where's your wheelbarrow, then?"

"Pardon?" he said, puzzled, as Ylsa choked. But neither of them explained, so he decided it was one of those colloquialisms he wouldn't understand even if he knew what she'd meant, and dismissed it from his mind.

Keren was probably Alberich's age, though with someone from Lake Evendim it was hard to tell. They were all lean, tall, and had the sort of face that appears not to change a great deal between the ages of twenty and sixty. She had been a Herald for several years by the time Alberich came to Haven, and people swore she'd looked pretty much the same as she did now on the day she arrived. She was an oddity among the

71

female Heralds, as she wore her brown hair cropped close to her head, but then, the only "hairstyle" she was interested in was how to braid up a Companion's mane and tail for parade.

"Since Dethor his Second made me, prowling the streets I have been," Alberich confirmed. Keren grinned at him, with a glint in her eye that made her partner Ylsa sigh and cast a glance up toward heaven.

Ylsa was cut of similar cloth to Keren, though her hair was an ash-blonde and her jaw square rather than Evendim-narrow. Apparently they had been together from the time they were yearmates as Trainees. Ylsa tended to be the one who exercised more caution than Keren did; hardly surprising, really, since Myste claimed the Lake Evendim fishers were all descended from pirates. "And just how often have you been doing this?" she asked.

"Of late, perhaps every two or three nights. But during the worst of it, nightly, could I manage it."

"Bloody hell! When did you sleep?" Keren demanded.

"Infrequently, apparently," Ylsa muttered.

He had known he would have to let Ylsa in on the secret of his double life the moment he'd decided to recruit Keren; he had learned as a commander that the only way to ensure perfect cooperation from his men—or now, his women—was to make certain their partners knew what was toward. And although by the strictest Karsite creed, what was between Ylsa and Keren was—not to be thought of—Alberich had been a leader of men for far too long not to know that things that were not to be thought of were commoner than the Sunpriests admitted.

Back when he'd been a Captain of the Sunsguard, two of his men had had just such an "understanding" between them, though the rest of the troop had not known, and Alberich doubted that even the two in question ever realized he had discovered their association. They had been very good at keeping it all to themselves, but Alberich had been better at reading subtle body language than they were at concealing it from him. Never once had it affected their performance; never once had they allowed it to affect their behavior in the troops. After careful soul searching on Alberich's part, he had finally decided that what did not affect the troops did not matter, and ignored it.

Several more of the men had clandestine marriages with women in one or another of the villages—ordinary fighters were not permitted to marry, at all, under any circumstances, only officers. Needless to say, those "understandings," too, had been kept very quiet. Strange, that whoring was tolerated, if preached against, but an honest marriage was absolutely forbidden . . . on the grounds that it was a distraction to the soldier.

This had all conflicted with what the Sunpriests decreed, and as their leader, his responsibility was to report every irregularity to the Sunpriests. Except that if he did that, he'd earn the hatred of half of them, and see the other half cashiered before six months was over. Eventually he had come to a decision on his own about what the men did or did not do. If some behavioral trait of one of his people did not affect performance and honor adversely, it mattered not at all. If it affected performance and honor positively, it mattered a very great deal.

So when confronted by similar "irregularities" as a Herald, he followed the same course, and that seemed to be the right way to go. It certainly fell right into line with the credo that "there is no one right way."

So far as he could judge, Keren and Ylsa were good partners. Keren gave Ylsa a boost to thinking imaginatively. Ylsa steadied Keren down, something that hellion badly needed. If they had lovers' quarrels, they kept it to themselves, or at least, never involved anyone but a counselor. And although Keren was permanently stationed at the Collegium—there hadn't been a better riding instructor in the past fifty years, so it was said—and Ylsa was a Special Messenger, which took her out of Haven all the time, neither of them complained about being separated far too often. If they'd been Sunsguard, he'd have called them fine soldiers, and written them up for commendations. As it was, since there was no such thing as officers in the Heraldic Circle and thus absolutely nothing he could say or do that would get them any advance in rank, he merely considered it a pity that there weren't more Heralds like them.

"And you want me to help you out?" Keren continued, still with that glint in her eyes.

"From time to time. Not often. But there are some things women tell not to men. And some places men are welcome not." He shrugged. "That there is the greatness of threat to Valdemar that there was once, I think not. That there is the threat still existing, however, I do think. I know not why there was that man paying for grumblings against the Queen, for instance, and this troubles me. Valdemar was not impoverished in the Wars as it could have been—"

"Thanks to you," Ylsa pointed out. "If you hadn't gone after those children, and got the lion's share of the Tedrel loot in the process, we would have been."

He waved that aside. "Still, seasoned fighters were lost; Valdemar hires not from the Mercenary Guild, so weakened will Valdemar be for some time. A weakened land is a land that others may seek—to exploit."

"Hmm." Ylsa sat back in her chair, and stroked her chin speculatively. "That could be . . . though we've friends on the east and south."

"There is the north," Keren pointed out. "Northern barbarians are always a danger, and the gods only know what Iftel might do—just because it's been quiet for centuries doesn't mean it won't suddenly roar up and turn into a menace. And there's always the west. Pirates on Evendim. Bandit bands large enough to qualify as armies. Weird stuff out of the Pelagirs. Gods only know what comes farther into the west than the Pelagirs."

"Even so." Alberich nodded. "The Northern Border and the Western are—"

"Fluid," Ylsa supplied him. "And what's more, Selenay inherited a Kingdom where war has allowed other problems to be ignored. And I suspect you know that at first hand." She raised an eyebrow at him; Special Messengers saw a lot, and were chosen as much for their ability to keep their mouths shut as their riding prowess.

He shrugged. "Indeed. The enemy I fear most lies within our borders. In Haven, the City Guard shorthanded still remains. Opportunists come in all stripes, and all ranks. Perhaps this is why someone seeks to agitate against Selenay. While we look to that as trouble, we miss some other evil he may do. Where there are fortunes to be made, men will seek to make them, be the source never so vile."

"And once you start selling one vile thing, further vileness comes easier. Especially when the price is good enough." Keren shook her head. "Well. How would you like me to start?"

"By learning to act a part," Alberich told her immediately. "The hellion will not always welcome be, where I would ask you to go. Sometimes, the serving wench. Sometimes, the whore."

Keren snickered at that. "Me! I'd never pass as a whore! Nobody'd look twice at me!"

"You are not old, not raddled with drink, have all your teeth, most of your mind, and no disease," Alberich said pragmatically, before Ylsa could jump in. "In the quarters where I go, that is enough."

Keren snorted. "*Most* of my mind! I like that!"

Ylsa laughed. "You're a Herald. You are volunteering to spy in the worst parts of Haven, dear. That's not exactly anything I see sane people queuing up to do."

Keren made a face. But she didn't argue.

"So. There it is. Can you act a part?" Alberich asked. "Can you act *those* parts?"

Keren scratched one eyebrow thoughtfully. "I'm pretty sure I can, at least, as long as you don't expect me to bed anybody. Not for days and weeks at a time, but then, you aren't going to want that, I suppose."

"No," he agreed. "If it must come to days and weeks, another solution sought must be. Not you nor I can be spared our assigned duties. A few hours at most, is what we will need. And no—if the whore you play, it is *my* whore you will be."

"For a few hours, I can manage anything," Keren decreed. "I suppose I could even manage pretending to be a lady."

"I'd pay money to see that!" Ylsa chortled.

"If it is a lady I need, to Talamir I should take myself," Alberich told them both. "Better to find one within the Court who is a friend—and I assume that he has more than one such already."

"Probably," Ylsa agreed, and Keren nodded. "There are highborn Heralds, too—*probably* no one would tell them anything directly, and since everyone would know they were Heralds, they'd be useless as spies, but people do gossip, and gossip alone might be worth something."

So, there it was. He had agreement, not only from Keren, but from her partner—which basically meant that Ylsa agreed not to interfere. He felt a little of the weight lift from his shoulders. "Well, then, I thank you both." He stood up, and motioned them both to remain seated. "I shall myself let out. Not soon will this be—nothing have I that needs a female, at the moment."

"Better to have the gaff in your hand before you try to land the sturgeon," Keren observed. "Take me with you a time or two when you've not got something on the boil, and I can get used to playing your doxy."

"I shall," he promised, and let himself out of their somewhat cramped quarters. They shared a room meant for one—well, it probably wasn't as crowded as it could have been, since both of them tended to keep personal possessions at a minimum and Ylsa was often away. But it felt very claustrophobic to him.

All things considered, he wasn't unhappy about being down in the salle. If he wanted or needed more room, he could just add on, as apparently, generations of Weaponsmasters had done before him. Quarters in the Heralds' Wing were best described as "tight" by his current standards, and he wasn't at all certain he would care to have neighbors on either side of his walls either.

That went very well, he decided, and knew that it could have turned out a flat failure. Keren might not have been interested—Ylsa might well have objected. And Keren's suggestion of going about in persona when there was nothing particularly that he needed to do was an excellent one. It would establish *her* personae and allow him to correct her, if need be, at a time and place where breaks in the particular persona would not be dangerous. Better to clear all that up before it could be fatal. Prowling the slums when there was nothing in particular he was watching for could be tedious at times; at least with Keren along, it might be less tedious. And having her with him when he changed into one of his varied costumes would also be useful. She could double-check the face paint he wore to cover his scars. The stuff was a damned nuisance; it had to be peeled off when he was done with it, and in hot weather it itched, but it was the only way he could keep from being recognized.

He'd better warn her about the food and drink in The Broken Arms, though, before they entered what passed for its door. There were some things even Keren's famously iron stomach could not digest safely.

Perhaps I should lure those whom I suspect there, and buy them meals. After a single bite I would have the truth out of them in no time.

Selenay chased the last of her servants out and closed the door to her bedchamber, even though she hadn't the least intention of going to sleep. It had been a long day, and unfortunately, it had also been a very dull one. It had not helped that every moment of it, she had been poignantly aware that just outside the Palace walls, virtually every creature of Court and Collegia—with the possible exceptions of the two scamps who'd broken the salle mirror—was taking the time to have some winter fun in the heavy snow. Even the oldest of codgers was out there, standing by one of the braziers, watching the younger folk skate or stage snowball fights. It made her feel very forlorn.

It had also made her miss her father very much. Sendar had loved the winter; had he still been alive, he'd not only have chased her out to play, he'd have contrived a way to join her. At night, during a full moon, he'd have huge bonfires in the gardens, and serve ice wine to the skaters. He was always the first one to inaugurate a sled run, and, as he said so often, "Royal dignity be damned."

She bundled up in a fur-lined robe over her nightdress, and took a book to the window seat in her bedroom, though she had no intention of reading it. Instead, she rubbed a clear patch through the frost on a windowpane with her sleeve, and looked out over the gardens.

The moon was just up, shining through the branches of the trees as if it had been trapped there. It was just a half-moon, with a little haze around it, and a faint golden cast to its face. Light from other windows in the Palace made golden rectangles on the surface of the snow beneath, with the occasional shadow passing across them as she watched. She had retired early tonight, but life in the rest of the Palace went on as usual. Even as she watched, she heard a giggle from outside, and a vaguely feminine form bundled up in a cloak and hood ran across the snow, followed by a second, then a third, scudding across the white snow like clouds across the moon. Three of the young ladies of the Court, out for a moonlight frolic? Were they meeting young men, or just having some girl-fun? Slipping out to skate on the frozen ponds by moonlight? Or were they servants, or even Trainees? They couldn't be Heraldic Trainees, for the cloaks had been too dark to be Grays, but they could be Bardic or Healer Trainees. . . .

Perhaps not Healers, who tended to be *very* serious indeed, and not likely to be out for a moonlit frolic in the snow. But Bardic, perhaps. Or even—well, no, probably not three of the common-born female Blues, either, the ones who got into the Collegia on merit. Those young ladies, fewer than the males by far, tended to be even more serious than the Healer Trainees, spending their evenings in study, except for taking the rare night off to go to the Compass Rose. Their positions were hard-won; many of them had come here over parental opposition, and they were not going to hazard what they'd gained by frittering it away.

Selenay sighed, feeling a wistful kinship to that handful of young women. She was in a very similar position, or at least, it seemed that way to her. She, and they, were prisoners to their duty and their responsibilities

Except that they were self-imprisoned; she was bound by blood and rank as well as duty. Surely self-imposed bonds were less galling than ones imposed from the outside.

She sighed again, more deeply, and rested her chin in her hand, and wondered what it would be like to be ordinary.

:*That rather depends on what it is that you mean by "ordinary,"*: Caryo replied. :*An ordinary Herald, for instance?*:

:*I suppose,*: she replied, unable to even think of what her life would be like without Caryo.

:*You've had some taste of it, when you accompanied Herald Mirilin down to the City Courts in Haven,*: Caryo reminded her. :*The real difference between you and the other Heralds is that you can never escape being Queen, and they can sometimes escape being Heralds for a candlemark or two.:*

:Exactly.: Selenay was relieved that Caryo hadn't started in on a lecture about how she should be grateful, that there were hundreds of young women in her Kingdom who had gone to bed hungry and would wake up with no better prospect of breakfast than they'd had of supper. That there were young women who had done extremely unpleasant things in order to get a supper, or a bed, and would do the same tomorrow. She knew that; knew that very well, no matter how much Talamir and Alberich tried to shelter her from it. She also knew that there wasn't anything much she could *do* about it with the limited resources at her behest. She knew that children went to bed hungry and cold, or even curled up in a doorway without a bed at all. She was doing what she could about that, with what she had—the mandatory schooling was a help, as were the "Queen's Bread" meals she'd managed to get instituted, so that at least every child had *one* meal in a day that it could count on. . . .

But never mind that now. She was just grateful that Caryo understood.

:Of course I understand. The wild songbird that's had its wings clipped and been clapped in a cage doesn't feel much like trilling, no matter how comfortable the cage is, nor how good the food in its cup.:

She felt her throat close a little, and blinked back the urge to cry—she was tired of weeping, tired of feeling sad and beaten and alone. That was a pretty accurate summing up. And no matter where she looked, it seemed that someone around her was trying to install yet another set of bars.

She wanted some fun again. She wanted to be irresponsible for just a little while. She wanted to tell the Council, the courtiers, the petitioners, to just *wait* for a candlemark or two while she went skating and sledding.

It felt almost as if she was being punished, and not only

had she done nothing to deserve being punished, she'd done everything she was *supposed* to be doing!

She didn't remember her father being so hedged about—

—*wait a moment*—

She blinked, and ran through that thought again.

I don't remember Father being so hedged about that he couldn't take a candlemark or two—

But the Councilors would be furious. There were so many things they wanted her to attend to, it often seemed that they even begrudged her the time she took to eat and sleep.

Just who is the Monarch here, anyway, me or them? Are people going to die because I take a little time to relax and have some fun?

:Exactly so,: Caryo agreed calmly. *:It would be one thing entirely if you neglected your duties to spend all of your time in pleasure and games. But since the moment the Crown was put on your head, the most you've stolen was a candlemark or two at bedtime to read.:*

:But how do I—: she began, then stopped, thinking back to her father. All right; Sendar'd had the authority to simply stop everything and say, "I'm going out for such-and-such." She didn't. So—

:I'll have to schedule it. Won't I?:

:Better still, decree it, in such a way that it becomes a duty—in their eyes—to take some pleasure.: And as she tried to work out how she could decree a few candlemarks off to go skating, Caryo added helpfully, *:There is a cold spell—a very cold spell—on the way. It's already frozen the verges of Evendim out to almost a furlong from the shore. It'll freeze the Terilee solid, and it should last for a fortnight at the least.:*

She blinked. She could barely remember the last time the Terilee had frozen solid. And when it had—

:I declare an Ice Festival?: she hazarded.

:Announce there will be one if the Terilee freezes, and make the announcement public,: Caryo agreed. *:Your Councilors will*

be so certain it won't that they'll just smile and ignore the decree. Then, when it does, it'll be all over the city, and they won't be able to cancel it.:

:But—what does one do—:

:Leave that to the merchants, for the most part,: Caryo said wisely. :Once you make the decree, they'll do exactly what they do for a Midwinter Fair, except that they'll prepare to set the booths and tents up on the ice. And you know, merchants being merchants, if you don't decree a Festival, they'll do this anyway. At least by making a royal occasion out of it, you can set a time limit on it. All you need to do is send someone to rummage through the attics for some prizes for skating contests and other competitions, and arrange for a Royal Pavilion out there with some provisions and cooks for the highborn. And talk to the Deans. Perhaps the young Bardic Trainees could perform gratis? Certainly there should be at least one day off from classes.:

The more she thought about it, the more excited she became. :But what if the ice starts to break—:

:Just find some people that know ice to be ice wardens; if it starts to break up, there'll be plenty of warning.:

Competitions. There ought to be skating races, of course, short and long. Perhaps something for trick skating? A prize for the best ballad on a winter theme. One for the best spiced cider and mulled wine?

:And hot meat pie,: Caryo said, with a mental shudder. :There are so many wretched hot pies, any encouragement to make them better would be a boon to your people.:

Ice fishing. There should be a prize for the biggest fish caught ice fishing.

:One- and two-horse sledding races.:

That was just about all she could fit in a single day, she thought with regret. And she wouldn't dare to take more than one day off herself—

:So have all of the elimination contests before the Royal

day,: Caryo advised. *:That way there will be some real anticipation building up, and you won't have to taste more than five
or six final entries in the food and drink contests.:*

Or listen to more than five or six ballads on the subject of
winter. . . .

*:And end with a feast and entertainments by moonlight on
the ice, with the feasting supplied by the Crown,:* Caryo said.
*:Have a Royal Ball at the Pavilion to coincide with the common
feast. It will be very romantic. Some of your young ladies have
been trying to get their young men to come to the question
since you were crowned, and if this doesn't do it, nothing will.:*

She thought of those giggling girls out in the snow, and
sighed wistfully. The last year of the Tedrel Wars had put paid
to a great many romances, and placed obstacles in the paths
of many more. Young men who had survived that last battle
had sometimes not had the heart for much after what they had
been through. She could certainly understand *their* frustration!

Not that she had anyone she wished would come to the
question with her. Far from it. No, she wished mostly that for
once a "courtship" didn't consist of her Council shoving
names and portraits at her. It would be so nice to listen to
poetry, even bad poetry, about the beauty of her eyes. It would
be wonderful to listen to stammered, clumsy compliments in
the moonlight, and to pull away from an attempted kiss at the
last possible, and most coquettish, moment.

Was it so wrong of her to hanker after romance, to long for
a circle of adoring young men who *didn't* adore the crown
rather than the girl? Oh, she knew that most young women of
her Court went off to arranged marriages rather than romantic
ones, but still, they usually weren't bartered off to the highest
bidder like prize cattle. They usually had some choice in the
matter.

Well, she had one choice, she supposed. She could always

say "no." They could badger her and nag her, but they couldn't force her to marry anyone.

:Think about your festival,: Caryo advised. *:You've taken all the steps you need to about the marriage plans. Think about something pleasant.:*

But would Talamir and Alberich approve? They were in charge of her safety, after all. . . .

:Alberich has already supposed that you were going to do just this, and has been making his own plans,: Caryo said instantly. *:Or so Kantor tells me.:*

What? Her head came up, like a hound suddenly sniffing something it did not expect on the breeze. But how—

:Partly knowing you, partly knowing you need some pleasure in your life about now, but mostly, I suspect, that Fore-Sight of his giving him a nudge in the right direction. It doesn't always have to be a disaster that he Foresees. And when it isn't—he probably doesn't realize that it's ForeSight.:

Well, that made perfect sense to her. And it was comforting, knowing that someone she trusted as much as she trusted Alberich thought this was a good idea.

:Oh, yes. For the people as much as for you. There's been too much sadness. When you mourn for too long, you start to forget how to feel joy.:

She bent her head at those words, feeling sadness overcome her again for a moment, and felt Caryo sighing with her. That struck to the heart of the matter, and had been something she had not felt comfortable voicing aloud. It had felt somehow disloyal to her father's memory to be weary of weeping for him. And yet, how many tears could she, should she shed?

So Alberich, who had been as loyal to Sendar as anyone could have asked, felt she was ready, and Valdemar was ready, to let go and move on?

Perhaps she didn't need to feel guilty, then.

But Talamir?

:Rolan says that Talamir will have no problem with this.:

Well, she wouldn't expect Talamir to participate; it would be unkind. She wouldn't really *need* the Queen's Own for something like this, just some good bodyguards. Alas. She wished she could have done without *those* as well.

But probably the monarchs of Valdemar hadn't been able to do without bodyguards since—well, for as long as she could think. Certainly as long as there had been difficulties with Karse.

So, there was one good thing; if she had to have bodyguards, they could at least be people she knew would be able to enjoy the Festival with her.

:Heh,: Kantor said, just as Alberich was choosing a book to read by his fire before going to bed. *:I doubt that you're going to be surprised at this. Caryo has just told me that Selenay has decided to hold that Ice Festival.:*

He settled down in his favorite chair, and adjusted the lamp behind him so that the light fell properly on the page. His window had an interesting look to it, with the light falling on it rather than through it. Rather like colored stone set in a mosaic. No doubt the Glassmaster had considered this as well, when he'd chosen the glass and the colors.

He hoped no one would ever take a shot at him from the other side of it. Getting those colors matched would be impossible. He'd probably have to have the whole thing made again.

At least it would take less time to craft a new window than that blasted mirror.

:Good,: he said firmly. *:It will be good for her, and good for Haven. But we'll need to slip it past the Councilors, so tell Caryo to suggest that Selenay wait until she's holding public audience, then make a decree tomorrow that if the Terilee freezes solid, there will be the Festival.:*

:What difference will that make?: Kantor asked.

Alberich sipped his hot wine. *:First, the decree will be in public, which will make it more difficult for the Councilors to object. Secondly, they'll applaud this in public as being a grand gesture, and think in private that it's about as likely as pigs flying. Then, since the decree will have been posted all over the city, when the river does freeze solid, it will be too late for them to do anything about forbidding any such festivities.:*

He was rather pleased with this. He wanted Selenay to have a victory without having to fight for it. The more of those she got, the more her Councilors would become accustomed to the idea that she *was* the Queen and *was* a ruler. Sooner or later, she was either going to have to rule in truth, or become the mouthpiece for her Council, a figurehead, but not a leader.

The sad part was, he could see even the *Heralds* who were on her Council gently maneuvering her into that role, all the while telling themselves that it was for her own good, that she was still too young to take the burden of the Crown, that they would just *guide* her. . . .

It was always easier to hold power than to give it up. That was how the Son of the Sun and his strongest Priests had come to rule Karse. And look where that had gotten them.

Kantor seemed to be following his thoughts. *:Good idea. I'll tell Caryo.:* And after a moment, *:Who do you want for Selenay's bodyguards? I doubt she'll be able to take more than a day away from her duties, but she'll need guards when she does.:*

Bodyguards . . . someone out there was trying to cause trouble over Selenay's rule, and even if he was doing it as a distraction, it was *still* possible that his words would find fertile ground in some poisoned mind and bear unexpected fruit. Maybe she wasn't in quite as much danger as she had been during the Tedrel Wars—

But maybe she was. He was in charge of her safety. He could not take the chance. So . . . that meant very good bodyguards, all over again.

Good question, who he should assign; assuming that the Collegia would be taking a full set of holidays, the various teachers and their assistants wouldn't be needed up here, but the Royal Guard *would,* in its full strength, both at the Palace and at the Festival. They would be busy keeping watch over all the highborn; he needed someone watching over Selenay and only Selenay. *:Might as well make it Keren and Ylsa for the daylight hours.:* He gave some more thought to what this Festival should involve, for lowborn and high as well. *:I suppose she'll have a feast and entertainment for the highborn in a pavilion on the ice the same evening that she attends the games? Or should I say, there will be two feasts, one for the common folk, and one for the Court? And I mean* all *of the highborn, as many as can come at short notice in winter? It would be good for building loyalty.:*

Kantor was taken by surprise by that question. *:I don't think she'd even considered a Court Feast for the entire roster of the highborn throughout the Kingdom, but it's a good idea. A very good idea. I'll pass it on.:*

Alberich felt a certain amusement that he, born poorest of the poor, and bastard to boot, should be the one to be making suggestions about what the great and grand would find appropriate. Still. He'd been raised on tales of it, after all. Virtually every child had. And he'd been watching *this* Court for years now. *:A grand feast for the Court will help lighten things considerably. Midwinter was shadowed; the first one without Sendar, and Selenay still in mourning. I don't think anyone had the heart for it. But this won't have any memories, any connotations. It's the sort of thing that ought to make the Councilors happy with the whole idea, since they'll be able to haul in all their so-called eligible candidates for her hand and hope that one of them charms her.:*

He added that last, with just a touch of sourness. Sourness, because, truth to tell, it annoyed him to see these supposedly sensible men trying to force the poor young woman into a destiny of *their* choosing. And because they were wasting so much time and effort on the project, time and effort that could be going to some task more useful. If they would put half the concentration they put into working together that they put into finding a mate for the Queen, three quarters of the current difficulties besetting the Kingdom would vanish overnight.

And for just a little while, it was a relief to think about something other than plots and intrigues. He had never been very comfortable in dealing with plots and intrigues, except for his singular talent of being quiet and unreadable. He was better at it now, but that didn't mean he enjoyed it.

Well, except for the occasions when he had an excuse to let off some of his tension by breaking a few heads. Hmm. This Festival just might give him a chance at that form of relief—

He quickly sealed *that* thought away from Kantor.

:She can be impartially charming right back to any would-be suitor without giving any of them hope,: Kantor agreed. *:I wish that more of them were worth being charming to.:*

:So do I.: The fact that so many potential mates had been systematically disqualified by Selenay in public meant that anyone who was dredged up and hauled in for the Ice Festival was bound to be marginal at best. Unsuitable in the extreme, unless some distant cousin out of the back of beyond happened to get dragged out of his manor, Chosen on the spot, and proved to be the man of Selenay's dreams. If she even had any dreams on the subject. It was hard for Alberich to tell. Selenay's mind was often opaque to him; he didn't have a great deal of experience with young women. Come to that, he didn't have a great deal of experience with women in general.

:And whatever suitors are hauled in will probably be stone-deaf and ninety at worst,: Kantor sighed. *:Poor Selenay! It will be a shabby lot of dancing partners she'll be getting.:*

Another aspect that hadn't occurred to him. With things so subdued at Midwinter, she hadn't seemed to want any dancing. The Selenay he remembered had loved dancing. Well, maybe he could do something about that.

:I think at an occasion like an Ice Festival, she ought to dance every other dance with a Herald, don't you?: he asked Kantor. *:In fact, isn't there some sort of mandate about that, somewhere? So that no highborn can claim two dances with her in an evening?:*

:If there is, Myste can find it,: Kantor replied, with a chuckle. *:And if there isn't—:*

:Myste can still find it,: he replied, thinking with real pleasure of how Myste and Selenay together had foiled the entire Council plan to get her safely betrothed to someone of *their* choice. It had been a thing of beauty, according to Myste. He was just glad that he had kept himself out of it, so that when he'd been asked, he'd been able to truthfully disclaim any knowledge of it all.

Not that he'd wanted to be anywhere near the room at the time the entire thing unfolded. Whenever certain members of the Council were thwarted, they always looked at the Karsite as the source of their troubles. Funny. They suspected *his* hand behind even this without his being anywhere near the Council Chamber that day; they'd entirely overlooked Myste. *:I'm not entirely certain about all those cross-cousin links Myste was finding. Surely the highborn of Valdemar aren't that closely inbred.:*

:Chosen! You don't think Herald Myste would concoct information, do you?: Kantor asked, pretending to be aghast at the thought.

:You're forgetting she was a clerk before she was a Herald,: he replied. *:They spend a quarter of their lives writing things down, a quarter finding what other people have written down, a quarter in hiding what was written down, and a quarter in making sure if it should have been written down and wasn't, it is now.:*

Kantor had no real reply for that, but Alberich didn't really expect one. And no, in the case of something important, he really did not think that Myste would stoop to forgery. But in the case of something like this, where nothing was hanging on a little judicious creativity but Selenay's all-too-rare pleasure, Myste could and would unbend her rigid ethics in order to ensure that the "tradition" existed, even if it hadn't been a tradition until a few moments ago when he'd thought of it.

Apparently Kantor agreed. *:Consider it a tradition that's been in place for centuries. You know, Myste is very good at aging documents.:*

Well, she had to be; she had to know how to forge them in order to detect forgeries. And it wasn't as if she'd be doing anything really unethical, like forging the Great Royal Seal. She could just insert it in a list of protocol from the last Ice Festival, hand it to the Seneschal as the guide to how he should conduct the feast at the end, and no one would be the wiser. And Selenay would get dancing partners that she could relax with. In fact, he'd handpick them. Or rather, he'd handpick them after consulting with someone who knew which Heralds were adequate dancers.

Which reminded him of something else.

:Don't the wretches generally sneak off to some private, Heralds-only party as soon as they can when there is an enormous fete like this one?: he demanded, recalling that they had done *just* such a thing at Selenay's Coronation.

:Um—: Kantor began, with overtones of guilt.

:Well, not this time, and that is an order, and have Talamir enforce it,: he said firmly. *:Not until Selenay is ready to leave. By Vkandis' Crown, if she doesn't get to enjoy most of this affair, it'll be no fault of mine, and it won't be for lack of good company, friends among the rest, as well as dancing partners!:*

:Yes, sir!: Kantor replied, for once, with no hint of mockery or irony whatsoever in his mind-voice.

Hmph. He settled into his book with a feeling of satisfaction, as Kantor and the other Companions—and whatever Heralds would be involved in the plot—coordinated themselves. Myste, Talamir, the Seneschal's Herald, presumably. Those here at the Collegium who were young enough to make decent conversation with her, good dancers, or both—

—and he wouldn't have to worry about a Herald as a risk to her safety either. Not that it was likely that anyone would try anything in so great a throng, but—

Grand, something else to worry about.

:What about—: Kantor interrupted his pretense at reading. *:—if we concoct another point of protocol? That any final-year Trainee of appropriate age and gender can serve as the Queen's dance partner?:*

He thought about that for a moment; it would effectively double the number of young faces at the occasion, and what was more they would be people Selenay already knew and would feel comfortable around. It wasn't that long ago that she'd been a Trainee herself.

:Perfectly reasonable. While we're at it, throw the doors open for the Bards and Healers as well. No reason why they can't be included. Every reason why they should be.: And Bards and Healers were just as trustworthy as Heralds. With any luck, there would be so many of them that no one else would even get a chance at taking a dance with Selenay.

He felt Kantor's approval. *:Good. Bards make better dancers anyway.:* And, once again, he sensed Kantor's withdrawal.

He felt himself smiling; there was something to be said for this particular kind and purpose of conspiracy. It made everyone who was involved in it feel good. And it got their minds moving in directions that had been sadly unfamiliar for far too long. Poor Selenay had been spending the last six moons and more thinking only of the welfare of those around her and dependent on her. It was about time that they all returned the favor.

:If Keren and Ylsa are going to be her bodyguards,

shouldn't she have an official escort?: Kantor said, coming "back" from wherever he'd "been."

Good God, another sticking point, another point of vulnerability. Not one of the suitors—oh, no. That would be opening the door to all sorts of potential trouble *and* danger. But who? *:Since this is a Festival, what about a Bard?:* he asked, thinking about all the really handsome-looking Bards he'd seen in and around the Collegia. *:Besides, with a Bard around, you never lack for conversation. It's their job to be witty.:*

:Good idea. Then she can't be accused of favoritism for the Heralds, but she won't be stuck with one of the suitors.: Kantor "vanished" again, and Alberich was left alone with his book.

He might even manage to get a page or two read, in between thinking of yet more security holes, and coming up with schemes to block them. While she was up *here,* behind her walls, she was secure. But down there, for the God's sake, out on a solid sheet of ice—

But her people love her. Even down there, in the worst part of Haven, there was anger when that whore tried to make trouble. He had to take comfort in that; had to remember that this was *not* Karse and Selenay *could* move among her people without fear.

Most of them, anyway—

He sighed, and put down the book. No point in trying to read now. It was time to start making some lists, or his mind would be buzzing and he'd get no sleep at all this night.

"When do you sleep?" "Infrequently."

He sighed, and fetched a pen and paper.

C LEAR sky of a brilliant, cloudless blue, and it was cold enough to freeze the— Well, it was colder than Alberich had ever been without also being wet clear through. It got cold in Karse, but never quite like this, a dry, biting cold that didn't penetrate so much as stab. He was grateful for the extra pairs of socks he was wearing, as well as for the peculiar contraptions that Keren had cobbled up for everyone at the Collegium, leather straps with five or six tacks in them that you could strap on over your boots to give you traction on the ice. She said that people used them for ice-fishing on Lake Evendim. Well, he would take her word for it, because if it was cold enough to freeze that lake this thick every winter, he never wanted to go there.

He'd never learned to ice skate, and at this point in his life, he was a bit dubious about the odds of his success if he started, so it was a good thing he had these so-called ice cleats on his feet. They kept him from measuring his length on the slippery river ice more than once.

He just wished there was something for sun glare off of ice and snow that made him wear a squint that was beginning to feel permanent. He had his hood up and a hat on top of it to shade his eyes, but that did nothing for the reflected glare. It was also beginning to give him a headache.

Still, this Ice Festival was something to be seen, and worth the cold and the rest of it. He didn't often get out during the day down in Haven in one of his disguises, and for once, he wasn't even down here on "business."

Whoever the jolly lad had been who'd been paying for people to foment dissension over the Queen, evidently getting his hireling arrested had frightened him off. Not a rumor, not a sign, not a *breath* of trouble had there been since then. Talamir reckoned that the whole scheme *had* been hatched up to create a distraction at some point—and that the hatcher of said plot had gotten cold feet when his agent had been unmasked.

Maybe, maybe not—but thanks to the Festival, Selenay's star was very high with the common folk, and grumbling was going to get someone's head broken. And *that* would quickly bring the City Guard and constables, which meant that Alberich's job was being done for him, at least in part. So—if this excursion, intended so that Alberich could listen to people talking, spend some time in and around the places where liquor flowed freest and tongues were loosest, wasn't entirely pleasure, it wasn't entirely business either.

As he traveled with the flow of the crowd down the improvised "street" of booths that had been built on the solid ice of the Terilee, he was covertly watching the reactions of those around him to his current guise. This costume represented more of a middling class of working man, someone who was, unlike many of his personae, *not* a particularly dangerous fellow, and he wanted to make sure he had the nuances down. The last thing he needed to do was to alert people when what he wanted was for them to be careless and at their ease around him. Normally he would have worn a clever cosmetic paste that covered his scars, but that wouldn't pass muster in the daylight. Fortunately, it didn't have to, not when he and almost all of the other people down here had their faces wrapped in scarves against the cold. He was experimenting with false beards and other facial hair, but those didn't stick too well in the cold.

That meant a lot of work on his part: moving easily, schooling his eyes and eyebrows into a vacantly pleasant expression. People reacted to the language of body and expression without even realizing that they were doing so; he knew very well how to read those things now. He'd been good as an officer, but now, thanks to no end of schooling, he was very, very good. That instruction had been not only at the hands of his mentor Dethor, but with the help of Jadus, who before becoming a Herald had been a Trainee of Bardic Collegium, where the Trainees were taught drama and acting as part of the curriculum. It had taken him years to get to this point, where he was willing to try going about among the middle classes, attempting to be unnoticed.

He thought, judging by the way that he was jostled, shoved, and occasionally grumbled at, that he was succeeding. None of his bully-boy personae would have been blundered into like this; the folks of the daylight hours would have taken one look at him and given him a wide berth. Assuming they didn't report him to the City Guard as a suspicious person. It was too bad he couldn't find a thief, especially a pickpocket, to teach him how to blend in. If there was one person whose very life depended on blending in, it was a petty thief.

He'd been on the lookout for those, just to keep his hand in at spotting them, but oddly enough, he hadn't seen any. Possibly that was because they were keeping to the nighttime hours in order to work the crowd in more safety, but possibly the issue was that they were no better on the ice than he was. If you had to run for it—well, you couldn't run for it.

:If I was a petty thief,: Kantor observed, *:I would work the*

booths on the bank and stick to the nighttime. A couple of hours past sunset, and it's not only dark enough to make a good getaway, people are a lot drunker than they are now.:

:Glad you aren't out here?: Alberich asked.

:Profoundly. I shudder to think of me on the ice. Keren hasn't yet come up with cleats for us, and neither has the blacksmith managed shoes that will work out there.: Kantor did not mention how much he disliked the cold; that was a given. Alberich had taken pity on him, and hadn't even ridden him down to the Bell today; he'd borrowed an ordinary horse from the Palace stables.

Alberich snugged the hood down around his ears, adjusted the scarf, and pulled the floppy felt hat down tighter. There was another thing to feel grateful for, and that was the quality of his costume. The good, thick, homespun wool with the old-fashioned hood was better than anything that the young bucks were sporting out here, and his clumsy-looking boots had room for three pairs of socks in there.

As he had predicted, the Councilors had thought the idea of the river freezing solid enough to hold the Ice Festival extremely amusing when Selenay brought up the idea before them. They ignored it in Council, and chuckled as she issued the proclamation in front of the Court. Well, the ones that weren't Heralds did, anyway; the Heralds already knew it was going to happen, but nothing would have convinced the Councilors of that. The news got down into Haven, and with a feeling of anticipation, people began making quiet preparations.

Then the cold wave rolled in silently at night, and everyone woke to find ice in the water jugs on their bedside tables, ice so thick on the glass of windows that you couldn't see out, and down along the river, reports that it was frozen over.

And all of the townspeople, who had, of course, been certain that anything the Queen made a proclamation about would come to pass, had sent watermen out to test the thickness of the ice daily. It had taken three days until everyone was certain that it was strong enough for the festivities. No one wanted accidents, however much they wanted a holiday.

Then, overnight, an entire Fair sprang up, with the more timid arraying their tents on the banks, and the bolder setting up right on the ice. Predictably, the merchants on the ice were heavily weighted in favor of hot food and drink stalls, while the ones on the banks featured fairings and other goods. The Midwinter Fairs, not only in Haven but all around the countryside, had been something of a failure, for the weather had been bleak and no one had had much heart for frivolity; this was going to more than make up for it, if the merchants had any say in the matter.

There were stalls doing a brisk business in crude skates, basic wooden blades with simple straps to hold them to the soles of the shoes. They could be made for you right there on the spot and fitted to your shoes or boots. There were several more booths set up to wax or smooth the blades. Then there was a knife grinder who'd set up to sharpen the blades of good steel skates. Those were blacksmith-made, of course; no one in the crowd that Alberich was moving in now could afford such things. Those with the money for steel skates who hadn't already gotten a pair were queuing up to get theirs, though, and the blacksmith who'd had blades going a-begging at Midwinter was getting double the price for them now. There were two kinds; you could get the ones that strapped on as the wooden skates did, or, if you really had money to spare, you could bring the blacksmith a pair of your boots or shoes, and he'd fasten the blades permanently to the soles. Anyone with those, though, was someone dedicated to the sport.

A kind of protocol had sprung up in the first day of the Festival about who got what part of the ice, since there were both skaters and walkers among the booths. Skaters got the middle of the lane, and those who were slipping and staggering about on their own shoes kept to the sides. The lane had been laid out wide enough that there was room for both, though occasionally a skater would go careening into the crowd, and the walkers would curse and try to cuff the skater. Most of the time people took it in good part, and if they saw someone skidding toward them, they often did their part to rescue him before he cracked his skull.

The contests had begun as soon as the booths were set up; informal races at first, which soon weeded out those whose bravado exceeded their skill. By the time that the Palace had sent down real judges, the would-be competitors had been winnowed down to a manageable number.

There had been those whose skill exceeded the limits of their equipment, but Selenay had a good plan to take care of that. She'd ordered preliminary races and games among those with the cheap wooden blades only, and the winners of those got steel skates—still of the strap-on sort, but made stoutly and of good steel—as prizes. That put the competition on something like a level field when the real contests started.

The booths began at the largest bridge across the river, where there were steps built into the banks. The racecourse began and ended where the booths did; going upriver for a set distance, carefully marked on both riverbanks, then returning. Anyone who cared to come to the bank along the race route could see the races; some enterprising souls along the bank were renting their rooms for the final day of racing, so that people could watch in comparative comfort. Alberich couldn't quite see the point of that—being crowded up to a window that gave you less of a view than the worst spot on the bank itself—but then, from what he was hearing, there would be so much in the way of drinking and carousing going on in those rooms that no one would be paying much attention to the races anyway.

Then there were the competitions in trick skating, being held in a particularly smooth section. Real seats had been set up there, and there were contests in jumping over barrels, fancy skating in singles and pairs, and sprint racing. When the trick skaters weren't performing or competing, someone had come up with a strange game involving two teams of eight men each, armed with brooms, a ball, and two goals. There didn't seem to be many rules, except that the participants evidently needed to be drunk enough not to care when they fell down or crashed together, but not so drunk they couldn't manage to play. Fights frequently broke out, but no one got seriously hurt, as far as Alberich had been able to tell. There were black eyes, a few lost teeth, and broken brooms, but no broken bones. Perhaps that was due at least in part to all the padding that the players wore in the way of extra clothing. The games tended to have no set duration, lasting either until everyone was too tired to go on, or the fancy skaters wanted to use the ice again and got the Guard to chase the gamers off. Whereupon the gamers would pick up their goals—made of eel traps—and move to rougher ice until the good patch was free again. To Alberich's inexperienced eyes, the game looked something like a game played on ponyback by some of the hill shepherds, who had allegedly got it from the Shin'a'in.

There weren't any prizes for the broom-ball game, so the people playing it were doing so purely for the sheer enjoyment of the mayhem they were engaging in. And, perhaps, for the hot wine and mulled ale that their supporters brought out for them whenever they took a break.

It never failed to amaze Alberich how much effort some people would go to for a "free" drink.

Skating competitions weren't the only ones that had been announced. Ice and snow sculptors had been hard at work, too, with their creations ranged wherever the artists' fancy had chosen to put them, with the traffic left to deal with them. Alberich had never considered ice as a sculptural material before, and he'd never seen anything made of snow other than a child's snowman, but these pieces were quite astonishing, and he thought that it would be a pity when they finally melted. There was one entire snow castle, with blocks of ice for windows, and furniture made of ice and snow, and a clever tavern-keeper inside selling ice wine in glasses made of ice. Some people were said to be paying him for the privilege of sleeping on the ice beds, but to Alberich's mind that was going more than a bit too far for novelty. Still, the place was pretty at night, with light from colored lanterns making the walls glow from within.

Probably the most popular places of all were the warming tents, prudently set on the riverbank, where braziers of coals kept the worst of the cold at bay and allowed frozen feet and hands to thaw out. Sellers of hot wine and hot pies provided the tents, and the benches inside. The Crown supplied the fuel (a gesture of good will that was much appreciated, for otherwise it would have cost something to be admitted) so even someone without the penny for a pie could get warmed up. And if you were clever, you brought your own drink in a metal can, and your own pies from home, to warm at the brazier.

The pies themselves were something new to Alberich—not that he'd never seen them before, but in this cold, they served a new and dual purpose. The pie itself served as a hand-warmer, in fact; most people made or bought sturdy offerings with a hard crust that could stand a great deal of abuse, wrapped them in a scrap of cloth as soon as they came right out of the oven, and tucked them into pockets and muffs to act as a heat source until the owner got hungry. By that time, the pie would probably have suffered enough that the owner could gnaw through the tough crust without losing a tooth—and if it had gotten too cold, you could always rewarm the thing without worrying too much about it. Or, as one old fellow said to Alberich, "Wi' my wife's cookin', a little char improves the flavor."

And the pies were as universal as the snow and ice, even for the denizens of the Collegia. If they presented themselves to the Collegia cooks before coming down, the Trainees were given pies as well, for the same dual purpose, but nothing like the common sort, which could have stood duty as paving stones. Alberich had one in each pocket right now, as a matter of fact, providing a comforting source of heat for both hands.

:You know, that might be another reason why there are so few pickpockets,: Kantor said. *:Your purse is somewhere inside your coat or your cloak and hard to get at. Your pockets are full of pies of a dubious nature.:*

Besides testing his disguise, a matter of curiosity had brought Alberich down here today. The Dean of Bardic Collegium had intercepted him yesterday to tell him that she thought she knew where the two mirror breakers had gotten their mad ideas for gymnastic fighting. Her information had brought him down to the booths at the bridge end where, as part of the Festival, a troupe of players had set up a tent to display their talent. There weren't many of those—it was, to be honest, too cold for anything but unaccompanied singers to be performing out-of-doors, and as for the sort of acrobats and dancers that plied their trade at Fairs, they'd be risking their skins to bounce about in their usual skimpy attire. This set of players, however, usually performed several times in a week at one of the bigger inns off the Trade Road; they'd moved to this venue just for the Festival, and as Alberich neared the canvas walls that held their makeshift theater, he saw that the move must have been very profitable for them. He joined the end of a longish line just forming up for the afternoon performance with some interest.

Well, "tent" was something of a misnomer, he discovered, as he got to the entrance, paid his entry fee, and filed inside with the rest. Only the area over the back half of the stage was roofed over and curtained, the rest was simply canvas walls to prevent the show from being viewed by those who had not paid, with an overhead scaffolding of rigging for stage effects and nighttime lighting reaching out into the area of the audience. Crude benches in rows fronting the stage were supplied to the public, and the show must have been popular, for the

tent was half full when Alberich arrived, and by the time of
the show, the benches were packed and so was the standing-
room area along the walls.

The drama was called—or so the banners outside proclaimed—"The Unknown Heir." The banners could have fit
any one of a hundred standard stories, and probably served
for every play these actors ever put on. They looked superfi-
cially new, but Alberich could tell that they'd been freshly
touched up just for the Festival.

The audience was ready to be entertained, and when the
back curtains finally parted and a single actor took the stage,
they erupted in cheers that must have gladdened his heart.

Alberich sat back on his bench, arms folded under his
cloak, and prepared to see just what it was that had "cor-
rupted" two Trainees.

First came the declamation of the Prologue. The plot, what
there was of it, concerned a highborn child, stolen from his
cradle and sold to slavers, subsequently bought or rescued (the
prologue was rather unclear on the subject) by a troupe of poor
but noble actors, and raised by them to adulthood. All of this
was laid out in a spirited fashion by that single actor before
any of the real action took place.

Alberich had to admit that the fellow knew what he was
doing; he had the right mix of flamboyance and humor to keep
the audience's attention. He finished his piece, gave an elaborate bow, and retired to great applause.

Then the curtains parted on "A Sylvan Glade," represented
by two rather sad little trees in pots, and a painted backdrop,
against which marched the troupe, portraying the actors on
their way from one town to the next. The *real* action opened
immediately with the Unknown Heir and his adoptive family
being attacked by bandits, and the Heir proceeding to single-
handedly, acrobatically, drive the bandits off. But not before
the bandits had managed to mortally wound the Heir's adoptive father—though how they got a knife blade through the

four or five layers of costume he was wearing was beyond Alberich's comprehension. This worthy managed an amazingly long set-piece while dying in his "son's" arms. He explained the young man's circumstances, presumed highborn heritage, and handed over the medallion the child had inexplicably still been wearing (even though it was solid gold) when taken from the hands of his kidnappers. It was an astonishing monologue, especially from the lips of someone stabbed through the heart quite some time ago.

None of this evidently stretched the credulity of most of the audience.

With tears and histrionics, the Heir proclaimed that he would regain his rightful place, and wreak revenge for his father's death.

Riotous applause called up many bows from the actors before the action resumed.

The rest of the play consisted of one improbable fight scene after another, taking advantage of the acrobatic abilities of— Alberich guessed—roughly four of the actors in question. And there was no doubt in his mind before the first act was over that this was, indeed, where the two miscreants had gotten their misguided ideas, and given the wild applause that these bizarre fights managed to garner, he was a lot less surprised that the boys had become enamored of the idea of fighting like *that*.

As the Heir and his Best Friend—both in love with the same girl, of course—battled their way through throngs of evil henchmen attempting to keep them from claiming the Heir's rightful place as the Duke of Dorking, Alberich had to admire their stamina, if not their style. In the conclusion to the first act, the Heir plummeted off the top of a "cliff" to flatten half a dozen evildoers, then engaged four at once, sword-to-sword, and after being disarmed, defeated his enemies with a bucket. In the second act, the Heir and the Friend, ambushed in a Peasant Hovel, made the most creative use of a ladder, a table, and a stool that Alberich had ever seen. In fact, what they most closely resembled was not a pair of fighters at all, but a pair of ferrets trying not to be caught. In the third act, the Best Friend met the end that Alberich had expected from the first, after yet another acrobatic exhibition, dying in the arms of the Heir and bravely commending the Heir and the Girl to one another, with the Heir vowing revenge once again—

:*You know,*: Kantor commented, :*I'd steer clear of that man. People trying to kill him seem to keep missing and hitting his friends instead.*:

But it was in the fourth act that something entirely unexpected happened, and it had nothing to do with the script.

Now, Alberich had noticed something a bit odd just before the play began. In the front benches, just off to one side, was a group of young men in clothing far finer than anyone else here was wearing. When the action started, he quite expected them to begin jeering and catcalling, but to his surprise, they did nothing of the sort. In fact, they were quiet and attentive to a degree all out of keeping with the quality of the drama unfolding. And it wasn't as if they weren't *used* to better fare, either; he recognized two of them from having seen them moving in the fringes of Selenay's Court.

Now, that was odd. So odd, in fact, that he felt a tingle of warning and kept his eye on them all during the play.

Then came the fourth act, and the "Grand Climax and Exhibition of Sword-play with Astonishing Feats of Strength and Skill, Never Before Seen on Any Stage" which was laid in the Grand Hall of the Duke of Dorking's Castle. The Heir's enemies held both the Heir's real parents *and* his True Love captive and were engaging in a spot of gloating.

And the Heir swung in over the heads of the front of the audience on a rope.

Alberich had to give them credit; it was a spectacular entrance. Not a very bright one for a real fighter, since while the Heir was swinging about on a rope he was an easy target for anyone with a knife, crossbow, spear or lance, all of which were in evidence among his enemies—but it was a spectacular entrance. The Heir let go the rope, did a triple somersault in the air, hit the stage, and came up fighting.

No mistaking that move, which was one the boys had tried (in vain) to copy. The actor might be a phony fighter, but he was a superb athlete and tumbler.

There was more of the same wildly unrealistic combat and Alberich noted in passing that the actor who *had* been playing the Best Friend was now, with the assistance of a beard, playing the Chief Villain. And then—

—then came the break with everything Alberich had expected.

If he hadn't been watching so closely—*and* watching the audience, in particular, his lot of young nobles—he might have thought it an accident.

But in the middle of the duel with the Chief Villain, a prop-sword went clattering across the stage, right under the lead actor's feet. He apparently stepped on it, because the next thing that happened was that his right foot shot out from under him, he staggered and tried to catch his balance, and then he went blundering right over the edge of the stage and down onto the audience in the first row—landing atop the same young highborn that Alberich had noticed—to the gasps and shrieks of the crowd.

But all was not as it seemed.

The thing was, someone as good a tumbler as that actor was shouldn't have gone off the edge of the stage at all. What was more, he *hadn't* stepped on or tripped over the sword—

No, as Alberich saw, just before he surged to his feet along with the rest of the audience, the actor had actually kicked it off to the side before making that spectacular "fall."

Furthermore, the young men he'd landed among *had been tensed and ready to catch him.*

If he'd *really* fallen by accident, they'd have scattered instinctively away from his path, not gathered under him, broken his fall, and set him down.

He was up in a trice, as the audience applauded, bowing to them, apologizing to his "victims," even brushing one of them off—

Which was when Alberich distinctly saw a folded set of papers pass from the actor to the young highborn man, vanishing inside the latter's cloak before he could blink.

:*Great Gods!:* Kantor exclaimed, as Alberich struggled to keep his expression precisely like that of everyone else around him. :*What in the nine hells*—:

:*I don't know,:* Alberich said, as the actor got back up on the stage and resumed the play. :*But I am going to find out.:*

"—and I do not know who it was," Alberich told Talamir, feet stretched out toward the fire in Talamir's somewhat austere chamber. He had come here directly from the Festival, so directly that he hadn't even had a chance to properly thaw out, though he had stopped long enough to change out of his disguise at the Bell. But Kantor had warned Rolan that Alberich needed to speak to Talamir, who had in his turn informed Talamir that Alberich was coming and was in serious need of defrosting. And Talamir had arranged for hot drinks and a well-stoked fire as well as getting free long enough for this quick meeting.

"A young man you've seen in the Court. No one you clearly recognized." Talamir frowned. "I wish the young people were a little more distinctive, or at least wore the same badges they put on their retainers' livery. Your description doesn't resonate with me either."

Alberich shrugged. "That being the case, until I discover, I am going to have to spend more time around the Court than it is usual. Most probably, it is you who shall have to identify him for me, once his face I see."

"I can do that, certainly, but what do you suppose was the meaning of this?" Talamir asked, leaning over to refill Alberich's tankard. Alberich shifted a little, and shrugged.

"What it probably *wasn't,* much more easily can I say, than what it was," Alberich replied, absently taking another drink and half-emptying the tankard again. "Not an assignation do I think; better ways there are, of passing love notes, than the midst of a play. Not contraband of the usual sort; papers, these were, nothing more."

"Unless the contraband is too large to hand off, and the papers were directions telling where it was," Talamir observed. "It could be something else less-than-legal. Stolen goods, perhaps a valuable horse—or—perhaps money to pay for it?"

"Only papers," Alberich countered. "And what would the purpose be, of the poorer actor paying the highborn, rather than the reverse?" He shook his head. "No. And I think not, the papers were directions to something stolen. Which leaves—information. Paid for by the highborn, gotten by the actor. So—why the exchange in the midst of the play?"

"Because our highborn fellow does not want to be seen making clandestine visits to a mere player." Talamir seemed very certain of that point. "Someone like that would never come up the hill or be allowed even in the gates of one of the manors. Let me tell you, there is *nothing* more certain about the Great Houses than access to them."

"Surely as an actor, easy would it be to feign to be the servant?" Alberich hazarded.

Again Talamir shook his head. "Every servant in a Great House will either have worked for the family for generations, have come from the family's country property, or have been personally vouched for by other servants. Every delivery person will be from a particular set of shops and will be known to the servants. Even the folk who come to take off the trash are personally known to the servants—what the highborn discard is picked over by dozens of lower servants before it gets to the bins outside, and then the right to cart off what is left is jealously guarded."

"Hmm." Alberich blinked; he hadn't known that. Well, so much for ever trying to insinuate himself into a Great House as a servant! "And the boy could not come to the actor in a more secret way?"

"Hah." Talamir raised an eyebrow. "Not where they are. And people take note when they see someone richly dressed hanging about a 'common' venue. No matter how careful he was, someone would see him. Unless, of course, he was as practiced in deception as you are, which is highly unlikely."

"And the resources have, as well," Alberich reminded the older Herald. "Without the Bell, my movements could not possible be."

Talamir's lips formed into a thin line. "The question is, what information, why, and to whom is it going?"

"And does the Crown have interest?" Alberich added. "It could be, we need do nothing about it. It could be, this is only to do with the rivalries among the titled."

Talamir looked thoughtful as Alberich put the empty tankard aside on a little table that stood between their chairs. "It could be, I suppose," he admitted. "But it seems a great deal of trouble to go to simply to acquire information about a rival. And why the connection with a troupe of common players?" He shook his head. "No. I don't like it. I scent something else here."

Alberich was willing to bow to his experience. "So, you think it is something surely to do with a larger issue? Still, it could signify only that someone has an interest, and is not hostile."

"Or not. The Karsites are not our only enemies." Talamir looked pensive. "Or it could be agents of a putative ally, who wishes to learn more than we've told him. In which case—we need to establish if there is any harm in letting him continue to operate."

Alberich snorted at that. "Allies can cause as much harm as enemies, and are less suspected."

"Hmm. There are times, my suspicious friend, when I am glad that you are who and what you are," Talamir replied after a long silence. "That had not occurred to me."

Alberich shrugged. "I am, what I am," he replied. "In Karse, one keeps one's friends close, and one's enemies closer."

"And in Karse, suspicion is no bad thing." Talamir pinched the bridge of his nose and closed his eyes in a grimace. "Let us start with the obvious. You might as well add yourself to Selenay's bodyguards tomorrow. The entire Court will be down at the Festival, and I've no doubt that your mysterious young man will be in the midst of the throng. You'll have your best chance to spot him then, and I can identify him for you."

That was a shortened version of "You'll show him to Kantor, who'll pass the image to Rolan, who'll show it to me, and I'll put a name to him." Alberich nodded.

But he wasn't happy. "Hoped I had, the crush to avoid," he sighed. He still wasn't comfortable rubbing elbows with the titled, even when he was playing so "invisible" a part as that of a bodyguard.

"Well, you can't," Talamir retorted, with an unusual level of assertion. "I won't be around forever, and it is well past the time when you began taking up the duty of spy within the Court as well as down in Haven."

If anything, that made Alberich even more uncomfortable— because no matter what he did, he *couldn't* take Talamir's place within the circles of the Court. For one thing, even if he'd been Valdemaran, he wouldn't fit. For another, no one was ever likely to confide anything in *him*. He just didn't have the face for it.

But he held his peace. There were more ways of undoing a knot than splitting it with an ax. There were Heralds permanently assigned to the Collegium who might serve as his eyes and ears among the highborn, especially the women. Ylsa, perhaps. And there were Trainees coming up who were highborn themselves who might be trusted to play clandestine agent.

"My best, I will ever do," was all he said, and he and the Queen's Own got down to the business of trying to find other ways for Alberich to set eyes on the young man in question again—just in case, against all probability, he did *not* show his face at the Festival.

Because in Alberich's experience, the thing that you planned for always turned out to be the one that was least likely to happen—and the one that you had never thought of was the one that landed in your lap.

SELENAY'S day at "her" Festival dawned cloudless, bright, and bone-chillingly cold. Alberich and the others had planned on forgoing Formal Whites for the sake of warmth, but the ever-resourceful seamstresses had provided the entire escort with heavy woolen capes lined and trimmed with white fur, white fur mittens (fur inside and out), and heavy stockings trimmed at the top with fur, which would make the boots look as if *they* had been lined and trimmed with fur. As a result, they all looked smartly turned out and entirely festive.

When they had all arrived to escort Selenay down to the river, one wag suggested that they ought to have their capes festooned with the same bridle bells as were on the Companions' parade tack, a suggestion which had earned him a handful of snow down his back. After that, he kept his thoughts on costume to himself.

They made quite a little parade, going through town. Fortunately, no one had thought it necessary to make a real procession out of it, though people were lining the streets, waving and cheering, the whole way.

"I think your people love you, Your Highness," said one of Lord Orthallen's hangers-on, patently hoping to curry favor, for he still had his mouth open to continue with a compliment when Selenay laughed.

"I think they love the Queen's Bread they're getting today, and the feast I've arranged for tonight," she replied, and Alberich smothered a smile. For this, the final official day of the Festival (although people would probably stretch things out for as long as the ice held), she'd arranged for bread to be distributed in the morning until the supplies ran out, and meat, wine, and bread for the same time as the Court Feast this evening. If the fountains weren't running with wine instead of water, it was because it was too cold; instead, there would be hot wine available in huge cauldrons along the bank, alongside fires where various beasts were roasting on spits, and more of the bread that had been baked well in advance, and stored cold. Although the notion of "whole roasted oxen" was a romantic one, for practicality's sake, what was going to be offered was just about any beast that could be spitted and roasted and would provide enough meat to satisfy a portion of the crowd. There were quite a few sheep, for instance, and a great many pigs, domestic and wild.

Selenay had been as generous as her purse would allow. If anyone had seen these creatures alive, he would have been well aware that they were all, well, not exactly prime. Most of them had come from the Royal Farms, and were past breeding or working age. Still, they'd been well tended all their lives, and if they were going to provide somewhat tough eating, well, as one old man once told Alberich, "Forbye, much chewin' makes it last the longer, and tough be tasty." Most of the people who would be swarming the fires didn't taste meat more than a few times in a year, and it was almost never anything like beef or mutton.

And as for those who could afford better, well, they could take their purses and go buy it.

In fact, the fires were already being set up for the cauldrons, and the carcasses turning over *their* flames when they arrived at the river. It occurred to Alberich, as the scent of roasting meat filled the air, that the food merchants were not going to do badly out of this, after all. The meat wouldn't be ready for hours, but people would be hungrier with the scent of it in their noses.

For all that he disliked the crush, the sidelong glances, the discomfort of his position as Selenay's shadow, Alberich could not begrudge the Queen a single moment of her day of relative freedom. All he had to do was to catch a glimpse of her face to know that she was enjoying herself for the first time in—well, in far too long. She was smiling a great deal, even laughing, and there was a glow on her that made her look more alive than she had in months.

It didn't take a MindHealer to know why either. This day at her Ice Festival was, perhaps, the only time she had spent since her father's death that wasn't shadowed with memories. Sendar had never presided over such an occasion; guided only by old Chronicles, her friends, and her own imagination, this was something that Selenay had created for herself. It had taken Alberich a little aback to see her *smiling*.

With special nail-studded shoes to give traction on the ice (for the blacksmith had finally come up with something that worked as well as the ice cleats) the Queen, her escort of Heralds, and their Companions came down onto the rock-hard river just about a candlemark after dawn to view the ice sculptures. When a winner had been chosen and rewarded, she went on to watch the childrens' races and present medallions, money, and skates to the winners. Alberich enjoyed that; the children were enthusiastic and excited without turning it into the cut throat competition he'd seen watching the preliminary races of the adults. The losers were disappointed but consoled by the sweet cakes Selenay passed out to all the competitors, and the winners so bursting with joy that they could hardly contain themselves.

By midmorning she was ready to taste the three finalists in the meat pie, the mulled ale, the spiced cider, and the hot and ice wine competitions. Then, fortified, she returned to the exhibition area for the fancy skating.

By this time, Alberich was both cold and frustrated, for he hadn't yet seen the young highborn fellow he'd been hoping to identify. When Selenay retired to the Royal Pavilion set up on the ice for a hot meal and a chance to catch her breath, *he* left her in the guard of Keren and Ylsa, and went prowling.

Selenay never had her noon meal in the presence of her Court; by the time she had a chance for that respite, she was generally sick to death of most of them, and wanted nothing more than a little privacy to go along with her food. She wasn't going to change that habit now, so Alberich had a good candle-mark to roam about the Royal Enclosure to see what, if anything, could be seen.

There wasn't much. Just a few of the younger set who were already sport-mad, and some of the older ones who never missed a chance to hover in the presence of royalty, and had done so even in Sendar's time. Alberich decided that he would have the best luck if he sidled in near the former and tried to eavesdrop on their conversation, so he got a skewer of basted meat from one of the cooks serving up food *al fresco,* and stood just behind a likely pair, slowly eating and staring off at nothing in particular, doing his best to be ignored.

". . . Jocastel may think he's clever, taking the whole house for the day," one of them sniffed, "but they shan't see anything but the middle of the races."

"Well, none of them will, except for Redric. He took that warehouse." The other nodded at a warehouse on the opposite bank, whose docks were festooned with greenery and a few pouting girls wrapped up to the eyes in expensive furs.

"Oh, yes. Well, trust *him*. That entire set is gambling-mad. They'll be there all day."

"And so will Jocastel's, and I doubt that any of *them* will be watching even the middle of the races." A knowing tone crept into the young man's voice. "Redric may have snared most of the ladies, but Jocastel got the keys to his father's wine cellar."

The first one snorted. "Idiots. The lot of them. You can guzzle wine anytime, but when is there likely to be another Ice Festival in our lifetimes? The last one was over fifty years ago, and every champion skater who could get here in time is going to be in the races today! Listen, the big races will begin as soon as the Queen comes back out—*I'm* for hunting down one of those broom-ball tournaments I've heard of. The Terilee might thaw, but the pond up at the old pile will hold for months yet, and I've a mind to get a bunch of the lads together and try the game out ourselves!"

"Oh, now there's a plan!" enthused the second, and both of them moved away, gesturing at each other.

Well, that explained why there was no one here to speak of . . . a gambling party in a warehouse, a drinking party in a rented house, and that pretty much accounted for most of the youngsters of the Court.

Alberich wandered over to the vicinity of a quintet of older men, who were glaring at the young ladies on the dock with disapproval and muttering at each other. "What are their fathers thinking?" grumbled one, just as Alberich got within earshot. "The idea! Going off to some rented hovel unescorted—"

"Oh, it isn't the daylight hours that I would be concerned about," said another sourly. "But who's to say what's going to happen when the Feast is going on and some of them slip off, unsupervised?"

Alberich eavesdropped shamelessly a little more, learning only that most of the "younger sets" weren't even planning to come down to the Royal Enclosure until the sun set. The older courtiers would be trickling in during the late afternoon, but they weren't the ones Alberich was concerned with.

He returned the skewer to the care of the cooks, and drifted back to Selenay's Royal Pavilion feeling heartily annoyed at humankind in general and that feckless lot of highborn in particular. Hang it all! Why couldn't all those eager parents insist that the young men come down here to dance attendance on the young—and eligible—Queen? Why were they allowing their offspring to gamble and drink away the afternoon without even trying to steal moments of Selenay's time? What were they thinking?

:They're probably thinking that if Selenay hasn't indicated her interest in any of them by now, there's no point in freezing their manhood off to try to impress her today,: Kantor observed dispassionately.

:Hmph.: Alberich nodded to the Guards at the entrance, and pulled back the door flap, feeling entirely disgruntled. *:Then there's no damned point in my being here now.:* The Royal Pavilion had been set up with a kind of antechamber to keep out the coldest air; he parted a second set of door flaps just inside the first.

:Yes, there is. It will get everyone used to seeing you playing bodyguard, so that no one will think twice about it tonight,: Kantor retorted.

It wasn't much warmer inside, but at least there were carpets laid over the ice, and braziers of coals on sheets of slate atop them that provided little pockets of warmth. The light in here was a lot more restful than out on the frozen river, too; the pitiless sunlight glowed through the painted canvas rather like the light coming in through his precious colored window. And it was out of the wind.

"Alberich!" Selenay called from amid a heap of furs and cushions piled on a high-backed settle that had been brought down from the Palace, her cheeks glowing, her eyes sparkling. "What's to do between now and the Feast?"

"More races," he replied. "The really serious ones; all the champion skaters that could get here in time are going to be competing. Out there will be some intense rivalry; the prizes for the adult races are considerable, and to claim one bragging rights will bestow for a decade."

"Really!" She looked entirely pleased. "How exciting! Have we referees along the course?"

"Absolutely," Keren replied, before Alberich could answer. "Not only is there the prospect that someone is likely to cheat, there's the fact that if someone goes down, there might be a fight over it. He'll probably claim he was fouled, and he might take a part of the field with him. We have this sort of thing every Midwinter where I'm from."

"And there is, I hear, much gambling over the outcome," Alberich added. "So, more incentive there is, to cheat."

"And if someone's accused of cheating?" Selenay looked from Keren to Alberich and back again. "What do I do? Whoever is accused will deny it, no doubt."

"Depends on how and where in the race, and if a referee saw it," Keren said judiciously. "Let the referee handle it, unless enough people got taken down. Then, if you're inclined, you can have 'em run the race over again. Presumably, everybody'd be equally tired, so they'd all be on the same footing. If I were a betting person, I'd lay odds you'll have to rerun at least one race this afternoon. This is going to be the climax of the Festival for a lot of people—not even the Feast is going to eclipse it. Feelings will be running high."

"Which is why I have plenty of the Guard stationed on the course and off it," Selenay replied, nodding. "The Seneschal warned me about that, after he watched the semifinals."

"You won't be able to jail everyone who starts a fight—" Keren began dubiously.

Selenay laughed. "And we won't try! Instead, anybody who

gets out of hand is going to find himself hauling wood and chopping wood for the spits and the cauldrons!"

Keren laughed, too. "Good enough! Work the energy out of a hothead and leave him too tired to fight!"

"That was the plan," the Queen agreed, looking pleased with herself. "So, besides the races, is there anything else for me this afternoon?"

"Only a skating pageant," Alberich replied, having seen the preparations going on for the thing nearly every day since the Festival began. "Like a street pageant."

"Only instead of *you* riding along the street and stopping at every display, you'll be the one sitting, and the groups doing the displays will pass in front of you, stop, and make their presentations," Keren said helpfully.

Selenay made a face. "I suppose," she sighed, "that everyone would be very disappointed if I didn't watch the whole thing."

Alberich didn't blame her. There were only so many badly-rhymed paeans to one's beauty and goodness, sung by shrill and slightly-out-of-tune children's choirs, that a sensible person could stand.

"Very," said the Seneschal, who had just entered the Pavilion himself, in his firmest voice.

"Can I watch it on Caryo instead of in the grandstand?" she asked hopefully. "It's warmer on Caryo—"

"But the purpose of the pageant is as much for you to be seen as for you to view the presentations," the Seneschal pointed out, in a tone that made it very clear that Selenay would not be watching the affair from her saddle.

She sighed. "I hope you have lots of these furs," she said.

The races were just as exciting as Keren had predicted. And a great deal more dangerous for the participants than Alberich

had anticipated. In fine, the contestants were no longer holding back, at all, to save something for the climax. This *was* the
climax, and every one of them was determined to go home
bearing the champion's medal. The putative honor of entire
villages depended on the results, at least for the next year or
so, and the skaters were in competition not only for themselves, but for all of their backers.

They wore a lot less for the actual racing than Alberich
would have thought wise, but then, moving at the speeds
these folks did, perhaps they burned up so much energy they
simply didn't feel the cold once they got moving. Or maybe
their exertions kept them warm. Whichever it was, when it
came time to form up along the starting line, they all left off
coats and cloaks, keeping only thin, knitted woolen trews
bound closely to their calves, and thin, sleeved, knitted woolen
tunics, with scarves wrapped close around face and mouth,
and knitted hats and gloves. They all looked somber, focused,
and purposeful. By this point, anyone left in competition had
steel blades on their feet, and they were wickedly sharp, too.
It was when he was looking at those blades glinting as the
skaters warmed up before the first race, that Alberich suddenly
realized that the races could be *dangerous* as well as competi-
tive. These folk were wearing knives on their feet, and if they
went down in a heap. . . .

Well, they must know that. Presumably, they would take
care if they did go down. Or at least as much care as could
be taken. The idea just made him shake his head, though; he
couldn't imagine taking the chance of getting a leg or arm
slashed to the bone for the sake of a race.

Interestingly enough, it was the longest of the races that
started first, because by the time this race, of several leagues,
ended, the shorter races would be long over. They called it simply the Long Race, and those who competed in it were specialized skaters indeed, and would not take part in any other race
today. It was a lonely sort of race—far, far down the river and

back again, a test of endurance as well as speed, and the organizers had supplied each of the volunteer referees stationed along the route with a fire, blankets, and restoratives so that they could go to the rescue of any racer who failed.

That race began with a preliminary scramble, but as the skaters passed out of sight beyond a bend in the river, it was clear that the pack had quickly sorted itself out, and the race had turned into an orderly skate in which each man would play out a strategy that he had predetermined for himself.

Then the fast races began. First the sprints, which were *very* fast indeed, and just as contentious as Keren had promised. There were falls, and the predicted fights among both skaters and spectators, and some sorting out by the Guard. Selenay declared that two races would be rerun.

Then came the longer races, which was where Alberich got a good look at the sort of pace that could rival that of a Companion at full gallop. The skaters bent low over their feet, with their hands clasped behind their backs, making strong, sure, gliding strokes that were most like the oarstrokes of men in sculls. Only at the beginning and the end did any real fight for position take place, although there were some minor exchanges back in the pack. It was fascinating to watch, and the slightest mishap could change everything. More than once, a bit of bad ice caused a fumble that could drop a skater one or more places, and once, a fall took out the entire back half of the pack, with the resultant scrambling that meant there was no chance that any of them could fight for one of the top positions.

The dock at that warehouse was full of people the entire time, and highborn though they might have been, they were shouting, gesticulating, and jumping up and down just as much as any of the commoners on the banks until all but one of the races was over.

And the crowd settled down to wait, eyes straining to the

bend in the river, ears cocked for the first sounds of approaching blades.

Then, at long last, the first of the exhausted endurance skaters hove into view—that is, Alberich assumed they were exhausted, though the ones in the lead showed no signs of it, just gliding on with long, sure strokes, swinging their arms for added momentum, looking neither to the left nor the right. The crowd bellowed encouragement, and in the last few furlongs, the final bits of strategy played out; and a skater who had been steadily in third place, hanging so close to the man in front of him that it looked as if they were bound together with a rope, suddenly pulled away. As people screamed and shouted, he put on a final burst of energy; he passed the man in second place. The man in first heard the shouts and made the mistake of looking behind him, faltering for just a moment.

That was just enough.

The fellow behind him somehow found the strength to surge ahead.

And he crossed the finish line with scarcely the length of his forearm ahead of the man he had just passed.

The crowd went mad, and flooded toward the skaters, screaming wildly, while the rest of the skaters staggered over the finish line.

Only then did the exhaustion hit the skaters, as friends swarmed the ice with blankets and cloaks, and legs gave out, sometimes with breathless cries of pain. . . .

Alberich found himself shouting and screaming along with the rest.

There was a brief period for the skaters to recover; then, wrapped warmly in their cloaks again, there came the moment of their glory, when Selenay rewarded the first three finishers with medals, purses, and pairs of the finest skating blades made.

It was at that point that, much to his shock, Alberich realized that he had screamed himself hoarse.

The skaters were all taken away to recover, and Selenay and her bodyguards settled into the reviewing stand, her ladies around her, and Alberich *under* the stand to ensure nothing could get to her from that point. Then came the pageant. And Selenay sat in the reviewing stand, patient as a statue, with a footwarmer under her boots and a handwarmer tucked into a muff someone had brought for her, smiling, while her servants showered the participants with sweets and small coins by way of reward. Alberich felt sorry for her; she was musical by nature, and the kind of cold they were experiencing did not do good things to instruments. Nor did all the screaming that the singers had been doing during the races help the quality of their voices.

Yet when the afternoon wound to a close, and the sun sank over the river, lending everything a tinge of red, he thought that Selenay looked as if she would have gladly sat through another three or four pageants rather than see the day come to an end.

But, of course, it hadn't. Not yet. As the horns sounded to signal that the common folk could begin queuing up to the roasting beasts and simmering cauldrons, Selenay retired once again to the Royal Pavilion to exchange her clothing for a gown created for this particular event. A floor of wood had been laid over the ice, and a special tent pitched over it. Tapestries and hangings brought down from the Palace to hang against the walls of the tent provided further insulation from the punishing cold. While it would not be *warm* within the canvas walls, it would not be nearly as cold as it was outside.

Outside, there was music, and a peculiar and very attractive kind of ice dancing, skaters carrying torches either in round dances or following one another in a close file through intricate figures that were made up on the spur of the moment by the skater in the lead. Inside, there was also music, and fires in firepits, and candles and oil lamps wherever it was safe to put them. Outside, the common folk feasted on meat and bread and well-watered wine drunk hot. Inside—

Inside, it would be another Court Feast like so many others, the only novelty being the cold.

Alberich waited on guard just inside the main entrance to the Royal Pavilion until the Queen appeared, newly-attired and ready for her Feast. When she emerged, he saw that Selenay's gown—white, of course—was of heavy quilted velvet, with a fur-lined surcoat and a heavy gold belt at her hips. Her hair was surmounted by a fur hat rather than her crown, with one of the great cloak brooches of the Royal Regalia pinned to the front of it, a great blazing diamond surrounded by lesser diamonds, and instead of slippers, she wore boots. Most of the garments would be like that tonight, he thought, and the wind would shake the canvas walls, reminding all the courtiers present that although they might mock winter by holding their feast on the ice, the winter could take them if it chose.

Still. When Selenay emerged from the back of the Pavilion, she was still smiling, and Alberich thought that she looked both charmingly young and utterly regal. He took her arm himself, and led her out into the torch-lit darkness. He brought her over the treacherous ice as far as the door to the Feasting Tent, where her official escort took over. He found himself a little reluctant to let her go, but that could have been because of the man she had chosen to partner her at the Feast.

Her official escort for the Feast was Lord Orthallen, who had had his tailor copy Selenay's garb in a lush and warming golden brown. He looked extremely handsome, and the surcoat—his ending at his calves, rather than trailing behind in a train as Selenay's did—suited him very well. To Alberich's mind, he looked rather smug as well.

:Hmm,: Kantor commented. :He does, doesn't he? One wonders why.:

Well, it could only be because Selenay was showing him

such preference tonight. Alberich hoped so. Fortunately, Orthallen was safely wedded, and there was no way that he could divorce his faithful, fruitful, and obedient wife without a major scandal—so there was no way that he could imagine this sign of preference to be anything but Selenay's choice to honor her "Uncle" Orthallen in what was, essentially, a meaningless gesture.

Meanwhile, he had a job to perform, and he set about doing it, following immediately behind the pair as they walked up the aisle between the rows of lower tables. The two Heralds he'd chosen to play bodyguard at the High Table were already waiting there, flanked by Royal Guardsmen in their blue formal uniforms.

He and the other two Heralds he'd picked as bodyguards for tonight—Alton and Shanate—had taken the precaution of purloining some dinner from the cooks before the Feast began, just as the Guardsmen had. So they were able to keep their minds on the surroundings and not the food.

Not that there was even the slightest hint of trouble. Just a great many excited, animated people, who were showing clearly with their high spirits that this entire Festival had been a very good idea. No one looked at *this* High Table with that shadowed glance of regret. The very different setting kept any memories of Sendar's High Feasts from intruding.

So did the food, though not as much as the setting. There were some novelties, which was only to be expected; a soup served iced rather than hot, many small ice sculptures on the tables, and clever combinations of chilled food seasoned with hot spices. There were sherbets and shaved ice with fruit and syrup spooned over the top—something that would not have survived more than a moment in the heated Great Hall. There were other concoctions that were actually doused in liquor and set afire, that made a fine show as well, though those made Alberich more than a little wary until they'd been doused.

With Orthallen on Selenay's right, and Talamir on her left,

unfortunately Selenay could not have gotten much novelty in conversation. Well, she couldn't have everything. And she did appear to be enjoying herself.

On the whole, Alberich thought about halfway through, he and his fellow bodyguards had gotten the better part of the meal—by the time the stuff got to the table, with the exception of dishes served flaming, quite a bit of it was lukewarm at best.

He scanned the tables for his suspect, but the full Court wasn't here—it wouldn't have been possible to serve them all under these conditions for one thing—so those at the table were the most important members of the most important families, and his *young* highborn wasn't among them. Alberich stifled his disappointment. The time to really look for the elusive fellow was coming.

Finally the last subtlety was served and eaten, Selenay and her escort parted company with smiles, and everyone cleared back to huddle around the firepits and braziers to let the servants swarm over the place and clear out all of the tables and most of the benches, setting some against the tapestries so that those who were not dancing would have a place to sit. Now the evening could really begin.

And now people literally poured into the grand tent; the Royal Pavilion was even now being laid out with refreshments to save room here, for this was where the dancing was to be held. The small dais where the High Table had stood now held a single proper seat—Selenay's portable throne, which she took as soon as it had been set up. The musicians, teachers at Bardic Collegium all, sat near her, on stools, where she could give them any instructions she might have on what sorts of dances to play.

The musicians carefully tuned their instruments, and at a nod from Selenay, the first notes cut across the milling crowd. Those courtiers who did not care to dance cleared away to the side; the rest, including most of the younger ones, taking the floor, forming up into four rows of couples, waiting expectantly for Selenay to take the lead spot.

And Selenay's first dancing partner came forward, a very tall, very clever-looking fellow in full Bardic Scarlet. He bowed over her hand; she stood up, and they took their positions.

Every dance had been arranged in advance, of course. The only deviation would be if Selenay elected to sit any of them out, at which time her partner would be expected to attend her and offer conversation. Alberich doubted that Selenay would do any such thing, though; she loved dancing, and she'd been keyed up all day without having much of an outlet for her energy.

If ever his young nobleman was going to appear, it would be here. But not, Alberich thought, among those nearest to the Queen.

And in fact, the evening was half over before he caught a glimpse of the young man. It was only a glimpse, too—too quick to be certain, much less pass the sight along to Kantor. But Alberich was good at remembering details, and the young man was wearing a hat that was reasonably identifiable. Alberich kept his eye on that hat, watching as it swam through the crowd, as it swayed and bent in a dance, as it huddled with several more hats off to one side—

And, for one horrible moment, he thought it was going to duck out of the entrance.

But it hesitated, then bowed to an elegant plume. It joined with the plume—escorting it?—and the pair moved along the side of the dancing-floor until, at last, they moved out onto it.

As luck would have it, it was a round-dance, and eventually the figures brought the hat, and its owner, into Alberich's line-of-sight.

He felt Kantor absorb the young man's image through his own eyes; felt Kantor "absent" himself for a moment.

Then Kantor "returned."

:*Devlin Gereton, third son of Lord Stevel Gereton,*: Kantor reported. *:Talamir will tell you what he knows about the young man, and his family, later. It isn't much; it's an old family, but not particularly prosperous, and they haven't done much to draw attention to themselves or distinguish themselves. There's only one thing; there's no reason why this young man should be so interested in common plays or actors. His eldest brother's a sound amateur poet, and the only thing that Devlin is known for is that he has a good ear for poetry and letters and is considered a budding expert in drama.:*

Well. Wasn't that interesting.

Wasn't that very interesting indeed. . . .

SELENAY woke just before dawn; if she had had any dreams, she couldn't remember them.

Yesterday everything had gone perfectly. With one exception. One glaring, aching exception.

Her father hadn't been there.

A weight of crushing depression settled over her.

She opened her eyes and lay quietly in her bed as thin, gray light crept in through the cracks in her curtains. She closed her eyes again, and hot tears spilled from beneath her lids and down her temples to soak into her hair.

Her throat closed, and a cold, hard lump formed in it. Selenay tried to fight back the sobs, but one escaped anyway, and she turned over quickly and muffled her sobbing in her pillows. She didn't want to wake her attendants, or alert the servants on the other side of the door. She didn't want anyone to know she was crying.

They wouldn't understand. They would think that she should be thrilled, not choked with tears. After all, her Festival had been a triumph, and people would talk about it for years. The Court had loved it. The common folk had adored it. Even the Seneschal and Keeper of the Treasury had been happy, for she had been very frugal, extracting the maximum benefit from every coin she'd spent, either overseeing the preparations herself, or sending people with stern demeanor and sharp eyes to do so for her. The Feast for the common folk had been a wild success, going on long into the night as folk brought or bought food of their own to extend that supplied by the Crown.

As for the entertainments for her Court, their Feast and dancing had been as much of a success, and for once, she'd had nothing but perfect dancing partners. Alberich had been right; having Heralds and Bards (and even a few Healers) alternate with her young nobles had made all the difference. Her gown—the first time she'd been out of mourning—had made her look beautiful; she hadn't needed dubious compliments to tell her so, for her mirror and the frank gazes of the Bards and Heralds had made that clear enough.

But Sendar hadn't been there, and it might just as well have been a total failure because of that. She'd tried to lose herself in the preparations, then to immerse herself in the happiness of other people, and she'd actually forgotten for a little—just a little. She'd smiled and even laughed, and when she'd come back here to her rooms, she'd been so tired she'd fallen straight asleep.

But she'd known, the moment that she awakened, that one day, one week, hadn't changed anything, hadn't filled the emptiness, hadn't given her back the part of herself that was gone.

Her father would have loved this. He'd have reveled in her triumph. He would have had so many ideas for the Festival, so many more than she had—

The brief respite she'd had was just that—a moment of forgetfulness, nothing more. And now, with nothing but day after day of gray sameness stretching ahead of her, she missed him so much she thought she was going to break beneath the weight of grief.

So she sobbed into her pillow, inconsolable. How *could* anyone console her for this? She and her father should have had years and years together; she should have had him to cast stern eyes over would-be suitors, to advise her how to deal with the Council, to scold her for working too hard and send her to read a book or ride. And if she ever married—he should have been there to see it, to see his grandchildren, to spoil them as he'd often threatened to do. All of that was gone, taken from her before it ever had a chance to happen.

She didn't want anyone to hear her crying; they wouldn't understand. They'd tell her stupid things—that it had been long enough, that she needed to "pull herself together," that it was "time to move on."

How could they know? How many of *them* had a beloved father cut down in front of their eyes? How many of *them* were facing what she faced, the rest of her life without the man who had been father *and* mother to her, and friend, and counselor? None of them understood. None of them could. None of them wanted to. What they wanted, was for her to be something else, some biddable creature they called "Selenay" that had no feelings but the shallowest, and no thoughts of her own. *Her* feelings were an inconvenient obstacle to that.

Or worse than telling her to "get over this," they'd spew some kind of platitude about how he was surely watching her from somewhere and was proud of her, but would be unhappy that she was still mourning for him. How could they know? How could anyone know?

It wasn't fair. It wasn't right. Sendar had been *good;* he'd given up so much, he'd always done so much for others—it wasn't *fair!* She'd always thought that when you did good, good came to you. What kind of a cruel god would do this to her, and to him?

For that matter, she wasn't entirely certain that there *were* any gods out there, not after this. And if there weren't any gods, then that meant that when you died, you just *died,* and her father wasn't "out there," looking after her. He was just gone, and all those platitudes were nothing but empty lies. . . .

Damn them. Damn them all, and their needs, and their platitudes, and their plans. They would never, *could* never, understand. She'd lost her best friend as well as her father; she had been cheated out of *years* of things that they all took for granted.

How could she possibly ever "get over" that? There would be a great, gaping wound in her for the rest of her life that would never be properly filled!

Except with tears, the tears that never seemed to heal anything inside her.

She had tried, these past moons at least, to do things that would keep her moving, keep her busy, keep her too concentrated on things outside herself to think. For a while, the sheer desperation of having to learn how to rule, of having to outwit her Council when they tried discreetly to shunt her aside or maneuver her into something she didn't want to do had filled that need to keep moving. She would work and plan and learn until she fell asleep, exhausted, and wake early to work again—and that had helped, at least, to keep things at bay. Keep moving, keep busy, keep her mind full, keep it all at a distance. Then, just as the urgency of all that began to ease, there'd been the preparations for the Festival to fill the silences, to force her to work, think, and not remember.

But now—now she had awakened this morning, knowing there was nothing, nothing between her and that vast, aching void that used to be filled with her father's presence.

And anyone who found her crying like this would just never understand. They'd wonder why, after yesterday, she could be unhappy. Even if she tried to explain, they'd stare at her without understanding, then tell her that it was time she moved on, that it was time to leave her grief behind her. As if she could!

:*Of course you won't,*: Caryo said, very, very quietly. :*And you shouldn't. That would be wrong. How can you leave it behind you when it's a part of you?*:

The feeling that Caryo had somehow put comforting arms around her only made her sob harder. But Caryo didn't seem to think there was anything wrong with that.

:*They keep telling me stupid things like "Time will heal it—"*: she said, around the sobs that shook her entire body.

There was an ache in Caryo's mind-voice that matched the aching of her heart. :*Time doesn't. All that Time does is make it more distant, put more space between you and what happened. It doesn't heal anything. I don't know how or what does the healing, but it isn't Time.*:

:*Oh, Caryo, I miss* him *so much!*: she cried.

:*So do I.*:

Somehow, that was exactly the right thing for Selenay to hear; it let loose another torrent of weeping, but this time, it seemed as if she was weeping herself out, until at last she lay there, curled in her bed, her nose stuffed and her eyes sore, her pillow soggy—

:*Turn your pillow over, love.*:

She sniffed hard and obeyed without thinking, and closed her aching eyes. She was exhausted now, limp with crying, and if the ache in her heart didn't hurt any less, at least she was too tired to cry any more.

:*I keep thinking, if only I'd gone after him—*:

:*If only. Those must be the two saddest words in the world,*: Caryo sighed. :*The best thing that I can tell you is that there is* nothing *that could have happened that would have allowed you to follow him. And there was not one scrap, one hint of knowledge or even ForeSight that any of us had that would have let us guess what he was going to do, or enabled us to prevent it. If there was ever a moment in history where a man took his own fate in his own two hands, that was it.:*

:Then I wish I could go back—: But there was no use in pursuing that line of thought. She couldn't. No one, not even in the tales of before the Founding, had ever said anything about being able to go back into the past and change things.

:I don't want to get up, Caryo.: And she didn't. She didn't want to move. She didn't want to leave her bed. Ever. The weight of depression pressed down on her and filled her with lethargy. She wanted to close her eyes, and fall into oblivion, and never come out again. She didn't exactly want to die—but if only there was a way to *not live*—

And Caryo didn't say any of the stupid things that other people might, about how she "had" to live for Valdemar, or how she was being hysterical, or overreacting. *:If you don't get up, I'll miss our morning ride,:* she said instead, wistfully, as if she was deliberately misunderstanding the "I don't want to get up" as merely meaning "this morning," and not "forever." Maybe she was.

But—the thought of the morning ride, another of those times when she could forget, for a little, as Caryo moved into a gallop, and she could lean over that warm, white neck and let the movement and the rush of air and the rhythm all lull her into a kind of trance, that same state of *not being* that she was just longing for—that broke through the lethargy. It was hard to tell why, but it did; it made her decide that she *had* to get up, to keep moving, to try for another candlemark, another day. And as she forced her legs out from under the covers, it occurred to her that as long as she just kept moving, even if she didn't find any peace or escape in movement, she might at least find a little more distraction.

Distraction. She had to distract anyone from knowing she'd been crying, or they'd want to know why, and then there would be all that stupid nonsense that she didn't want to hear.

She slipped out of bed and went to the table where a basin

and pitcher waited; she splashed some of the cold water into the basin, and bathed her face until she thought that most of the signs of her tears were gone. Her eyes were probably still red, but with luck, no one would remark on it. After all, with all of the snow glare out there yesterday, probably they'd think it was that. If anyone said anything, she'd claim it was snow glare. And maybe she could claim a headache, too, and cut the Council session short.

She blew her nose, and went back to her bed, and crawled back into it, feeling as exhausted as if she hadn't slept at all.

:Just close your eyes,: Caryo advised. *:They'll expect you to sleep late after last night. You really did look lovely, you know. All of the young Heralds, at least, were saying so. I can't speak for the Bards; they don't have Companions to gossip about them, but the Heralds were very taken with how you looked.:*

:They were?: That was—if not comforting, at least it was satisfying. Nice to know that she did look as good as she had thought.

:Believe it or not, even Alberich thought so. In fact, I think he might have had just a twinge of jealousy when he handed you off to Orthallen.:

Well, that penetrated the lethargic depression, a bit. *:Alberich? Surely not.:* And anyway, it was probably only that he disliked Orthallen. Well, apparently the feeling was mutual, and there wasn't anything she could do about that. When two men decided to take a dislike to one another, there really wasn't anything to be done about it. It was like trying to get a pair of dominant dogs to be friends; no matter what you did, each of them was going to be certain that *he* should be head of the pack, and all you could do was to try and keep them separate as much as possible. Orthallen was one of the few people who *didn't* say anything stupid about her father. He didn't even say that she ought to be over her grief by now, and that made him one of the few people she felt comfortable being around, even if he did tend to treat her as "little Selenay" instead of the Queen.

Besides, it wasn't Alberich that she wanted to make jealous.

Though, on second thought, there really wasn't *anyone* in her entire Court or the Heraldic Circle she wanted to make jealous. Honestly, if the whole business of trying to get her to marry someone who was tied to a whole pack of special interests was put aside, the real reason she didn't want to marry any of the Council's choices was that they all *bored* her. There wasn't one of them that was worth spending an entire afternoon with, much less a lifetime. There wasn't a single unattached male in the entire Court that even gave her a flutter of interest.

She was just so tired of it all; tired of the ache in her soul, tired of the loneliness, tired of trying to outmaneuver the people she *should* have been able to lean on. It seemed as if her entire life was nothing more than dragging herself through an endless round of weariness and grief, and she just wanted an end to it all.

She buried her face in her pillow, not to muffle more sobs, but to block out—everything. If only for a moment.

It was when she woke again to the sounds of her servants and attendants bustling around the room that she realized she must have fallen asleep again. And if she didn't feel *better,* at least she felt a little less tired.

Enough so, that she felt she could probably face the day. She didn't want to, but she could.

:I think,: she told Caryo, as they came to get her out of bed and dress her, *:I think we'll have our morning ride before breakfast.:*

:Good,: Caryo said simply. *:I'd like that. Thank you.:*

Keep moving. That was the only answer. Just keep moving. . . .

And if that wasn't an answer, at least it was a way to keep her from just—stopping. Stopping and never starting again.

For Alberich, the day after the Festival's climax began just as any ordinary day did—the only differences being that now, at least, he didn't have to concern himself with making preparations for Selenay's appearance, and now that he knew the identity of the young man he'd been looking for, he could concentrate on thinking of ways to find out what was going on.

But as far as the young Trainees went, apparently, the end of the Festival meant restlessness and discontent. They'd had an unexpected break in their routine, and as Alberich was woefully aware, any break in a youngster's routine generally meant trouble in getting him back into that routine.

As a consequence, the first class of the morning was a disaster. Far too much time was wasted in trying to get his students back on track after the excitement of the Ice Festival. And they fought him every step of the way, performing their warmups lethargically, running through the initial exercises in a state of distraction, and wasting time in chattering about the pleasures of the day before.

And part of him was still puzzling over the question of Devlin Gereton, why he would be receiving information from a play-actor, and what that information could be. It took real effort on his own part to put that aside and concentrate on getting some results out of the class.

But it was a futile effort. The Trainees were utterly disinclined to settle down and work, and finally, in desperation, he decided that if all they could do was chatter about ice sports, well, he'd *give* them an ice sport they would never forget!

After all, they were going to have to learn to work together, in coordinated teams. . . .

"*Silence!*" he barked. "Weapons *down*."

Startled, they shut off the chatter, dropped weapon points, and stared at him.

"Weapons put away. Get the staves," he ordered grimly. "*Now*. Then on with cloaks, and follow me."

Now looking apprehensive and guilty, they obeyed. He snatched up his own cloak, hid a little surprise inside it as he did so, and stalked out, followed by a suddenly subdued tail of Trainees of all four colors.

Out into the snow they went, out past the practice grounds and into Companion's Field, following a path beaten by others into the thigh-deep snow. It was another cloudless, bone-chilling day, and sunlight poured pitilessly down through the skeletal branches of the trees. He led them to one of the frozen ponds in Companion's Field, one that had been cleared off so that it could be used for skating, but was far enough from the Palace and the Collegia that it wasn't in use very much. In a welcome release for his temper, he kicked three basket-sided holes in the snow at the edge of the ice, one at each point of an imaginary equal-sided triangle laid on the pond, then divided the class into two teams. He made sure that the Trainees were fairly evenly distributed between both teams, and he made a point of dividing up friends as much as he could. If they were mad for sport, well, he'd give them bloody sport indeed. . . .

:*Chosen, I hope you aren't releasing a wolf from a trap, here,*: Kantor said, full of amusement. :*Are you sure you know what you're doing?*:

:*No,*: he said honestly. :*But at least they'll get some stave practice out of this.*:

Then he dropped what he had picked up onto the ice in front of them.

It was one of the little round cushions that they used over their knuckles when they were practicing bare-fist fighting. They looked at it, then at him, then back down at it, without any comprehension at all.

"Pah. You are two teams of fighters now. *There* are your goals. First team—there, second team, there." He pointed, He thought he saw comprehension beginning to dawn. He hoped so. They'd *all* seen the broom-ball competition. He hoped they weren't so dense that they couldn't figure this out! "The third goal neutral is. Either team may score there. The cushion, into the opposite goal, or into the neutral goal, you are to put," he said icily and moved carefully off the slippery surface of the ice with as much dignity as he could muster, heaving a sigh of relief when he reached the bank and could stand there with his arms folded over his chest, under his cape.

"But is this like broom-ball? What are the rules?" someone asked, and "But we don't have skates!" protested another.

"There are rules in war? I think not," he retorted. "Skates you will be carrying in the field? Enough. No rules. The cushion, in the goal, you will put. How it comes there, your problem is. Hit it, you may. Kick it, carry it, I care not. You have staves. Use them. Fight with them. *No rules.*"

He hadn't been altogether certain what their response would be. On the one hand, they were Trainees, and had a modicum of training in organization. On the other hand, they were overstimulated adolescents with too much restlessness to settle down. They *could* settle in and make some rules, assigning tasks and responsibilities before they set to their new version of broom-ball.

They *could.* But they didn't.

With a yell, someone broke and swatted at the cushion with his stave, and the melee began as someone else jumped for the cushion, and half of the other team piled onto the one making the move. It was, in a sadistic sort of way, rather entertaining for the onlooker. Staves went everywhere—though not as successfully as if the fighting had been on solid, unslippery ground. Bodies went everywhere. Most of them ended up sprawled on the ice. The cushion tended not to get anywhere near a goal.

He had been counting on the ice to ensure that no one was able to get in any dangerously hard blows with the staves, and the ploy worked. Even the ones that were good skaters found the going slippery, and none of them were used to trying to stay balanced on the ice while simultaneously swatting with a stave. And all of them were fairly good at stave work to begin with, so if someone swung for an opponent instead of the cushion, there was a good chance that he'd find the blow blocked. But none of them were doing much in the way of coordination or teamwork; it was pretty much every man for himself, and Alberich had ensured that the little amount of teamwork that *might* have occurred naturally was sidelined by breaking up friends onto opposite teams.

It got pretty wild out there, though, before it was all over. He didn't know if any of *them* were keeping track of the number of goals that were made. He certainly wasn't. All he was interested in was to make sure that no one was injured beyond falls and bruises and bumps on the head. Putting them on the ice had another effect; even when someone connected with a stave, most of the force of the blow went into sending the opponent flying like a giant version of the cushion. Oh, they were going to be aching and stiff when it was over.

:*There's going to be competition for the bathtubs today,*: Kantor observed, sounding highly amused. :*And calls for liniment, I suspect.*:

:*They wanted excitement,*: he told his Companion.

:*So they did.*:

If they were going to act like a lot of wild hill brats, then by the Sunlord, they were going to learn why discipline and organization were necessary if you wanted to win a fight.

By the time that class was over—more to the point, by the time he broke up the melee that the "game" had turned into and sent them all back to their other classes—it didn't appear that the lesson had sunk in yet.

But he was relatively certain that eventually it would, as

they thought back over the chaos on the ice. Certainly they were, one and all, winded, weary, aching in every limb, and there wasn't one of them that wasn't sporting some sort of injury. There were a hefty number of black eyes, and lots of bruises in places that didn't show. And a strain or two, and lumps on the skull. And he would have laid money on the fact that not one of them was going to give the other instructors any trouble for the rest of the day.

But most of all, for the sake of the lesson in teamwork, it was painfully clear that no one had any idea who had won.

So when the next class showed the early symptoms of the same "disease," he administered the same "cure." It was only when he got the final-year students that he got any signs of sense and steadiness out of them, and managed to run a normal class.

He didn't have the option of thinking much past the fact that at least he'd gotten some work *out* of them, and a lesson of sorts *into* them. After classes were over, some of the Guard appeared for a little training, and he was able to work out some of his own frustration in a satisfying series of bouts. When the last of the adults had gone, and the last of the daylight faded, leaving the salle in blue gloom, he was more concerned with a hot shower than anything else.

He went back into his quarters and got himself cleaned up, coming out of his bathing room to find that the servants had come and gone from the Collegium, leaving behind both his dinner and a visitor.

"What in the bloody blue blazes did you infect your students with today?" Myste demanded, peering at him through her thick glass lenses, pausing in the midst of laying out plates, cups, and cutlery. "They look like they've been through the Wars, and they're chattering like magpies about some ice exercise you invented."

He stared at her for a moment, bemused both by her presence and by the question. He hadn't thought much beyond exhausting the worst offenders; it hadn't occurred to him that they'd actually *take* to the exercise. Well, not really, anyway. Maybe some of the Blues, the courtiers' children, who hadn't anything better to do with their time. "They would not settle," he replied after a moment. "So, to exhaust them, I decided. And to show them, organization is needed, a battle to win."

"Well, your little experiment in ice warfare is being talked about over all three Collegia," she said in a rueful tone, as if she could hardly believe it. "And the ones that hadn't tried it yet were mad to, while the rest are trying to come up with rules, so-called 'proper' equipment, scoring. It's all anyone could talk about over luncheon *and* dinner, and they want to do it in their free time—"

He interrupted her with a gust of incredulous laughter. "No—they mean to make a *sport?*"

"Evidently." She shook her head, and dished out food for both of them. Then she sat down, next to the fire, with a bowl of stew in hand. "I suppose we should be grateful. It's new, it's a good alternative to tavern hopping and getting into pranks, *and* it's exercise."

"And they will weary of it, soon enough," he said. "If they do not, when the ice melts, over it is." He couldn't believe that anything as ridiculous as the foolish melee he'd put them through had suddenly become an all-consuming interest.

"Hmm." She ate a little, chewing thoughtfully, as the fire crackled beside her. "I think what's likeliest to happen is that they'll all try it, but the only way to keep from getting bruised up and battered over it is to have a lot of rules, and maybe purloin the padding and helms used for weapons practice into the bargain. But having a lot of rules means that they'll have to *agree* over the rules. No two sets of would-be players are going to have the same idea of what the rules should be. And in the end, they won't have agreed before the ice melts."

"Probably," he agreed, feeling relieved and irritated at the same time. Cadets would never have been allowed such foolishness. But then again, as he had noted before, Heraldic Trainees were not Karsite Cadets. . . . "I had noted that on the river, the players of the broom-ball game required much drinking of wine and beer to continue the game past the first few goals."

"And without that, it isn't *nearly* as much fun." She chuckled. "Right. That's what I'll tell the others. They were afraid it was going to take over the Collegia."

He thought about that for a moment. Thought about the fact that a certain level of madness seemed to come out of the confinement of winter. And thought about all the high spirits generated by the Festival. "It will, probably, for a short time," he decided. "But that gives a painless punishment as well. For those of the Collegia at least, who will not settle and study, *forbid* them from playing. Make playing contingent upon good marks. Blues, we can do little about, if they are highborn children. But then again—time, they have, to waste. At least melees on ice harm them only."

"Oh—ouch. Very good indeed," Myste laughed. "That should do the trick."

They finished dinner quickly; so much time spent out in the cold used up a lot of energy, and he was wolf-hungry.

Only after they had cleared the dishes away into the hampers did it occur to him to wonder why she had come there tonight. It couldn't have been because she wanted his company—could it?

At that thought, he got a very odd feeling in the pit of his stomach. Not unpleasant, no, but—fluttery. It disconcerted him. It disconcerted him so much that he just blurted out what was in his head.

"Why are you here?" he heard himself saying, and could have hit himself for how it sounded.

But she didn't seem to take offense at his words or his tone.

"Well—" she began, and hesitated. "Mixed motives, actually. I wanted to find out what you'd done with the youngsters.

I must say that the ones who *had* gotten your lesson were nicely subdued for my classes; it was only the ones that hadn't gotten to 'play' that were wound up like tops. And, um—" another hesitation, "—I, um, enjoy your company. And one other thing—" she added, hastily, before he could decide if she was blushing or not. "Keren slipped a little. Well, she didn't really *slip,* so much as I browbeat it out of her when she brought me a dress, of all things, to mend for her." She laughed. "I mean, Keren? In a *dress?* Please! That was odd enough, but a dress that looked like *that?*"

"Like what?" he asked, unthinking.

"A dockside whore," she replied, with cheerful bluntness, and it was his turn to flush. "She said she didn't want to take it to the Collegium seamstresses, because it was supposed to be a secret, and then tried to backtrack. Well, needless to say, I got the whole story out of her."

"So you know?" he asked, feeling a little guilty that he hadn't told her before this, seeing that he'd been thinking about asking for her help anyway.

"Hmm. I guessed, before this. Too many evenings when you weren't here in the Complex, too many times when you knew things you shouldn't have about parts of Haven you weren't supposed to have ever visited," she said thoughtfully. "I mean, I can put two and two together—and unlike some of our colleagues with some rather lofty ideas about Heraldic duties and honor, I know a bit about the practicalities of life. Anyway, I just wanted you to know that if I can help, without getting in the way, I'd like to. Keren might fit in some of the wilder parts of Haven, but I know the craftsmen's districts inside and out."

That stopped him cold. It hadn't occurred to him that Myste might want to *volunteer.* Or that she would actually have some inside knowledge that he *didn't.* He'd thought he would have to persuade her, then train her.

"It's not as if I'd have to act a part, like Keren," she continued. "I'd just have to be what I was before I was Chosen. An accountant, a clerk, ordinary. Believe me, people like me are just invisible as long as we keep our mouths shut. No one thinks anything about having us around. We're a kind of servant, and no one ever pays any attention to the servants."

He didn't know how true the latter statement was, but the former was true enough. "There could be danger in this," he warned.

She raised an eyebrow. "You might not think it, but there's danger in being an independent clerk. You don't always know just who is hiring you, or for what—or at least, not until they ask you to run two sets of books, or you get a look at papers you weren't supposed to see. That never happened to me, personally, but I know those it did happen to. And there's stories about people turning up missing after taking certain jobs." She chuckled weakly. "Well, that's probably what most of the people who knew me think is what happened to me. I know for a fact that none of them realize I was Chosen."

Well, she was on that last battlefield for the Tedrel Wars, and she'd volunteered for that, too. She'd faced danger there, certainly enough. "I might then ask you for help," he said carefully.

"Ask, and you'll have it," she said. And then seemed at a loss for anything else to say.

But he didn't want her to leave. They sat in awkward silence for a long time. And when the silence was broken, they both broke it at once.

"Can you tell me—"

"What of interest have you—"

They both broke off, flushing. Alberich was just a little angry—at himself. Surely he was more than old enough to have a simple conversation with an interesting woman without blushing like a boy! Particularly this one, that he had shouted at, cursed at, and forced to learn things she adamantly did not want to learn!

"You first," she said, gesturing.

He paused. What *did* he want to say? It suddenly occurred to him that there was a lot he didn't know about her. He might as well start with that.

"So. What was Myste, the clerk, like?" he asked. "What was her life?"

She laughed. "Boring. But—" Her eyes grew thoughtful behind those thick lenses. "But you don't know much of anything about the ordinary person in Valdemar, of the middling classes, do you? I know a lot about all of that, in Haven, in particular. So even if I'd be bored by it—"

"Please," he said, with a slow smile. "Tell me."

And so, she did. And being Myste, she got as much about Alberich of Karse out of him, as he did about Myste of Haven.

It was, on the whole, an equitable exchange. And perhaps, best of all, it was one that would take some time in telling.

8

THE Ice Festival had taken place a fortnight after Midwinter. Now, another fortnight later, the deep cold finally broke with a gray day, vastly warmer than the ones that had brought the Ice Festival, and with a dampness to the air that warned of snow. By a candlemark after sunrise, the snow had begun, and it fell, thick and soft, all day and into the night. Alberich, for one, was very happy to see it, for it meant that all the frozen ponds were covered over, and at least until the would-be athletes shoveled them clear again, there would be no more ice melees.

Or, as the Trainees had decided to call it, *Hurlee*. Yes, they had given it a name. They had agreed on that much, and more. It had taken on a life of its own.

He had, unwittingly, created a monster. Yet at the same time, it was a very useful monster. If, at times, it seemed that the vast majority of the free time of both Trainees *and* young courtiers was taken up with creating rules and scoring for this combative game, and arguing over both endlessly, at least they were learning about teamwork, cooperation in combat, and negotiation. If they seemed obsessed, at least, as several teachers said with a sigh, there were worse things to get obsessed about, and the slightest *hint* that falling marks would occasion being forbidden to play or even *discuss* the game often worked miracles.

Still, it seemed that there was nowhere in Court or Collegia that one could go to *escape* the wretched game. Even some of the younger Guards had started to take it up. For all Alberich knew, it was spreading down into Haven by now, and many older members of the Court, decidedly unamused by the racketing teams of youngsters surging here and there and practicing on every open bit of ice, or even *creating* unauthorized bits of ice to practice on, often gave Alberich unfriendly glares when he saw them.

The cushion had been replaced by first a child's beanbag, then a tough leather ball filled with heavy buckwheat in its husks, of the sort that jugglers practiced with. The staves now had small scoops on one end. The holes in the snow were now nets, and the teams had been stabilized at five members each, one of which was supposed to guard his team's net.

Combat with the staves was still very much allowed; Alberich had the feeling that no few little feuds were being worked out during the games. Half-helms of padded leather and elbow, kidney, and kneepads had been agreed upon. Skates were *not* allowed, on order of the Healers, who didn't want to deal with the results. Other additions were being argued about, or rather, forcefully argued *for* by Healer's Collegium, which did not want an influx of Trainees and other youngsters with missing teeth or broken jawbones. At this point, Alberich had washed his hands of the entire project and disclaimed any involvement with it. Like the other instructors, *he* had declared that inattention and falling marks would be grounds for being forbidden to play.

He was rather desperately hoping that a thaw would put an

end to it, and depressingly afraid that, given the new changes in it, they would be able to play without ice.

At least, by this point, it was very clear that no more than half of the Heraldic Trainees, and substantially, very substantially *less* than a quarter of the Healers' and Bardic Trainees, were going to actually be playing this game. The rest lacked the coordination and, after the initial excitement was over, the inclination. That did not, however, mean that the rest weren't interested. Oh, no. They were still just as mad about watching it as the rest were about playing it.

But he could not spare much time to worry about a mere game. He had decided to start taking Keren out on some of his prowls through Haven. And he had yet to come up with a plan to let him discover just what Devlin and that actor were up to.

The main stumbling block was that he could not think of a way to shadow the young courtier *or* the actor without alerting them to the fact that someone was watching them. For one thing, he was more than a little wary about trying to disguise himself around the actor, at all. He could fool ordinary folk, but an actor? The fellow might have a style that was ridiculously flamboyant, and exaggerated, but that, Alberich suspected, was for the benefit of his audience, which was not going to react to a subtle performance. The man could not have come up with so clever a plan for passing information if he was not clever and subtle himself. And if Alberich tried to pass himself off as someone who had business being around either Devlin or the actors—

It seemed impossible; Alberich was certain he'd be caught. He might be able to pass off his Karsite accent as Hardornan or Rethwellan down in the slums, but actors had an ear for accents, and might even be able to correctly identify his. And just how many Karsites were there in Haven? Not many; not many that still had their accent. The paste he used to disguise his scars passed muster after dark, but actors knew about makeup and false hair—he'd never get by an actor without

him noticing. How many Karsite Heralds were there? A sufficiently clever man could easily put two and two together.

As for getting in close, that *was* impossible. The man—
finally Alberich had learned who he was (Norris Lettyn), and
where his troupe was operating from (the Three Sheaves in the
Cattle Market area)—seldom went anywhere outside of the
inn, and never consorted with anyone except his fellow actors
and exceedingly attractive, buxom, adoring women. Neither of
which Alberich was—nor were Keren or Myste. They might be
able to feign the adoration, but the kind of ladies that Norris
kept company with were the sort that made men turn in the
street and stare after them.

Not surprisingly, no few of them were ladies of negotiable
virtue, but the price they placed on their services was very,
very high. They were nothing like the common whores of the
Exile's Gate neighborhood. And Alberich could not make up
his mind if Norris was paying for their company, or getting it
on the basis of his reputation, popularity, stunningly handsome face, and muscular body. If he was paying for it—where
was a mere actor getting the money? On the other hand, someone who looked like Norris did generally had women fawning
on him, and Alberich saw no reason to suppose that expensive
courtesans were any less likely to fawn than supposedly "honest" women.

Thanks to Norris' face and flamboyant style, the troupe
was certainly prospering, as was the inn to which they were
attached. They didn't even have to give plays every day for the
public anymore. Once every two days, the courtyard was
packed with spectators for one of the repertoire of plays they
put on, and it certainly wasn't because of the high literary
standards of the things. Moving to that tent on the riverbank
during the Festival had been a shrewd move—putting on their
play there spread their reputation to the entire city, and the
city evidently followed them back to their home ground when
the Festival was over. Norris even was beginning to get some-

thing of a following among the highborn of the Court—while the plays they put on for the public were hardly great literature, evidently they had in their repertoire a number of classical works, and the troupe had been hired to give private performances at least twice now. There would, without a doubt, be more of those, though how lucrative they were in contrast to the public performances, Alberich had no way of telling.

Which created another problem. It seemed to Alberich that Norris was living somewhat beyond his means, but without getting close to the man, there was no way to know that for certain. *He* didn't know how Norris was paid, or if, now that he had a bit of a following among the highborn, he was getting gifts or patronage.

If so, then young Devlin would have the perfect excuse to add to that patronage, and even visit the actor openly. So Alberich still did not know what was being exchanged, whether or not it mattered to the Crown, nor how dangerous it was, and at the moment he had no way of finding these things out.

And there was another thing that worried him, that had nothing to do with the Devlin problem. It seemed to him that Selenay was not looking entirely well. It wasn't that she looked *ill,* exactly, but that she looked far more subdued than he liked. It was the death of her father, of course; it couldn't be anything else. The Festival had been an all-too-brief diversion from her grief, he suspected. He wished he could do something for her, but the honest truth was that *he* was completely unsuited to that sort of task. All he could do was what he was good at, and let others—Talamir, who was, after all, Queen's Own—do their job without any interference.

Assuming that the Hurlee players didn't drive him utterly mad before spring.

"The problem is," Myste said, over a good slice of beef in the Bell, "you don't understand the sports-minded." Both of them were in disguise; he as a middling craftsman, she in some of her old garb from her previous life, including the spectacles she had worn then, lenses held in frames of wire. This was the first time he had brought Myste down into Haven to try out her disguise, but it was more for his benefit than for hers. He wanted to look like an ordinary craftsman in the audience at the Three Sheaves, and if he didn't have to talk, he stood a better chance of passing as Valdemaran.

"The bloody-minded, not the sports-minded," he muttered under his breath, then said, louder. "And you do?" It seemed unlikely. Bespectacled Myste held as much aloof from the Hurlee madness as he did, as far as he could tell.

"As a matter of fact," she retorted, "I do. *I* was raised here, in an ordinary family, and not in a Cadet School. People with a bit of leisure time. Ordinary folk *like* sport, even if they don't play a game, or at least, don't play it well. That's why they like to cheer on those who do."

"That, I do not understand, at all," he admitted, reluctantly.

She sniffed. "You ought to. It's part of what makes it easy for a sufficiently unscrupulous leader to get his people involved in a needless war. Look, it's like this, as I reckon it. People like to be in groups, on one side, so they can tell themselves that their side is better than the other. They can get the excitement and the thrill of being worked up about just how much better they are than the other side is. And when they're in a group doing that, then the excitement is doubled just because everyone else is doing the same."

"That, I understand," he said darkly. "So you are saying that being sports-minded, a little like being in a war is?"

"Without the bloodshed," she replied, and sighed. "Without the consequences. People like competition, but at the same time, they like cooperation almost as much. With something like Hurlee, you get to either be *on* a team, or *for* a team, and you get cooperation, like being in a special tribe. But then, your team goes against someone else's team, and there's your competition. It satisfies a whole lot of cravings all at once. It's like a bloodless war, and then you get to go out and buy each other beer afterward, and you get cooperation all over again."

He shrugged. It made sense, he supposed. He thought about how he had been shouting at the end of the last skating-race, along with everyone else. If even *he* could get caught up in a sport to that extent, then what Myste said made sense.

And there wasn't any warfare going on. People who had been used to living with a conflict and an enemy now found themselves with nothing of the sort. Maybe those who had actually *fought* were perfectly comfortable without having an enemy, but those who hadn't—particularly all those young-sters—might be looking for a focus for all that energy.

So maybe that was why Hurlee had suddenly become an obsession. And probably, as Myste expected, within a couple of months it would turn into a sport like any other. At least, now that the rules had been agreed on, and things had sorted out into a round-robin of regular teams with exact rosters, the situation wasn't quite so out-of-hand. Certainly the whole scheme of forbidding participation if marks fell off was work-ing—miraculously, even with the highborn Blues, and hereto-fore, if their parents weren't concerned with marks, there had been no way to effectively discipline them.

Maybe Hurlee wasn't so bad after all.

"So where exactly is it that we're going?" she asked.

"The Three Sheaves Inn," he told her. She nodded, though she looked surprised. He had explained his situation with re-gard to young Devlin and his contact Norris, and the difficulty he found himself in trying to get close enough to make some sort of judgment about it. "I thought, at the least, into the play-going crowd we can insert ourselves. Good for me, for open my mouth I cannot, without myself betraying, so you can do the speaking for us both. Good for you, it would be, and it may be that an opportunity you will see that I cannot."

"Fair enough," she agreed, and glanced out the window into the thickening gloom of twilight. "And I might. You never know. Besides, I wouldn't mind seeing this actor fellow, if he's setting young hearts afire."

Alberich snorted. "Not just young," he corrected, and finished the last of his meal.

"All the better, then." She chuckled at the expression on his face, and pushed off from the table without another word.

"Now, something did occur to me," she said, as they moved out into the cold, snowy streets, passing a lamplighter who was climbing up to light one of his charges. "Had you considered paying one of those low-life pickpockets you hang about with to snatch young Devlin's purse when you think he's carrying what you're looking for? Tell him you want the papers, he gets anything else."

Since it had *not* occurred to him, he almost stopped dead in the street to stare at her. "Ah. No," he managed at last.

"Should be easy enough," she pointed out. "I suppose you'd have to make up some cock-and-bull tale about *why* you wanted it done. And you'd have to work the whole setup just for the other lad to do the snatch-and-run so he'll get away clean, maybe even interfere with some of the constables to keep them from nobbling him. But between what you paid the fellow and what he'd get off Devlin, I'd have to think that it'd more than pay him to keep his mouth shut about it."

His mind was already at work on the problem. He could sacrifice one of the problematic personae if he needed to. If one of *them* was never seen again after getting the papers, it wouldn't matter if the thief in question couldn't keep his mouth shut, because there'd be no one to betray. It was definitely an idea, and a good one. Not perfect, but—

—but it opened up a whole new set of ideas. It hadn't occurred to him to make use of the criminal element. There were other possibilities here. If, for instance, he could discover which room in the inn Norris used, perhaps he could send someone to search it. . . .

"You do know that someone might recognize me at this inn, don't you?" she continued conversationally. "Not as a Herald, of course—I'm certain nobody actually knows that's where I went when I quit my job. My Choosing was pretty quiet, actually, and since I was right in Haven, I persuaded Aleirian to let me finish out my work for the day, hand in my notice, and slip out without a fuss."

"Modest of you—" he began.

She laughed. "Hardly. I didn't want anyone who wanted a favor showing up at the Collegium looking for me. Anybody who knew me would recognize me as Myste Willenger, the accountant and clerk, not Herald Myste. Except for the Wars, I haven't set foot outside the Collegium Complex since I was Chosen."

"Really? Well, that would not harm anything." He pulled the hood closer around his neck; this damp cold seemed to be more penetrating than the dry cold of Festival Week. "In fact, it might be a good thing."

"Reestablish myself in my old haunts?" She glanced at him sideways. "Well, if you want me to do that, I can. I'll think up something to tell anyone who asks where I've been—"

He had to snort at that. "Where else, but for the Army working?" he asked. "At least until the Wars ended."

She stared at him a moment, and stumbled over a rut, then smiled. "You've got a good head for this," she said. "You're right, of course. All those soldiers needed feeding, supplying, paying—that needs clerks."

"And now, half of them disbanded are, and no more need for extra clerks." That was certainly true enough. Just as it was true that an Army the size of the one that Sendar had assembled had required a vast force of people to support it.

"Which is why I'm back—" Her smile spread. "But of

course, the reason I'm not back at my *old* job is because I was replaced. Which I was, but when I was Chosen. So—"

"A job you must have." He frowned over that thought.

"Not necessarily—"

"No, wait—an idea I have. The Bell. That is safe enough. A note I will leave; it will be arranged, should anyone ask." Not that anyone would; no one was likely to ask about a minor clerk and accountant, but it was best to cover every contingency. "For the master, you do the records, and the taproom clerk you are, also. You board there as well." This was common enough. Just because people were *supposed* to be literate didn't mean they were good at reading and writing. Often enough, they were willing to pay someone else to write a letter for them—and of course, any legal documents absolutely *required* a clerk to draw them up.

"That'll do." She sighed with satisfaction. "I like to have everything set out, just in case."

"As do I. Alike, we think, in that way." And before he could say anything else, although there were a couple of half-formed ideas in the back of his head, it was too late to say anything.

Because the Three Sheaves was looming before them, and with it, a good-sized crowd milling about at the door, waiting to get into the courtyard for the performance. They joined it, and at that point, kept their conversation to commonplaces.

The one excellent thing about having Bardic Collegium right on the grounds of the Palace was that there were always musicians of the finest available at a moment's notice. The Hardornan Ambassador from King Alessandar had expressed an interest that afternoon in hearing some of the purely instrumental music that Valdemarans took for granted, and Selenay had been able to arrange for that wish to be gratified with an impromptu concert after dinner. Ambassador Isadere was finally rested enough from his journey and formal reception to show some interest in the less formal pastimes of the Court—which meant, to Selenay, the ones where she wasn't required to pay exclusive attention to him, or indeed, to anyone. Bardic Collegium responded to her request for an instrumental ensemble with what almost seemed to be gratitude; she'd been puzzled by that at first, but then, after a moment of thought, she realized that she had not made such requests more than a handful of times since she'd become Queen, whereas her father had called on Bardic, either for simple musicians or true Bards, at least every two or three days. Perhaps they took this as a sign that things were getting back to "normal."

Well, even if *she* didn't feel that way, was it right for her to impose her depressed spirits on everyone else?

No, it wasn't. No matter what she *felt* like, wasn't it her duty to put on a sociable mask?

Besides, entertainments like this meant she wouldn't really have to put on more than the mask. When she thought about it, she realized that anyone who was really listening to the music wouldn't require anything from *her* except that she not be dissolved in tears.

So when she sent a note back to Bardic thanking them, she asked if it would be possible for them to supply musicians of the various levels of expertise to her as they had to her father—and as often. The immediate response was that they would be overjoyed to do so, and would even save her the trouble of trying to decide on informal entertainments by setting them up with her household, as they had done for Sendar.

With great relief, she let them know that this was perfect. And she led her Court into the Great Hall for the concert, then settled into her seat, enthroned among the courtiers, with Ambassador Isadere at her left, thinking that tonight was turning out to be something of a respite after all. And the gods knew she needed one. She wasn't feeling up to an evening of bright conversation with her foreign guests tonight; she'd been fighting melancholy all day, knowing that it would take next to nothing to make her break out in tears. Now, with not only the ambassador, but his entire entourage listening with rapt attention to the musicians, she could lean back in her chair and wait for the evening to be over.

Or so she thought.

"Majesty, are you well?" whispered Lord Orthallen. He leaned over the arm of his chair toward her, his voice pitched so that it would not disturb anyone else, and to his credit, he really did look concerned.

She smiled faintly at him, and nodded. He raised an eyebrow, as if he didn't entirely believe her, but turned his attention back to the music.

She glanced over at Herald Talamir, who did not appear to have noticed the interchange. But then, it was difficult to tell, these days, what Talamir did and did not see. It was even more difficult to tell what he thought about what he saw.

In fact, he was sitting back in his chair, eyes half-closed, and he looked exactly like a statue—except that there was nothing of the solidity of a statue about him. How he managed this, she could not tell, but these days Talamir didn't entirely seem to be in the *here and now,* as it were. His manner was often preoccupied, as if listening to and watching something no one else could hear or see. And to her mind, there was a suggestion of translucency about him, the spirit somehow shining through the flesh. When there was something that really *required* his attention, he was almost like his old self, but when there wasn't, he was almost like a ghost-made-flesh, and not altogether contented with that state.

He made a great many people uneasy, without any of them being able to articulate why. He made Selenay uneasy, as a matter of fact; she could never glance at him—except in the times when he *was* very much in the here-and-now—without an involuntary shiver.

And yet, there were plenty of people who saw no difference

in him at all. People like Orthallen, for instance; they acted in Talamir's presence now exactly as they had acted in Talamir's presence before the last battle.

Before he died, and was dragged back to life. . . .

That was the crux of it, of course. Heralds, Healers, and Bards almost all sensed it. Talamir was a man in two worlds now, and most of his concentration seemed to be taken up with the unseen world. That was why Selenay just could not bring herself to confide in him, even though that was what the function of the Queen's Own was supposed to be.

How could I sit there and tell him things? she wondered wearily. *Even if he wasn't a man, and as old as my father. It would be like trying to share girl-secrets with a particularly unworldly priest. . . .*

And anyway, Talamir had been her father's closest friend—which was only as it should have been, of course, but how could she tell him how much she missed her father and cry on his shoulder, when surely Talamir missed him as much, or more? It would be too cruel, too cruel for words. Talamir had already suffered so much pain, losing his own Companion to death as well as Sendar and so many other friends— No, it would be too cruel to inflict further pain on him that way.

As for sharing her scarcely-articulate longing for, well, *romance*—

Oh, no. He would never, ever understand. And she'd get a grave, well-considered, perfectly reasonable lecture about her duties as Queen, and how great power required great responsibility.

As if she didn't know, as if she didn't feel all that with every pulse of blood through her veins.

But that didn't stop her from wanting it. Even though most of the younger members of her Court were probably going to make arranged marriages in the end, that didn't stop them from flirtations and even outright courtship. After all, there was always the chance that both sets of parents would be pleased to find that an alliance had been made.

And even if they weren't, well, as one young lady had tearfully put it, unaware that Selenay was eavesdropping from the other side of the hedge, "It will give me something to remember when I'm wedded to that awful old man—"

But a Queen couldn't have flirtations. And of course she knew that only too well. Knowing she *couldn't* was bad enough, but being reminded of that fact by someone like Talamir would only make it worse. Her father would have understood; *he'd* been able to marry for love. He'd always said he didn't want to see her sacrificed to a marriage of state, but with him gone, and with no telling what needs might arise, she had to count on sacrificing herself.

She felt a lump rising in her throat and closed her eyes against the sting of tears, fighting them back. This was neither the place nor the time to display weakness.

It was at that moment that she felt, with a sense of shock, someone press a folded bit of paper into her hand.

Her eyes flew open in time for her to see Lord Orthallen, removing his hand from hers. Their eyes met, and he nodded gravely, then sat back again.

For one brief moment, an incredulous thought came into her head. *A love note? From* Orthallen?

No, surely not. He was married. He was older than her father. And besides, every other Councilor would spontaneously combust with rage at the very idea.

She looked down at the scrap of paper, and opened it.

Selenay, you used to call me your "Lord-Uncle," and told me all your childish woes, she read, *And if I have, in recent days, often forgotten that you are no longer my "Little Niece" but my Queen and fully adult, please forgive an old man for clinging to his illusions longer than he should have. I have seen you fall into melancholy more than once these past few days; I think you might be in need of a friend with whom you can unburden yourself freely; if that is the case, will you honor your father's friend by putting me in that place as he did, so that this old man can begin to see the grown lady of reality instead of the child of the past? Perhaps we can help each other in our shared sorrow.*

Selenay blinked. This was unexpected. First of all, Lord Orthallen was, above all else, a very proud man. He seldom apologized. Secondly, he had been one of those on her Council that had seemed the most adamant about keeping her from taking the reins of power into her own hands—

But this *was* an apology, and a tacit admission that he was ready and willing to see her as the Queen in fact as well as in title.

And the part about shared sorrow—that made the lump in her throat swell all over again. Orthallen had been her father's good and trusted friend. She hadn't thought about how *he* must be feeling. But that pride of his might well have prevented him from making any great show of his own grief. . . .

And who better to *talk* to? He was safe enough, with a wife he honored; he had never, ever given rise to a single rumor about his fidelity (unlike far too many men in her Court). She had known him all her life; she'd cried on his shoulder before this.

Who else was there, really—and she was beginning to think that if she didn't find *someone* she could talk to, someone besides Caryo, that is, she was going to crack. Talking to Caryo was a little too much like talking to herself. And besides, even Caryo was getting tired of how depressed and burdened with grief she was.

She looked up and met his eyes. He tilted his head to the side, in grave inquiry. She nodded. He smiled; it was a sad, weary smile, the same sort that she often found on her own lips of late.

She smiled back, folded the piece of paper, and put it into her sleeve pocket for safekeeping, feeling a little better already. Better enough, at least, to give the musicians her full attention for the rest of the concert.

Rather than joining the people in the courtyard on their benches, Alberich paid out enough for seats on the second-floor balcony that ran along the inside walls facing the courtyard, a balcony that made up a sort of makeshift gallery. It was marginally warmer here, and the folks in the cheap seats were notoriously rowdy. When the troupe had been playing in that tent, there had been no balcony, and the expensive seats had been in the first several rows. Not so here.

The courtyard was entirely enclosed by inn buildings. Behind the stage and the curtains that closed off the back of it, were the stables. Not the sort of place where anyone would care to sit, so using that wall as the back of the stage wasted no valuable space that could have accommodated paying customers. The other three wings were the three stories of what was a typical market inn, with an arched passage in the middle of what was, in this configuration, the "back" of the courtyard leading out into the street outside. The ground floor of that wing, divided as it was by the passage, held two separate dining rooms, a taproom for the common sorts of folk, the drovers, the shepherds, the farmers who came to the market, and the second an actual set of dining rooms, one large dining room for the better-off sort, and several private parlors for the "gentry," or at least, those with enough money that the inn-keeper's servants called them "m'lord" and "m'lady," whether or not they had any right to the title.

Above that, in the second and third stories, since that wing both had the noisy dining areas on the first floor, and faced the street, were the cheapest of the sleeping rooms. These were the sort where strangers packed in several to a room together, on pallets laid so closely together that the room might just as well have been one big bed.

The right and left wings held more expensive sleeping rooms on the second and third floors, with the kitchens on the ground floor of the left-hand wing, and the servants' quarters on the ground floor of the right-hand wing.

When there wasn't a play on, the balconies gave access to those rooms. Now, however, there were benches there, where those willing to spend a bit extra could sit along the balcony railing. The view was good from here, and you weren't going to find yourself harassed by someone who'd paid less than the cost of a pint for his seat.

Normally, at least with most acting troupes, the truly expensive seats were *on* the stage itself, to the left and the right. Not with this lot—their energetic acrobatics made that a dangerous place to be, and the entire stage was free of any such obstructions.

Myste laid her arms along the balcony rail and parked her chin on them, peering down at the stage with interest. The courtyard was lit almost as well as the Great Hall of the Palace, with torches in holders on every supporting beam, and shielded lanterns around the stage. The thing about holding a play at night meant that the players could actually do some things with the scenery—like a paper moon with a lantern behind it, or using foxfire smeared all over someone's face if he was a ghost. Or, as had occurred in the scene they'd just watched, the softer, dimmer light had made the shabby costumes and tinsel and paste gems of the "lords and ladies" at a grand Festival look positively genuine. *:This isn't as bad as I thought it would be,:* she remarked to Alberich in Mindspeech.

:True,: he replied. *:This is actually one of the plays they do privately.:* It was a tale of unlucky lovers, who came from feuding families, who met by accident at some celebration, and of course, were lifebonded at first sight. The troupe were playing on current events by making the place of their first meeting the Ice Festival—which worked out very well, since it allowed them to bundle up in their warmest costumes. And of

course, the feud allowed for several of the signature acrobatic fight scenes.

Down there on the stage, the feud had been acted out by means of a confrontation in the first scene, then several of the youngsters of both clans had gotten caught up by accident in the party following a wedding. The hero and heroine had met and fallen instantly in love, and had retired. Down on the stage, the stagehands were scuttling about in the pause for the scenery change between the first and second acts.

:*I suppose they're both going to end up dead in the end,*: Myste sighed.

Alberich had seen this play before. :*Well, it* is *a tragedy.*: And in fact, that was exactly what was going to happen. Hero and heroine would be wedded in secret in the second act. In the third, the feud would escalate into open warfare, isolating them from one another as the city turned into a battlefield. In the fourth act, the lovers would arrange a desperate meeting, intending to flee the city and seek the help of the King. The heroine's brother would discover the hero waiting with horses, and challenge him. The hero would attempt to placate him, but to no avail. He would find himself forced into the duel, the brother would disarm him, and just as the heroine arrived, fatally wound him. She would run screaming toward them both; startled, the brother would turn, and she would be accidentally impaled on his sword, and the lovers would die in each other's arms.

Not before forgiving the stricken brother, however, and extracting his vow to end the feud for all time.

Not the worst of plays, by any means, and with enough action to please the male members of the audience.

:*I see at least a dozen people I know down in the audience,*: Myste remarked. :*The most interesting thing is, though, that— Look, see that bald-headed fellow down there, stage left? The one who seems to be in charge of the scene changing? I know him* very *well. The last time I saw him, he was the butler for*

*an officious little mercer I did regular work for. I wonder how
he got this job?:*

:Really?: Well, that could be interesting, if he happened to
recognize Myste.

And even as that thought passed through Alberich's mind,
the man looked up at their gallery, blinked, and peered upward
at them, through the torch smoke and lantern light.

He gave a tentative wave. Myste nodded, and waved back.
He grabbed a passing boy, said something to him, pointed at
Myste, and shoved him in the direction of the stairs. A few
moments later, the boy clambered toward them.

" 'Scuze me, mum, but Laric wants t'know, if you're Myste,
Myste Willenger, the clerk?" the boy asked.

"That I am," Myste replied, without a moment of hesitation.

The boy grinned. "Well, mum, then Laric 'ud like ter talk
with you arter the play, if you've time, an could use some
work," the boy continued. " 'Cause he's got a job that needs
doin'."

Myste grinned. "Tell him, thanks. Who can't use extra
work?"

The boy grinned back. "I'll tell 'im, mum."

With that, he scrambled back down the stairs, presumably
to find the now-vanished Laric. Myste settled down for the second act, with a smile like a cat in cream.

*:Well. How about that for an opportunity dropping into our
laps?:* she asked.

Alberich could only shake his head in amazement.

9

ALBERICH and Myste lingered after the end of the last act, assuming that Laric would seek them out as soon as the audience cleared out, It was a reasonable assumption; both of them assumed he would not have interrupted his urgent work to send up a boy if he hadn't intended to get to Myste as soon as he could. It wasn't comfortable, sitting out there in the cold, on the hard benches, but both Alberich and Myste had the feeling that it just might be worth the wait.

And they were right. As soon as the actors took their final bows, the audience began to shove its way out. Once the actors were gone, the audience lost interest in what, to Alberich, was actually more interesting than the play itself. In the torchlight, there had been a certain—something—that had given an illusion of reality to the play. Now the illusion was coming apart, bit by bit, and it was fascinating to Alberich to see how it had been put together in the first place.

First, the lamps at the edge of the stage were blown out and gathered up, and the stagehands began clearing away the properties on the stage, carrying them back behind what *had* looked like a false front of several buildings made rather solidly of wood. But it was now apparent that it wasn't wood at all, nor solid, but another canvas backdrop of the same sort that the troupe had used during the Festival. With no one being careful about how they moved around it, the thing rippled and waved as people went behind it. Two other bits of business that stood on either side of the canvas, hiding the edges, looked a bit more solid. They were only a single story tall, though they had a pair of doors in them that the actors had used to come and go. As two stagehands hauled off the "horses" that the hero and heroine were to have escaped on, Laric dashed out of one of the doors in the scenery onto the edge of the stage, and peered up at the balcony. "Heyla!" he shouted, and waved at her. She waved back. "Myste! Stay right there for a bit while I tie things up!"

Myste nodded vigorously; evidently that was enough for Laric, who dashed back through the false door again. "Tie things up, hmm?" she said cheerfully to Alberich. "I hope that isn't literal."

"That, I could not tell you. I know nothing of—all this," Alberich admitted, waving vaguely at the stage. And at precisely that moment, the painted cloth at the back of the stage, depicting the outer walls of several buildings, dropped down to the stage with a *bang,* along with the pole it was fastened to along the top. Behind it was another, with a forest or garden scene; it came down next. And finally, a third, showing stalls of a market and sky—that was the setting for the Ice Festival. Down it came, revealing the bare front of the stables, which was three stories tall, like the rest of the inn, though Alberich could not for a moment imagine what they would need three stories for.

Well, this was a busy place, with a lot of animals coming and going. Maybe they needed all that space for hay and straw storage.

A cheerful-looking little boy had been up at the top, where there was a crane and a pulley with a rope still hanging from it. Apparently that was what the backdrops had been fastened to. Now he slid down from the upper loft of the stables on the rope there, and he and another stagehand began rolling up the three backdrops on their poles. With another *bang,* one of the two pieces of scenery that screened each side of the backcloth fell over, and two more men came up to haul it away. The second one followed in short order. In a remarkably short period of time, not only had the sets and properties vanished into the stable, so had the stage itself, which apparently came apart, although it seemed solid enough even with all of those actors leaping about on it. That explained how the troupe had been able to get a stage into their tent that could take the amount of abuse they had been delivering with every performance. Alberich watched in fascination until there was nothing to be seen but a perfectly ordinary-looking inn courtyard with the stables at the rear.

And that was when Laric emerged from the stable door again and wearily climbed the nearest staircase, heading in their direction. He mopped his red face with a handkerchief the size of a small sail as he came. He was a very big man, with an imposing belly, red-faced, with hair going thin at his temples and surprisingly honest eyes. Not that Alberich was going to trust how someone *looked* to tell him anything about that person's real nature.

His clothing was ordinary enough: a sheepskin vest over a heavy knitted tunic and moleskin breeches. He wore shoes, rather than boots, but most city dwellers did. If you *had* to go out in fresh snow that hadn't been shoveled or packed down yet, and you didn't have boots, you just wrapped your feet, shoes and all, in canvas, and tied it around your calves with twine.

"Damme, but if makin' an honest livin' ain't the hardest work going!" he exclaimed as they both stood up. "Myste, where you been? I got hauled in to stage manage for this idiot lot, and just when I had some work for ye, ye ups and vanishes!"

She shrugged. "Army needed clerks," she said simply. "Now it don't, so they let me go. Back I came. Got some work at the Companion's Bell, but it ain't full-time."

"Well, that's a break fer both of us," he said genially. "Who's yer friend?"

"Bret," she said, without batting an eye. "Carter. From down-country, on the border. Army don't need carters now, neither; nothing more to haul down *or* up."

"Ah, hard luck, man," the stage manager said, with sympathy.

"Don't feel too sorry for him!" Myste laughed. "The Army may not need 'im, but damn-near everyone else does! He paid *my* way in tonight!"

"Owed her one," Alberich said, gruffly, but with as much good humor as Myste, and doing his level best to minimize his accent. "Bet 'er a meal an' a raree-show, an' she picked this. Warn ye, man—don't play cards with this one!"

He hoped that someone who *wasn't* an actor wouldn't think twice about his accent, and took the chance on actually saying something. It was worth the risk; the big man let out a belly-laugh without a single look askance.

"Myste! You conned another country boy! Listen, man you're lucky the stakes wasn't more than just a meal and a seat at a play!" Laric responded, wiping his eyes with that kerchief. "I learned that one a long time ago!"

"Well, a man looks at her face, he don't think of card sharp!" Alberich replied. "He thinks pen pusher!"

"Which she is, she is, but she's got some *system*," Laric replied earnestly. "It ain't cheatin', but she's got the cards in her head, somehow, an' she can figger the odds of what's coming' up—" he shook his head. "*I* can't make it work, but she can. So we know better'n t' play against her."

"You get along, Bret," Myste said, in a kindly tone of voice. "You got a load in the morning, and we might be a while. I can get back by myself."

:I'm safe enough with Laric,: she added. *:Just go wait at the Bell, and I'll catch up with you.:*

"Right-oh," he responded, as if he was just a casual friend, and left—though with a lot more reluctance than he showed. He didn't like leaving her alone, even if she knew the man. He didn't like the idea that she would be walking back to the Bell alone, even though this neighborhood, and the ones between here and the Bell were safe enough.

But he had no excuse to linger, once Myste had "dismissed" him, and no place to wait for her to finish her business with the stage manager. Now he was sorry he hadn't scouted this area beforehand and found some place he could have holed up nearby. If she was going to actually get involved with these people—

Still. She had her "throwaway purse," just like he'd taught her. If someone tried to rob her, she'd toss that purse away and run in the opposite direction. And the Three Sheaves was very public. Even near the sleeping quarters, there were people coming and going all night. If something happened, her Companion would be out of the Bell's stable in a trice and on the way to help. Surely she couldn't get into trouble. . . he hoped.

He returned to the Bell alone, going in through the hidden door in the back of the stable to the secret room. There he changed his disguise for his gray leathers, and waited impatiently in the Heralds' common room for her to return, sitting right at the window so he could see her when she did. Or at least, see her if she came anywhere near the front.

:She won't,: Kantor reminded him. *:She'll use the back, just like you did. Alberich, she's more used to moving around in a city than you are.:*

Well, that was true enough. Especially this city, at least the reasonable parts of it.

It felt like half the night, rather than just a candlemark or so, before he "heard"—rather than saw—the Herald-Chronicler at last.

:I'm back. Everything went smoothly; it's a distinct advantage to go disguised as yourself. Don't get yourself in a knot, Alberich,: she said cheerfully. *:I've got good news for you. Just let me change into my uniform.:*

He signaled a girl and ordered hot wine for both of them, knowing that by now she must be frozen. She was, thankfully, faster at changing her clothing than most women he had encountered. The hot wine he ordered was barely on the table when she came in, lenses glittering in the lamplight—and fogging up in the transition from cold outside to warm and humid inside.

"So," she said, without preamble, sliding onto the bench across from him. She took off her lenses to polish them on a napkin before replacing them on her nose. "Here's what we've got. You want to know how Norris started up this whole show in the first place?"

"All information is useful," he admitted.

"So I've learned." She took a sip of wine. "There were a lot of people displaced by the Tedrels as you know, and quite a few of them ended up here in Haven. Your boy Norris is supposed to be from near the Rethwellan Border, and managed to get separated from the entertainment troupe he'd been with. Laric didn't say how, and I didn't ask. Supposedly, he hitched up with a caravan, doing acrobatics to amuse everyone around the fire at night, and ended up at the Three Sheaves along with the caravan. Supposedly, the rest of his group was going to come up to Haven and find him, and they never did. He wasn't minded to sign up with the Army, but he was running up a big bill at the inn, when he got the idea to put together his own new troupe from some of the other ragtags of entertainers that were drifting in so he could *pay* that bill without getting put to work in the kitchen. That's the story, anyway; I suspect at least part of it's true. He's definitely an actor, and he's better than anyone else of the bunch. He's got 'em all charmed, that's for sure, and now that they're doing just as well as he promised they would, there isn't a one of them will hear a word against him. I don't know if he's from Rethwellen, because he's damn good at putting on and taking off accents. He did at least four in my presence."

Alberich almost choked on his wine. "You *saw* him? You talked to him?"

Myste shrugged. "It was after I made the bargain with Laric; we were looking over the office I'm going to use. He swanned in with two women on his arms, Laric told him I was going to be checking the books. He looked at me, saw a dowdy lump, wafted a little charm in my direction just to keep his hand in, and promptly forgot me as soon as he turned around and headed out the door. I *told* you that it's useful being a clerk. Nobody ever pays any attention to us. Even that business with card counting; Laric's the only one who ever caught on I was doing it. Everybody else just figured I was lucky."

"Evidently so," Alberich managed. How close a call had it been? He wished he had been there to see Norris' reaction with his own eyes.

"Anyway, here's the thing; the innkeeper is the one taking in the receipts at the door, because he takes his room and board for the troupe right off the top, and now that they've gotten popular, Laric think's he's skimming. But nobody else can manage to cipher for the numbers that they're bringing in of an evening now. So from now on, I'm going to go every night they're putting on a play—which is once every two nights—and go over the books, the head-count, and the innkeeper's tally." She grinned. "And I'm doing it all from the room next to Norris', which is Laric's office. Which means that I'll be in a position to tell you when he's there, where he's gone if he isn't, when he's likely to be back, and to leave my own window open for someone to come and go. If you want to search his room for papers, I can make it happen."

Alberich stared at her. "And for how long will this go on?"

"That, I don't know," she admitted. "Laric wants me to come regularly at first, then taper off. He thinks, and I agree with him, that if the innkeeper *is* skimming, it's going to be better not to confront him on it, just bring *me* in. They know what I was at the Three Sheaves, and they'll know why I'm in Laric's office with the tally boards. If the innkeeper knows we're watching him, he'll be honest, and by comparing the take over time, we'll know if he's *been* honest in the past. And knowing that Laric has me on tap will probably keep him honest when I stop coming around."

"So, earliest on the best of our chances will be." Alberich didn't like that, particularly, but there was an old saying that beggars didn't get to pick what they were given. And another that it didn't pay to inquire too closely about the age of a gift horse.

:Or, in my case, the color of his eyes,: Kantor said wickedly.

And Myste was right. The best way to find out what Norris was passing was to search his room for the papers before he got rid of them. Which meant that Alberich was going to have to find a way to copy them, because they might be in code, and he certainly wasn't going to be able to memorize them even if they weren't—

"Is there, perhaps, a way to copy such things?" he asked.

"Several," she assured him. "Rubbings, if he's using graphite or a crayon, damp-paper transfer if he's using ink. I can show you. We do that all the time to make emergency copies. Of course," she added judiciously, "when you do that, you get a mirror-image, but that's no great problem."

Alberich took in a deep breath, and let it out in a sigh. "Myste—very well have you done. Thank you."

She made a face. "Well, if you're doing the dangerous bit— and I assume it'll be *you* climbing in that window and not some lowlife from around Exile's Gate that you hired—I'm doing the tedious part. Here I was, pleased I'd finally gotten *out* of doing accounts, and here I am back into it!" Then she sighed and looked out the window. "And on top of my real work, too."

"Worse, it could be," Alberich reminded her. "On the battle-field, we could be."

She gave him a wry glance. "Well," she admitted. "There is that. I'll try to keep it in mind when I'm trying to hide you or throw you out a window because your lad Norris came back early."

And there just wasn't much he could say to that, so wisely, he said nothing at all.

But as Myste had pointed out, just because they were involved in this after-hours clandestine work it did not make their normal duties go away. He had his full set of classes to train, and as the season edged toward spring, the snow began to thaw, and the blustery winds began to blow, it became more and more of a challenge to hold classes out of doors. At least that wretched game of Hurlee was put on hold, for the ice on the ponds was getting rotten and not to be trusted, but the ground was alter-nately frozen mud or slushy snow, so the game couldn't be transferred to some sort of playing field. And, oh yes, he had already heard that there were plans afoot for *that,* though the players would have to run, rather than sliding. The next thing he'd probably hear was that the Heraldic Trainees were going to try it Companion-back. . . .

Meanwhile, the replacement mirror finally arrived and was installed. The two miscreants who began that particular ad-venture were as responsible for creating the new one as de-stroying the old one, being the ones who had spent an interminable amount of time polishing it to rid it of as many

defects as possible. Both Deans decreed that their term of punishment *at the glassworks* was at an end although they would
still be serving double-chores at the Collegium for well into
the summer. They had missed the entire Hurlee season, and
whenever an animated discussion of the game began, their
faces were a study in adolescent disappointment. Alberich
wasn't at all surprised. If ever there were two rascals who
might have been born to play a game like Hurlee, it was those
two. And it occurred to him that this, alone, might be the worst
punishment that could have been inflicted on them. They had
missed out on the creation of the game, they had missed out
on becoming some of the first experts. From now on, the best
they could hope for was to play catch-up to some other ascen-
dant star.

And in a way he felt just a little guilty, for if it hadn't been
for his own curiosity about where they had picked up their
wild ideas, he would never have investigated the actors, and
never have known that there was something going on.

He still didn't know *what* it was, of course, but at least he
knew there was something. Now he had a fighting chance to
discover what it was, and whether or not it was dangerous.

Nevertheless, he had an important duty to perform, right
there at the Collegium, and it was one that he could not give
less than his total attention to during the hours when he was
teaching, and no few of the hours outside of that time.

He was training those who would one day become Heralds
how to stay alive, when other people wanted them dead.

And that was a massive task.

It began with the youngest or the least experienced—not
necessarily the same thing, as his tutelage of Myste had
proven—and the basic skills of hand and eye, coordination,
and familiarity with weapons. And while they were learning
these things, he was studying them, to determine what their
lifelong weaknesses would be (for there had never been a per-

son born who had so perfect a physique that he *didn't* have one) and how to make them aware of the fact.

Then, he would move them into the next stage of their training—how to compensate for those weaknesses.

By then, they were roughly halfway through their years as Trainees; they had mastered basic skills, and they were as strong and flexible and coordinated as they were ever likely to get. There were exceptions to that last, of course, but those were the exceptions that proved the rule. If they had found him a hard master before, he was harder still at that point, because no one, *no one,* ever likes having a weakness pointed out, and human nature is such that when one *is* pointed out, the natural reaction is to try to deny it exists.

Which was why he would go from master to monster at that point, until not even the most persistently self-delusional could continue to believe anything other than that the problem was real, and Something had to be done about the problem.

Sometimes the weaknesses were physical—restricted peripheral vision, for instance. Sometimes they were mental. Often, they were emotional, and the biggest lay in the very natures of those who were Chosen as Heralds. These youngsters did not *believe* in the goodness and decency of their fellow man, they *knew* it. It was fundamental to their souls.

And he had to, somehow, prove to them that their fellow man was very likely to plant a knife in the middle of their backs without destroying that deep and primitive *knowledge.* As Heralds, they had to go into every day expecting that the people around them would all act as ordinary, fallible, but decent human beings who, given the chance, would act decently and humanely. They also had to be prepared for the eventuality that those around them would do nothing of the sort—and be able to cope with such a contradiction without going a little mad.

Not that all Heralds weren't already a little mad, but—not *that* kind of mad.

Then, once the weaknesses had been identified and ac-
knowledged, he had to train them to compensate for the weaknesses.

It would have been infinitely easier to do this had his students been, say, Karsite Cadets. Only physical and mental
weaknesses would have to be dealt with, because emotional
weaknesses literally did not matter to the Sunsguard so long
as they were locked down tightly—and he could have proven
those weaknesses to them with sheer, brute force, by persistently attacking them at those weak points until even a blind
man could see what was wrong. Persuasion always took a lot
longer than hammering something home.

He was generally in that last stage only with those who
were in the last year of their Trainee status—it was far, far
easier to work with these Trainees, who were quite ready for
Whites if only they had a little more experience and skill. For
them, he was a mentor, not a monster.

It had occurred to him, and more than once, that here in
the Collegium the Trainees were put through a kind of forced-
maturation process that sent them out into the greater world
at eighteen, nineteen, or twenty with the mental and emotional skills of someone well in his thirties or older.

Alas, most of his time was spent in being the tyrant with
the heart of stone.

This was never more true than when the energy level of
those in his class was such that the students were near to
bouncing off walls as they entered the door of the salle, and
he turned them right around and took them outside to run
their drills in the mud, the slush, the half-frozen snow, and no
matter if it *was* too wretched out to be doing any such thing.
Cold, dampness, and dirt weren't going to harm them any; if
they got too cold, he knew the signs and always sent them
back into the salle to warm up at the oven. Not that there was
any chance of getting cold enough to fall ill, unless something
odd happened to keep them standing about soaked to the skin.

The Blues, of course, were exempt from this if they chose. However, if they declared their unwillingness in such a way as to be insubordinate, rather than merely electing not to show up for lessons, he had a weapon to either bring them to heel or get rid of them entirely.

Such as today—with one of the classes that was in their middle, and most difficult period of development.

And they roared into his salle already in full antagonist mode.

The battle lines were already drawn; Blues versus Trainees, one ringleader facing off for each side. The insults were flying. Blows would follow, in a moment.

Except that Alberich waded right into the middle of it, and sent both of them to the floor with a blow to the ear, and the silence that descended was absolute.

"Well," he said crisply. "Before it begins, I care not how it started, nor *who* started it. You brought it into my salle. You will take it out again. There will be no second mirror to be replaced."

A nervous titter came from behind him. He didn't turn to look. Neither boy had moved, and he gave them both looks that should have turned them to ice. "I said," he enunciated carefully. "You will take it outside. You wish to fight? Well enough. Outside. It ends when I say it ends, and *I* will be the judge of the winner."

The Trainee on the floor had the sense to go pale; he, at least, must have some inkling of what Alberich meant—which was to let the fight go on until they were both too exhausted, bruised, and battered to stand. There would be no winner, short of one of the two being knocked unconscious, which, with the bare hands of a pair of boys fundamentally unskilled in bare-hand fighting, was unlikely. This was, actually, *why* Alberich did not teach bare-hand fighting to anyone who had not passed into that third and final stage of development. . . .

But the Blue was one of Alberich's personal headaches. Arrogant, assertive and, unfortunately, skilled enough to have earned the right to a part of that arrogance. Alberich would have gladly rid himself of the boy—Kadhael Corbie—if he could have. Unfortunately, that was out of his hands. Kadhael was in the class unless and until he took himself out of it.

The boy looked him up and down, and sneered. "No," he said.

Someone gasped.

Alberich did not move, and did not change his expression by so much as a hair. "I do not believe I heard you correctly," he said evenly, trying to suppress the thrill of glee the boy's insolent answer gave him. "What, precisely, did you say?"

"I said, *no.* No, I am not going outside. No, I am not fighting by your rules. Who are you to give *me* orders, old man?"

Alberich smiled—and Kadhael took one look at the smile and suddenly realized that he had made so fundamental a mistake that there was not going to be any evasion of the consequences.

"I," he said quietly, and with the perfect and precise control of Valdemaran grammar that came upon him in moments of stress "am the Collegium Weaponsmaster. As such, *when I choose to exercise my rank,* within the four walls of my salle and on its grounds, I outrank, by Valdemaran law, every man, woman, and child in Valdemar save only the Monarch. And within these four walls, the Monarch is my equal, not my superior."

And it was all perfectly true. How else could he properly *teach* the sons and daughters of the highborn? How else could he train high-ranking Guards? How could he drill the greatest warriors and nobles of the realm? How could he *ever* train the Heirs, if he did not outrank them? To properly train, there would be injuries. They might be serious. And the Weaponsmaster could not be held responsible for such injuries. To *be* trained, the Weaponsmaster must know his orders would be obeyed, and the only way to be sure of that was to see that his rank on these grounds was higher than anyone else's in the land.

Which was why—though he had not learned this until *after* Dethor had retired—he had that special status within the salle and on the grounds.

Kadhael looked as if the blow Alberich had given him had knocked every particle of sense right out of his head. He stared, he gaped, he looked as if he could not rightly understand a word of what had been said. "But—"

"And since you choose not to abide by the laws of this, *my* Kingdom," Alberich continued, still smiling. "I banish you. Now and forever."

"What?" Kadhael stammered.

"Out. Go. Do not *ever* present yourself as my pupil. You may tell your father why you are not here, or not. I care not. I will report this matter to the Queen, the Lord Marshal, and the Provost Marshal—since you are not a Trainee, I shall not trouble any of the Deans with it."

"You can't *do* this!" Kadhael protested wildly, paling. Alberich knew why. Kadhael's father had watched Alberich fight and train the Guards for months before the boy had been sent to the salle with a class. Kadhael's father *knew* that there was not enough money in Valdemar to purchase the services of a trainer as good as Alberich.

Kadhael's father would be very, very unhappy about this.

"I can. I have." Alberich eyed the boy consideringly. Should he?

:Oh, go ahead, do,: Kantor answered.

He bent down, and grabbed the boy by the back of his tunic and hauled him to his feet. Without much effort, be it added—Kadhael was just about Alberich's size and weight, but he was still an uncoordinated adolescent, not a trained, honed warrior. Alberich tightened his grip *just* enough that the fabric half-choked the boy, eliminating any more babble out of him.

"I will, because you do not seem to understand your own

tongue properly, repeat myself," Alberich said, with no anger whatsoever. "You are banished from the salle and the grounds. You are no longer a student here. You are leaving now, and you will never return. If you do, I will personally thrash you until you cannot stand, and throw you off the grounds again. Training here is a privilege, not a right. You have just proved you do not deserve to enjoy that privilege."

And with that, he frog-marched the boy out the door, down the path, to the very edge of the training grounds. And with great care and utmost precision, he pitched the insolent brat right into the biggest, muddiest patch of slush that he thought he could reach.

He did not even wait to see if Kadhael went headfirst into it, or managed to somehow save himself. He turned on his heel and marched back into his salle.

No one had moved. This was good. He wasn't going to have to discipline anyone else—yet.

He raked them all with his stony gaze. "More objections, do I hear?" he asked, raising one eyebrow.

Silence.

"Then outside you will go. All of you." He turned a stern gaze on the Trainee, who was still sitting on the floor—Osberic, that was the boy's name. "Osberic," he continued, and the Trainee flinched. "Since no opponent you have now, yet equally of guilt you are to have brought a *fight* within my walls, it will be me that you face. Fetch two staves, and follow. Even practice swords, I will not ruin in this muck."

He would not be *too* hard on him. Putting him on his face or back into the mud two or three times would be enough.

:He started the fight,: Kantor put in. :Not that Kadhael wasn't trying to goad him into starting it, but he did start it.:

All right. Four. Teach the boy to hold his temper.

:Good answer. I'm going to watch.:

Alberich smiled as he walked out into the cold again and

saw that there was no sign of Kadhael, other than a vaguely human-shaped depression in the slush. *:Please do.:*

The boys had formed up in a rough circle, and Osberic came up to Alberich with two fighting staffs and a hangdog look. Alberich took one without looking at it.

"Consequences, Osberic," he said as he squared off against the boy, who began circling him warily. "Say I will not, that a Herald loses not his temper—but aware a Herald is, that consequences there are for doing so."

His staff shot out at ankle-level, tripping Osberic. Down he went.

He picked himself back up, and aimed a blow at Alberich's head. Alberich blocked it, riposted, and let the boy block him. "So think you—had there a fight been, what consequences there would be?"

"Uh—" Osberic tried again, was blocked again. "Lord Corbie would get me in trouble?"

"Wrong." Alberich flipped the staff at Osberic's ankles; the boy dodged, and Alberich flipped the other end around to thwack him in the buttocks and send him into the slush again. "Lord Corbie would protest to the Queen, who would be forced to go to the Dean, who would have to answer to why discipline was so lax among the Trainees that a highborn fought a Trainee."

Osberic picked himself up, flushing. "My fight would get the *Heralds* in trouble?"

"Correct." Alberich let the boy try a few more blows; not bad, but he wasn't going to get through Alberich's defenses any time soon. "And who else?"

"The Queen?" Osberic hazarded.

"Correct. Now, why will there be *no* trouble for what I did with Kadhael Corbie?"

Osberic didn't answer, being a little too busy fending off a flurry of blows from Alberich, only to trip over a hardened lump of snow and land on his backside in an icy puddle.

:That should count,: Kantor said from the sideline.

:I agree.:

"Because," Alberich continued as Osberic picked himself back up for the third time, "A proper and correct order gave I. Insolence I was given. My proper authority I exerted—no temper, no beatings, no punishments, and only when more insolence and refusal was I given, did I remove Kadhael with prejudice. To his father he will go, yes, but his father will likely box his ears. Now, know you why *I* am drilling you thus?" Osberic came at Alberich yet again, Alberich let the boy drive him back.

"To punish me!" Osberic shouted, his cheeks burning with humiliation. "To make me look stupid in front of everyone!"

"No, that would the act of a bully be," Alberich told him. "So that, should Lord Corbie protest it was *you* who began the fight, *I* can tell the Queen that you were punished, and all here will swear to that. This is not for *you,* it is for the Heralds, that all know that we tend to the misdeeds of our own in proper measure." He then neatly sidestepped the last rush and tripped Osberic as he went past. Once again, Osberic measured his length in the mud. "A Herald cannot merely *right* be, Osberic. A Herald must guided by the *law* be. He cannot dispense the law, if he follows it not himself. He cannot dispense the law, if he thinks himself immune from it. He cannot dispense the law, if he will not deal it to his fellows in the same measure as he does to those whom he has in charge."

"Yessir, Herald Alberich," Osberic groaned from the ground.

"And that is why, for fighting, you have also been punished in this way," Alberich continued. "Now, back into the salle. There is work to be done."

They were all quick to follow the order, but none so quick as Osberic.

KADHAEL Corbie disappeared from the Court and Collegia entirely. Not that Alberich would have noticed his absence, having banned the boy from the salle, but it wasn't long before there were murmurs and speculations among his students and the Court—and being that it was his business to know things, he heard every one of them. Rumor had it that the boy's father was so enraged that he had gotten himself thrown out of Alberich's class and forbidden to enter the salle that he'd sent the boy straight down to the family manor, there to languish in what the young lords and ladies called "rustification." Since it was said to be a particularly dull and cheerless place, lacking in anything that a young man might find amusing, and since rumor also had it that Lord Corbie had sent orders for his son to be confined to the house and grounds until further notice, Alberich was perfectly satisfied that the punishment fit the crime.

On the other side of the table, Lord Corbie went to Selenay and also demanded the punishment of "the Trainee who started it," and allegedly was nonplussed to learn that "the Trainee" had already been punished. And that the punishment fit *his* crime, since all he had done was to bring a fight into the salle and after being reprimanded, had behaved with the proper respect for the Weaponsmaster. The trouncing—with lecture—at the hands of the Weaponsmaster in front of his peers was deemed both painful and humiliating enough, even for Lord Corbie.

And Lord Corbie had been quite taken aback to learn that it had all happened within moments of Kadhael's expulsion.

Without knowing much about the man, but intuiting a great deal from the behavior of his son, Alberich doubted that humiliation of Kadhael at the hands of "that foreigner" would ever be forgotten or forgiven, but at least there was nothing overt that Lord Corbie could do about the incident. Alberich had exercised *precisely* the correct amount of authority: he'd been defied, he banished the offender. Not from any other classes at any other part of the three Collegia, only from his own. He had indeed ejected the boy by force—because the boy would have gone on defying him if Alberich hadn't physically thrown him off the premises. He had not exceeded his authority, and in point of fact, Alberich *could* have given the boy a taste of what Osberic had gotten, and hadn't. In fact, Kadhael had gotten off lightly at Alberich's hands, and not only was there no denying it, but both the Lord Marshal and the Provost Marshal (who was in charge of discipline on and off the Collegia grounds) said loudly and publicly that *they* would have boxed both his ears until he was deaf.

Nevertheless, Lord Corbie would not like the man who had rejected his son; he would not like the Collegium nor the organization that had given him the authority to do so.

One more enemy . . . but Alberich was used to those by now. He would have to watch his back, but when had he ever done anything else? And sure enough, within days, there were rumors in the Court about how the Weaponsmaster was abus-

ing his pupils, abusing his authority, treating Heraldic Trainees with indulgence and punishing Blues arbitrarily. A few
Blues were quietly absent from his class after that. But there
was not a great deal that he could do about that—nor, truth
to be told, wished to do.

As for Osberic—according to Kantor, that very evening,
when the Trainee's bruises started aching and he started feeling particularly sorry for himself, his Companion had given
him a good talking-to. Whether this was delivered in the form
of a lecture or with sympathy, Kantor didn't say—but one
thing was certain: when Companions took it upon themselves
to correct their Chosen, the lesson tended to stick. Osberic was
certainly properly contrite the next day, and if there was still
a great deal of moaning about Alberich's hardheartedness, at
least no one among the Heraldic Trainees was claiming he was
a bully or a sadist. Hardhearted, he could live with. In fact, the
more hardhearted they thought him, the better off they would
be in the long run.

Though shortly after the Kadhael incident, there was one
little lad who would not have agreed with that estimation.

He was one of the "Tedrel orphans," brought in by the Companion Cheric the very same day as Osberic and Kadhael's
chastisement. It took a day or two to get him settled into the
Collegium, so Alberich didn't see him until his mentor, Trainee
Rotherven, brought him by himself to the salle, shortly after
the last class of the day.

Alberich was overseeing a set of Guards working out with
maces, when the door to the salle opened and a final-year
Trainee came in with a very small boy at his side. Alberich left
the two to continue their bout, and walked over to the door
where they waited politely.

"This is a new Trainee, Weaponsmaster," Rotherven said,
leading the young boy by the hand—a *very* young boy indeed,
no more than seven, if Alberich was any judge. He was rather
angular, with an unruly thatch of no-colored hair, but very

intelligent eyes, and a look about him that was vaguely familiar. And when he got a good look at the Weaponsmaster, the boy gaped at him with shock—then awe—then spun to look up at his mentor with a look just short of accusation.

"You did not tell me this was the Great Rider!" the child exclaimed, and Alberich knew immediately by the trace of a Karsite accent that this must be one of the children brought out of the Tedrel camp after the end of that final battle.

"Great rider?" Rotherven said, his brow furrowed with puzzlement. "But—"

"Never mind, I understand him," Alberich interrupted. He looked down at the boy with some bemusement. So *that* was why the boy looked vaguely familiar; he was Karsite, or at least, half Karsite. Most of the hill-folk shepherds were mongrels by Sunpriest standards anyway. "So," he said—in Karsite, "we have another of the Sun's children come to be a White Rider, eh?" This one must not have been too damaged by his experiences, or he wouldn't have been Chosen so very young. "There are others here, not as White Riders, but as Selenay's pages. You won't be alone."

"Oh." Relief suffused the boy's features. "I did not know that, Great Rider—"

Alberich looked up at Rotherven. "Selenay has perhaps five or six Tedrel orphans; in her service as pages they are. See that this lad meeting them is, please. Perhaps a playfellow he will find among them."

Then he looked back down at the boy and continued the conversation in Karsite. "Also, there is Priest Gerichen, a true man of the Sunlord. You may go with the others to the Temple of the Sunlord if you wish—though they do not call it that here, but rather, the Temple of the Lord of Light. And if you do not wish to do so, you need not. You are free to serve who you wish, here."

"I still serve the Sunlord, Great Rider," the boy said quietly. "The Sunlord of the Prophecy."

"Then you will find His House yonder in Haven, and Gerichen at His altar," Alberich replied, suppressing a smile at the child's solemn demeanor. It was quaint and charming, but a little sad also. Those children had been forced to grow up far too quickly. "I have it on the best authority that He approves of the White Riders and all they stand for, and that there is nothing in the pledges that a White Rider must make that run counter to His will. Quite the opposite, in fact. In serving as a White Rider, you will also serve Him. You will be a hope and an example to our people, and repay some of the debt to those who saved and succored us, as I try to do."

The child's face took on a look of fierce pride and determination. "I will not fail you, Great Rider!" he said, in tones that made it a vow. "I will not fail the Prophecy!"

Rotherven's expression of bemusement, as he looked from Alberich to the boy and back again, made Alberich very glad that he had a great deal of practice in keeping his own face under control, or he might have laughed aloud.

"It is a great responsibility," Alberich replied, as gravely as if the child was three times his actual age. "And a signal honor."

"I do know that, Great Rider," the child said, nodding. "Cheric has told me so. And it is—all I could ever wish to be."

"Excuse me, Herald Alberich, but I was supposed to tell you that young Theodren here is one of the orphans," Rotherven said, then laughed self-consciously, "but obviously you already know that."

"I do, but I thank you," Alberich replied, and turned back to the boy. "So. I am glad to see you, Theodren. You will be learning weapons at my hands—as any other Trainee. And you must call me Herald Alberich, not Great Rider. I am no greater than any of the other Heralds—the White Riders. We are all brothers and sisters."

"Yes, Herald Alberich." The boy gave an odd little salute that he must have learned from the Tedrels. "I was afraid, when my friend Rotherven said I was to be given over to weapons lessons. Now I am not." He smiled. "I was afraid the training would be like—the bad place."

"It will be hard, but not like that other place, I promise you," Alberich said, and turned back again to Rotherven. "He will be in the beginner's class, of course—just following luncheon, that would be."

"Yes, sir." The Trainee's expression told Alberich everything he needed to know; evidently Theodren had been properly terrified when he'd been told he was to learn weapons' work, and Rotherven's solution had been to bring him directly to Alberich so that he could see his teacher for himself. Or, perhaps, the suggestion had come from Rotherven's Companion, who had been no mere colt when Rotherven was Chosen. "Thank you for talking to him; I think he'll settle now, and I was a bit worried about him—"

Alberich nodded. "You have done exactly what was needed, bringing him here. My thanks." And to Theodren, "This young man is also my pupil, and he will be as a brother to you as well as a Brother Rider. You may give him your trust. He will also see that you meet the others brought out of the camp that are now in Selenay's service, and perhaps you may find a friend or two among them, as well."

The child's eyes shone with gratitude. "Thank you, Herald Alberich."

Then Theodren looked up at Rotherven, and said, in Valdemaran that was much better than Alberich's, "Thank you for bringing me to the salle, Rotherven. Herald Alberich is the chief of those who came to save us, and I am honored to be taught by him."

It was so formal, and so charming, that Rotherven couldn't help but smile. It was a kind smile, and Alberich knew at that moment that the older boy had been a good choice to watch over Theodren. "Well, good. And now you've met all your teachers, so let's get some dinner. You'll be back here after luncheon tomorrow."

Alberich escorted them to the door of the salle, then watched the two of them off up the path back to the Collegium. As they disappeared into the twilight shadows, he felt Kantor coming up beside him. He put his hand on Kantor's shoulder, and felt the Companion's silken hide beneath his palm, warm and smooth.

:Cheric can't Mindspeak him very clearly yet, and the little lad was petrified,: Kantor told him. *:He thought he was about to be put into one of those vile Boy's Bands that the Tedrels used to "toughen" the boys. Nasty training, if you could call it training. Kept them on short rations, more or less forced them to steal if they were going to keep from going hungry, but beat them within an inch of their lives if they got caught. Weapons' training with real, edged weapons—if you got hurt or died, too bad. Every infraction was punished with a beating, in fact. Small wonder he was terrified.:*

:Well, I'm glad he recognized me. I only hope he doesn't hero-worship me.: Alberich sighed. *:Though it might be pleasant for me, it would do him no good.:*

:I wouldn't necessarily agree with that.: Kantor nudged him affectionately. *:You could do with a little hero-worship.:*

:Adoration is for the Sunlord. I am content with respect,: Alberich replied, but rubbed Kantor's ears with affection. *:So long as I have the friendship of my Companion and a few good comrades, I am content,:*

:Piff. I can think of one other thing you could do with.: Kantor's eyes sparkled with mischief, and Alberich had a very good idea what he was talking about, but he pretended otherwise. After all, it was usually Kantor who managed a jest on Alberich, rather than the other way around.

:Yes, indeed,: he replied blandly. *:I could do with my dinner.:*

And he laughed aloud at Kantor's exasperated snort.

The following day was very much business as usual, although
during the day he found himself looking forward much more
than usual to dinner, because Myste had sent down a note
asking if she could join him then. He didn't know why, and
she didn't tell him; probably it had something to do with the
players. Since she clearly was comfortable with them and was
not going to have to *act* in order to fit herself into a persona,
he had elected to leave her to get used to the situation, and
her "employers" to get used to her, before he asked her to
actually do anything. He'd told her to let him know when she
thought she was ready, and that was probably why she
wanted to meet him over dinner.

And yet—well, he wouldn't be disappointed if it wasn't the
business of the actors that brought her.

When she arrived with the servant that brought his dinner,
as usual, helping to carry the baskets, he did note that her
step was definitely light, and that there was more than a mere
suspicion of a smile on her face. But she only spoke of com-
monplace things—more rumors about Kadhael, in fact, and
more slurs about Alberich himself—until the servant had
gone. And when he bent to uncover the first of the supper
dishes, she held out a hand, forestalling him.

"Dinner can wait for a moment," she said, as always when
she was with him, speaking in Karsite. It was an effective
hedge against anyone who might, somehow, have gotten in
close enough to be listening. Not that Alberich expected anyone to manage, for he'd have to get past the Companions to do
so, but sometimes Trainees dared each other to particularly
stupid pranks and it would be just his luck for one of them
to sneak in to eavesdrop on the Weaponsmaster and overhear
something he shouldn't.

"I assume you have a reason?" he replied.

She nodded. "First, I want you to see these."

And she handed him a folded packet of paper; the paper itself was odd, thin, very light, very strong. He unfolded it.

And knew immediately what it was, because it was in cipher, and there was only one place at the moment where Myste would have gotten a packet of papers in cipher. They were the same papers—or more of the same—that he'd seen passed from Norris to Devlin!

"No, they're not," Myste said immediately, as if she had read his mind. Not that she needed to; she would know exactly what he was thinking at that moment. "In this case, it's a packet that was passed the other way, from Devlin to Norris."

He looked from it, to her, and back again, speechless for a moment. "But—how did you—"

Her grin widened, and she sat down with an air of triumph. "He gave them to me."

Alberich also sat down, then. He had to. His knees wouldn't hold him. "If you're joking—"

"I'm not," she replied with satisfaction. "I swear I'm not. He gave them to me with his own lily-white hands. And do you know *why?*" She laughed, a rich and satisfied chuckle. "Because, my friend, he wanted me to copy them for him."

Alberich had thought himself too surprised to react to anything by that point, but he felt his mouth gaping open, and shut it, and swallowed. "I think," he said at last, "that you must tell me this from the beginning."

But first, he leaned over and poured both of them a full cup of wine. He had a strong need for a drink, just now. Myste laced the fingers of both hands together over her knee, and looked as satisfied as a cat with a jug full of cream in front of her. "Sometimes," she said, with a touch of pardonable smugness, "the person you need to keep an eye on someone isn't a spy, or a tough bully-boy. Sometimes it is *exactly* the kind of middle-aged, dowdy, forgettable little frump that no one looks twice at."

"You aren't dowdy or forgettable," he said without thinking. "Or a frump."

She looked inordinately pleased at that, but didn't interrupt her story. "It didn't take me long to get their books straight, and yes, the innkeeper has been skimming, and yes, he stopped *immediately* when he knew I was there to check on him. So since I was there anyway, both the players and their other staff started coming to me for other little things. You know, the odd letter from home to be read or written, arranging with a goldsmith to put something away for a rainy day, that sort of thing. And King Norris would come sailing by now and again, vaguely note that I was there, and be off again— and whenever he came by, I always made sheep's eyes at him, which is exactly what he expected. Women throw themselves at him all the time, and if I *hadn't* acted infatuated, he might have suspected something. Well, that was how things stood, right up until last night, when we had an—interesting situation."

"Oh?" Alberich prompted.

"They'd done a reduced-cast play for a private audience in the afternoon, and all the leads had to hurry back to the inn to do the main play that evening," she said, her lenses gleaming. He didn't have to see her eyes to know that there was great satisfaction in them. "So I'm sitting there in the office with folded hands, nothing much to do, and in comes Norris himself and for once, he's *looking* for me. 'Can you make a fair copy of something without knowing the language?' he asks. I gave him a look—"

She tilted her head slightly, and showed Alberich the expression of dazzled infatuation she must have given Norris.

"—and I said, 'Of *course* I can, I'm a clerk! If we stopped to actually read what we're copying, we'd never get half the work done that we do! Eye to hand to paper, and no stopping at the brain, that's us—' And before I can say anything else, he dropped this in front of me." She indicated the packet. "And some paper—if you can believe it—that's even lighter than this is. 'I'm in a hurry,' says he, 'and I haven't time to do this myself. I need *that* transcribed in the smallest hand you can manage onto that paper, then burn the original. And I need it by the time I'm off the stage tonight.' I looked at him like I didn't care so long as the job was for *him,* and didn't ask why. He didn't tell me, he just rushed straight out, and I heard the wardrobe mistress screeching for him, so he must have been late for costuming. The rest is easy enough. I made his copy and tossed the original out the window to Aleirian, who carried it away."

"Good God," he breathed. "I wouldn't have thought of that."

"I didn't," she admitted. "Aleirian did. Anyway, then I kept an ear out to gauge the progress of the play, copied as many pages of the original again in the original size as I could fit in the time left, made them the top sheets in a stack of blanks, and when he got offstage and came for his papers, he saw *that* packet merrily burning away and assumed I'd burned the original the way I was told. He was damned careful, too; he stayed there until all the papers were burned, then broke up the ash until there wasn't a fragment the size of the head of a nail. Then he went off. I assume that he must have gotten the originals at that private performance. And I guess that my copies must have gone out that night, because he just flew out the door with them. It wouldn't have been hard. You could have rolled the lot up and hidden them practically anywhere."

"I can probably find out who and where when we know what is in these," he replied absently, unable to believe his good luck. "What did he do when you gave him the copy, besides watch the papers burn?"

"Well, he made an excuse for hanging about while he made sure the papers were gone by pouring charm all over me until I was practically gagging on it," she replied, a chuckle in her voice. "And I gazed at him adoringly like he expected me to,

and hung on his every word, and vowed that if I could ever do
something for him again, he had only to ask. He went away
never thinking twice about having entrusted me with papers
in cipher."

Surely they couldn't be *that* lucky. "You're sure it wasn't
some sort of trap—" he said warningly.

"Well, of course anything is possible," she replied. "But he
wasn't expecting a Herald, or Aleirian, and, well—Alberich, I
know that kind of man. I ran into them all the time when I
was a girl and my best friend was the prettiest girl in our quarter." She sighed, and for a moment, that good humor and spar-
kle faded. "The first time, and even the second and third, that
a handsome boy came and poured that kind of charm and flattery all over me, I fell for it—but after three times of being
fooled and finding out that they were only being nice to me
because they wanted to meet my friend, I became immune to
it."

His mouth formed a silent "Oh."

She shrugged. "It's one of those things that plain girls
learn, Alberich. You just get used to it after a while. Well, your
lad Norris might be one of the best in Valdemar at charming
people, but someone like me—" she shook her head. "Actually, he's never encountered someone like me, I suspect, because we *won't* throw ourselves at him; we know better. He'll
never even see the plain ones who are on to his little game—
they might be at the performances, and they'll certainly admire his acting ability, but so far as lingering on the off chance
they'll meet him, it will never happen. So he looked at me and
saw a plain, frumpy little mouse with a little mouse's job, who
looked at him with eyes of adoration, and figured he knew
exactly what I was and how he could use me. And best of all,
he wouldn't have to actually do more than give me a bit of
attention, because someone like me would never, ever expect
someone like *him* would want to romance me." The cynical
laugh she uttered at that moment made him wince, and he

wondered then about the young girl in lenses who'd been tricked three times by manipulative boys. "Oh, no, a crumb of attention to cherish in the darkness of my little closet of a room, that's all he needed to give. I'd be his slave forever, and never demand anything out of him."

"Myste—" He swallowed. "I apologize."

She started, and stared at him. "For what?" she asked.

"For people like him." He shook his head. "I am sorry."

She laughed again, but this time the humor was back in her voice. "Good gods, Alberich, don't be. Trust me, the injuries to my heart, such as they were, scabbed over a long time ago, and the scar is a useful reminder. If I *hadn't* been hurt and used by all those heartless boys back in the day, I'd never have been able to see right through your lad Norris, would I? So don't think I'm living with a tragic past! Good gods, compared to at least half of the others that have gone through these walls, it's a teacup tragedy at worst, and a farce at best." She winked at him. "Besides, I saw my pretty best friend not long ago. She's tripled in size, she's had a baby a year, and her handsome husband chases tavern girls. Have pity for her, not me."

"Ah." He felt a good deal better. At least she wasn't likely to reject him out of hand if—

"Besides," she chuckled again, "it gives me an appreciation for men who blurt out 'you're not a frump,' and not some carefully rehearsed speech, who say it without even *thinking* about it, and who then go on to apologize for the vagaries of their sex."

"Ah—" he felt his face burning. "Er—"

"I think you might be sitting too near the fire," was all she said then. "Now, about dinner? We shouldn't let it get cold."

Lord Orthallen had asked, had *requested,* in writing, an informal meeting with Selenay. She had invited him to dinner, in her own suite. Not alone, of course; they'd be surrounded by servants, but it would certainly be informal. She was intensely curious; the note had a certain apologetic tone to it that she couldn't quite put her finger on.

The first course arrived, and was complimented, without her curiosity being satisfied. She sipped her wine as the second course was plated and served. She felt she could afford to be patient.

"My dear Selenay," said Lord Orthallen at last, over the third course. "I have done you a grave disservice."

She motioned to a page to refill his wineglass. "Yes, my lord," she said somberly, "I think you have." She was not going to pretend that she did not know exactly what he was talking about. *He* had been the prime instigator of that wretched plot to get her married off, and she was not in the least happy about it, and what was more, she intended for him to know it.

He sighed, and grimaced a little. "In my own defense, I was trying to protect Valdemar from being in the precarious position of having no Heir. But I am afraid—truly and sincerely, Selenay, I *was* afraid, I was dreadfully afraid, and I still am. I never dreamed we would be in this position. Sendar should have been King for decades yet. You are a very young woman, and we have just fought a hideous war—"

"And Valdemar needs to look strong, not vulnerable, I know, Orthallen," she replied with spirit, and with some heat. "But didn't it occur to you that rushing me into a marriage is going to do the very opposite of making us look strong? *Why* would I suddenly wed the first candidate presented to me, if I wasn't desperate? I might as well send out letters to every likely ally we have, saying that I'm up for sale to the highest bidder!" She frowned at him, and he looked pained.

"I know, I know," Orthallen replied, flushing. "And if I had possessed any sensitivity or common sense where you are concerned, I would have come directly to you, rather than laying it all out in front of the Council—"

"So it *was* your idea." Selenay gave him a hint of the anger she felt in her gaze. She'd been certain it was all along, as had some of the others, but now, at last, he had admitted it.

"To my shame." He nodded. "Not that the men we presented are not fine—"

"My lord," she said, interrupting him with exasperation as well as a feeling of real depression, "although I would give a very great deal to be like other young ladies and at least be able to *dream* of finding a great romantic love, I am not, and I know it." She heard her own voice retaining its steady, reasonable tone, despite the lump in her throat, and felt a moment of pride at her own self-control. "I am Queen, and when I wed—which I must, for the people would not accept an Heir born out of wedlock—it is for Valdemar, not myself. But my father *did* find a lady who suited him well enough that he never remarried, and I at least hope to be able to find a friend, if not a lover. I will not find such a Consort by being rushed into an imprudent marriage. And I cannot find one if I have twelve dozen potential husbands shoved at me every time I turn about!"

Orthallen flushed again. "Sendar might not have been in love with your mother when they agreed to marry," he said quietly, "but he came to love her, deeply, and she him. And they *were* great, good friends before they wed."

She spread her hands wide, ignoring the fork in one of them. "So you see that I am right."

"Indeed, I do see," he agreed. "And I was wrong, very wrong. I was just afraid that—" he laughed, self-consciously, "—well, there are a number of fine young foreign princes out there, younger sons, whose fathers would be very happy to cement an advantageous alliance with us. Perhaps too advantageous. Especially if one of them managed to make you infatuated with him. My thought was that— Well, at the least, we could keep your interest here at home."

She sniffed. He took the hint. "Well, you have given me every reason to agree with your point of view, and I believe you have convinced me. I will approach my fellow Councilors and suggest that the subject should be tabled for the foreseeable future—and I will insist that our Queen is wise enough to choose her own future husband *without* our help."

She exhaled a long sigh of genuine relief "And I thank you for that, Orthallen. You cannot know just how much easier that makes me feel."

"Oh, perhaps I do, I little," he replied genially. "Your father was none too pleased at the prospect himself, and he was not even King when the idea of marriage was first broached to him."

As the meal progressed, Orthallen first told her about her father's reluctant search for a prospective bride, and how he had eventually settled on her mother when after a month went by *without* her throwing herself at his feet, he asked her why—or rather, why not. After all, every other young woman of rank and spirit had. . . .

"And she told him that she would, on the whole, prefer to be his sister than his wife!" Orthallen laughed, shaking his head. "And when he asked her why, she told him that she had more desire for his library than for him!"

All this was new to Selenay; she stared at him, not quite believing it. "And what did he say?"

"That *he* would rather at least have someone he could talk to, and that anyone who wanted his books that badly was someone who could hold an interesting conversation." Orthallen smiled. "She certainly intrigued him; and I think most of what intrigued him at first was that she wasn't *trying* to intrigue him, she really felt that way. She was inordinately shy, you know. And then, when she proposed to him, she made him agree that she would participate as little as possible in Court life before she'd even entertain the merest idea of marriage with him."

"But she was happy?" Selenay felt she had to know.

"Oh, very," Orthallen assured her. "And by the end of a year of marriage, as much in love with Sendar as any woman could be. And he with her. Remarkable, really. Usually the most one can expect from a marriage of state is an easy partnership—a business relationship, of a kind."

Her heart sank a little at that, and Selenay couldn't help wondering if that was what she was fated to have. And she changed the subject.

Nevertheless, before the dinner was half over, she found that she had confided a great deal in Lord Orthallen, and not the least of those confidences involved her own, barely-articulate wishes for—well—romance.

She was rather surprised at herself for spilling so much into his willing ears, and even more surprised when he seemed sympathetic and not at all dismissive.

:He's certainly easier to talk to than Talamir,: she said to Caryo, after he'd gone.

:On that subject, a doorpost would be easier to talk to than Talamir,: Caryo replied sadly. :At least Orthallen is well rooted in the here-and-now, enough to know that a young woman, Queen though she is, deserves to at least be able to dream. Poor Talamir.:

Poor Talamir, indeed. But at least now, and with Caryo's tacit approval, Selenay had someone she could confide in.

And to her mild surprise, she found that it helped, a little.

Enough that she went to sleep that night, for the first time since the end of the Wars, without first lying awake for a candlemark staring into the darkness.

11

SOMETHING teased at the back of Selenay's mind for the next several days, making her feel restless, full of nervous energy. Perhaps it was the season; spring was *almost* upon them, the early crocuses were already pushing their way up through the flower beds, the last of the snow was gone, the really wretched end-of-winter rains had begun, and now the days were long enough to make you believe that winter might actually end, after all. The air still felt raw, and other than the optimistic crocuses there was no sign of anything growing, but there were moments when the sun felt warm as a hand on the cheek, and when there was a hint of green-scent in the wind.

Winter would end. Spring would come, and after it, summer, and a year would have gone by without her father. Time, they said, was a great healer. Some of her depression eased a little more with the lengthening days, certainly. Maybe it was due to the season, maybe she was just getting used to Sendar not being there anymore; there was no longer the blow to the heart when she entered the Throne Room and did not see him

there, nor quite the feeling of emptiness when she took what
had been *his* chair at the Council meetings. Not all of it—oh,
by no means. But enough that she was sleeping the night
through, and not waking up to weep in the darkness.

Sometimes she even slept until her maids woke her, and it
was a deep and thankfully dreamless sleep.

Orthallen was as good as his word. At the next meeting of
the Full Council, before it was called officially into session, he
asked for a moment to address the group personally. "This is
not Council business, precisely," he said. "But it is something
that I would like the Council to hear."

They all looked at Selenay; she nodded. The Seneschal
called the meeting to order, and gestured to Orthallen. And
when he had the silent regard of everyone around the table,
he cleared his throat awkwardly, which was not like him at
all. That alone got him the full and alert attention of everyone
sitting there.

"My lords, my ladies, I believe that we have been pressing
the Queen on an issue that really has no urgency at all," he
said, looking embarrassed. "And by that, I mean the issue of
her choosing a spouse immediately. After due consideration,
and more thought, I believe we have been overly hasty."

Selenay inclined her head, accepting what he had said
without saying a word herself. This was not the time to add
her own thoughts. She wanted Orthallen to explain it all to the
rest of the Council in his own words. Though there was one
thing that struck her as odd, and that was the phrasing Orthallen had used. Spouse was a peculiar choice of word, when it
came to the Queen of Valdemar. Why not say Consort, which
was the traditional title if the ruler was the Queen, and the
husband was not a Herald?

Perhaps it was because she had shown no real interest in
any of the Heralds, but Orthallen did not want to make that
too obvious. Now if she'd had a candidate among the Heralds,
she'd have made her choice known immediately. It was a given

that unless her husband was also a Herald, he could never be King and co-ruler. But still—given that none of the candidates *were* Heralds, why not just say 'Consort?'

Maybe it was just that Orthallen was keeping the options open in their minds, eliminating neither the possibility of Consort nor King. *It's been a long time since Valdemar had a Queen. Maybe it's just slipped their mind that no husband of mine can rule unless he's a Herald.* It might be just as well not to remind those of the Council who had forgotten that fact.

"It should be obvious to all of us by this time, that while the Queen is a *young* woman, she is not only capable, she is wise enough to know when she needs advice and guidance. She could lawfully have replaced all of us, and has not, because she trusts us as her father trusted us, and believes that we, who were her father's advisers, are capable in ourselves." He coughed, as a murmur went around the table. "We may be flailing about in the wake of our loss and casting for solutions to situations that are not actually problems."

Selenay exchanged looks with the other Heralds on the Council; Kyril, the Seneschal's Herald, Elcarth, and Talamir. Although Orthallen had included the rest of the Councilors in this "admission," it was a signal departure for him to admit to making a mistake.

And they *had* been flailing about, as if she herself was a problem, before there had been any evidence of anything of the sort!

Orthallen cleared his throat again, and continued, reluctantly. She held her breath. Was he? Was he going to admit it? "Furthermore, by seeming to cast about frantically for a suitable candidate, we may be giving an impression of weakness to those who do not wish us well. As if we do not trust our Queen and our own ability to carry on in the absence of her father. We could be giving the same impression as a herd of sheep, milling about anxiously without a shepherd, and I do not need to tell you that there are wolves about."

Another murmur, and Selenay stifled a smile, hearing Orthallen borrowing so heavily from her own argument. *He did.*
He admitted I'm right. I may only get apologies from him in
private, but at least he's admitting that I'm right in public. It
was a triumph, but she was not going to gloat over it.

"I know that I was the one pressing most eagerly for such
a wedding—or betrothal, at least—but I should like to urge
that we drop the subject for now." He shrugged, and no few of
the other Councilors looked as embarrassed as he did.

"If you recommend so, Orthallen," Lord Gartheser said hes-
itantly. "You know more about foreign affairs than the rest of
us do."

"I think it would be the wisest course." And in that moment, Orthallen all but said, *I was wrong.* But he went on
quickly, making an attempt to regain the face he had lost. "In
all events, having the Queen so blatantly unattached can also
work to our benefit. There are a number of young men of rank,
of valuable connection—princes, even—in other lands, who
are also unattached. No doubt, their rulers will soon see that
there is a way to bring Valdemar into close alliance by the
closest of ties. So let us table this search for now, and get on
with the business of the realm."

Nods all around the table, a few reluctant—well, not surprising that the oldest Councilors were less than comfortable
about a *Queen,* and a young one at that, and the oldest men
were the ones least inclined to trust her to rule alone. *Only*
time will cure that, she decided. *Time—or perhaps a change of*
Councilors. It wouldn't hurt for the Bardic and Healer representatives to retire, for instance. It would be better if there
were more women on the Council. *A woman who has made her*
own way in the world will be more inclined to see me as a
leader and less as someone needing to be led. Perhaps she
should also add an entirely new seat or two. Someone from
one of the newer Guilds, perhaps? To have more people whose

wealth was self-made rather than inherited could be of real benefit.

Orthallen moved on to some dispute between the Guilds of the Mercers and the Weavers while Selenay's thoughts were elsewhere. She quickly brought her own attention to bear on the situation; it would not be a good idea to undo all of Orthallen's work by seeming to be lost in other thoughts. She did notice that several of the Councilors actually waited to hear her opinion before voicing theirs, which was a pleasant change. The rest of the meeting proceeded in the same atmosphere, and if she felt a momentary resentment that she'd had to get Orthallen's "approval" before being granted the respect she was due, at least now she had that respect. And though it might be temporary, having gotten it once, it would be easier to regain it.

But once the meeting was over, as she and she and her escort of Guards and ladies wound their way back to her quarters, she allowed her thoughts to tend in other directions. Orthallen's comment about foreign princes—*that* struck a chord, and told her that *that* was what had been nagging at her all this time, since the Councilor had first voiced that idea over dinner.

What foreign princes? Certainly there had been no hints of such a possibility before now. No envoys had presented themselves, no inquiries had been voiced via ambassadors.

But perhaps they had all been waiting until her year of mourning was over. That would only be appropriate, really.

Assuming there are such mythical creatures, she told herself, as she entered the door to her suite, and the Guards took up their stations outside.

But they might not be mythical—

Surely, though, if there were such young men wandering about unpartnered, she would be aware of them. Granted, her knowledge of highborn families outside of Valdemar was sketchy to say the least, but the only royal that she knew of was the King of Hardorn, and *he* had married an allegedly lissome young creature out of his own Court a little more than a year ago.

But would Orthallen have mentioned the possibility twice if it didn't exist?

So just what foreign princes *were* there, out there? She dismissed her ladies, and selected a gown to be worn at dinner while her maids drew a hot bath.

Did the Shin'a'in have princes? She couldn't remember anything of the sort. :*Caryo, is there such a thing as a Shin'a'in prince?*:

:*I've never heard of one.*: Caryo sounded surprised. :*I think they don't have things like Kings and Princes. I think they are an alliance of Clans.*:

That tallied with the little that Selenay recalled, but perhaps some of the Clans were big enough that their Chiefs would qualify as princes. There were a great many Shin'a'in after all. It was an—*interesting* possibility.

She stepped into the bath that had been prepared for her, and chased the maids away while she soaked. As she relaxed in the hot lavender-scented water, she had a silly little vision of a strong, wild warrior, raven hair down to his waist, riding into Haven dressed in black furs and leathers, astride—bareback, of course—a horse as black as his hair. And wouldn't that make a pretty picture, the two of them riding together, she all in Whites on Caryo, he on his midnight steed. . . .

She gave herself a mental shake. Ridiculous, of course; what Shin'a'in nomad would ever leave the Plains, much less do so with the intention of marrying a foreign, civilized queen? Besides, even if he came here looking for her, he wouldn't stay. The Shin'a'in never stayed away from the Plains for long, and *she* could scarcely leave Valdemar. What would the Shin'a'in get out of such a marriage, anyway? Valdemar was too far from the Plains for there to be any advantage in an alliance at all. No, no, no—too easy to burst that particular bubble of illusion.

But who else did that leave? Rethwellan? Were there unmarried princes in Rethwellan? If there were, well, they at least shared a border with Valdemar, and it would be an advantage to them to have such an alliance, if only for trade advantages. Menmellith? Menmellith was a principality of Rethwellan, but she couldn't really recall anything at all about their ruling family. Not Karse, of course—

Could there be interest as far away as Jkatha or Ceejay, which were just names on a map to her? Surely not; Valdemar didn't even trade directly that far away, so why would any stray princeling come wandering up here?

But there might be places she had never heard of. To the North—well, Iftel was out of the question; no one ever came past their borders except a few favored traders who were remarkably close-mouthed about the place.

The bath was cooling; time to finish and get out, before someone came in here to scrub her. Stupid; she'd bathed herself for the last fourteen years and more, so what was it about being a Queen that rendered her incapable of bathing herself now?

But the splashing as she emerged from the bath seemed to be some sort of signal that caused maids to swarm around her with towels and robes and scents and lotions. And for once, involved in her own thoughts, she let them fuss over her.

Once she was properly clothed in a lounging robe, they messed about with her hair while she continued her ruminations. North, other than Iftel, were the barbarians above the Forest of Sorrows. Surely not. *Surely* not. The idea of a greasy, violent, fur-clad brute was even more repulsive than some of the octogenarians the Council had suggested.

Were there little secretive kingdoms out in the West, in the Pelagiris Forest or past it? It was possible. There were certainly *people* out there, and not just the half-mythical Hawkbrothers.

There were entire villages that looked to the Hawkbrothers for protection, so maybe there were Kingdoms in the West. But still—what possible advantage could they have in an alliance with Valdemar? Nothing that she could imagine.

Or were there men in other Kingdoms who were like the Great Dukes of Valdemar, who held enough power that they qualified as princes? There might well be; she hadn't had time to study such things. In such a case, for a younger son, there would be a great deal of prestige and advantage in marrying a Queen, even if it left the young man as nothing more than a Consort without ruling powers. His children would rule, if they were Chosen, and that might be enough. Separate trade agreements could be made with the family, and *that* might be enough. There was a great deal of difference between royal marrying royal, and royal stooping to wed a rank below hers. In that case, the advantages to be gained were almost all on the side of the lower rank.

:Surely there's something in the archives of letters from ambassadors and trade envoys,: Caryo said helpfully. *:Or Seneschal's Herald Kyril will know where to look. I should think that someone would know if we might expect a spate of foreign suitors.:*

A foreign prince—or more than one—the idea gave her a kind of fluttery feeling of excitement inside. Oh, they might well all be as impossible or even repulsive as the candidates she'd been presented with so far, but—at least they would be someone different.

And surely one would be older than an adolescent and younger than a graybeard. Maybe even handsome—though she wouldn't necessarily care, as long as he wasn't a monster. Someone she didn't know, that she couldn't predict, someone with entirely new ways and manners— Even if she didn't want to marry him, it would be interesting to have him in her Court.

It would be more than interesting—it would be fascinating!

She licked her lips, and hardly noticed the maids tugging at her hair.

I mustn't get my hopes up, she told herself. *There might not be any such thing. If they exist, they might all be old. Or feeble-minded. Or already married.* She shuddered involuntarily, as she realized that she'd had a narrow escape without realizing it. If King Alessandar *hadn't* gotten wedded to his sweet young thing—if he'd still been alone—

Well, he would not have let the opportunity to propose slip past, no matter how many sweet young things were in his Court. And the Council would *never* have allowed her to reject his suit. Hardorn and Valdemar had been allies for so very long that there had even been cases of Heralds coming to the rescue of Hardornans in the past. Even Herald Vanyel had done so; that was how he earned his title of "Demonsbane." There would have been no way to gracefully turn down such a proposal.

Bright Havens, what a narrow escape!

She suddenly needed to *know,* and know with certainty, if there really was a possibility for a foreign suitor.

I have to know. And I truly have to know if there are any unwedded Alessandars just waiting for my year of mourning to be over—

Well, there was one person to ask, and it wasn't Herald Kyril, however knowledgeable Kyril might be. No, Orthallen would be the one to ask. After all, he was the one who had brought it all up in the first place. If there had been such a position in her Council as Foreign Minister, he surely would have been the one to fill it; his knowledge of the lands outside of Valdemar was as exacting as hers was vague.

A foreign prince. . . . An easy thought to kick off daydreams, and it was a good thing that she was safely away in her own suite where no one would notice if her attention wandered.

When the maids were finished with her, she chased them

out, all but one, whom she sent off with a note to Orthallen. They would discuss this tonight, after her dinner with the Court, for certain.

Alberich had a meeting of his own after dinner, and he had, with some regret, decided against inviting Myste to share it. No, there could only be one invitee to this "gathering," and it had to be the Queen's Own.

Talamir was, for once, very much alert and in the *here and now* as he examined the documents that Myste had purloined. Alberich had been reluctant to let them out of the salle; he was even more reluctant to let them out of his sight. Fortunately for all concerned, Talamir had no trouble in getting about, though he was still—well—fragile.

It was hard on a man to have been through all that Talamir had—dying and being dragged back to life again must have been unthinkably grim. At Talamir's age, it had been more that, and Alberich was still surprised that he was reasonably sane afterward. In a way, he was doing far better than anyone had any right to expect.

:*Yes, he's fragile, rather than frail,*: Kantor agreed. :*And a good half of that is mental, I'd say.*:

Except when something that required all of his attention was before him. Then he was the old Talamir again. It was the old Talamir that had appeared, unescorted, at the door of Alberich's rooms. It was the old Talamir, alert and in possession of all of his wits and wiles, who heard him out, and examined the documents with great care. Alberich hoped—wildly, he knew, but stranger things had happened—that Talamir would recognize the cipher, even be able to read it a little. The odds were very much against it, but—well, ciphers and secret messages were *not* part of the training of a Karsite Cadet, and the denizens of the vile dens down near Exile's Gate that he usually trafficked with were barely literate. Asking them to manage a cipher would be like asking a pig to dance on a tightrope.

"Well," the Queen's Own said, putting the pages down carefully. "I don't know enough about ciphers to make any sense of this. In fact, there's something we should consider, and that's the possibility that this might not even be in Valdemaran."

Curses. Oh, well.

"Actually," Alberich said with extreme reluctance, "it probably is not. If consider we do that it was intended for someone in another land, in that language it would be. Which could be anything."

"So we have two puzzles to crack; the cipher itself, and which language it's in. Still—" Talamir rested his index finger along his upper lip, his eyes opaque with thought. "Still, we're very much further on than we were before. If someone is going to this extreme to send messages in cipher, I think we can be pretty certain it isn't just Guild secrets or messages to a mistress. I will need to take these to an expert, I think."

"I should, the originals prefer to keep here," Alberich ventured, wondering how Talamir would take that. "Evidence, they may become."

"Oh, certainly!" Talamir waved his hand dismissively, as if the idea of taking the originals was out of the question. "I would rather you did, too. Myste can make copies for me to give to—" He hesitated a moment. "Well, forgive me, if I just tell you it is a fellow whose hobby is ciphers, one I've taken such problems to before this. Odd little chap, but solid and true, and you'd be surprised if you knew who he was. I won't tell you his name, though, if you don't mind."

"Safer for *him,* if you do not," Alberich agreed. "Secrets are secrets between two, in danger between three, and often lost between more than three."

Talamir nodded, but with an air of assurance that he had

been certain that Alberich would understand before he'd asked the question.

"And, if you don't mind my saying it, it would be safer for Myste if she can get away from those actors," Talamir replied. "But I doubt either of us could persuade her."

"Of that, you may be sure," Alberich sighed, having spent several marks fruitlessly attempting to persuade her to do just that. *"If I leave now, they'll be suspicious, and* you'll *never get a chance to follow Norris and find out who he's meeting!"* she'd said, which, alas, was true enough. *"And if he trusted me once, he'll likely trust me again. Think of what else I could get! What if he really runs out of time some day, and asks me to do the ciphering!"* "More of these, she hopes to obtain," he added.

"Well, the more samples, the better. If they change the cipher key, my man will spot that much right off." Talamir pushed the papers across the table to Alberich. "Put those somewhere safe, and I'll come and get the copy—"

"Tomorrow, Myste says," Alberich began. "Two copies—"

Talamir smiled. "Good! Then instead of my coming alone, let's have a little get-together with Jadus, and Crathach, too. With the originals hidden, you should be all right bringing the copies up to the Collegium—we can meet in Jadus' rooms. No one would see anything amiss in that, and you can safely give me the copies then. Clandestinely, if you like. Or just come along to my rooms to 'remind me' of our gathering, and pass me the copies then."

"That is the best plan. And I should like to see the others. Jadus is—I have not seen much of him—" Alberich said, feeling guilty.

"Because it isn't easy, learning to get about on one leg, and once he got his strength back, he's been working hard at it," Talamir replied. "He hasn't had much time to spare for any of us but Crathach, my friend, but I think he's well on the road to feeling useful again. He won't be doing any dancing, but there'll be a vacancy for a Herald in the Courts of Justice in Haven, and he'll do well there."

Alberich was relieved; Jadus probably would do well there, for his sound common sense if nothing else, and his soft ways would put frightened people at their ease. But when the time came for stern justice, Jadus was not a man to be put off by anything, or anyone.

"Tomorrow night, then," Alberich agreed, and gathered up the papers.

Talamir stood. "I don't want to see where you put them, so I'll take my leave now." He glanced at the stained-glass window, and raised an eyebrow. "Now I see why you put that bit of artwork in. Or one reason, anyway."

"Yes. We cannot be watched, through such a thing," Alberich replied.

"Hmm. And when I think of all the people who said you were the last person to put in Dethor's shoes. . . ."

"Myself, included," Alberich replied. Talamir gave him a penetrating look, then shrugged.

"I wouldn't have picked Myste as a spy either," he said. "Good night, Weaponsmaster."

When he was gone, Alberich folded the papers into their original packet, and felt carefully under the table until he found the catch that released a little drawer inside one of the thick legs. Dethor had shown it to him, so he was reasonably sure that no one else knew about it. There were hiding places like this all over the private quarters of the salle, but this was the only one that he could use without getting up. Probably there was no one out there trying to make sense of the shadows on the other side of the colored glass, but just in case there was, there would be no way to tell that Alberich had hidden something. It only looked as if he was reaching for his drink.

And there was another set of papers on the tabletop, just in case the shadows had betrayed that Talamir had been looking at papers. This was a report about bandit activity along the Karsite Border, something that Alberich could reasonably have an interest and expertise in. If someone came to the salle in the next mark or so, Alberich would take great pains to mention that report. It wasn't just that he was taking precautions about the papers Myste had stolen, he was protecting *himself.* There were a great many people in Court circles who distrusted "the Karsite," besides those who had no reason to love him because he did not cosset their children. Sometimes he grew very tired of it all.

Layers upon layers; he envied Jadus and Elcarth and all the others who didn't have to live their lives weaving webs of subterfuge. He wished—

Well, it didn't matter what he wished. He would, as a gambling friend of his had often said, play out the cards he had been dealt.

Complications, complications.

"My life is full of complications," he said aloud. There was no answer. Vkandis knew it was true enough.

Another complication: Myste herself. She'd been on his mind all day. There had been *no* doubt in his mind that Myste had been discreetly flirting with him last night. And he'd liked it. He'd even tried a little clumsy flirting back—

:Not as clumsy as you think,: Kantor put in. *:I was pleasantly surprised. You've got a light touch, when you care to use it.:*

He felt himself blushing, but it was at least partly with pleasure. But what would the other Heralds think of this, if they realized that she and he were attracted to one another.?

:If they bothered to take any notice, they'll wait to see if you mind teasing, then give you both a bit of a word about it, now and again,: Kantor told him. *:Other than that, they'd probably begin a betting pool as to when the two of you decided to stop flirting and get down to something serious.:*

:Serious—: he ventured.

:Bedding,: Kantor said bluntly.

Alberich bit his tongue. Quite by accident—Kantor had startled him. *:But—:*

:Sorry. Didn't mean to shock you. But if this gets past flirting, Myste is going to expect it to go there. Heralds are—well, by the standards of a Karsite, they're flagrantly immoral and utterly hedonistic when it comes to the ways of man with maid. Not that she is. Myste, I mean. She's not a maid.:

Maybe he should have been shocked, but he wasn't. Startled, yes, but not shocked. Well, not that Myste wasn't a maid, anyway.

In fact, he was relieved. It had been a long time since he'd—well—and then it had been someone he'd paid. He didn't have any practice in the more polite forms of congress, and he was probably going to step on his own feet more than once if things—got past flirting. And the ache in certain parts of him let him know in no uncertain terms that his *body* certainly wanted it to get past flirting. *Far* past flirting.

As for how she came to be not a maid, well that was her business.

Unless she made it his. And then it was even more her business. . . .

:Good man. Slow and cautious. She's in no hurry and neither should you be.:

:As long as she doesn't run in terror from my face,: he said dryly, *:I doubt there is anything else about me that cows her. Underneath, that woman is someone that would appall people if they only knew her. There are things she will not compromise on. And things that she would kill over, if it came to that.:*

Which was, of course, how she was getting away with purloining secrets out from under the very noses of the owners, and with their cooperation. At some point, perhaps in that last battle, Myste had found, or gotten, her courage. Now he doubted that anything could effectively stand in her way if she believed in or wanted something badly enough.

Like me—?

He sat firmly on *that* thought and crammed it back into the little mental cupboard it had come out of.

Back to business. *:What do you Companions know about ciphers?:* he asked. After all, better to cover all possible avenues with this one.

:Nothing much,: Kantor said with regret. *:Nobody here at the Collegium for sure, and I think not anybody alive. Just because we're good at Mindspeech doesn't mean we're good at everything. Working ciphers takes a particular kind of mind— the kind that can see patterns where the rest of us would see only chaos.:*

Well, he'd had to ask. *:Should I just leave all this to Talamir, then?:*

:He knows more about who to trust in this than you do. I think I know who he'll be taking the papers to, and no one is safer.:

Well, that was a dismissal if he had ever heard one. Time to stop worrying about that end of the situation, and think about the part he could do something about.

Such as discovering just who, besides young Lord Devlin, his contact in the Court, Norris was meeting.

IT was spring, at long last, and the gardens were bursting with greenery and blossoms, as if to make up for last year's sorrowful season. With every breeze, the ornamental cherries carpeted the ground beneath their boughs with pink and white petals; the air was full of a hundred different scents. Kingdom business be hanged; Selenay was going to walk in her gardens before the season ripened any further into summer.

So she told the Seneschal at their morning meeting over breakfast that she wanted him to shorten the usual afternoon audiences by half.

"If I stay within walls for much longer I'm going to shred something," she said a little crossly, expecting him to object. "I'm tired of never seeing the sun except through windows, and I am exceedingly tired of hearing *people whining*. I would like to hear birds for a change, and if I must hear voices, I would prefer it to be the voices of people who are not complaining to me, at least for a candlemark or two."

But he only nodded his graying head, and regarded her

kindly. "If Your Majesty will recall," he told her, "your father was exactly the same, in the spring."

And now that he had reminded her, she *did* remember it, but not as a memory of him ordering shorter audiences, but as seeing him in the gardens every fine afternoon, and walking there with two or three friends in the evening, too. But she—

I was taking classes, or practicing, and he'd always done that, every spring, so it never struck me as odd, she decided. *I didn't know then that the business of government takes up so much time, and that he must have been stealing time from it for a little while.*

Or perhaps, it wasn't that he had been stealing time at all, though she would certainly have to, and the only place where she felt she could in good conscience take it was from the Audiences. Now that she thought about it, her father had definitely had more "leisure" time than she seemed to.

But then, he had been King for all of her life (obviously) so he'd had some practice at it. Maybe it would get easier as she went along; perhaps the more practiced she became, the less of *her* time it would take . . . perhaps, some day, she would have some candlemarks of leisure for herself.

She felt guilty; then decided that feeling guilty was stupid. If she was ready to rip someone's throat out now, how would she be *without* taking some time, at last, for herself? A pox on that. Bridges were not going to fall down, nor buildings collapse, because she walked in her garden and played at games a little while with her ladies.

"Well, then schedule fewer petitioners for the foreseeable future," she ordered, adding, "if you please."

Surely some of those people can manage to sort out their troubles by themselves.

"Certainly, Majesty," the Seneschal said, with a little smile. "If Your Majesty will forgive my voicing my own opinion, you are just a trifle *too* accessible. Restricting your availability will make people think before they request an audience for which they might have to wait several days."

She blinked, then nodded. And here she had thought he was going to disapprove! But the prospect of a simple walk in her gardens was enough to elevate her spirits for the entire morning, even though the Exchequer occupied her for most of that time with budget and tax allotments. Just the simple knowledge that she *was* going to escape his stuffy little office was enough to set her to work with more energy than she'd had in weeks for such things.

And the audiences did not seem as tedious either. And when the Seneschal announced that she would not be seeing any more petitioners that day, it was all she could do to keep from leaping up out of the throne and flying out the Privy Door behind the dais to get to her chambers and out of her robes of state.

She changed into a simple, split-skirt gown without calling for her maids, collected a ball and racquets, then gathered up her rather startled ladies-in-waiting, and bustled them all down the hall like a goose-girl hurrying her geese to the pond.

And when they were out into the garden, she acted like a child newly-freed from lessons, dropping every bit of her dignity to lead them all in a game of "tag," then taking each of them on in turn at racquets. In fact, she wore some of them out with her energy, until they all begged, laughing, for a moment of rest.

Which she graciously gave them. And while they sprawled on the lawn, or lounged on benches, she walked alone among the flower beds. She hadn't intended to actually pick any flowers, but this spring there was a superabundance of blossoms, and she found herself taking one here, one there, not deliberately selecting anything, just picking them from places where the blooms seemed crowded or scents were especially intoxicating. *I'll put them in my bedroom,* she decided, feeling an unaccustomed glee. *Just stick them all in a vase full of water. No formal flower arranging, no careful selection of "harmonious colors." The kind of bouquet—no, bunch* of flowers!—*I used to pick for myself as a child!*

She didn't—thank goodness—have to think twice about wandering about here alone either. It was safe enough for her to be unguarded here in the Queen's Garden. There were Royal Guards all around the grounds, and the grounds themselves were walled off, of course. No one could come here who wasn't a member of the Court or Collegia, and it was a matter of etiquette not to invade the Queen's Garden when the Queen was in it unless you were specifically invited.

So she was a little surprised to look up from picking another bloom and see the Rethwellan Ambassador, followed at a slight distance by a young man she did not recognize, coming toward her on the path.

He dropped to one knee when he reached her, and she automatically extended her hand for him to kiss, then gave it a slight tug, indicating that he should rise.

"Ambassador Brenthalarian, whatever is it that brings you here?" she asked. "I hope you aren't going to trouble my afternoon with a problem—"

"Nothing of the sort, Majesty," the Ambassador said smoothly. "Indeed, I only wished to inquire if your Majesty would be willing to receive King Megrarthon's second son, Prince Karathanelan. He has come bringing His Majesty's belated personal condolences, for you have already had His Majesty's official ones."

"Yes, I recall," she replied, looking at him with a feeling of interest tinged with excitement. So—here was her answer to the question "what foreign princes were there?" before she had even asked anyone about it. A foreign prince, from Rethwellan! Princes did *not* travel abroad unless they had very compelling reasons for doing so. . . .

She cast a surreptitious glance at the young man who waited just out of earshot, and felt another thrill, this time of pleasure. He was handsome. *Very* handsome. His coloring was an intriguing mixture—dark chestnut hair, quite curly and almost shoulder length, and blue eyes that were a lighter color than her own, the color of a sky with a thin, high haze of cloud over it. He had a long nose, high cheekbones, and a narrow face with a cleft chin. He looked—

:Like centuries of inbreeding,: Caryo said sardonically.

:Oh, hush, silly!: she replied keeping a watch on him out of the corner of her eye. *:What he looks like is* not *like a Valde-maran, which is a refreshing change.* I *think he's lovely.:*

"When could the Prince come to Court, do you think?" she asked, pretending that she had not already guessed that the Prince was right here in her own garden. The Ambassador knew very well that she knew, and so did the Prince, but greeting him straightaway would spoil the game. And it was likely to be a very amusing little game. *Surely this is one of the "foreign princes" that Orthallen was talking about!* "I would, of course, be delighted to receive him at any time."

"Then in that case, gracious lady, let the Prince prevail upon your noble nature and present himself!" the young man said, flinging himself at her feet in the most romantic posture possible. "My curiosity brought me here, but my heart will not allow me to remain outside of your regard for a single moment more!" He seized her hand and kissed it, and she flushed with pleasure. He spoke very good Valdemaran, with scarcely a trace of accent.

"Then, welcome, Prince Karathanelan," she said, tugging his hand. He took the hint and rose gracefully. "How could I be less than gracious enough to welcome you when confronted with such a gallant gentleman?"

She was trying to be queenly and dignified, but she felt her flush turning into a blush. He gave her a sidelong glance and smiled. "You are as gracious as you are beautiful, Queen Selenay," the Prince replied. "Will you permit me to conduct you back to your ladies?"

"With pleasure," she said. And now it was the Rethwellan Ambassador's turn to smile.

The Prince offered his arm; she took it. The first play of the game was over, and it had been *very* pleasant. Selenay could hardly wait to see what the next move would be.

One of the most difficult things Alberich had ever done was to put that cipher out of his mind and concentrate on the rest of his duties. And yet, there was nothing he could *do* about the message except to guard the original. He'd sealed the panel of its hiding place shut to make certain that it wouldn't be tampered with, and short of locking it in a strongbox and burying the strongbox under the floor of his room, he couldn't make it any safer. So at this point, there was nothing *he* could do about it. No man could be an expert at all things, and it was a bit late in his life to begin studying ciphers.

Instead, he went on with his own double life. He taught his students, and drilled those Heralds and Guards who came to him for extra tutoring and practice by day. And when his work for the day was over, and everyone assumed he was resting in his own quarters, he went out into the city by night in one of his assumed personae.

There was one distinct improvement in his clandestine tasks, however, and that was that the City Guard and constabulary were back up to full strength. He no longer needed to ferret out ordinary criminals; they had their *own* agents for that again. In fact, he knew one or two City Guards who did such things by sight, and they knew him. If he spotted them in one of his haunts of a night, he would move on to a different spot, knowing that they were probably on the trail of something or someone, and the very best thing he could do would be to get out of their way. There was, after all, no point in spoiling someone else's hunt, and too many hunters in one spot sometimes made the "game" shy of being around.

And he suspected that they did the same, on seeing him.

At any rate, with the Tedrel Wars over and Karse busy with its own internal problems, the market for information on Valdemar's strengths and weaknesses had dried up somewhat. He also suspected that the market for information of interest *to* Valdemar was not what it had been. For now, anyway, there just was not as much trafficking in that sort of thing going on. Now the highest prices were being paid for more mundane information—usually having to do with who was in possession of what valuable goods, and how strongly a treasure was guarded, and so on. The most interesting trafficking he saw now was the manufacture of new identities, and he had the strong suspicion that the people who were buying these identities had once called themselves "Tedrels." How they managed to get as far north as Haven he could not imagine; even he hadn't done it without having a Companion. The journeys must have been terrifying. He was not, however, concerned. Selenay was in no danger from them; there were no Tedrel leaders for her to be taken to as hostage or as forced-bride, and he doubted that any of the men purchasing new lives for themselves wasted a moment of thought on her.

Well, as long as they stayed on the right side of the law, he'd be hanged if he turned any of them in, or the people who were helping them (for a price) either. And if they broke the law, well, he might be the one to catch them, but it was up to the Guard and constabulary to deal with it.

Information trafficking was mostly going the other way now, and even those prices were deflated. He could almost feel sorry—almost—for the fellows whose sole stock in trade was in intelligence.

On the other hand, this made two of *his* personae very popular fellows with those selling information about Valdemar's neighbors, since both those personae were still buying. Though for information about Karse, he was relying on Geri and the informal network that the Sunpriests who had escaped to or been born in Valdemar had built over the years.

As a consequence, he had known well in advance of today that one of the younger Princes of Rethwellan was arriving "secretly" with the intention of paying court to the Queen. He had told Talamir, and neither of them had seen any reason to spoil the surprise by informing Selenay. "Let her have a little romance," Talamir had opined, and his opinion was seconded by Herald Kyril. "She is sensible enough to know that whatever courting or romantic attention he pays her is only an illusion, and that he is here purely for the purpose of making an advantageous alliance. She will bear in mind, I am sure, that he would pay her the same compliments if she was stooped and squint-eyed. This will amuse her, and she has had little enough pure amusement since the Ice Festival."

Illusion or not, romance was not in Alberich's area of expertise, nor were the doings of princes. He would leave that to Talamir, and had said as much. His personal opinion was that the arrival of this princeling was a damned good thing for *Talamir*. Between the discovery of the ciphered papers and the advent of the Rethwellan Prince, Talamir was looking more centered than he had since the Coronation.

Alberich had filed that observation away for further thought, but there was one conclusion to be made from it that was obvious—Talamir needed *real* things to do, too, things he could get his metaphorical teeth into, things that focused him on what was going on around him. Alberich made up his mind to find more such tasks.

Now, following that actor fellow—*that* was something he could do.

Though once the weather turned and spring was well and truly in bloom, he began to wonder where the man got his energy, and whether he *could* manage to follow him without dropping over.

It wasn't only that Norris was performing every evening

with the full company at the inn *and* rehearsing new productions every afternoon—

That is, when he wasn't performing with a reduced company at special private performances of an afternoon—

No, it was that once those evening performances were over, he scarcely had time to wipe the paint from his face and change out of his costume before he was off somewhere. Most of the time it was with a female. Alberich couldn't call them "ladies," though some of them had that title, even if they acted more like cats in heat. When he wasn't with a female, he went roistering off with a gang of male friends, drinking and carousing through several taverns—and usually then ended up in a woman's bed in some bawdy house anyway.

It was astonishing. Because then, no matter how late he'd been out, there he was again, looking alert and fresh and ready to go, no later than noon, to rehearse with the company.

"I know not how he does it," Alberich said, as he accompanied Myste, in his guise as "her friend from the Army, the carter," back to the Companion's Bell where she was ostensibly staying. They had just watched Norris drink enough to make Alberich's head reel, then take three whores up to his room. Only one thing was certain; he wouldn't be going anywhere tonight. Thank the Sunlord. Alberich didn't think he could have made another late night of it himself.

"Nor does anyone else," Myste admitted. "Especially not his head for drink! That man can drink any three under the table, and I am not exaggerating, because I've seen it with my own eyes. And the next day, you'd never know he'd taken a drop."

Alberich licked his lips thoughtfully. "A useful talent, for an agent."

"Damn right it is." She tucked her hair behind her ears, and adjusted her lenses. "What's more—and this is a woman's intuitive observation, so take it with whatever grains of salt you choose—I don't see that he has anything that you could exploit as a weakness. Not even for women."

Alberich gave her a dubious glance. "Pardon?"

"He *uses* them," she elaborated, "but he has no *use* for them. I think, they're like food for him—he satisfies his appetite, and he does have a hearty appetite, but once he's through, he pays no more attention to them than he would to the shepherd's pie he just finished eating. He pushes away the leftovers, and wants them cleared away. I've watched him with his women, remember. Quite a lot more than he thinks I have, actually. I have yet to see him show any emotional attachment to anyone, woman *or* man. He acts as if he does, says all the right things, and it is superb acting, yes—actually quite a bit better and far more subtle than anything he does on stage. But so far as I can tell, there's nothing genuine behind the words and the gestures."

"Well," Alberich said thoughtfully. "Well, well, well. I think it is good that I have never tried to come too near to him, or I might have been swiftly found out. But that makes me concerned for you—"

She nodded. "It makes *me* concerned for me, too, believe me, and the only things I have in my favor are that he thinks I'm besotted and under his thumb, that I'm not ornamental to look at so he spends as little time as he can get away with doing so, and that he does not think that women in general are particularly intelligent. I expect," she added thoughtfully, "that he regards *me* rather in the line of a trained dog. Quite clever at performing the tricks I've been taught, and utterly devoted to my masters, but not really capable of thinking for myself."

"Which would make, I think, other women his lap dogs," Alberich pointed out, continuing the analogy. "Good for ornament, and sensually pleasant, but otherwise utterly useless."

She laughed aloud at that. "Oh, I wish some of his light'-

o'loves could hear you say *that* of them! How he manages to keep them from tearing him to bits in jealousy is beyond me."

"Perhaps they are in truth as utterly besotted as he thinks you to be," Alberich observed. "Or else, he has the gift of golden speech."

"Both, I think." She shook her head. "You know, as often as I see it, I'm still amazed at how self-deluded a lot of women are. A man says one thing, and does something else, and they believe the words and not the actions."

"That behavior is not restricted to women," Alberich pointed out. "Are his fellow actors not equally deceived in thinking him a grand fellow?"

"Hmm. That's true enough." They were nearly at the Bell, but neither of them made the turn that would take them into the alley and the back way. "Alberich, I don't believe we're alone."

"So you have noticed." Someone had been following them for some time. Alberich had been certain of it about a third of the way back.

"I'm not usually good at this, but I heard a footstep that I know just before I said something. It's Norris."

Well, that put a different complexion on things. "So the three bawds—?"

"A ruse. Maybe he isn't as sure of me as I thought. So— hmm. Now what do we do?"

"You go up to your room, and I say good night. Then I see what your friend does next."

They had, because Alberich always liked to plan for every possible contingency, planned for this one as well. Myste *did* have a room here—in fact, it was one of several that Heralds could use if they needed one; if, for instance, there was a major convocation of Heralds and all the beds at the Collegium were full. They were very spartan in nature, hardly more than closets with bunks in them, identical to the servants' rooms and exactly the sort of thing that a clerk would get in trade for his services to an inn. So when they reached the door of the Bell, they parted company as old friends rather than anything more intimate, and Myste used her key to the side entrance where the long-term residents and inn servants had their rooms. Alberich clumped off, made certain that their follower hadn't followed *him,* then reversed his coat to the matte-black side, and ghosted back.

Sure enough, there was Norris, hidden, and hidden relatively well, in a shadow across the street. After a moment, one of the little windows in the garret rooms glowed as a candle was brought inside. Alberich was about to suggest to Myste with Mindspeech that she go to the window, when she did just that without his needing to prompt her. She not only went to it, she opened it, and sat in it for several moments, as if enjoying the warm, spring night. Even though she was probably dying to peer down into the street to look for their follower, she did nothing of the sort; instead, she took off her lenses, rubbed her eyes as if she was tired, and sat back with her head against the side of the window frame and her eyes—as far as Alberich could tell—closed.

:Is the kitty still stalking me?:

:Yes, he is,: Alberich replied.

:Persistent beast. I don't suppose you can think of anything that will make him go away?:

:I am working on just that,: he told her, although in truth, he was coming up rather dry as to ideas.

After all the times when his admirers have been a nuisance to get around, this is one time when I wish some of them would appear, he thought crossly.

:How many would you like?: came Kantor's interested query.

He blinked. *:Why do you ask?:*

:Because there is an entire table full of young women from the audience this evening here. They wanted to get a table there, but you know how it is—:

Yes, indeed, Alberich knew very well how it was. Norris'
company was, by far, the most popular in Haven in a very long
time. On the nights when there were plays, it was impossible
to get a table in his inn, either before or after the play. The
innkeeper had taken to doing the unheard of—making *reser-
vations* for tables. There were people who had waited as long
as three weeks before being able to take their pre-play dinner
or after-play supper in Norris' presumed presence.

:—*at any rate, all they've done is talk about Norris since
they got here. They're very loud, and I think, a bit tipsy.*: There
were distinct overtones of snigger in Kantor's voice. :*I can't
imagine how they'd be useful to you, though.*:

:*Oh, I can*—:

He slipped away from his hiding place, went into the alley,
in through the secret room at the back of the stables, and
changed into, not his clothing, but his uniform. This was not
even his gray Weaponsmaster's garb, but the Heraldic Whites
that he seldom, if ever, wore. He had kept a set down here for
just this reason. He wanted to be noticed this time, but he
wanted all the attention to be on his clothing, not his face.

Then he strolled openly into the Bell, and listened for the
sound of female voices. It didn't take him long to hear them,
for as Kantor had said, they were both loud and tipsy, the latter probably being the cause of the former.

:*All right, Myste,*: he Mindspoke. :*Yawn, stretch, put out
your candle and go to bed. You shouldn't have to stay there
much longer.*:

:*I'm alive with curiosity.*:

The Bell had more than one public room; there was the
main tavern area, and several supper rooms that were intended more for eating in than drinking. He entered the room
where the young—and not so young—women were, as if looking about, possibly for a place to sit.

They were, so far as he could tell, not highborn. But they
definitely were prosperous; their gowns were all new, of good

quality, and they wore a moderate amount of silver jewelry. Middling well-off merchant or craft families, he guessed; the younger ones had probably persuaded their families to let them see the players, and the older ones had come along as chaperones, and they *all* had fallen under the spell of the handsome leading man. They were already planning their next outing to see him perform.

A Herald always got noticed, even in Haven, and when he entered the room, they all looked up and at him. He concentrated very hard on his words, and his accent. This was not the time to sound like a foreigner. If Norris went to the effort of trying to track back who betrayed him—Alberich just wanted to be "a Herald." He gave a little bow, and said, "Your pardon, my ladies. I wouldn't want to interrupt your party—"

One of the older ones giggled; it was one of the young ones who called out, "Oh, that's quite all right, Herald, you weren't interrupting anything. We were just talking about the play we've been to."

"The play be hanged!" said one of the tipsier ones. "It's that actor Norris' way of filling out tights that *we* were talking about!"

Some of them laughed hilariously, some with embarrassment, and Alberich smiled. "He's a fine actor, that one," he said agreeably. "Very impressive indeed. I think all of us managed to get to one or more of his performances during the Ice Festival." Then he added, as if the idea had suddenly struck him, "He wouldn't be waiting for any of you, would he?"

Oddly enough, it was one of the drunker ones who caught the implications of that last question, which slipped right by most of them. "What d'ye mean, waiting for one of us?" she asked, not quite slurring her words. "Y'mean, now? Right now?"

"Why, yes," Alberich replied, feigning surprise. "I saw him just across the street, lingering in the doorway, as if he was waiting for someone to come out of the Bell—"

Well, that was *all* he needed to say, and the only thing he needed to *do* was to press himself against the wall to get out of the way of the avalanche of gowns heading for the door.

They piled past him and rushed for the front exit. A moment later, and there was something like a little chorus of squeals as they tumbled out into the street. "Is that—" "It is!" "It's him!"

:*You wicked, wicked man!*: Myste chortled, as the sounds became a bit inarticulate and much louder.

There was a single, masculine voice, saying desperately over the torrent of giggles and little shrieks, "Ladies! Ladies!" and the owner was clearly getting nowhere.

Alberich strolled out to the door, and stood there with his face in shadow, leaning against the doorpost with his arms crossed, enjoying the havoc he had created. Norris was in the center of a tight knot of women, all of them breathlessly telling him of their admiration at the tops of their lungs, all of them trying to elbow each other aside to get closer to him. He looked like a very desperate man at the moment.

:*Oh, this is choice,*: Myste said. :*I can't resist.*:

From overhead and to the right came her familiar voice. "Will you please be *quiet?*" If Alberich hadn't known Myste so well, he would have been certain that she was angry, not trying with might and main to hold back gales of laughter. "People are trying to *sleep!*"

Her window slammed shut.

Then Myste's plaint was joined by several other, genuinely irritated voices, calling down to the gaggle of women surrounding to *shut up!* and *go away!* and *I'll get the constables on you, see if I don't!*

And it wasn't long before a constable *did* appear, and suggest to Norris (as the apparent center of the disturbance), that "It would be very nice, sir, if you and your friends were somewhere else right now."

And there was nothing else that Norris could do at that

point, except to bow to the inevitable. He was going to be stuck with these women for the next candlemark at least. And the only way he was going to get rid of them was back at his own inn, where he knew the ground, and could slip away from them under the guise of attending to nature's call or something of the sort—or getting one of the cast to find one of his regular bawds to come down and drag him back to his room. The one thing that would embarrass them enough to go away even in their present state of intoxication *would* be the presence of a real whore.

But it would have to be done there, not here—

Somehow, perhaps by sheer force of personality, he got the group moving, and away they went, still surrounding him on all sides, chattering like a flock of noisy little birds, and he with the look of a man being nibbled to death by ducks.

When they were all out of both sight and hearing, he Mind-called up to Myste. :*I think you can come out now.*:

:*Just a moment. I was not exactly dressed. I wanted to add some verisimilitude to the illusion that I had gone to bed.*:

Now he wished he'd looked up when she leaned out of her window.

Then it struck him; there'd been a hint of—something—in her mind-voice. Was it what he *thought* it was? Should he? Did he dare?

:*If you didn't read that as an invitation, you're denser than I thought,*: said Kantor.

He couldn't clear his throat in mind-voice, but he managed a combination of eagerness and diffidence. :*I don't suppose you would care for me to come up instead?*:

He heard the purr in her mind-voice, and almost tangled his own feet together, trying to whip himself around and head for the stairs. :*Ah, yes. Indeed I would. Please, do.*:

13

THE journey back up to the Palace was surreal. Dreamlike, as the four of them made their way through peace-filled, cool air scented with honeysuckle. Alberich held onto the moment fiercely; no matter what had happened in the past, or what would happen in the future, he'd had this night, this time. His heart was, for the moment, at peace, and he could not have been more content with his lot. He hoped—he thought—Myste felt the same.

They parted with a touch of lips and hands at the branching of paths, one leading up to the Heralds' Wing at the Palace, the other to the salle. He and Kantor moved off into the velvet night.

:*I told you that you were worrying too much,*: Kantor said, when he and Alberich were finally settled back in their respective "beds," in, and beside, the salle.

:*Hmm. You were right.*: Still—no, there was no "still." Kantor was right. The benefit of being Gifted; there was no question of how one's partner felt. There had been a little initial fumbling, but—

No "buts."

He sighed, and started to settle into sleep—

Then something popped up into his mind and jolted him into wakefulness again. *:Now,* why *did she tell you "Thank you, you were right"—?:*

:Ah. You weren't supposed to hear that.: Kantor sighed. *:I gave her some advice, some time back. Through her Companion, of course, but she knew it was from me, because she asked me directly.:*

:Yes?: He decided that, no matter what it was, he wasn't going to be annoyed. After all, look what it had gotten him.

:I told her, "He won't make the first move; you'll have to. And don't be subtle. In this situation, he's trying so hard to be a gentleman that he won't notice if you're subtle." But if you're wondering, I don't think this was planned, I think she just seized the opportunity when it was too good to be passed up. I know she's felt diffident about approaching you here, in your own place, and more than a bit shy about inviting you up to the Collegium where—:

:Where everyone would notice and gossip.: Alberich finished for him, and mulled it all over. No, he definitely was not going to be annoyed. *:Thank you. You were right.:*

Of course, now that the first move had been made in the game. . . .

He chuckled to himself in the darkness. The *next* time she showed up here, it wasn't all going to be business. Not that he was going to forget his duty, far from it.

Now he did let his doubly-tired body relax. And his last thought was, perhaps not oddly, *Norris is a fool.*

Selenay sat at her open window, and breathed in the honey-suckle-scented air dreamily. Karath—he had insisted almost immediately that she call him Karath—had been officially presented at Court two days ago. He had gone out of his way to be charming, and Selenay was by no means the only one to have been affected by that charm. But his attention had been directed, like a focused beam of light, on her.

This was not the first time that she had been the focus of someone's attention, but it *was* the first time the attention had been completely positive, and universally directed to the sole object of pleasing her. Heady stuff.

And it didn't hurt at all that Karath was so very good to look upon. . . .

No, not at all. But there was more, as impossible as it seemed. Karath understood her.

It was magical, how well he understood her. Already they had shared commiserations on how heavy the burden of duty was for a royal child, and how unfair it was that they had less freedom than the lowest of their subjects. How very unfair. . . .

And he had looked straight into her eyes and said, "It is a sad pity that you have no one to share your burden with."

Oh, she had laughed at that, and demurred that she had an entire Council to help her, but his words had rung very true, and she wondered if there was something behind them. As if—could it be—

No, of course not. He's a Prince of Rethwellan. If he can charm me into giving Rethwellan advantages, he will. He may even be courting me with an eye to a marriage of state. Right now, though, he's simply being friendly; he's a Prince, and there can't be too many people that he can confide in. It isn't as if he has a Companion to talk to, or even someone like Lord Orthallen. He was, she thought, a very proud young man. It would be hard for him to confide in anyone that he considered below him. *Yes, that is certainly it.* She rested her head against the window frame, feeling suddenly melancholy, for herself, for him.

No, there could be nothing more to it than that. *Besides, he can't possibly stay for very long. He'll have to return home soon.*

The thought made her feel cheated, somehow, and even more melancholy.

But after a moment, she shook it off resolutely. The Seneschal had decided that having a Prince of the blood here was an occasion of great import, and had arranged that his days should be enlivened by all manner of amusements, and that it was Selenay's duty to take part in at least some of them. The Vernal Equinox was in a few days, and although it was the wrong season for hunting, it was the best season for other sorts of outdoor excursions. They were all going to watch a new version of the Hurlee game, played Companion-back by the oldest of the Trainees. Others had been trying to come up with warm-weather variations on Hurlee, but this was by far the most exciting and successful. And there were those who were trying to get horses to do what the Companions were doing, but it would probably take a couple of years to train horses to put up with balls rolling under their hooves and sticks whizzing about their ears. For now, at least, the only mounted version of the game would be played by Heralds or Trainees.

It made an excellent excuse to sit out on lawns, with hampers of refreshments, in the warm sunshine, rather than in the stuffy Audience Chamber, listening to even stuffier old men complain about each other.

There would be supper in a pavilion on the lawns after the game, and then, a concert of music under the stars in the gardens. *It will be the most fun I've had since the Ice Festival. Actually, it will be much more fun than the Ice Festival; I won't be on show to an entire city.*

She smiled as she thought about it. To think that she would have most of a day devoted to something other than Kingdom business! But her Councilors all seemed very much in favor of the idea, even those who were reserved in their assessment of Karath.

Maybe he will *stay longer. . . .*

After all, Orthallen was convinced that he had come here with every intention of courting her. It was a time-honored means of cementing alliances, marriage. He *was* the younger Prince; he wouldn't be in line for the throne at this point, not even if his older brother died, because Faramentha already had a young son of his own. So—

She shivered, but with delight and anticipation, not dread. Oh, no, definitely not *dread.* Not like she'd felt with every other would-be suitor that had presented himself or been presented so far.

Now, wait and see, she cautioned herself. *Don't start chasing hares until the hounds have the scent. Orthallen could be misreading this. He might just be very kind.*

But if he *was* courting her—it was just a bit difficult to be loverlike when he never saw her except in the company of ten or twenty other people.

The question was, did she *want* him to court her? Actually, more to the point, did she want to marry him? She thought—perhaps—but she still wasn't entirely sure. It probably wouldn't be too much of a battle to convince the Council, but the rest of her subjects might not care for the idea of a foreign Consort. And while he had beautiful manners, and was extremely sympathetic, it was all words so far. She had no idea if he was truly attracted to her, Selenay, or was just being properly diplomatic and sympathetic to the Queen. *He* was one of the handsomest men she had ever seen, but how did she look to him, really? And how would he ever be able to say what he really felt with the constant audience that was around her?

If only there was a way to get rid of the audience—the courtiers, the ladies, all of them. If only there was a way that she could just slip away from them all, long enough for the two of them to be alone for just a little.

And then, she had an idea. It was a terribly romantic idea. And it just might work.

I'll have a masquerade, she thought with delight. *I'll have it when the year of mourning is officially over. Out in the gardens, spread out everywhere, with everyone in costume and masked. I'll have the same costume made up for me and all of my ladies, except I'll let him know by some little token which one is me. If he can't manage to get me alone for a little, then he won't be trying.*

Yes, that would do it. That would do it indeed. She chuckled at her own cleverness.

And meanwhile, she had tomorrow to look forward to, a half a day and all evening with nothing before her but to relax and enjoy herself. And perhaps Karath would show something more of his intentions.

She went to her bed and fell asleep, still smiling.

There were three stands set up along the three sides of the triangular playing field; the best one, reserved for the Queen and her Court, was on the side between the Scarlet and Green goals with a good view of both. Out on the field, the two teams faced each other, Scarlet and Green goalkeepers standing warily alert on their respective goals, the two goalkeepers on the neutral, third goal, watching each other as much as the teams.

There was a tension-filled silence as one of the referees placed the ball on the ground between the two teams, then ran off, well out of the way of what was coming.

A trumpet blast—

A single shout swelled a thousand throats, and the game was on.

"Explain to me what I am seeing, please," Karath asked, watching as the tide of riders collided, the ball somewhere under the churning hooves of the Companions. One half of the riders were wearing Bardic scarlet, the other, Healer Green— not because they actually were Bards and Healers, but because the two teams had been "sponsored" by the two other Collegia. It would; after all, have been impossible to tell which rider was on which team, otherwise.

"The players are all Heraldic Trainees, and they usually wear gray," Selenay said, as there was a loud *crack,* and the ball suddenly seemed to fly out of the scrum on a pair of invisible wings. "This came out of a game the Trainees made up over the winter, called Hurlee—" She interrupted to cheer, as the Bardic goalkeeper made a last-minute save, her Companion rearing and pivoting on hind hooves, letting her catch the ball in her net. The goalkeepers had nets, rather than club-ended sticks.

"Anyway, we wouldn't be able to tell the teams apart, so Bardic Collegium sponsored the team in red, and Healers the team in green." She shouted again, as the Bardic goalkeeper threw the ball back into play, and one of her own people caught it while it was still in flight and sent it whizzing toward the Healer goal with a mighty blow of his stick. The whole field went charging after it.

"But how are the horses so well-trained?" Karath asked.

"They aren't horses, they're Companions," she answered automatically. "Um—they're—" she searched for a way to explain it to an outsider. "They have Mind-magic, and so do the Trainees, and it's like having a partner. They can speak to one another."

"Ah, magic," Karath said wisely. "Of course. Like the Hawk-brother mages who control their birds in the strange places in the Pelagirs."

Actually, it's not like that at all, she thought, but that was probably as close as he was going to get until he'd been here a while, and saw for himself. Or until a Companion Chose him. "That's close enough, I suppose," she said instead, and turned her attention to the game.

It was absolutely vicious in its way; Alberich had insisted that the original version of Hurlee be played with no holds barred, and nothing short of murder against the rules, and this version was no different, with one single exception. No one was allowed to deliberately thrust a stick among the legs of the scrumming Companions. The idea of a Companion with a deliberately broken leg was just too horrifying. But the Companions were *certainly* allowed to ram each other, and shoulder each other out of the way; the riders could hit at each other with their sticks, and try to pull each other out of the saddle. Companions and riders alike wore hard helmets of leather over steel; the Companions wore neck guards, the riders wore padding and guards of their own.

It was war out there; Selenay, who had seen war first-hand, recognized it for what it was. Relatively bloodless, perhaps, but nonetheless, war. Which was why both Weaponsmaster Alberich and the new Equitation Instructor, Herald Keren, approved of it. You could study mounted combat all you liked; you could even practice as much as you dared, but you got no *sense* of what combat was really like—

Well, the fourth- and fifth-year Trainees certainly were now. By the time the first third was over, that was obvious. There was plenty of danger; one player was already out with a broken arm, and a second sidelined while the Healers made sure that the crack on the head hadn't resulted in a concussion. A third was playing with a broken nose, and there were two with black eyes, and no one would know until it was over how many bruises and strains there were. No Companions were injured, but that was always possible, too.

The second third began after a brief pause for water—both drunk and poured over heads—and a quick change of players. Then they were off again, with no less vigor than before.

"It seems very dangerous!" Karath shouted to her, over the cheers and shrieks. She glanced at him; he seemed just as excited as everyone else. His color was high, and he had a wide smile of enjoyment.

"It is!" she shouted back. "Our Weaponsmaster is using it for war-training!"

"Aha!" He nodded vigorously, then cheered wildly with everyone else as the Scarlet and Green goalkeepers on the neutral goal got into a clinch, and a Scarlet rider nipped in right under their noses and slammed home a goal.

Hurlee on ice had been exciting. This was beyond exciting—this was intoxicating. Even Selenay, who had been in the thick of war, was caught up in it, drunk as any of them on it, free to feel it, knowing that this time, there was no fear that anyone would die. One rider was actually knocked unconscious by the ball before it was over, and there was a broken wrist and a second broken arm, both caused by being unseated and falling badly. But Selenay knew that the Healers would soon put all of them to rights, and when the Healers were done with them, the congratulations they would get at the hands of the rest of the Trainees—and everyone else with an interest in the game—would soon make the pain just a memory. The Scarlets took the lead and held it for most of the game, but at the very end, in the final third, the Greens took the victory away from them by a single point.

When the winded and the exhausted winners and losers both had been mobbed and rushed off the field to their own celebratory feast, Selenay found herself hoarse with screaming and nearly as tired as if she had been out there on the field herself.

"My word!" the Prince said, his eyes still wild with excitement. "That's altogether more thrilling than any tournament I've ever seen! You say your Weaponsmaster is using this for war-training?"

Selenay nodded, and sat down so that everyone else could.

Protocol, after all—while the Monarch was on her feet, no one else could sit. There was some little time before the *al fresco* dinner, which would be served out in the gardens, and she wanted to give her staff plenty of time to have it set up before she led the ravenous hordes toward the food. Meanwhile, pages were going around with wine and fruit, and she availed herself of both. Karath sat down in the place of honor beside her, though he still looked as if he would like to go find a Hurlee stick and try the game for himself.

Not Selenay. She enjoyed watching the game, but once it was over, she couldn't help but think about why Alberich was so in favor of it. She didn't want any of those youngsters to have to see what she had seen. There had been too many no older than they who had not returned from the Wars.

"Indeed, he is, Your Highness," the Seneschal said, as both the Rethwellan Ambassador and the Ambassador from Hardorn leaned closer in order to hear. "He and the Equitation Instructor have found it an invaluable substitute for melee and skirmish training. They say they have found that both the mounted and foot versions are equally valuable. And it is all the better for the fact that the Trainees *want* to do it, and several of them spend a great deal of their free time in practice at it. We are restricting the mounted version to the final-year students, however, given the level of expertise required, and the danger involved."

"Better a broken bone or two now, than something worse in combat," Selenay said, sobered by her recollection of another spring day—nearly this time last year—

Then she shook off her melancholy. This was supposed to be a day given over to relaxation and pleasure, and she was not going to spoil it. "Well, gentlemen, you can tell your friends and kin back in your homelands that we here in Valdemar know how to provide both novelty *and* entertainment for our guests," she said lightly. "I do believe that was the first ever public game of mounted Hurlee."

"And I hope you will convey my admiration to your Weaponsmaster for finding so clever a solution for a training dilemma," the Prince said with a smile. "Though I will confess, if *that* is the level that he trains to, he is fully as expert as our own Weaponsmaster at home—though perhaps not *quite* to the exacting standard of Swordmistress Tarma shena Tale'sedrin, the famed Shin'a'in who trained my father and older brother."

"But not you?" asked the Hardornan Ambassador, and Selenay had the oddest sensation that *he* knew something about Karath that he would like very much for Karath to reveal. Something unflattering. . . .

Though *why* he would wish for such a thing—

Ambassadors are always jockeying for favor. I suppose he thinks that if Karath appears less than perfect, I will lose interest in him. Absurd.

The Prince frowned, and for just a moment, a shadow passed over his face. But in the next moment, he was all smiles again, and Selenay wondered if she had even seen it. "Alas, no," he replied smoothly. "The Swordmistress retired and closed her school before I was old enough in my mother's eyes to be sent away to it. And at any rate, from all I have heard, the lady is extremely ascetic in her ways and strict in her discipline; some might say, she is overzealous in both regards. And I—well—" he shrugged. "I am not much like my brothers. While I feel that every man of breeding should be adept at the use of arms, I fail to see why he should undergo the same rigorous training as someone who intends to live by them. Personally, I am afraid that the Swordmistress and I would be doomed to perpetually clash, so perhaps it is just as well. It would be a terrible scandal for a Prince of the blood to be thrown out of a school for mercenaries as an abject failure, or worse, a *discipline problem.*"

The Rethwellan Ambassador laughed, politely, but it sounded strained. Selenay was baffled. If *that* was all the

Hardornan Ambassador had been angling for, she failed to see what was so unflattering about it. Not even a Trainee who was unsuited to the martial arts was required to do more than learn how to defend him or herself. Why, look at Myste! Most of *her* training had been in the best ways of running away!

She decided to steer the subject away from the area that Karath was finding uncomfortable. "The Swordmistress—is that a Shin'a'in name?" Selenay asked, curiously, thinking wistfully of her earlier daydream of a wild Shin'a'in Clan Chief coming here to claim her hand. "I've never seen a Shin'a'in, though I believe some of our people in the south have traded with them."

"It is, indeed, Majesty," Karath replied. "Why do you ask?"

"Oh, only that I had never heard of Shin'a'in living outside the Dhorisha Plains, and I often think I would like to meet one, someday," she confessed. "I believe one came as far as Lord Ashkevron's manor in my father's day, to help the Lord with his horses, but it was before I was born."

"It is true that they do not often venture off their traditional grounds," the Rethwellan Ambassador said, after waiting for a few polite moments for all of them to nibble a little at their fruit and sip from their goblets of wine. "We see them from time to time selling horses, but as soon as the beasts are sold, they swiftly return to their homeland. The city of Kata'-shin'a'in is the only spot off the Plains where you will see them regularly. The Swordmistress is somewhat of an anomaly; she lives—or *lived,* since she was quite old, when last I heard—with her blood-oath sister, who had a school of sorcery alongside the school for swordsmen. Perhaps one day I will be able to entertain you with some tales of their adventures. They are rather famous in Rethwellan."

"I would enjoy that," Selenay said, wondering to see that faint shadow pass over the Prince's face again. "But today, it is incumbent upon me to entertain *you,* gentlemen, and I believe that it is time that we all went to supper."

She rose, and they all, perforce, rose with her. "And high time, Majesty," the Seneschal said lightly. "Watching the Hurlee game was nearly as exhausting as *playing* it, and just as stimulating to the appetite. These refreshments were welcome, but I swear, if you put butter on a brick, I would eat it at this point!"

"Pray, don't say that," she chided with a laugh. "Our guests will be afraid to try the pastries!"

She led the way down out of the viewing stands and into the gardens, with the rest of the Court trailing after. She wondered if she should ask the Prince about that Shin'a'in Swordmistress—perhaps there was some problem there that she should know about.

Well, perhaps not. Probably he was piqued that his older brother had the privilege of training under so famous a teacher, and he had not. She could understand that. As difficult as Alberich was, there was absolutely no doubt that he was the best Weaponsmaster that Valdemar and the Collegium had seen in a very long time. If she had a sibling who'd been able to train under Alberich, while she was not allowed to for whatever reason, *she* would be horribly jealous, too.

The meal was laid out along tables in the shade, protected from insects by tents of fly-gauze. Nothing was intended to be served hot. A guest had but to tell a page what he wanted, and go to find a good seat on the lawn, near the pavilion where the musicians were tuning up, and the page would bring him a laden plate and a cup of wine. It was all finger food of the sort that could be eaten with nothing but a little recourse to a napkin, and most of it was light and cool, meant to tease the palates of the diners with its subtlety. It wasn't the sort of heavy feast they'd shared at the Court Feast of the Ice Festival. Selenay made her selections, and went to take her seat. She wished that she could sprawl on a carpet or cloth, as she had on these occasions when she was only the Heir, but she was Queen now, and such an undignified pose would not be proper for her. Instead, she followed her page to a rustic seating arrangement of a garden bench softened with cushions inside a bower facing the pavilion, with a semicircle of chairs placed around it for her particular guests.

She was pleased to see that Talamir was already there, waiting for her. He hadn't attended the Hurlee game, pleading a need to see to something or other, but she had been a little concerned that the real reason was that he was feeling ill again. As the anniversary of her father's death—and that of his first Companion, Taver—approached, he had been looking distinctly frail.

But he seemed well enough now, and very much in the moment. He conducted her to her seat with all the gallantry of which he was capable (which was a very great deal) and to Karath's evident annoyance, took his traditional place at her left hand, leaving Karath to take the remaining chair at her right.

"I trust your business is taken care of?" she asked, as he made sure that she had all she needed before sending the page off for his own supper. She tried something sweet and spicy wrapped in a lettuce leaf; bits of spiced meat with crunchy little bits of vegetable in a light sauce, and decided that she would have *that* often this spring and summer. The cooks seemed to have outdone themselves; she hadn't recognized most of the dishes on the tables.

"More so than I expected, Majesty," he replied, with a definite twinkle in his eye. "I would hesitate to say anything, except that you will hear about it from any one of a dozen gossips before the end of the day. Apparently our Weaponsmaster is not as invulnerable to the darts of emotion as he thought. But he is skilled enough in deception that even *I* thought that his meetings with the Chronicler were all business until today."

Selenay wrinkled her forehead in puzzlement, trying to make out what Talamir was getting at. "Alberich? And—

Myste—" and all at once it dawned on her. "Alberich? And *Myste?* Oh, my word!" She began to laugh delightedly, as the Prince and the two Ambassadors looked puzzled. "Oh, but how lovely! Talamir, you must pledge me on your word that you will *not* tease him about it! Above all things, I do *not* want the poor man frightened off, just when he's taken the first steps into this venture."

"Not I, nor any other Herald, Majesty," Talamir promised. "We're too pleased, to tell you the truth. And we would rather that the Trainees didn't find out about it either—or at least, not until the relationship is so long established that they'll be as terrified of saying anything about it as they are of offending him in any other way."

Selenay turned to her guests, still smiling at the thought that somber Alberich, who seemed as destined to remain chaste as any sworn priest, should finally have found a lady who clearly found *him* fascinating. She and Myste were uncommonly well-acquainted, despite the differences in their age and backgrounds, and Myste had dropped more than one little remark after they had all returned from the Wars that had told Selenay that the Herald-Chronicler had definite leanings in the Weaponsmaster's direction. *He* treated her as she wanted to be treated, with respect for her learning and as an equal in intelligence. If they occasionally exasperated one another, that was only to be expected with two such strong personalities. But she had thought Alberich impervious to anything but friendship.

Apparently not. "You are puzzled, gentlemen; it is only a little romance among our Heralds, but a rather unlikely one, or so I would have thought until now. The season seems to have affected our Weaponsmaster, whom we all thought to be a man of iron. And the great irony is that the lady in question is the only Herald he was never successful in teaching the martial arts to—the Chronicler, Herald Myste."

The Prince smiled vacantly, clearly finding the subject of no particular interest, but the Hardornan Ambassador chuckled right along with Herald Talamir. "Well! So the spring has managed to melt the heart of stone after all! Good for Herald Alberich! And twice as many kudos to your Herald Myste; my guess would be that she was the one to do the stalking. These old warriors are as shy as partridge in hunting season when it comes to the matters of the heart."

Talamir laughed. "That, sir, would be telling Heraldic secrets. I will leave it to your imagination."

"And on that note, I beg that we listen to the music and enjoy our repast," Selenay said firmly. "Or else we will start to sound like a gaggle of village gossips."

The sun was just setting, making the gardens a wondrous place indeed. The day-blooming flowers wafted the last of their perfumes over the guests as they closed their blossoms for the night; the night bloomers were just beginning to open. As twilight closed over the garden, a soft breeze sprang up; the musicians kept to soft, lyrical melodies, and servants made their way about, lighting the torches unobtrusively. Selenay set her empty plate and cup aside, and suddenly felt a hand brushing hers, as if by accident.

Then it happened again; she glanced aside at the Prince, who caught her gaze for just a moment, touched the tips of her fingers with hers, and gave her a quick, conspiratorial wink.

She felt her heart give a leap, and an answering smile crossed her lips before she turned her attention back to the musicians.

But she sighed, and watched him covertly out of the corner of her eye. His *apparent* attention was on the musicians, too, but she had the feeling that she was being watched behind the screen of his long lashes and half-closed lids.

The breeze touched her cheeks, cooling the heat that had suddenly suffused them. She was glad for the shadows within the bower, so that her blushes would not betray her. *Surely that wasn't just the gesture of a gallant. . . .*

She reached for her wine cup, and her fingers touched

something else. Trying to appear as casual as she could, she managed to get both objects, and found that she was holding both her cup, and a red rosebud from which all of the thorns had been carefully removed. He turned his head slightly, lowered his gaze to the flower meaningfully, smiled, and looked back to the musicians.

Now her whole body seemed to vibrate with a thrill that she had never felt before. To cover it, and to moisten her mouth gone suddenly dry, she sipped at the wine. Then she put the cup back down—but kept the rose.

The half-planned masquerade took on a new importance and urgency in her mind. She would give him the setting. And she would see if he reacted to it.

And then—

Then things would fall as they fell.

SELENAY stood very quietly in the exact middle of her dress-
ing-room, while three maids fussed and fluttered around her,
making sure that every detail of her costume was just so. In a
few moments, she and her ladies would be going down into
the gardens to perform the masque that would open the Mid-
summer Masquerade. In fact, there was music drifting through
the open windows of her suite right now, making her both
impatient and nervous at the same time.

She stared fixedly at herself in the mirror on the wall opposite her. Her costume was identical to the ones her ladies
would be wearing; all of them would wear floating, ethereal
dresses composed of many layers of pale green silk gauze, the
topmost layer embroidered with tiny sprigs of leaves and
flowers, fitted to the waist and flaring outward like the petals
of a trumpet flower. It had a hint of a train, with long, trailing
butterfly sleeves and a round neckline that showed just
enough bosom to suggest, rather than reveal. With it, she wore
soft, silk slippers dyed to match the gown. None of them would

wear jewels, not even she, only a loose, trailing belt of ivy, and bracelets and anklets of flowers. All would be masked, the strange, featureless silver masks of the legendary Moon Maidens, ovals without even eye holes—a cunning layer of silver gauze where the eyes should be was perfectly easy for the dancers to see through, but gave no hint of the eyes behind the masks. Their hair, which otherwise would give their identities away, was covered with more silk gauze in the form of a wrapped coif with floor-sweeping veils crowned with chaplets of more flowers. And the only difference between Selenay and the rest of them was her secret; she wore a single rosebud tucked into the ivy at the waistband of her gown. She had not told the Prince this; he would have to discover it for himself. In fact, she had not told *anyone* this. And since no one was to unmask before midnight, she would be indistinguishable from any of her ladies except for that one detail.

Which meant, if she chose, she should be able to slip away from the rest without being missed and throwing everyone into a panic.

She surveyed herself in the mirror, and was satisfied with what she saw. In designing this costume, she and her seamstresses had taken every flattering aspect of every dress she had ever worn, and combined it into a single gown. In the past, as often as not, she had carefully selected her clothing to serve as armor. This gown, however, was meant to be a weapon. Now the only thing that remained to be seen was if the weapon would be used. She already knew, just from what she saw in the mirror, that it would be effective.

Was it so silly of her, to want to be *wooed* like an ordinary woman? To know that the man who asked for her hand wanted *her* as well as what she represented? She was sure, now, that Karath was here for the purpose of courting her, or else he would have gone home by this time. There had been several opportunities for him to leave, including when his own Ambassador was recalled because of an emergency in his family. He could have gone back to Rethwellan then, with the man who had brought him here in the first place. He hadn't. In fact, he had stayed even though the Rethwellan Embassy was virtually empty but for a few servants. Even though half of his guards had gone back to protect the Ambassador on his journey, and she had loaned him some of her own Guards until either the old Ambassador returned, or a new one with the rest of the entourage came to take his place.

She knew that most of her Councilors were devoutly praying for such a match. It would all but secure the southern Border, since Rethwellan would be obliged to help defend it if the Karsites somehow found the means to attack again. It would bring many, many trade advantages, since Valdemaran goods would probably be exempted from the onerous taxes on imported stuff. It would mean easy access to several great trade markets of the south. No one could or would object to a Rethwellan Prince on the grounds of either consanguinity or unequal rank.

But she didn't want a *trade alliance,* or a military advantage. She wanted a Consort, a partner, a confidant. Someone she could talk to; someone who—

—well, someone she could love. Someone who would love her. Who would treasure Selenay as well as the Queen, as her father had treasured her mother.

She thought, if things worked out as she hoped, that she would be able to tell if that was true of Karath. She knew already that she was deliriously infatuated with him. How could she not be? Nearly every woman of the Court was half in love with his handsome face and charming manners. Every time he looked at her, she felt a shiver of delight; every time she thought about him, she went hot and cold all over. She had dreams of him at night that made her wake full of aching desire.

They had shared several conversations now, which were, if not completely private, certainly *mostly* private. He really did

understand the terrible burden of the crown, of being unable
to ever have much real privacy, of having to be everything to
everyone. They had talked about all the times when, as children, they had lost entire holidays being on show for the people. They'd spoken of the difficulty of finding real friends. She
thought that he understood these things as not even a Herald
could. If he wanted her, well, he *had* her. But only if he truly
wanted her; she was not going to go into this *now* unless she
had him just as truly.

He would have to say so. More than that, he would have to
convince her that he meant it. Otherwise—

Well, in the end, she still might marry him. But it would
not be for a while, maybe not for years. If this was to be nothing more than an alliance marriage, then she was *not* going to
throw her heart after him.

:*That's the first sensible thing you've thought of*,: Caryo
said. She started; Caryo had been uncharacteristically silent
lately, and had not—until now—said a single word about the
Prince.

:*What was the point? I don't like him; I don't know why.
But you—you're in love with him. Or with his face and manners and fine words, anyway, and you're not going to send
him away just because I don't like him. I'd have to give you a
lot better reason than that, and I don't have one.*:

Selenay bit her lip and stared at her mirror. :*But if you
don't like him*—:

:*I'm also not going to try to stop you from doing something
you really want to*,: Caryo said, irritation clear in her mind-
voice. :*And if he can convince you that he's as much in love
with you as you are with him—well, there's nothing more to
say. It won't be the first time that someone in a bride's family
hasn't gotten along with the groom. If human families can put
up with such a thing, so can I.*:

Selenay found herself horribly torn between annoyance at
Caryo and gratitude—annoyance, that Caryo would have the

infernal gall not to like Karath, and gratitude that she was not going to stand in the way of what her Chosen wanted. She settled, finally, on the gratitude. There was no point in being annoyed, anyway. Caryo would do what Caryo did; the two of them didn't always see eye to eye.

:*It hasn't happened,*: she reminded Caryo. :*And what would be better—him, or someone that was beholden to one or more of my Council, someone we couldn't trust not to have a dozen people whispering in his ear?*:

:*Who's to say your precious Prince doesn't have that baggage already?*: Caryo countered, then softened. :*I suppose that you're right. And besides, if he doesn't take the bait tonight, and he can't convince you—*:

:*Then even if I eventually marry him* anyway *for alliance purposes, it won't be until I've managed to control my own feelings,*: Selenay said firmly. :*If I am doomed to an alliance marriage, it will be with all my armor on.*:

She said that, but underneath her words was the yearning, the hope, that she'd never be required to live up to those words. What was more, she wasn't entirely certain that she could. She thought that she covered it well, however. Certainly Caryo seemed mollified.

:*Then, in that case—go, and see whatever is to be seen with clear eyes,*: Caryo told her, and slipped out of her mind.

She heaved a sigh of relief. That could have gone very badly, and the one thing that she could not bear would have been for Caryo to be angry with her.

On the other hand, if Caryo never could grow to like Karath, well, too bad. There were even Heralds who didn't particularly care for one another, and not even all the Companions got along in perfect accord.

On the other hand, maybe she would mellow over time. When Alberich had first been Chosen, there had even been a group of young Companions who had tried to attack him. Now there wasn't one of them that wouldn't defend him to the death, and when he got into it with one of the Trainees—as he had over the broken mirror—even the Companions of those Trainees backed the Weaponsmaster.

If Karath truly loved her, then with luck Caryo would come around eventually. It could be just a matter of time and patience.

She dismissed the whole situation from her mind. Tonight would be hers—more truly than that moment on the battlefield when she became Queen, more truly than the moment of her coronation, because in both cases, it had been the Queen, not Selenay, who had received the accolades, whose life had been forever altered. Tonight, it would be Selenay, and not the Queen.

She glanced at the windows, and was gratified to see that the last rays of sunset were gone, and the light outside was deepening into twilight. It was nearly time for the masque. All the guests would have been assembled by now, and would be waiting for the appearance of the Moon Maidens to begin the real festivities.

"Are my ladies ready?" she asked one of the maids.

"In the antechamber, Majesty," the girl said promptly.

She nodded. "Good. Then that's enough fussing with the gown; it is never going to be more perfect than it is now. Hand me my mask."

Wordlessly, one of the maids gave it to her; she fitted it over her face, and the maid tied it in place over the coif, then settled the long, trailing veil over her hair, now so tightly braided and coiled under the coif that once the chaplet was pressed down over the veil and coif, not a hair was to be seen.

The world as viewed through the eye holes of the mask was clear enough, perhaps a little obscured, as if by a thin mist, but no worse than that. The face presented to the mirror, however, was a featureless silver oval, more than a bit uncanny.

The legend of the Maidens of the Moon was right out of Rethwellan, not Valdemar, and told of a young prince—

supposedly one of Karath's ancestors—who met a maid dancing in his garden by the light of the full moon and fell in love with her, only to discover that she was one of the twelve daughters of the King of the Moon. He went through many harrowing adventures to get to the Moon-King's kingdom to claim her, only to be faced by a final test—pick her out from among her twelve identical sisters as they danced before him. She hoped that was enough of a hint to Karath of what he was expected to do tonight.

"Let's go down," she told the maids, and went out to her antechamber to collect her eleven ladies.

But she was not the one in the lead; she let Lady Jenice have that honor. She was determined not to give Karath any more hint than that rosebud—and not to give *anyone* else any hint, so that no one could prevent her from escaping from the throng with him if he chose right. She had instructed all of her ladies to speak only in whispers and never to so much as hint as to their identities, pointing out that the whole purpose of a masquerade was to keep everyone guessing (insofar as that was possible) until the unmasking. And everyone taking part in the masque had agreed with alacrity. One or two of her ladies, she suspected, had certain suspicions of their own lovers and were thinking to see if they could be caught out. One or two she *knew* were hoping to use the opportunity for some clandestine flirtations of their own. The rest were all simply intrigued by the idea, which was more than enough to keep them in the spirit of the game.

She saw with more than a little amusement that she was not the only one of them to be wearing a flower tucked in the ivy-belt, but none of those flowers was a rosebud. Good! One more point of confusion, if Karath was not serious enough to be paying attention.

The guests were all in the garden by now, and she could hear the musicians playing incidental music. She and the other ladies would perform their dance on the torchlit terrace above the gardens, giving everyone a good view. She felt a flutter in her stomach, a nervousness greater than she'd felt even at her own coronation. Her hands felt cold and clammy, and her face flushed. She was glad that she wasn't going to have to *say* anything, or she was sure she would have stammered and stumbled over the words.

The ladies lined up at the terrace door in two lines, forming six pairs. Selenay joined her left hand to her partner's right—that would be Lady Betrice, though you wouldn't be able to tell that if you didn't know it. A maid ran outside to let the Bard in charge of the entertainment know that they were ready. Someone giggled nervously.

From outside, muffled by the closed terrace doors, she heard the Bard's staff pounding three times on the stone of the terrace, and a single trumpet sound a brief, silvery four-note call for attention. The chattering stopped; so did the music.

"My Lords and my Ladies!" the Bard called into the sudden silence. "In honor of His Highness, Prince Karathanelan of Rethwellan, Her Majesty and her Ladies will now perform the Masque of the Moon Maidens!"

The doors were pulled open from outside by two pages; the music began, and the twelve ladies danced onto the stone terrace above the gardens to the strains of a solemn pavane. Selenay felt her heart pounding and concentrated fiercely on the steps of the dance, watching the lady in front of her. *One-two-three, dip-two-three, turn-two-three, pause*—

To her immense relief, Selenay realized that she couldn't see a thing down below the terrace, that the light from all of the lanterns and torches quite obscured all of the courtiers and guests below. She could concentrate on the intricate patterns of the dance quite as if it was no more than just another rehearsal, even though her heart was pounding as if she was running, and her hands still felt as if she'd been holding them in ice-rimmed water.

In a way, it was just as well that this was *not* an easy dance, nothing like any of the normal dances of the Court. It began as a round dance in slow gigue-time, then moved into a double-round of two circles of six ladies with the pattern changed to a slow gavotte. Then it moved into a triple-round of three circles of four, back in a gigue. There were extra bows and flourishes of the veils and the long sleeves, extra circlings and glidings between the figures of the dance. In and out and around Selenay wove her steps, turning and bowing, touching the fingers of her next partner, then releasing them, turning again to face a new partner. Then it became a line dance as a pavane, then a six-couple line dance in a chassone, then a double line of three couples in minette, then three square dances as a pavane. And each time the dance changed, they struck a new tableau for a hold of six bars of music, until the music came around again to the first round dance, at the end of which they struck a twelve-person tableau. Selenay wasn't even in the center of that final tableau, she was over at the far right. There was literally no way of telling *which* of the ladies she was; she was quite certain of that.

As the music ended, the applause from below was enthusiastic, and very gratifying. She felt herself flushing with pride, and she was certain that she wasn't the only one. They all broke their tableau and stepped to the edge of the terrace in a line, holding hands, and took their bows, bending their knees and bowing their heads in a graceful acknowledgment of the applause. It sounded quite genuine, which was delightful, actually, since most masques in her experience were more endured than enjoyed, and the accolades tended to be dutiful rather than enthusiastic

Then they came down the steps from the terrace to the lawn to mingle with the rest of the guests as dance music began. And here was the hard part—other than getting through the Masque itself. Somehow she had to carry herself like one of the rest, neither with too much authority nor too little, neither with diffidence nor haughtiness. She decided to avail herself, first thing, of one of the fans laid out on a table just where the terrace steps ended, for the use of those who found themselves overly warm. A fan was an excellent thing; it served as a kind of shield as well as something to occupy the hands.

But before she could do more than pick one up, someone grabbed her free hand. Startled, she found that she had been seized by one of the more exuberant young courtiers and was being pulled into a rowdy country-style ring dance. She couldn't tell who it was, of course; he was wearing an ornate and rather antique uniform or livery, and a mask made in the shape of a rooster's head. It was clear he had taken her for one of her ladies and not the Queen.

Don't resist! she reminded herself, and allowed him to pull her into the circle. Everyone was laughing, sometimes tripping over the little uneven parts of the ground, and acting altogether like a lot of children. And somewhat to her surprise, she found herself having—fun!

And in a moment she understood why; she was anonymous, and she had been chosen by this young man for what he could see of her body, not because she was Selenay. Of course he assumed she was one of Selenay's ladies at least, but behind the anonymity of his mask and hers, they were able to act freely. As she romped her way around the ring, she realized that she hadn't felt this lighthearted since she'd been a Trainee, and just Selenay, who happened to sleep over in the Palace and not in a room on the Girl's Side of the dormitory floor.

She was very glad, however, that all the parts of her costume had been fastened securely. It wouldn't do to have the coif and veil, or worse, the mask fall off, and reveal her for who she was.

She took the precaution, in a moment between dances, to knot her sleeves and tie up her veil all the same. No point in getting them tangled and pulled off either.

A kind of madness infected her, and she was not the only one. That was the thing about a masquerade; you could be as wild and silly as you liked under the anonymity of a mask. Especially if you had one of the more common masks; as she whirled through the steps of another dance, she saw at least two roosters, three Horned Men, and no less than five bears. She, of course, was one of a dozen Moon Maidens, and there were cats, Wild Women, goddesses and butterfly masks that were no less popular.

Another dance struck up immediately, this one a brasle, where two lines of dancers ran at each other, then seized new partners and whirled madly until it was time to run at each other again. She went through four rounds of that, when suddenly she was seized by someone in a costume she did not at all recognize.

He wore a half-mask of gold surmounted by a huge hat crowned with feathers, the costume an elaborate doublet and trews of silk and velvet in reds and yellows. And as the young man paused in their heady rush, he bent over and whispered, "I am the Moon Prince. Have I chosen aright, Selenay, my Moon Maiden?"

She pulled back, startled, and he laughed in Karath's voice and boldly plucked the rosebud from her belt. "I see by this token that I have!" he said, the mouth beneath the half-mask grinning. "Here—run with me!"

He took her hand; she hesitated only long enough to snatch a handful of her skirt so she could run more freely, and the two of them sprinted hand-in-hand off into the depth of the gardens, laughing like a pair of children.

She didn't know where they were going; she didn't care. They ran through torchlight and shadow, the sounds of music and merriment fading behind them. She more than half expected him to run toward Companion's Field, or some other remote place, but instead, he ran toward the Palace. Once again, he had chosen correctly; there was no one in this part of the garden at all, and little light. They were right beside the windows of the Collegium kitchen, which at this hour was dark. There, in the shadows of a thick clump of bushes, he finally stopped, and pulled her into his arms.

"Won't you unmask now, Selenay?" he murmured, confronted with the featureless oval of her disguise. And as if to set the example, he pulled off his hat, which proved to be fastened to his half-mask.

She put up her hands to the back of her head and loosened the chaplet, but he was too impatient to wait for her fumbling fingers. He carefully took off the chaplet, then the veil, and untied the mask himself, discarding each on the ground beside his hat. With every item he removed, her heart pounded a little faster.

When he had laid her face bare, he looked into her eyes for a long moment.

Then, suddenly, his arms were around her again, his lips crushed against hers, and she felt a heat rise in her and overwhelm her. She felt as if she was made of butter, melting against him, pressing her body into his, wanting nothing so much as to have the kiss go on forever and ever.

But—too soon for her desire—she felt his arms loosen, and he lifted his face from hers to stare down into her eyes again. There was just enough moonlight for him to see her upturned face; his was all in shadow, and she strained to hear his voice.

"By the gods, Selenay, I have wanted to do that from the moment I saw you!" he breathed.

She lifted her face wordlessly to his, but he shook his head, and with every evidence of regret, loosened her from his grasp.

"No," he said, "I dare not, or I will not stop with but a kiss."

"No?" she asked, feeling obscurely disappointed. "Then—"

"But I can do this," he said, interrupting her. He dropped to his knees, clasping both her hands in his. "Here it is only you and I, not our countries, not our Councils, only ourselves to satisfy. We will please only ourselves; we will answer only to our own will, here. Selenay, I ask this for myself, and for myself—would you, will you, grant your hand to me in marriage?"

He had read her riddle; more than that, he had answered her invitation *and* her challenge and met it, his Prince to her Moon Maiden. And now—now, away from all witnesses, all eyes, he had asked her to wed him specifically for himself, and not for his country.

If this wasn't the answer to her questions, she could not imagine what could be.

"Yes," she whispered. "With all my heart."

He leaped to his feet and took her in his arms again, and her whole body thrilled to the caresses that he bestowed on it. She would quite willingly have torn off her own gown and melded her body with his there and then. It was his restraint that stopped anything more from happening.

And though a great deal of her was frustrated and disappointed, the rest of her was grateful and full of admiration at his self-control.

"Here," he said, as he actually stepped away from her, then took her hand and bestowed a tender kiss on the palm. "You may be only one Moon Maiden among twelve, but we should not take the risk that you are missed. Let me help you mask again."

And so she stood, burning with desire for him, as he, clever as her best maid, masked her hot cheeks with the silver ovoid again, and placed the veil over her head, and the chaplet atop it. Then he retrieved his own mask and resumed his guise as well. "Shall we walk?" he asked, "my own lady?"

A shiver went up her spine at the caress in his words.

"To cool ourselves," she murmured in reply, and he laughed.

"I think that cooling is what we both need, my Moon Maiden!" he chuckled. "It is just as well that our masks will hide our faces, or they would surely betray us to anyone with eyes in his head!"

He took her hand, and led her back toward the festivities, at a far more decorous pace this time. She was glad of the night air and the chance to get her pounding heart to quiet itself. Her hand trembled in his, and he felt the trembling, and tightened his fingers about hers for a moment.

They passed other couples on their way to the dancing-lawn, making use of the little bowers and grottoes of the gardens, standing or sitting together. They also passed places shrouded in darkness from which little sighs and murmurs came that made her cheeks flush again, and a stab of envy lance through her.

But Karath took no notice, or at least, did not appear to. They sauntered on together, like any couple on a leisurely stroll, until they stepped onto the lawn below the terrace and into the full glare of the torchlight.

She did not know what she would have done then, but the situation was taken out of their hands by a wild game of crack-the-whip that crossed their path the moment they stepped onto the torchlit grass. The trailing girl seized Karath's hand in passing, and since he still had Selenay's she was perforce now the running, laughing, end of the "whip" until she in her turn could grab another hand.

Before long, the scampering line was too unwieldy to be a whip, and became a dancing, running snake, winding its way among the more sedate and older courtiers, who either laughed indulgently or frowned and snorted behind their masks. Around and around they went, in and out of the ornamental bushes, until everyone that had any youth in his body had been caught up in it; the musicians seemed to have been infected by the excitement, for they did not stop or even pause in their playing, until Selenay was out of breath, her side aching, the corners of her mouth actually hurting from all of the laughing and smiling she was doing. When they snaked around a potted rosemary tree, she finally let go of Karath's hand and that of the person behind her so that she could drop out of the line. The person behind her ran up and grabbed Karath's hand to keep the line going, and he was soon out of her sight.

With her hand pressed to her side, breathing hard, she sought out a stone bench that was too exposed to be a choice of lovers, and sat down on it. She wished she had the fan that she had lost, somewhere back when the dancing began. But at least the breeze was cool, and her gown was light; she fanned herself with a piece of her veil, and took deep breaths, waiting for the stitch in her side to pass.

But she had not been there long before Karath appeared again, and wonder of wonders, he brought a fan for her! He handed it to her with a graceful bow, and she thanked him and wafted herself with it, wondering gratefully if there was *any* other man here who would have thought of such a thing.

He took a seat beside her on the bench, and covered her free hand with his own. "One thing only, my own lady," he said, quietly, his voice barely audible over the music. "Is it your pleasure that we make our choice known tonight, or would you—"

"Tonight!" she said quickly. "If we wait, if I go first to the Council—there will be objections, however trivial, and the Councilors will want to argue it over for days and days! But if we simply *tell* them, at the unmasking, they will accept what they must."

"You are as wise as you are beautiful," he said warmly, patting her hand. "I would not have thought of that. And— how fitting, for any who might recognize *my* costume if we are standing together at the unmasking—"

"Or better still," she said, suddenly seeing it all in her mind's eye, "—on the terrace!"

His eyes sparkled behind his mask. "Oh, well thought! How soon before midnight strikes?"

That, she could answer, for there was a time-candle visible from where they sat. She pointed, and they could both see that there would be just enough time for them to slip into the Palace and get into place before the trumpeter marked the moment of unmasking.

Giggling with a giddy exhilaration, she now led *him* in through an unguarded door in the public part of the Palace, then back through the maze of corridors to the terrace door where she had so lately stood. There was no one there now, not even a page, and the doors stood open. Together, hand in hand, they walked out onto the terrace at the exact moment that the trumpeter sounded the call of midnight.

With a cheer, the masks came off—all but theirs. With an instinct for the drama of it, they both waited until the rest of the guests noticed that there was a couple standing alone on the brightly-lit terrace where the Masque had taken place—

—that one of the figures was a Moon Maiden—

—began to grasp that the other *must* be Prince Karathanelan—

And at that moment, he pulled off his mask and flung it behind himself, as she pulled chaplet, veil, mask and coif all off, shaking her hair loose so that it fell down around her shoulders. And as the guests saw that it was *her,* he again pulled her to him, and bent down in their first public embrace and kiss.

She closed her eyes, as her ears filled with the great cheer that went up as her arms went around him.

And she thought, in that moment, that there could be no happier person in all of Valdemar than she.

FROM the moment it was announced, Alberich had deliberately planned to avoid the masquerade. This was precisely the sort of gathering at which he felt most uncomfortable. And after all, it was primarily a Court function, and not one at which he expected anything significant would happen either. Those older members of the Court upon whom he had his eye were unlikely to use such an occasion for any conspiratorial gathering; both he and Talamir were agreed on that. Of all the times and places in which one could talk with fellow conspirators, an occasion such as this, where there were dozens of people milling about, all masked so that you could not know just who, exactly, was around you, was not ideal. And furthermore (although many popular plays and romances would have attempted to persuade otherwise) a gathering that was held out of doors where you could never be sure there was not someone hiding and listening to you, was probably a very bad choice for passing on secret information.

Alberich hated this sort of entertainment with a passion.

And since Selenay was going to be costumed identically with eleven of her ladies, at least until the moment of unmasking, this was probably one of the few times when she would be safer without a bodyguard. Unless, of course, all *twelve* of them were to be granted bodyguards. So he had said, decidedly, that he was not needed nor wanted, Talamir had agreed with him, and had suggested that he might wish to actually relax that evening for a change.

He had, in fact, decided to keep an eye on Norris that evening.

He already knew where to find him; there was not a performance tonight, and with all of the young nobles up at the masquerade, there was little chance that Norris would be meeting any of *them* down slumming with the actors tonight. No, if he met up with anyone above his own station, it would be because there was something more than drinking going on. This was one of the things that Alberich was going to keep a watch out for; someone who *should* be at the masquerade who was not.

If anybody had asked him what he was hoping to discover, he would have told them that he was not, in fact, hoping for anything. He knew better than to expect a result from any given evening; results never came when you expected them. You got ready for them in case they cropped up, and you watched for them to make sure you didn't miss them when they came, but you never expected them.

Since Myste would not be there tonight as it wasn't a performance night, he decided to trot out a new persona, one that was designed to blend in as well as Myste did—the aging, cranky scholar. His station would be shabby middle-class, genteel poverty, but poor because he spent all his money on books, travel to confer with other scholars, and paying to print his own monographs on obscure subjects. He wore clothing that was of good material, but not new, a long-sleeved, high-collared, belted tunic and trews of heavy linen in a rusty black, with a shirt of white linen, and the flat scholar's cap. Not shabby, but also neither well-cared-for nor well-fitted. He had an old leather satchel stuffed full of papers and books. He brought a reading book with him, parked himself in an out-of-the-way corner of the common room, and apparently kept his nose in it while he ate, in an absentminded fashion. He had engaged a room, but it was a very small one and did not come with candle or lantern, so it was perfectly reasonable for him to take his book here to read. He had debated getting a set of lenses like Myste's, but decided against it. If *he* were checking to see if someone was in disguise and snooping about, the first thing he would do would be to arrange to knock their lenses off to see if they were real. A pair of plain clear glass lenses would be a dead giveaway. And for once, his scars were an asset rather than a liability; by enhancing them rather than trying to conceal them and at the same time enhancing those creases that would, in time, become frown-lines, he was able to age himself credibly by nearly thirty years.

He did not know for certain that Norris would be here tonight, but with no play on, there was a good likelihood that he would at least spend the afternoon in rehearsals, then have some dinner here, where he was fed for free, before going out anywhere. And at any rate, even if the man didn't start his evening here, there was a good chance that by careful listening, Alberich would pick up some gossip about him or his whereabouts.

But his luck was truly in tonight; not only did Norris begin his night here, but the rehearsal ran long, so that Norris came down from his room about two candlemarks after sunset, dressed in quiet elegance, all fawnskin breeches and fine linen shirt open at the throat, thigh-high boots nearly as tight as the breeches.

He stepped up to the bar and ordered himself a drink. And shortly after that, so carefully timed that Alberich did not for a moment think it was coincidence, someone came looking for him.

Except that the man didn't exactly come *looking* for him, the way an admirer would. He didn't begin by asking the door-keeper if Norris was about, for instance, and he didn't come up to him openly, as a simple admirer would.

The stranger cast a glance around the common room; his eye lit on Norris, standing beside the bar and chatting, mug in hand. Since Alberich was watching Norris very carefully, he saw the actor catch the stranger's eye and hold it for just a moment. Then the newcomer took a seat of his own, in the same out-of-the-way corner that Alberich was already in. It was an awkward little cul-de-sac beneath the stairs, big enough for only a couple of two-person tables. Alberich already had the most exposed of the tables; the stranger took the one that was the least exposed to the rest of the room.

Alberich went on reading. He did not even look up as the man brushed by him, nor when the serving wench brought him his order. Norris didn't pay any great amount of attention overtly either—but after some time, the actor left the bar and drifted over in his direction. By this time, the common room was at its most crowded, and virtually the only seats left were at two-person tables like the ones Alberich and the stranger each had. Somehow Alberich didn't think that Norris was going to ask if he could join the scholar.

Norris paused for a moment beside Alberich; Alberich's neck prickled, but he didn't look up from his book. Surely it wasn't possible that the actor was going to sit at *his* table!

Surely it isn't possible that he recognized me?

The actor certainly gave Alberich a good look-over. Alberich did just what his persona would have done: he read, outwardly oblivious to anything going on around him. Norris moved on, and said to the stranger, "Friend, would you mind if I sat at this table?"

"Be my guest," the man said with every sign of indifference. And that would have been perfectly ordinary, if it hadn't been that both of them pitched their voices just a little louder than if they'd been talking merely to each other, and not for the benefit of anyone who happened to be nearby.

Alberich turned his page, and furrowed his brow. It was appropriate to furrow his brow at this point; the author was taking a slightly controversial stance, and one that someone like Alberich was bound to disagree with. Alberich had chosen this book quite deliberately; he was very familiar with it, and if challenged, could converse knowledgeably about the contents. And tonight, he just might have to. Despite the heat in the overcrowded room, he felt a chill of apprehension.

He heard the scrape of a stool on the floor; the sounds of someone sitting down behind him. He didn't actually *hear* anything then, but the serving wench materialized, as they all did, whenever Norris summoned them, however imperceptible the signal was to anyone else. The actor ordered dinner, and when it came, there was a pause as the wench flirted a little with Norris then was summarily shooed away.

"Is it all right?" said the stranger, in a very, very soft voice.

"Safe as houses," Norris replied, casually. "Safer than my room. Can't tell who might be on the other side of the wall, there."

Well, thought Alberich, *That's what you get for insisting on the big corner room.* Norris had recently demanded—and gotten—one of the better chambers at the inn. Even with Myste keeping a jaundiced eye on the take, the innkeeper was doing a phenomenal amount of business thanks to the ongoing presence of the actors here, and couldn't afford to offend Norris at this point. The problem with the new room, however, was that while Norris had one of his fellow actors as a neighbor on one side, the other was a room that anyone could rent, and it was often taken by someone who wanted to be near the actor. That would practically *guarantee* a snoop with her ear to the wall.

"What about *him?*" persisted the stranger, and Alberich knew, by the prickling feeling on the back of his neck, that the man was pointing at *him* in some way. Probably with a little jerk of the chin; less obtrusive, unless you were watching for something of the sort.

"Hmm." There was a scrape; Norris this time; Alberich could tell from the position of the chair.

He's going to do something. Alberich thought he could guess what, and a moment later, it came. And now he had to do something that was against all of his instincts; he had to relax, not tighten his muscles in anticipation. The scholar would be deep in the book and would not even be aware of the rest of the world. You should be able to come up behind him and shout in his ear without his noticing.

There was the sound of a stumble, and Norris blundered into him, spilling his drink, knocking the book out of his hand, nearly knocking him over. Alberich did not try to save himself; he let the chair go over, and himself with it, as with a cry, he lurched for his book. Norris was there before him, picking it up, all apology, offering his hand, and when Alberich was on his feet, dusting him off.

"Horribly clumsy of me, I beg your pardon—" While Norris babbled on, he was managing to get a look at the book, in fact, at the place where Alberich had been reading. And thank the Sunlord for that, since it meant he was *not* looking closely at Alberich's disguise instead! He handed it back to Alberich so quickly, though, that it was unlikely anyone like the scholar would have realized that the actor had examined the book before relinquishing it. But an actor had to be a quick study; the man probably had both pages memorized by now.

Alberich snatched it away, glared angrily at him, and fussed over the book, making certain that none of the pages were bent, nothing stained. "You clumsy oaf!" he shrilled, pitching his voice to a whiny falsetto. "Curse you, fellow! Where did you think you were going?"

"I'll buy you a new drink," Norris was saying, as the serving wench bustled up with a towel to clean up the mess.

"If you've so much as creased a page, you'll buy me a new *book,* young man," Alberich replied querulously. "Copies of Canton's *Lives of the Philosophers* do not grow on trees!"

"No, they don't, I'm sure," Norris said agreeably, as the serving wench brought another drink and Norris paid her for it. "And I would be devastated to think I had ruined one. I particularly admire his scholarly treatise on Loval Hestalion, for instance."

Alberich simply gave him a good long stare, as if suspiciously certain that Norris was only trying to jolly his way past Alberich's anger. "It's *Lowal* Hestalion, young man, as you would know if you had actually read the book, rather than making something up to try and worm your way into my favor. And what is more, the man may be sound enough on other biographies, but his treatise on Hestalion is little more than a repetition of scurrilous rumor!"

Norris threw up his hands and laughed. "Caught! Well, I most sincerely apologize again, I *have* restored your drink, and I hope I haven't foxed your book, so are we quits?"

"The book appears to be intact," Alberich said icily, "I believe I am also intact. And I beg the pleasure of your absence."

"Yes, *sir!*" Norris laughed, and went back to his place while Alberich ostensibly and ostentatiously reburied himself in his book.

"So, there, you see," Norris said under the sound of the conversations all around them. "Nothing but a bookworm. We could burn down the place around him, and he wouldn't notice."

"Good enough. The game's in play tonight," the stranger said. "We think it will play out well."

"Good news," Norris said with satisfaction. "And my reward?"

"You'll get it when the bond is sealed," the stranger replied. "Even if all goes well, there will be opposition. We may need you before then. And don't forget, we'll also need you after, for a time, anyway."

"No, you won't," Norris growled, sounding irritated now. "The boy's a natural seducer. And the girl's untried. And *I* absolutely the finest instructor in the arts of seduction that was ever born. You say he's showing his hand tonight. If he doesn't have her well enchanted before the week is out, and wedded within the moon, I'll eat my hat without salt."

"All well and good, but he'll still need pretty speeches, and he's not bright enough to make them up on his own," the stranger said, irritation in his own voice. "Until there's an heir in the offing, we're not safely home."

"And *I* don't get my theater." Norris sighed, as if much put upon. "All right, then, I'll stay available. But he'd better not drag this on too long. It doesn't take *that* long to get a girl with child, and after that, keeping her bound will be up to him. I've never seen a woman born yet that didn't make every excuse in the world for the father of her child."

"After that, we'll have what we need," the voice purred. The tone made the hair on Alberich's head stand up. There was something very sinister about it, that made Alberich wonder uneasily just what it was that the voice and his cohorts needed.

And he felt very sorry for the girl in question.

But it seemed that, whatever was going on here and now, it had little or nothing to do with the security of Valdemar. Evidently Norris had been coaching some unscrupulous young man in how to seduce a young woman, into marriage. He could almost picture her in his mind as he carefully turned another page in his book, some young, lonely, plain thing, but wealthy—for surely only great wealth could be the cause for such a scheme.

Would there be any way to warn her, assuming he could find out who she was?

Probably not. Even coming from a Herald, she probably

wouldn't believe anything that anyone told her against her beloved. Not if she was as infatuated as Norris thought. And he was a practiced seducer, after all.

But he didn't fool Myste, a little voice in the back of his mind reminded him.

Yes, well, Myste had been fooled at least once in her past, when she was younger. You had to have experience in something before you could recognize danger when you saw it, and since the stranger called the unknown young woman a "girl," she probably wasn't old enough to have experience in much of anything. Poor thing.

He turned a page of his book, groped for his drink without looking at it, and took a sip. Well. Norris was very generous; this was much better beer than the stuff Alberich had ordered the first time around.

The scrape of a stool signaled someone's departure, and it turned out to be the stranger. He eased his way past Alberich, being exceptionally careful not to jar him. Alberich ignored him entirely, though he would very much have liked to get a good look at him. The best Alberich could manage was a quick glance at the man's profile. It looked faintly familiar, in the way that someone looked if seen once or twice. It could be anybody Alberich had seen around here. Alberich filed the face in the back of his mind.

Now Norris was alone—but not for long.

There was a bit of a commotion at the door, the sound of high, shrill voices, and a flash of bright color. Alberich heard Norris chuckle under his breath, and buried his nose even further in the book.

But Norris was the one who got up, and sauntered over to the trio of women who were clearly what Alberich's mother had been mistaken for.

Now, Alberich knew he was no expert when it came to women's dress, especially not here in Valdemar, but there were some commonalities among the ladies of negotiable virtue everywhere, and this lot showed every one of the sartorial signs. There were flounces and ribbons and curls and painted cheeks and lips, all done to excess. Colors were bright (including hair color, for all three sported hair of colors not normally found in nature), there was a great deal of cleavage, a great deal of bare arm and shoulder, and even a scandalous amount of leg showing. Jewelry was positioned the way a general arranged his best troops, with the intent of directing the enemy's sight to a particular object.

"Well, my lovelies," Norris said genially, as they clustered around him like gaudy butterflies around a tall flower. "What brings you here?"

By this time, Norris had the attention of everyone in the room, and very well knew it. He was playing for the crowd, and the crowd sensed it was going to get a free show—short, maybe, but nonetheless, free.

"You," said the boldest, flirting acid-yellow hair at him. "We've a bet on that you can't take all three of us at once."

The entire room howled with laughter, in which Norris joined, throwing back his head and roaring. "In that case," he shouted, and Alberich at last looked up with an affronted expression on his face, "You're doomed to lose, my bawd!"

"In that case," cried the second of the trio, with hair the same blue-black as a raven's wing, boldly twining herself around him, "we win!"

In the barrage of laughter that followed *that* sally, Norris seized the bold one, picked her up in his arms, and trailing the other two, went straight up the stairs to his room.

Now it was entirely possible that all that had been a ruse to cover Norris' exit through a window, but Alberich didn't think so. For one thing, that new corner room would be cursed difficult to get out of without being seen. For another, Norris had looked as surprised as anyone else with the whores' replies. So there it was. He might as well go home, since not even Norris could— Well, it would take him the rest of the night, if he was going to make good on his boast and not lose the bet. And that was one sort of bet that a man like Norris could not bear to lose.

He shut his book and went over to "his" room. He took off his tunic and turned it inside-out; now it was brown moleskin. He stuffed the hat in the satchel of books and papers. Now he looked like a well-off working man, probably enjoying a night out. He saturated a rag with sendal oil and used it to take off his "wrinkles," then doused his head in the basin to wash his hair clean of the streaks of gray he had painted in. He rumpled up the bed, making sure it looked slept in, and left other signs of recent occupation. And when he was certain that no one was watching, *he* went out the window. The room was already paid for. No one would raise a hue and cry, finding it empty in the morning. He had told them that he expected to be away by first light. They'd simply assume he had been as good as his word.

Still, he did have one thing; that rather sordid business about the unknown young woman. There might be something in that worth investigating later.

I suppose I can get some sort of list of wealthy young women who have full rights to their fortunes somewhere, he reflected. *And whichever one posts the banns in the next moon or so would probably be the one I'm looking for.*

He was so involved in his own thoughts that he actually wasn't even thinking about his Companion—until Kantor himself startled him.

:Great good gods!: exclaimed Kantor in his mind, surprising him so much that he stumbled over his own two feet. He recovered without falling, but he was thoroughly irritated when he answered back.

:What?: he snapped.

:The masquerade!: Kantor exclaimed. *:Selenay—at the masquerade—she just picked Karathanelan in front of everyone at the masquerade!:*

:Picked him for what?*:* Alberich began with even more irritation, and then, of course, it dawned on him. Kantor would hardly be this shocked over the young Queen choosing a dancing partner. *:She chose the Prince of Rethwellan as her* Consort? *But—:* Now he was bewildered a little, by all that he did not know about Valdemar. *:Can she do that? Just pick someone like that?:*

:She can, and she has,: was Kantor's reply. *:We had better get back up the hill and quickly. Every Herald in Haven is going to want to say something about this.:*

Since Alberich was already moving as fast as he could without being obvious, he saved his breath for running. Which he did when he got into the alleys where no one was there to see him. It seemed to take forever before he was safely in his little room at the back of the Bell's stables, though he knew rationally that he'd made good time.

In a remarkably short period of time, Alberich was back in his gray leathers, and they were cantering through the streets, heading for the Collegium.

:What happened, exactly?: Alberich asked, moving easily with Kantor's gait, and keeping a sharp eye out for unwary pedestrians.

Kantor told him.

:Didn't Caryo guess what was going to happen?: he demanded. *:Why didn't she warn the rest of us? We could have gone to more pains to investigate him!:*

:I don't know,: Kantor said, mirroring Alberich's irritation. *:Maybe she thought it would all blow over. This shocked everyone; no one guessed Selenay would do this. I suppose she didn't even confide in her own Companion.:*

He kept his thoughts on *that* subject to himself. All right, granted he wasn't the most competent when it came to matters of the heart and particularly of romance, but there were some things that were obvious. He hadn't set eyes on this Prince himself, but he'd heard from plenty of people that the boy was absurdly good-looking. When you took a young woman like Selenay, who surely cherished her own *dreams* of romance even though she knew very well she was unlikely to fulfill them—and you presented her with a handsome young man of the proper birth and with all of the advantages that a foreign minister could ask for—well, what did you *expect* to happen? The only reason that he, Alberich, had been blind-sided was because the young man himself had given no outward signs—*that Alberich knew of*—that he was interested in a marriage alliance with Selenay and Valdemar.

Clearly both he and Selenay had played these cards very close to the chest, if even Caryo had thought it would all blow over.

:So what does anyone know about this prince?: he demanded.

The way cleared; they were in among the manors of the highborn now. And the highborn were all still at the masquerade, so the way was clear. Kantor broke into a gallop.

:I don't know anything more than you do,: Kantor replied. *:But you'll shortly find out.:*

Alberich cut his questions short. But behind his silence, they were piling up, like stones before an avalanche.

"—and that is all any of us know," Myste concluded. Since she was the Chronicler, she had elected to be the one to collect all of the information there was about the Prince, and all of the information there was *concerning* the Prince and concerning the reaction this unique declaration was going to have on the Council.

Myste sat down on a bale of hay. They were meeting in the stables—the *Companions'* stables. The building had the advantage of being big enough to hold all of them, and away from prying eyes and eavesdropping ears.

No one seemed particularly ready to break the silence that followed Myste's words. Finally, someone coughed.

"And Caryo doesn't like him, but can't say why. . . ." said the Herald who taught some of the law classes. "I am reluctant to place too much weight on this. Not even all of the Companions get along all the time; there are Companions that dislike anyone who isn't a Herald, including their Chosen's own relatives. I would even hate to speculate."

"It could just be his natural arrogance that gets her back up," Talamir suggested. "The boy *is* arrogant. It's to be expected, in someone with that much rank and privilege, who is also that confoundedly good-looking."

"It could be jealousy," said someone else, in what sounded like the voice of experience. "Just as Peled said. We're not perfect, and neither are *they*. I know the first time I flirted with an outsider, my Jandal got as jealous as anything."

Someone sighed. "I don't suppose it would do any good to reason with her about it—"

"Not if you don't want her to call for a priest and wed the boy on the spot," Keren said flatly. "For those of you who don't happen to have experience with first love—"

"*Infatuation,* Keren, surely!" exclaimed someone else.

"First love, first infatuation, it doesn't matter because it's a strong emotion either way," Keren snapped back. "She's young, she *just* lost her father, and we can guess that he's been playing all the parts she needs right now in a single package—part comforter, part protector, part lover. *And,* may I add, her Council has been putting pressure on her to *make* some kind of marriage. With all of that going on, not only won't she hear anything bad about the boy, she'll turn on the one who tries to criticize him. *I've* seen that, time and time again, in my village. The fastest way to get a girl to marry someone is to tell her you don't want her to."

She nodded with an air of finality. Alberich saw her looking at him, and just shrugged. If anyone thought *he* had any insights on what would work with Selenay, they were going to be sadly disappointed.

"So what are we going to do?" asked someone in a small voice that sounded very bewildered in the darkness.

Now Talamir cleared his throat—and rose to the occasion.

"We will support her, and her choice," he said firmly. "No matter how hasty or ill-thought we believe it to be. Think! The worst, the very worst, he can do is to make her unhappy—at which point, since Valdemar law supports divorcement, he may well find himself packed back to Rethwellan with his tail between his legs!"

There were some chuckles at that. Weak, but laughter, nonetheless. And at least in Alberich's case, a sigh of profound relief. This was the old Talamir, seeing the larger picture and finding the cleanest path through what could turn out to be a quagmire.

"The best that he can do is to make her happy, and if he does that, even if we still do not care for him, who are we to object?" Talamir went on, the shadows cast by the lantern beside him making him look as ancient as a Grove oak. "Remember, *unless he is Chosen by a Companion* and becomes a Herald, he will never be more than the Queen's Consort, who will have only as much power, or as little, as she grants him— and all of it behind the throne." Talamir looked around, managing to meet the eyes of every Herald there. "So let us determine to put a good face on things," he continued. "Offer her our congratulations, singly, and as a group. Support her choice. Make sure that she knows that we are *there*, as we always have been, for Herald Selenay as well as the Queen."

And that seemed to be about all that anyone could offer.

Alberich went back to the salle, feeling very uneasy. He hoped that would be enough.

He was afraid that it wouldn't be.

But the game had been played out before any of them even knew it was *in* play at all. Now they could only ride along with it, and wait.

16

*T*HE *game was played. . . .*

Something about that phrase nagged Alberich as he fell into an uneasy sleep, but it wasn't until he woke the next morning that he realized where he had heard it last.

And it was only after the recollection jolted him that he realized that there might be a connection between where he had heard it first, and Selenay.

He had the flash of memory as he moved into wakefulness, and it brought him alert all at once, his mind moving from a standing start into a full gallop.

The game is about to play— It had been that stranger talking to Norris last night. He could hear the voice clearly in his mind. It had been a well-educated voice, and if there was one thing that it was hard for the well-educated to do, it was to counterfeit being a member of a lower class than their own.

The similarity of phrases was what had given him that shock to the system. What if the girl they had been talking about, the one Alberich had assumed was simply wealthy and plain, had actually been *Selenay?* And that the young man being tutored in seduction had been the Prince of Rethwellan?

It fit. It certainly fit. Untried, sheltered, accustomed to flattery but *not* to the kind of practiced seducer Norris was, she would be easy prey for a man of Norris' experience—or one coached by him.

And Selenay, alone in all of the Court, was the only young woman who would have been sheltered from such men. There was the irony; if she had spent any time among her peers, she would have *seen* attractive young men use their looks in such an unattractive way—and young women do the same.

Or—perhaps not. She *had been* the Heir, and even in the Court, that might have protected her.

Odd as it might seem, the cads in Court circles saved their wiles for two sorts of women—the lower-class girls that they seduced and abandoned, and the unattractive, wealthy ones they seduced and wedded and abandoned on their estates in the country, while *they* came back to Court to enjoy themselves unencumbered by the inconvenient wife. They wouldn't have dared to use those ploys on Selenay.

Still, she had been sheltered in another way. From the time she had been Chosen, she had been at the Collegium, and not the Court. She never saw the intrigues among her peers, because she was among another set of "peers" for whom intrigue was simply out of the question. Even when the occasion had called for it, *she* hadn't spend much time socially in Court circles, *she* spent her social time among Heralds. Or at least, she had until she'd become Queen.

But there should have been one creature above all who would have—or should have—*realized* what was happening before this. And even if she hadn't been able to stop it, she should have been able to warn the rest of them!

:Kantor,: he called.

:I follow you,: his Companion replied. *:I hope you don't mind; you jarred me awake and I just followed your thought.:*

Once he would have been angry; not now. Now, in fact, he was grateful. Kantor had become the perfect partner, in a way; the shield-brother, the man you could depend on to fall in at your side and match you, move for move.

:That's the way it's supposed to work.:

Well, he could see that. Clearly, it didn't always.

:You're thinking Selenay and Caryo.: There was a moment of hesitation. *:You can't understand why Caryo didn't nip this in the bud, especially since she doesn't much like Prince Karath. And why she didn't realize how far things had gotten.:*

:Exactly,: Alberich replied.

:You and I are—exceedingly compatible now. We are about the same age, with similar experience. Selenay and Caryo—aren't. I mean, they're compatible, but their experiences are vastly different.:

Alberich blinked in surprise. That hadn't occurred to him as a possibility.

:Think of Caryo as a maiden aunt, or a virginal, scholarly sister who is much, much older than Selenay. She's—well, to be honest, she's rather sexless. Kindhearted and stalwart, protective absolutely, ready to comfort when Selenay is hurt or angry, but as thick as two short planks when it comes to romance and especially sex.:

Oh. . . . This was beginning to make him feel a little ill.

:Caryo is the sort of person whose shoulder you cry on when your father dies, the wise and clever person you could ask for help with political and administrative problems. Not the person you go to when you're mooncalfing over a boy. And as for sexual attraction—you'd be horribly embarrassed even to hint that you had such a thing to her, because she would be horribly embarrassed if you brought it up.:

Now, suddenly, it all made sense. Terrible sense.

At least, insofar as he understood young women, and insofar as Caryo being in the dark about all this right along with everyone else. *:Dear God. . . . :* he replied, aghast. *:We've all been blindsided.:*

:Our own damned fault,: Kantor agreed. *:We, the Companions, should have known. We know Caryo better than anyone but Selenay—and she was exactly the right Companion for a girl who was bound and determined not to think too hard about anything that wasn't involved in being the Heir and a Herald. If Sendar was still alive—:*

:If Sendar was alive, he'd have sent the boy packing, after making him look ridiculous and unpalatable in Selenay's eyes first. That's the only way to handle such things.: Alberich was at least on surer ground there; as an officer, he'd had to break up many an ill-timed romance.

:But with Selenay alone, we didn't think about how Caryo should change, and you Heralds didn't think that Selenay would find herself looking for something outside of her duties.:

:We were fools,: Alberich said flatly. *:She was clearly drowning in duty and we thought a festival or two would be enough.:*

:Blind-sided. And there is only one way to deal with it, and that is to go along with it, just as Talamir said last night. Yes, even if it turns out that this Rethwellan princeling is a rounder and a cad who has been studying *how to seduce our Queen.:*

The very thought made him angry, made him want to get hold of the blackguard and beat him with the flat of his sword—but Kantor was right. And Talamir was right. Hadn't he *just* been watching plays all this winter and spring that proved that very point? The best way to get a young woman set on a particular young man, and vice versa, was to oppose the match. The only way to separate her from someone who was not good for her was to be reserved on the subject of the young man, while being supportive of *her.* Then, when things began to go wrong, and only then, did you make it clear that you were "on her side." The only difference between a cliche and a truism was the skill and intricacy with which the latter was presented. And, unfortunately, Norris was a much better actor than the tawdry plays he presented for the common folk would have suggested. If he was, indeed, coaching the Prince—

:Have you talked with Caryo about this?: he asked his Companion, as he rolled over on his back and stared up at the ceiling.

:Not yet. Right now she's very hurt that Selenay didn't even hint of this to her. And, frankly, angry with herself for not seeing it. And she should be.:

Well, *he* wasn't going to be the one to say anything, but Kantor was right. In retrospect, Selenay had virtually handed everyone a map to her feelings with that masque, and all anyone had thought, if they'd thought at all, was how clever she was to have devised something that would entertain and honor all at the same time. Kantor was right; in this case, Caryo *had* been as thick as two short planks. And so had they.

:Least said, soonest mended,: the Companion said philosophically. *:I am keeping my thoughts to myself until Caryo is ready to talk to the rest of us. But I think that where Selenay is concerned, our voices must be raised in a song with but a single refrain—:*

:Which is, "All we want is your happiness," I think,: he replied. *:It's true enough.:* At least the feeling behind that phrase would be absolutely genuine. All any of them *did* want was Selenay's happiness. They just wanted it without the Prince's presence involved.

:Meanwhile, I don't think you should give up chasing Norris,: Kantor continued. *:Now, I think that young Devlin was probably his contact in the Court to pass him information about Selenay herself. So I don't think you should take your eyes off Devlin either.:*

He smiled grimly up at the ceiling. *:Ah, now, nor do I. In the first place, Norris might not have been tutoring the Prince. In the second place, if that was indeed what was toward, we* *may someday need the evidence. Because what I overheard makes me think that once there's a wedding, the Prince will slip. Selenay might excuse him a time or two, but she won't put up with it forever. And then we can prove to her how she was manipulated.:* Then, because he was honest, he had to add, *:If she was. He might really be in love with her; he might be everything he seems. But my gut says he isn't.:*

He felt Kantor's satisfaction. *:You're better at this business than you were.:*

He sighed. *:I could wish that there was no reason to be. The Weaponsmaster is all I ever cared to be.:*

:We play the game we're put into, Chosen,: said Kantor, which seemed to be about the only possible answer.

After that, however, it seemed as if a whirlwind had suddenly engulfed them, and the whirlwind's name was Selenay.

Alberich never had a chance to voice any opinion at all, because it was never asked of him. Selenay simply seemed to *assume* that because she was enchanted by the Prince, everyone else was, too. She had never before had anything that she wanted, really and truly *wanted* so much as Prince Karath—except, perhaps, for her father to be alive again. But the latter was impossible and the Prince was entirely within her reach. She was lonely, she was in love, and at the moment, there was no more potent combination. She could not imagine living without him, and she was taking steps so that she wouldn't have to.

Alberich was not present at the Council meeting that day after the masquerade where she *announced*—not asked, not even for advice—*announced,* arbitrarily and making it clear that she would brook no opposition, that she and the Prince were going to wed. And that it would be within the month. He was told about it later that evening by Elcarth.

Elcarth, Kyril, Jadus, and Talamir were all in Alberich's quarters, which made it a bit crowded once Myste, Keren, and Ylsa joined the group. Elcarth was looking more than a bit dazed, Kyril a little grim, and Talamir very—quiet and contained. Inhumanly so, actually. It made the hair on the back of Alberich's neck rise.

But they all had other considerations at the moment.

"You ladies wouldn't have known her father when he was at his most stubborn," Elcarth said, rubbing his hands over his temples. "When there was something he *knew* he wanted done, and he wasn't going to take 'no' for an answer. He was a force of nature, and there was no point in getting in his way, any more than there is in standing in the path of an avalanche and expecting it to stop because you want it to. It was like seeing her father all over again, with the addition that she was positively *fixated* on getting her way in this, as if it not only would be, it *had* to be, or the world would end."

"She simply rode right over the top of any opposition," Kyril seconded. "Not that there was very much, not when Orthallen and Gartheser threw in on her side. But still—I've never seen her like this, she became a petty tyrant, in fact. It was as if anyone who said anything contrary to her just didn't exist—"

"She was afraid," Talamir said, into the silence. "Fear can make anyone a tyrant."

The men looked at him blankly; Alberich was among them. He couldn't imagine how Talamir had come to *that* conclusion; there was no logic in it.

But Keren and Myste exchanged an eloquent glance, and after Keren nodded, Myste spoke up.

"She was afraid that if she didn't force this through, now, she would lose him, you mean," Myste said. It was a statement, not a question. "And if she loses *him,* it will break her, and she knows it."

"I think so." Talamir passed a hand over one eye, and looked, for a moment, impossibly frail.

"How can it break her?" Elcarth asked, aghast. "Great good gods, she's been through much worse than having a love affair end!"

"She does not precisely *confide* in me, so I can only judge by what I see and sense, based on what I know. I have never been in love myself," he added, somewhat wistfully, "So all I can do is guess. But as for why it will break her—it is precisely because she has been through so much in this last year. I believe that she sees Prince Karath as—as a sort of lifeline."

"I think—maybe—it's *because* he's an outsider," Myste put in. "I mean, she thinks she can't unburden herself to the rest of us, because we're a part of that burden. And anyway, he's made himself indispensable now. If she loses him, it will be that proverbial last pebble that starts the avalanche. Maybe he's only a pebble, but sometimes that's all it takes."

"Think about it, think back to how you *felt* with your first loves, not what you know now. The first time a youngster falls in love, there's no way to tell the difference between love and infatuation from the inside," Ylsa added sadly. "So as far as Selenay and this situation are concerned, right now, the difference is negligible."

"You mean, we treat it as love even though it might be—is probably—infatuation." Kyril looked pained. "But—"

"Remember what I told you about supporting her," Talamir warned.

"But if she goes on like this, overruling everything before anyone even has a chance to object—" began Elcarth. But both Talamir and Alberich were shaking their heads. Talamir gestured to Alberich.

"I think she will not, for there is no fear there for her," Alberich said. "Such things do not rouse her passion or her fear, for they do not affect her love."

"Precisely." Talamir nodded. "Why should she be afraid

about a matter of budget, or of setting a law? None of this is going to going to wrench her love out of her arms. We should be far more concerned that she stops *caring* about these things, frankly."

"Actually," Jadus spoke up, making everyone turn to look at him, "I think the best thing we could do is get this wedding over and done with. If it could be done *tomorrow,* I'd say to do it."

"Because—" Alberich said slowly, *feeling* his way toward the words, "—if mere infatuation it is, the sooner reality comes, the better. So—let the Prince but think he has her, then revert to whatever his true self is, he will."

Just as that stranger with Norris said. He is not bright enough to make up his own speeches. When he has her, his control over himself will lapse.

"Something like that," Jadus agreed. "And when she *has* him, she won't fear she'll *lose* him anymore, so whether it's love or infatuation, she'll start thinking again instead of reacting with her emotions."

"That's what I meant by treating infatuation the same as if it was love," said Ylsa. "Even if *we* are certain it's infatuation, she's certain it's love, and that he shares it, and if you don't give the emotion the same respect as if it is love, she'll stop listening to you."

"Oh, gods," Elcarth groaned. "It's *hard.*"

"Because we all assume we know better than she does, we're so much older and wiser," said Myste dryly. "Believe me, that's exactly what she's most afraid of. She doesn't want to hear about our experience, she doesn't want to think that this intense emotional storm that is making her feel so good for the first time in months is based on anything less than truth. And hellfires, for all we know, she could be in the right. The Prince may be the best thing for her. He may *be* in love with her, and she with him. He's only a second son; there is no way that he is going to be able to aspire to anything but chair-warming at home; at least here, while he may not be a King, he'll be more than a hanger-on. Even if he isn't in love with her, he may see her as *his* escape from mediocrity, and he may treat her with all the respect and tenderness we could ask because of it. But until we have evidence to the contrary, *and* she's ready to look at that evidence, then—"

"—then?" prompted Alberich.

Myste sighed. "Then I believe we need to be planning a wedding."

The "we" turned out to be entirely rhetorical. With the opposition melted to nothing, and perhaps fearing tacit disapproval, if not of the marriage itself, at least of the haste with which she was insisting it be conducted, Selenay turned to the Court rather than the Heralds for her wedding plans.

Now, Alberich had no more notion of how such things were done than any other sisterless bachelor. A month seemed to him to be a perfectly reasonable length of time to plan even a royal wedding. After all, what did one need? A place, a priest, some new clothing, perhaps, and a feast—surely no more time was needed for that than for the Ice Festival.

Evidently not. And although he was *the* most certain man even among the Heralds that this Rethwellan upstart was nothing more than opportunism wrapped in a cloak of glamour, he was relieved to find himself excluded from the planning. Because the entire Court went absolutely mad. . . .

It was sheer bedlam. Just for a start, apparently *every* female of rank had to have a new gown. And every female of rank with any male relatives was bound and determined to shovel their males into new clothing as well. So there was a steady stream of seamstresses and tailors, jewelers and fabric merchants, furriers and shoemakers, going to and from the Palace and the manors around the Palace, from dawn to well past dusk, clogging the roads and getting in everyone's way.

Then there was the question of *where* to hold the ceremony, for there were at least four enormous Temples in Haven that demanded the privilege. That debate alone occupied the Council for an entire day, and was only resolved when, in desperation, the Seneschal suggested that the entire ceremony be held outdoors, on the Palace grounds.

And there was the question of how long the public celebration would be, for an occasion like this warranted feeding the populace at large for a whole day, at least, if not more; there was the problem of food, of course, and since it was now summer, the added problem of spoilage. A week was out of the question, but a day seemed too meager.

And once that was settled, there were the particulars of the wedding feast *and* the wedding breakfast here at the Palace, and why the Council should be involved in *that,* Alberich could not imagine, but evidently they felt they had to decide even the most minute details of the menu.

The next question that threatened civil war within the Court itself was that of precedence and who would serve as which ladies in attendance. It actually came to hair-pulling in the public gardens on one notable occasion. Myste solved this question when not even the Seneschal could, by tracing forward the pedigrees of everyone who had served as ladies in attendance at Sendar's wedding.

"I had the advantage," she admitted later to Alberich, "having that genealogical research at my fingertips to eliminate all those suitors." Having Myste settle the question did earn the Herald-Chronicler a few enemies among Selenay's ladies who discovered themselves placed farther *down* the chain than they wanted, but earned but the gratitude of everyone else, including the entire Council.

Although there was no question of who would perform the ceremony (the Lord Patriarch, of course), the question of *which* ceremony would be held was a pressing one. The Queen had her own personal choice of deities that she worshiped, but this was done privately, not publicly. There was no state religion in Valdemar. In fact, the Valdemaran credo was: "There is no one right way." And while this made for great tolerance and freedom—it also made for a problem. How to perform what was essentially a religious ceremony without offending any of the myriad religions and their adherents became a matter of hysteria, until Myste in exasperation unearthed a previous wedding that quoted from every major religion in Valdemar, including (to Alberich's shock) that of the Sunlord. At that point, as far as Selenay was concerned, Herald Myste could do no wrong.

"And I'll play on that later, if I have to," she told Alberich darkly.

The list of difficult questions, it seemed, only grew longer and longer with each passing day. It had been a very long time since a reigning Queen of Valdemar took a Consort, and many things had changed since that time.

Alberich held himself lucky to be well out of it. He understood vaguely that Lord Orthallen got himself put in charge of it all with the help of the Seneschal, and that things were being sorted out, and that was all he cared to know about it. He might not care for Lord Orthallen himself, but there was no doubt whatsoever that the man was a superb diplomat and administrator.

Nevertheless, the whole business was shattering discipline on the Collegium side. The Ice Festival had been bad enough; this was worse. He had to get positively savage with some of the youngsters in his classes, when the excitement over at the Palace started to ooze into the Collegia and some of the Trainees even had the temerity to *skip weaponry classes.*

It was all the fault of the Blues, actually. There was absolutely no point in expecting much of anything out of the highborn Blues, though, and he knew it. Half the time, they weren't even *at* their classes, having been pulled out for various reasons having to do with The Wedding (he was coming to think of it with capital initials). And the other half of the time, their minds weren't on anything that anyone was trying to tell them anyway. Some of them weren't worth the water in a bucket with a hole in it, but others had friends among the Heraldic Trainees, and unfortunately, they were the ones playing the part of the tempters, luring their Trainee friends away with the siren song of "Oh, come on! It won't hurt to skip just this once!"

The Blues were a lost cause, and Alberich knew it; even parents would look at poor marks this one time and say to themselves, "Oh, but it was all the excitement of the wedding."

As for the Trainees, at least he and the other instructors had ways and means of enforcing their authority. In Alberich's case, there was the threat of humiliation when a truant came back to class. The shame that the runaways would find themselves repeating a class brought some back into line, the threat of "no Hurlee" or other games got the attention of others. But in the end, what saved them all was that Selenay finally got around to declaring a fortnight holiday for all three Collegia, which at least solved the problem of keeping absent minds on study and would-be truants in their seats.

And it gave Alberich an opportunity all unlooked-for, to get back down into Haven and concentrate all of his attention on Norris.

And on a new problem.

The sound of music and laughter from the common room and taproom of the Bell was loud enough to reach all the way to the stables. Wedding fever had begun even down in Haven; the banners that had greeted the coronation were being hung again, more decorations were being hung every day, and it seemed to be all anyone could talk about. And of course, where there was an event, there would be commerce—medallions, flags, and banners to wave, portraits and statues, dozens of songs (most bad). There were even stalls with pairs of Selenay and Karathanelan dolls appearing—either dressed as the Moon Maiden and the Prince, or in what were fondly supposed to be the Queen and Prince's wedding finery.

And even the quiet Bell was abuzz. Alberich wasn't terribly unhappy about all the fuss—it made it easier to slip in and out, rather than more difficult—a good thing, since for a change he was here in broad daylight. He was actually in his secret room, changing into one of his personae, when he heard the stable-side door open behind him.

His heart leaped into his throat. He whirled with a knife in his hands, one small part of him wondering *how* anyone had gotten past Kantor, when he saw it was Myste.

He slipped the knife back in its hiding place, hoping she hadn't seen it, and was going to say something—something irritated, actually, since she wasn't supposed to burst in on him like this—when he caught the look of worry on her face. That, and the fact that she was wringing her hands together, made him bite back what he had been about to say.

"I'm in trouble," she said, and for one, startled moment, he flashed on the only thing *that* phrase meant, back in Karse—

"They want me to become their full-time clerk, accountant, and treasurer," she continued, oblivious to whatever expressions had flitted across his face in that brief moment. If any had. He'd probably looked like an idiot with his mouth hanging open.

Then what she'd *said* penetrated, and he realized that the situation was quite serious indeed. "Oh, hellfires," he said. *They want her to work for them and only them, and how is she supposed to do that* and *continue being Herald-Chronicler? Scratch that; spending that much time with them, how is she going to manage without getting caught?*

"Norris has found a backer, and he's getting a theater for

the company. The gods of actors and idiots only know where he's getting the money from, but it's quite certain. And the fellow that handles all the business matters—you met him, remember?—wants me to do all of the money things for them. It's a full-time job, I can pledge you that, between managing the take at the door, getting everyone and everything paid for, taxes, hiring things like cleaning women and laundresses." She shook her head frantically. "Thank the gods I got wind of this *before* they actually asked me. I think they're waiting—wisely, may I add—to be sure that the money for the theater is in hand before they say anything to an outsider." Now her voice took on the tones of a wail of fear. "But what am I going to *do?*"

She wasn't panicking, but she looked as if she was in knots. "Sit down, for one thing. You look as pale as a shirt." She did as he ordered, while he sucked on his lower lip and thought, hard. "All right, you *can't* take that job; I couldn't take it and stay undiscovered with a trained actor like Norris watching me. Which means we have to come up with some reason *why* you can't take it."

The moment he said, "You can't take the job," he saw relief suffuse her features. And he was very glad that it was Myste in front of him now, and not Keren, who would have been offended at the very thought that she couldn't keep up the deception. "I think we have these options to get Myste the Clerk out of range before the offer can actually be made. You can 'take another position'—tell them tonight, even, that you've been offered a job, say, on some Great Lord's staff but on his estate, so you have to leave. You can send them a letter saying that some wealthy elderly relative you didn't even know of before today is sick, and wants you to move in and take care of her, and if you do, you'll inherit everything. Or Myste can have a terrible accident and die."

"Myste *will*, if we can't figure out something," Myste said darkly, but looked infinitely more relaxed. "Well, the first one won't do, because every Great Lord is going to be *here* until the wedding is over, and I want to be able to tell them I'm leaving tonight. I'd just as soon not close off all options by killing my old self, so that leaves the second. And I want it to be by letter; I don't want to take the chance on arousing any suspicion by giving them a chance to start asking questions about my story."

"The best choice, I think," he agreed. "No one is going to seriously suggest that you give up a grand inheritance in favor of a position with a theater company that doesn't even have a theater yet. And in case Clerk Myste ever has to come back to Haven, it can either be as a visit after your wealthy aunt has died, or it can turn out that the wealthy aunt wasn't as wealthy as she made herself out to be, and you are back looking for work."

"Excellent," Myste replied, and closed her eyes and sagged back against the wall, "And I have to leave immediately. Better yet, I'm already gone. My aunt sent a coach, and I left in it. I don't mind telling you, I was panicked. Especially after last night."

Alberich nodded; he could well understand Myste's concern, for last night she had gotten to copy another one of those encrypted messages from Norris to—well, whoever they were *to*.

And that gave him an idea. "Writing a letter is perfect," he said, "In fact, write *two*. One to the manager of the company and one to Norris. If you were as infatuated as he thinks you are, he'd think it strange if you didn't send him a personal good-bye. As your old friend, I'll take them both over, and you can go back up the hill as soon as you change."

"What—" Myste began, and then she nodded. "Right! So that Norris *doesn't* suspect, after last night, that I'm a spy who is running off now that I have what I need. I think I know just the tone. The brokenhearted farewell letter of the hopelessly infatuated woman who knows she had less chance with him than a lapdog, but can't bear not to tell him about how her soul will be empty forever without him. It'll take some clever writing—"

"And hold out the offer that if he is ever in—Three Rivers, I think that's far enough, and rustic enough—or if he ever finds himself down on his luck, he can call on you for anything he needs." Alberich chuckled a little as Myste made a face. "You might as well spread it on thick."

"Oh, I will." She stood up and went to the small chest that held writing materials. "This won't take very long."

And it didn't. By the time he was finished changing into his guise as the carter, she had finished both letters, sanded them to dry the ink, folded, and sealed them with a blob of candle-wax and her thumbprint. On the outside of one, she made a little drawing of a pen, and on the other, a mask. "The mask goes to Norris," she said, handing them to him.

"Good. Would it sound loutish of me to say that I am re-lieved that this is over for you? And that I have never liked having you in this position?" he asked, taking them and stow-ing them in his pouch.

"No, and not half as relieved as I am," she replied, and unexpectedly kissed him. "I make a good historian. I make a mediocre spy."

"But if it had not been for you—" He kissed her back, feel-ing warm and peculiarly *protective.* It was a very pleasant sen-sation, now that she was going to be out of danger. He had deliberately not thought about her being *in* danger while all of this was going on. It wouldn't have done any good in the first place, and in the second, well, it might have done both of them quite a bit of harm. They were, first and foremost, *Heralds.* They had duties. Only she could do what she was doing, and they both knew it.

But now he certainly knew what people meant by the phrase, "having your heart hostage to fortune." It was not a feeling that he had welcomed.

"I still make a mediocre spy," she replied. "And I hope you never need my peculiar mix of talents again."

"Oh, I shall—but I hope not as a spy." He raised an eyebrow and she flushed, but laughed. "Don't forget to tell the innkeeper before you leave the Bell where Clerk Myste is going, and that she left in a private coach for Three Rivers a candlemark ago."

"I won't," she promised. He gave her a little bow, and slipped out the back way.

The last thing he was going to do, especially after this, was to go directly from the Bell to his destination. Instead, he cut through back alleys and even through a few unfenced yards to get him to the part of town where the tanners and dyers had their workshops, before he finally headed for the inn. He never came at it from the same direction twice if he could help it, and today it would be especially important that there be no association between himself and the Companion's Bell.

Other than that his "friend" Myste had lived there, of course.

He discharged the first errand by leaving the letter in the room that served as an office, for the business manager was out on some errand or other. But as for the second—the troupe was rehearsing in the stables, and he had heard Norris' voice when he passed by. Now he went in, and waited patiently until there was a break in the action and Norris left the group that was declaiming at each other to get himself a drink of water from the barrel Alberich stood beside.

"Message for you, sir," he said, making sure that his voice was pitched low, his tone harsh, rather than high and shrill as the "scholar" had been. He thrust the folded paper at Norris, who took it automatically, but with a look of annoyance.

Still, the man did open it, and read it, his mouth twitching with amusement. Alberich was rather surprised to find himself wanting to punch that mouth and make him eat that amusement. . . .

"So, the little mouse has got herself a granary, eh?" he said, carelessly. "Well, I can hardly blame her for running off to secure it. Lads!" he called to the rest of the group, whose heads all turned in his direction. "That drab little clerk of ours has fallen into the cream! Some rich auntie's got sick, and she's run off to nurse and inherit!"

"Cor, I could do with a rich auntie," said a beardless fellow enviously.

"Hey, Norris, if she's rich enough, reckon she can afford you?" catcalled another, as Norris made a face.

"She'd have to be richer than the head of the Goldsmiths Guild," Norris scoffed back.

Throttling down the urge to throttle Norris, Alberich started to turn away to leave. Because if he stayed a moment longer, he might hear something that would make him lose his temper.

"Say, fellow, could I get you to run a similar errand for me?" Norris asked. "For, say, a silver penny?"

Alberich turned back. "Aye," he said curtly. "As long as it don't take me out'o town."

"Oh, it won't." Norris pulled an embroidered handkerchief—masculine in style, rather than feminine—from a pocket in his trews. "A friend of mine left this here by accident last night. I'd like you to take it back to him. He lives at a rather grand place on Hoberd Hill. It's the one with the wyvern gateposts; you'll know it when you see it."

Alberich took the handkerchief and the penny, successfully concealing his surprise. Because he knew that address; knew it very well indeed.

It was the location of the Rethwellan Embassy.

All the time he was on his way, he wondered what *exactly,* he would learn when he got there. He knew what the handkerchief business was about, of course, for sewing a packet of papers between two identical handkerchiefs to conceal them was an old play. The bit of fabric had been neatly folded, but he'd felt the thin papers when he put the object in the belt pouch that had lately held the letters. Myste had written these last night, he was certain of it, for the paper was very thin and light.

So this time Norris was prepared to send his—whatever he was sending—openly. Probably more instructions to the Prince on how to handle a woman. Couple that with Myste's certainty that Norris had found a "backer," and it was clear that Norris was under the impression that his job was complete. So maybe he was willing to take a risk he would not otherwise have dared.

Or perhaps he doesn't care now.

Or both. Or—one more possibility—Norris knew that his "handler" would be as busy with the wedding preparations as everyone else, and figured he could afford to be lazy this time, for he wouldn't be caught.

When Alberich reached the Embassy—he went around to the "tradesman's" entrance. Not for the likes of him, those wyvern-carved doorposts and the imposing worked-iron gate. Oh, no.

He followed a narrow passage between the walls until he came to the back of the property, where there were signs of life. Quite a bit, actually, which was hardly surprising considering that the Prince was marrying the Queen of his host country. It took Alberich a while to get the attention of someone who looked as if he was in charge of things.

"What do you want, fellow?" asked the harried-looking man in Rethwellan livery—who then interrupted himself to shout, "look, how many times must I remind you, the Prince does *not* like lilies!"

"Actor by the name of Norris sent this," he said, thrusting the folded cloth at the man, who took it, then gave it a second, startled glance. "Says someone up here left it down at his inn."

"Ah—yes. Of course." From the man's expression, Alberich

knew that they must be the Prince's own handkerchiefs—and that the man had not expected to get them in quite this way—*and* that he knew very well there was something inside them. "Thank you, my man; I'll see it gets to the Pr—owner. Ah—" he fumbled in his belt pouch, came up with a couple of coins, and thrust them at Alberich without looking at them. "Here. For your trouble."

So you think about the tip and forget about wondering why I needed to march up here to return a handkerchief. "Thankee, sir," he said, with a little bow. "I'll be off out of your way."

"Yes, yes, of— *No! No, no, no!*" The man was off, chasing down a couple of fellows with what looked like a rolled-up carpet. Alberich absented himself.

Quickly.

Because he didn't want anyone here to get a good look at him, he didn't want the man to think about questioning him, and above all, he wanted to get back to talk this over with Talamir.

For what the man had almost said was, "I'll see that it gets to the Prince."

IT would have been a satisfactory end to the tale for Selenay to have realized, at the very altar, that the Prince was a cad who was manipulating her for his own purposes. It would have been equally satisfactory for Talamir and Alberich and Myste to have presented her with the evidence they had gathered, including the decoded papers outlining—well *something* rotten—in time for her to come to her senses and send the blackguard packing.

In fact, nothing of the sort happened.

The papers were still not decoded, and even if they had been, Selenay would neither have looked at them nor believed what was in them. No one who saw her could have doubted that she was insanely, deliriously happy. The Prince appeared to hang on her every word, *she* certainly did on his. The wedding plans swiftly turned into preparations, without even an incident that could have been thought of as ill-omened, and with no more problems than any other major undertaking. In the end, of all things, it was probably the Tedrel Wars that were due the credit for organizing so much, so well, in so little time. After putting together armies and encampments and battle plans, then seeing to it that everything was smoothly executed, Selenay's people had more than enough experience to pull off a Royal Wedding in a moon.

Alberich stayed away from the Palace as much as possible; during the last week he never even left the salle. Myste brought him some meals from the Collegium kitchens, for there were no servants to be spared to bring them to him; others he simply prepared for himself. They assiduously avoided the topic of the wedding, concentrating instead on any other matters that could possibly be considered useful.

And in a curious and careful exploration of each other. In fact, with the shining example of what *not* to do so blatantly in front of them, somehow they had both come to the conclusion, simultaneously, that they ought to take a very long time in simply talking about things. It was very curious. Alberich suspected that their Companions had a hand in it. But he wasn't going to object. . . .

These long talks provided the pleasant interludes in what was otherwise a period that was not so much ridden with anxiety as resignation.

He knew that he wasn't the only one who felt this way. Most of the other Heralds that he knew, if they were not actually supposed to be taking part in the proceedings, were avoiding the Palace altogether. The feeling that they all seemed to share was most adequately described by one of the fellows from the south, who had seen some terrible mudslides when he'd been a child. "You see it start," he said, "and it's so slow, and so big, it seems impossible that it can be happening. And then you realize that it's actually impossible to stop—and impossible for you to get out of its way. And if you aren't in the path, all you can do is stand there and watch, knowing that there isn't one damn thing you can do except try and pick up the pieces when it's all over."

He had simply made sure that the Guards he trained as the Queen's bodyguards, who were suffering no such misgivings, were at their absolute peak of performance and knew in their guts as well as their heads that no matter what happened, they were always to protect Selenay from *anyone* that threatened her. Including her husband. When people came to the salle looking for a workout, if they were up to his level of expertise, he gave them one. If they were not, he found them partners, and supervised.

Then the day of the wedding arrived; it was a Collegium holiday, with all the Trainees serving as helpers, additional servitors, or actually participating with their families. It was very quiet at the salle, and Alberich made himself a solitary breakfast, then took the time to give the salle a thorough cleaning and checking. The wedding breakfast was for family, the highest ranking Court members, and the three highest ranking Heralds. After the breakfast would come the preparations. No one needed to turn up in the gardens for hours yet.

By midmorning everything was in perfect shape, and he was sitting on a bench outside, in the sun, working on mending training equipment while Kantor watched. Every so often, a bit of breeze carried a snatch of music from the Palace gardens, but otherwise he could have been all alone out here. He had thought about going down into the city, but couldn't bring himself to face the crowds partaking of the public festivities.

Finally he couldn't put it off any longer. He went back to his quarters, donned his Formal Whites, and made his way to the gardens.

Any checking of invitations was going on at the gates in the wall around the Complex itself; anyone on the grounds was already part of the festivities. There were far, far more people crowding into the gardens than Alberich felt comfortable around, and the ones who were not in formal uniforms of white, scarlet, or green were, for the most part, so laden with ornaments and so vivid with embroideries that they hurt his eyes. And the sound of dozens and dozens of people all chattering brightly at the tops of their lungs was nearly enough to drive him mad.

Fortunately for his sanity, the Heralds actually had a job to do and a place to go until the moment of the ceremony itself. The Queen's Garden was the assembly point, and he made his way there.

The first person to greet him was not, somewhat to his disappointment, Myste. It was Keren, looking unexpectedly sharp in what was clearly a brand new set of Formal Whites.

"Like me new duds?" she asked, in a heavy Evendim accent, and laughed at his expression. "Never had a set of Formals made for me before; just had a set that was a hand-me-down from the stores. Neither has Myste, actually. We're both odd sizes, and neither of us had the money for a tailor the way the highborn Heralds have. And somewhere along the line somebody figured this out in time to have some tailored up for us." She backed up a pace and looked Alberich over critically. "Now you, you've got the proper military bearing and figure. Must have been a doddle to find a set to fit you."

"I suppose," he replied, noting that her eyes were a little too bright, and figuring that Keren was using inconsequential chatter to cover her unease. "There is, it seems, some merit in being average."

"You, average? Bite your tongue," said Myste, worming her way between two Heralds Alberich didn't recognize. "You couldn't be average if you tried."

He was saved from having to answer anything by the sound of the trumpet that signaled their part of the ceremony.

Heralds at the entrance to the garden formed into a double line and began filing out; the rest of them joined one or the other line in no particular order. Somehow Alberich, Myste, and Keren ended up at the end of their lines; this didn't displease him on the whole. He did not particularly want to be near the center of attention.

The Heralds lined both sides of the path that Selenay and her wedding party would take from the door of the Palace to the bower where the Lord Patriarch waited. Alberich was actually nearest the door in his line, and Keren was directly opposite him. At a mental signal that was passed via their Companions, they smoothly and simultaneously unsheathed their swords and crossed them overhead, forming an arch of shining steel.

As the swords left their sheaths, the chattering stopped. There was a moment of absolute silence.

Then the musicians struck up the processional march, the door of the Palace opened, and the first of the ladies in attendance emerged.

There were twenty of them, strewing rose petals on the path from silver baskets. Last of all came Selenay.

He could not have told what she was wearing, though he knew that even Heralds who were female would be discussing it for days if not weeks; he *was* only a man, after all. It was white—no surprise, she *was* a Herald as well as Queen. It was made of some soft, shining stuff, overlaid with some gauzy stuff, and embroidered with gold and pearls. She was swathed in what seemed like furlongs of veil, which made it difficult to see her face; he thought, as she passed, that she looked terrifyingly happy, though. She stared straight ahead, both hands holding a huge bouquet of white flowers and ivy.

Her step was firm and brisk, and in a moment, she was past him, and all he could see was the back of her gown. It trailed for quite some distance on the ground behind her, and there were two of the little Tedrel orphans carrying her train. And one of them was that little lad in Formal Trainee Grays, an exact duplicate of Formal Whites, except done in gray. He looked terribly solemn and a little scared, but when he saw Alberich, he brightened, and Alberich raised his free hand in a formal salute that made him look still happier as he passed.

Fortunately, the children were too young to have been infected with the doubts that plagued their elders.

The Heralds held their pose until the entire wedding party had assembled at the altar. Then, with another signal passed by the Companions, they pulled their swords into a formal salute, and simultaneously sheathed them. As the musicians ended the processional with a flourish, they turned as one to face the altar.

Alberich was just as glad that all he could see was the back of the Herald in front of him. He was reminded of all of the ceremonies he had attended as a member of the Sunsguard, after he had realized how many of Vkandis Sunlord's Priests were corrupt and venial creatures with no more calling than a cat. Then, as now, he had made his mind a blank, and set his face in an expression of bland attentiveness.

The ceremony, which made reference to every deity worshiped in all of Valdemar *and* Rethwellan, was a long one. Before it was over, long before, in fact, he sensed the restlessness of some of his fellow Heralds who had not spent their youths in military training. Anyone who had been a soldier got used to standing at attention for unconscionably long periods of time. . . .

This should have been a joyful occasion. It struck him as inexpressibly sad that it should have become one that was merely endured.

At long last the final vows were spoken, somewhere up there ahead of him. The rings were exchanged, Selenay's veil lifted, the first marital kiss given.

Bells rang out all over the Complex, which signaled the bells of the city below to begin pealing. A cheer rose over the assembled crowd—

And it might have been noticed that the Heralds were not cheering, except that someone had decided that they should form the sword-arch again at full attention. Whether that someone had been Talamir or even Myste, the action made certain that no one was going to have to try and force out something he didn't really feel.

The procession came back through the arch, led by Selenay and her new Consort. He had his arm around her possessively, but Selenay was between him and Alberich, so the Weaponsmaster didn't get much of a look at him. They all retired back into the Palace to be divested of parts of their costumes—veils and trains being highly impractical for outdoor receptions and feasts—and make a first appearance on a balcony above the gardens.

Once again, the Heralds saluted—each other, this time—and sheathed their swords. But now the double line swiftly broke apart, to be absorbed into the milling crowd, some heading for the formal gardens, others on errands of their own.

Myste was one of the latter; Alberich gathered that she had some little wedding duties to attend to in the matter of protocol. He loosened his collar and, feeling heavy in spirit, swiftly separated himself from the throng and headed back down to the salle.

Once there, he stripped himself of the detested finery as quickly as he could, and donned a set of his oldest and most comfortable leathers.

:What did you have in mind for the rest of the day?: asked Kantor.

:I suppose—: he began, then heard footsteps on the path and looked up to see Elcarth approaching—with a bottle in one hand.

"We might as well stay out here," he said, by way of greeting. "The others will be here shortly."

"Others?" Alberich inquired, raising an eyebrow.

"You'll see soon enough," Elcarth told him, with a sardonic twist to his lips.

And within the candlemark, Jadus, Keren, and Ylsa all arrived bringing *their* bottles. And last of all, bringing up the rear, came Myste, with Healer Crathach, more bottles, and a hamper between them.

The last, evidently came as a surprise to the rest; Myste and Crathach set down the hamper and the Healer surveyed them all, hands on hips, as they tried not to look guilty. "Myste advised me of what you were likely to do," he said, and Alberich tried not to wince or feel betrayed. "Or shall I say, the state you were likely to get yourselves into." But Crathach was only warming up to his theme.

"Now, all things considered, I am somewhat in sympathy with the idea of finding a bit of ease in drink, at this particular time. But I told her that you were *not* going to undertake this without me. We are going to get drunk," he announced. "We are going to get *genteelly* drunk, pleasantly drunk, and we will remain in that state with careful application of food as well as drink. We will not drink ourselves sick, we will not drink ourselves stupid, or maudlin, or unconscious, and I will make personally sure that when we finally seek our beds, we will do so in a state that will permit us to sleep and wake without hangovers. Are you with me?"

They set out a kind of *al fresco* area under the trees, since none of them really wanted to be inside, and at any rate, Alberich's little sitting room would have been horribly cramped with all of them crammed into it. "I certainly don't need to be up there now. There are a couple dozen people who'll be giving me their notes," Myste said sourly, jerking her head in the direction of the gardens. "Including Talamir."

"I can't figure Grandfather on this at all," Keren replied, waving vaguely at the Palace; Alberich wondered if she'd gotten a start on all of them back in her own quarters, for although she walked and moved perfectly well, and her speech was clear, she had a glazed quality to her eyes as she passed him a full mug of wine.

"Grandfather?" he asked. Keren had her nose in her mug, so it was Myste who answered.

"Talamir is Keren's grandfather; her people marry off early, and it's usually arranged between families," Myste replied. "Since he was the only boy in his, he had to take a break during his Trainee period to go home and fulfill his—ah—obligation."

"Four breaks, to be precise," Keren added, with a smirk. "Fortunately for me, I'm half of a twin set, and traditionally only one of us had to do the duty. So when I was Chosen, that left my brother Teren as the one."

"But is Teren also not a Herald?" Alberich asked, puzzled.

"He got Chosen after he'd provided the family with a litter," Keren replied and shrugged. "What can I say? With so many close relational ties, my people have to be more pragmatic about marriage. You marry who's available, and if it turns out there's a love match, all well and good, but if not, nobody cares who you sleep with for love or pleasure as long as no one is harmed by it."

"About your grandfather—Talamir," Alberich prompted, wanting to change the subject back to its original topic.

Keren lay back on the old, worn rug she'd appropriated, and stared up at the branches waving overhead. "I don't understand why he isn't *doing* something about this," she said finally. "I mean, it's wrong, we all know in our bones that it's wrong, though—"

"We can't put a finger on why," Elcarth interrupted. "That's the reason, I think. We don't *have* a reason, and somewhere down inside, we're all uncertain that the only thing we can object to is that the Prince is an outsider."

"But none of us objected to Sendar's choice of wife," Jadus said slowly. "None of us had this feeling of wrongness about her, and she was not a Herald."

"But she was Valdemaran," said Crathach, and turned to Alberich. "And have you anything to contribute?"

Alberich shrugged. "No ForeSight, if that is what you mean," he admitted. "Only the same feeling, that this marriage will prove to be a grave mistake." He did not mention the things he had learned about the Prince's contacts with the actor, in no small part because it was not yet proven. But he exchanged a look with Myste, who gave a small shrug.

"Which could all too easily be nothing more than prejudice," Ylsa pointed out shrewdly. "He certainly has gone out of his way to be agreeable to everyone."

"Too agreeable?" Keren asked, then snorted. "As if it matters."

"Well," Myste said slowly, "it *does*. If we aren't just making a mountain out of nothing, if this is going to turn into a bad situation, then the best thing that we can do for the Queen is to support her in every way. Including keeping an eye on *him,* so that if he does something against her, or against Valdemar, we can do something about him."

"That's more or less what Grandfather said," Keren admitted. "But of all things I hate, I hate having to play a waiting game the most."

"Don't we all," Jadus replied, and that seemed all that anyone could say.

They passed the remainder of the evening assiduously avoiding the entire subject—but it was with them, as an unseen presence, a kind of specter at the feast, the whole time. Alberich left them early, feeling that not all the wine in the world could wash away his unease, and feeling wearier than he ever had in his life. He sought forgetfulness in sleep, and for the first time in his life, actually found it. Whatever was wrong, it was not immediate enough even to give him uneasy dreams.

The Collegium was back in session; things were getting back to normal again. The last of the classes was over for the day, and Alberich was working with Kimel of the Guard, while two more of Kimel's fellows waited their turn to bout with him. They were outside, on the practice grounds, rather than inside the salle—whenever possible, since the mirror incident, Alberich preferred to run practices that were, by their nature, unpredictable on the grounds outside.

Alberich caught movement on the path long before the Prince and his entourage arrived; he sensed it, identified it as "outsiders" by the lack of Whites or Guard uniforms, and dismissed it as currently unimportant, all in a heartbeat. The group of seven or eight paused a prudent distance outside the edge of the practice ground and watched.

There was some murmuring, but nothing more than that; certainly there was no hint of scorn or scoffing in the tones of the muttered conversation. Perfectly acceptable, that was. Alberich finished the bout in a draw with Kimel. He probably could have beaten him; he usually did but caution made him decide not to do so in front of outsiders. The two of them drew back and saluted, and only then did Alberich turn his attention to the audience.

It could not have been clearer that the one in the middle was Prince Karathanelan. The man was, Alberich supposed, handsome enough. He could certainly see that Selenay would have no reason to find the arrangement of his features less than pleasing. The cut and style of his clothing was a bit different from roughly half of the young men around him; the effect was of "foreignness," but was reasonably flattering. The others were apparently friends of his from Rethwellan; Alberich had heard something of them, that a number of the Prince's landless friends from Rethwellan had arrived in time for the wedding, and that Selenay had already granted them holdings of their own from unclaimed properties on the Border with Karse and Rethwellan. Alberich wished them joy of their new lands. They weren't the most prosperous even at the best of times, being mostly sheep country.

What Alberich didn't like was the posture of those around

him. These were sycophants; nothing more. They devoted themselves to pleasing someone stronger; if any of them had ever had an original thought in his head, he had quickly suppressed it. A man who surrounded himself with men like these, in Alberich's experience, was a man who had a great deal of difficulty in understanding that the world did not happen to run itself to his desire.

There were a great many Sunpriests like that. . . .

Still, the look on the face of the Prince suggested that he had some respect for Alberich's ability.

Alberich gave him a sketchy sort of salute, while the Guards gave him the full bow due to his position as Consort. He waited, resting, to see what the Prince would do or say.

Although a brief shadow passed over the Prince's face, aside from that flicker of displeasure, the Prince's expression did not change, and his voice, when he spoke, was polite and pleasant enough.

"You are the Weaponsmaster?" he asked. "The Karsite?"

"Weaponsmaster Herald Alberich," Alberich confirmed. "Karsite-born, yes, Your Highness."

The Prince looked him over carefully. "And Karsite-trained, I am told. Interesting." As he was surveying Alberich, the Herald was doing the same for him.

:There's muscle there,: he observed to Kantor.

:No matter what he's been doing since he got here, he's not soft,: Kantor agreed.

"I should like to bout with you," the Prince said abruptly.

Alberich did not bother to point out that the Prince was hardly dressed for a round of vigorous exercise; he was clearly one of those who did not trouble himself over the ruin of a suit of clothing. He merely glanced at the two Guardsmen, who quickly effaced themselves with a little nod, making it clear that they were perfectly willing to yield their time to the Prince. One of them picked up a set of practice swords and offered them to the Prince, as some of his entourage helped him to take off his elaborate doublet and relieved him of some of his jewels.

"Would Your Highness make a choice of practice weapons?" the Guardsman asked.

But the Prince waved them off. "Live steel is the choice of men," he said, with a touch of arrogance that made the Guardsman flush.

:*Stupid. Overconfident,*: Kantor said acidly.

:*Testing me,*: Alberich countered, as he took up his own sword from where it was lying with the Guardsmen's. :*And he knows that there is no way that I would dare harm him. He has me at the advantage, he thinks.*:

The question was whether that advantage was real or only in the Prince's mind. There was muscle under that silk, but somehow Alberich doubted whether the Prince had ever had a Weaponsmaster who really tested the Prince to the limits of his ability. There was too much sly arrogance there.

Nevertheless, Alberich was not at all certain that he wanted to show the Prince which of them was the superior fighter. The Prince was the enemy here, but he was an enemy who had not yet truly shown his hand. He knew far more about the Prince, he would warrant, than the Prince knew about him. So there was a distinct advantage in leaving the Prince with the impression that his expertise was less than it actually was.

All that flashed through his mind in a few moments, as he made sure that his weapons were in good condition and his own muscles thoroughly warmed up.

Then they faced off, and the combat began.

It was no real challenge; Alberich was not only able to react automatically to the Prince's blows and feints, his mind was free to *think* about what he was doing, despite the fact that they were using live steel weapons.

The Prince's style of fighting was a curious combination of aggression and stealth that told Alberich far more about the Prince's personality than the Prince would ever guess. He did not—quite—engage in the underhanded moves of the street-fighting bravos that Alberich had encountered in his own nighttime prowlings, but the things that he did left Alberich with no doubt that he was perfectly well acquainted with such tactics. And while Alberich himself made no bones about teaching his Trainees those moves, he doubted that the Prince had any notion of this. So he pretended that he had not noticed those little suggestions of a feint, and proceeded exactly as if he was fighting in the "classical" style. And he thought that he saw the Prince's lips tighten in a self-satisfied little smile when Alberich failed to respond to those feints.

So much for the testing; having established the perceived limits of Alberich's expertise, the Prince abruptly switched tactics, and went for a very aggressive, straight-on attack. Alberich kept up a purely defensive strategy, and did not respond to any of the openings that the Prince gave him. This was surely puzzling Kimel and the other Guards, but Alberich wasn't working for their benefit, only for this audience of one. The impression he wanted to leave the Prince with was that Selenay's Weaponsmaster was skilled, competent, strong, but limited in his vision—and thus, in what he was teaching the Trainees.

I'll have to have someone watch the boy when he *practices,* he realized. There was a lot he could guess from what the Prince had done so far, but if it ever truly came to a fight between the two of them, he wanted to be sure of what the Prince could and could not do.

Gradually, the Prince's style began to drift, and for a moment, there was a nagging sort of familiarity to it that Alberich could not pin down. It was flamboyant, definitely overconfident, and grew more so as time went on.

Then, as the young man committed to a traveling lunge with a shout, a lunge that would have gotten him into a world of difficulty if he had not had lightning reflexes and stupendous athletic ability, Alberich realized where he had seen this style, and *knew* who had been teaching him.

Norris.

Should I let him beat me? he wondered, then.

:I wouldn't,: Kantor cautioned. *:He might guess that you did. And besides, you want him wary of you, yet sure he can beat you if he really puts his mind to it. Wait until he gets a little careless, and take advantage in such a way that it can be a draw—there!:*

But Alberich had already spotted the momentary distraction, and drove in, so that the two of them ended up body-to-body with their blades hopelessly entangled. A draw.

And the Prince withdrew with a salute that was not—quite—mocking.

"An excellent bout, Weaponsmaster!" he said jovially, removing the practice helm and tossing it carelessly to Kimel, who caught it unthinkingly. "Thank you!"

Alberich gave him a grave bow without speaking, and as the Prince and his chattering entourage sauntered back up the path to the Palace, he disarmed and turned his attention back to his Guardsmen.

Kimel gave him a questioning look, but said nothing. The others took their lead from him. Alberich nodded.

"Sometimes," he said quietly, "it is as well, not to reveal all."

Kimel grunted and nodded. "I wondered," he said and left it at that.

But Alberich was not quite done. "I would be grateful, should anyone an eye to that man keep, should he be found in weapons' practice."

Kimel nodded again, and this time, so did the other Guardsmen. "We'll see to it, Weaponsmaster," he said, and Alberich clapped him on the shoulder with a feeling of satisfaction. The undercurrents of that simple conversation had said more than the words themselves. Kimel and the others had seen the hints of underhandedness and had not liked what they'd seen. And perhaps they had already observed some things in the Prince that made them uneasy. For the first time, Alberich had some coconspirators who were *not* among the Heralds (or in Crathach's case, the Healers).

And that would be very useful indeed.

Nevertheless, this was hardly something that needed to be pursued immediately; it was unlikely, having had this round of exercise, that the Prince would choose to go find another sparring partner and continue the practice. That was not how Alberich was reading his nature. He would bask in the admiration of his friends and sycophants, none of whom had or ever could have taken Alberich to a draw, and after he tired of the admiration, he would probably either find another subject or move into a dissection of the bout. But he would not, now that he was warmed up, follow it up with more practice. Nor would he make much of an effort to find out what his cronies knew about Alberich.

So the immediate need was to continue the practice that had been interrupted, perhaps now with an eye to drilling in the counters to those abortive moves that the Prince had displayed.

"So, Rusken," Alberich said, picking up a wooden blade and gesturing to the Guardsman, "your turn it is, I believe?"

Dutifully, though her heart was not in it, Selenay forced herself to concentrate on the dull details of the Council meeting when what she really wanted to do was to lapse into a daydream. She felt like a cat full of cream; she wanted to smile and purr and generally make a spectacle of her contentedness.

And of course, she could do nothing of the sort. She had to look grave and attentive, and pay attention to her Council debating over the details of the trade agreements with Rethwellan that were a consequence of her marriage, when she didn't want to think about trade at all, she wanted to think about tonight, and what would happen when she and Karath were alone at last.

No wonder that people would do and say nearly anything for love!

She had known that it would not be pleasurable at first; she'd had plenty of instruction from a sympathetic Healer named Anelie during the weeks before the actual wedding. But the "at first" had not been long—

Ruthlessly she dragged her attention back to the meeting, in time to nod gravely as the Councilors finally agreed on a trade package, then went on to the relatively simple matter of signing off on the grants of property that Karath had asked her to settle on his friends. It was a small enough thing. There were properties along the southern Border whose owners were no longer among the living, thanks to the Tedrel Wars, and here were landless second sons out of Rethwellan, who were eager to take responsibility for them. The Councilors had no great objections, and the papers were quickly written up.

So ended yet another tiny problem—with the income from these properties, those landless second sons would now be able to support themselves in Haven at least half of the year. Karath would have friends here. something that had worried her—though he did seem to be getting along very well with some of her own young courtiers.

That was, in fact, where he was now; out hawking with some of the young men of the Court. He had also said something about wanting to test the mettle of her famed Weaponsmaster; she hoped that Alberich would go easy on him.

The Council meeting went on for what seemed to be an interminably long time. Yet she had to admit that there was a great deal of business to take care of, as much had been set aside in the rush attending on the hasty wedding and the week she had stolen for herself thereafter. But it was concluded at last, when it appeared that if it was *not* concluded, the Councilors would be forced to do without their dinner.

And as this was not an emergency, sending the pages out for cold viands and drink and continuing the business—even if Selenay herself had been prepared to put up with it—was not to be thought of. The Councilors like their comforts, too, and were not prepared to do without them, having been forced to do so for the last months of the Tedrel Wars.

She took her leave of her Councilors, and all but flew to her quarters and the hands of her maids; as she changed her clothing and submitted to their attentions, she heard, with an internal thrill, the sounds of laughter as Karath approached the door. He and his friends must have had a grand day while she had been working. And after all, why not? He was not co-Ruler and could not be unless he was Chosen, which was looking less and less likely as time passed, so why shouldn't he be spending his time in sport? In fact, by socializing with the courtiers, he would be taking the burden from her of doing the same.

"Ho, Selenay!" he cried, bursting through the door, waving some of his friends, who laughingly tried to follow, back into the hall. "I have met your Weaponsmaster, and tried his blade!"

She leaped up from her seat, as the maid who had been fixing her hair waved her hands in fruitless protest. He enfolded her in his arms and kissed her; her lips parted beneath his and his tongue teased hers as she tasted the salt on his mouth.

She felt herself melting, as always; it was he who pulled away first. "And what came of that, my Prince?" she asked breathlessly.

"Oh," Karath said carelessly, "I think, had I exerted myself, I could have taken him. But he is a fine swordsman, conservative, but fine. I am sure he is a good Weaponsmaster."

Selenay almost said something then, for that certainly did

not sound like Alberich—Alberich, conservative?—but then she thought better of it. Alberich was certainly doing *her* a favor, letting Karath think himself the finer fighter, and where was the harm in that? In fact, now that she came to think of it, she felt a surge of warmth toward dour Alberich, that he would compromise his own reputation in order to make Karath feel the superior.

So she resolved not to say anything about it, she simply smiled and said, "I doubt it not," and let him lead her in to dinner.

The contest turned out to be something of a topic of conversation among Karath and his friends, with a great deal of gesturing and boasting. She discovered, with a flush of pride, that Karath was very much considered to be the superior swordsman among his cronies, and she thought, given the apparent sincerity of their talk, that this was not just flattery. That he had fought Alberich to a deadlock was considered to be amazing by those of his friends who were Valdemaran, and their admiration was considerable. Karath warmed under their regard, and expanded on the theme, describing other bouts he was particularly proud of. She smiled and paid little attention to the chatter, which sounded to her ears very like that of the younger Trainees when they first began to gain some success in arms, and concentrated instead on merely watching him. He was hardly insensible of her regard, and looked as if it gave him a great deal of pleasure.

Bless him—let him preen and strut a little! He had never been forced to *use* that sword of his, and if she had her way, he never would. It was all still a game to him, and not the deadly business that she knew it was; she took great pleasure in that.

From dinner, the Court went out into the gardens, where there was music and some simple dancing. He remained assiduously at her side, showing by means of a smile or a casual, whispered remark that he was as eager to withdraw as she was. But of course, this sort of thing was as much of a duty as the Council sessions, and she carefully exchanged pleasantries and conversation with, not only the Rethwellan Ambassador, but all the other notables present.

It did give her a great deal of pleasure, however, to be able to tell Karath's friends over the course of the evening, that they were to receive official word of their grants from the Council on the morrow. She loved the way that Karath smiled and accepted their effusive thanks graciously.

Finally, it seemed that to her that they had distributed their attention enough for one evening, and when she whispered to Karath, "My lord, shall we withdraw?" he smiled knowingly and nodded.

It was not the custom in Valdemar, much to her relief, for the Monarch to leave a social gathering with any fanfare. So they simply drifted off under the ever-watchful eyes of her Guards, and took the private entrance back into the Royal Suite.

Once there, her maids descended on her like a swarm of ants, while he sauntered off to his dressing room to the like attentions of his servants. The days were long gone when she could dress and undress herself; being Queen apparently meant wearing gowns that it was impossible to get into or out of without help. But once her maids had taken down her hair and gotten her stripped down to her shift, she dismissed them all, slipped into a silken bed gown, and with a shiver of anticipation, got into bed to await Karath.

He was not long in coming. With a knowing grin when he saw her waiting for him, he extinguished the last candle, and she felt the mattress take his weight in the sudden darkness.

In the next moment, he had slipped the gown from her shoulders, and his lips were on hers, insistently; his tongue probing at her mouth. Her lips opened immediately as she felt her skin flush, and for a moment, his hands cupped the sides of her face as his tongue teased hers.

But then his hands were moving lower, caressingly, clever fingers making her skin tingle, and when his hands reached her breasts, she gasped at the sensations he awoke in her body, and with that now-familiar feeling of melting, lay back into the softness of the mattress.

As one hand slipped still lower, his mouth took over where his hands had been, evoking still more intoxicating thrills of pleasure, and she moaned softly under his caresses. By this time, she was nearly mindless, all of her attention bound up in the sensations that he was creating in her body, feeling herself on fire with pleasure and desire and an urgency driving her towards that peak she now not only knew existed, but which had become so very necessary to her life.

So that, when he finally took her, she was all animal, crying out as she raced toward the goal, nothing else mattering in all the world but their bodies moving together to that moment when she exploded in pleasure, convulsed and paralyzed at the same time, a cry escaping from her that she could not have stopped and didn't want to.

And before she had fallen from that pinnacle of sensation, he had come to his own shuddering climax, so that they fell together, tangled in sweat-gleaming limbs, into dreamy, euphoric lassitude, and then, when he had pulled the covers over them both, sleep.

18

Karath was eating and talking at the same time, and it always amazed Selenay that he managed to eat as much as he did and still look trim and fit. At the moment, he was eating his way through the plate of breakfast pastries like a fire going through dry timber. Selenay was just as happy to let him have all of them to himself; a little dry toast and some tea was all that she could bear to stomach at the moment, and her stomach was not altogether pleased about *that*. And alas, this was no mere illness, which she could expect to recover from in a day or so. Oh, no.

She had, somewhat to her dismay, discovered that eternal truth that most women learn, soon or late. The pleasures of the bedroom, undertaken without precautions, end in babies. Three days of discovering that she could not rise in the morning without recourse to a basin had told her that much.

Of course, in her case, the pleasures of the bedroom were *supposed* to end in babies, and in fact, were required to end in babies. As many as possible, in fact—but at least the typical "heir and a spare," so that there were two chances of being Chosen. That was, after all, what her Council had been nattering about for *months*—why they'd wanted so desperately to find her a husband in the first place. When she let them know—well, they'd be thrilled. At least, right up until the moment that it occurred to them that there was some risk in childbearing. Not that she was worried; she was in the best of health and positively surrounded by Healers. She'd been in a lot more danger of injury watching a Hurlee game.

I just didn't think it would happen so quickly, she thought mournfully, and told her stomach sternly to behave itself while Karath went on with his meal and his one-sided conversation, utterly oblivious to her discomfort. Of course, the Healers would have things that could help in this case—but that would mean going to the Healers, and then they would know she was pregnant, and then *everyone* would know she was pregnant, and that would open up an entirely new set of things for the Council to natter at her about—

Yet another worry. Why was it that she always seemed to add concerns, and never seemed to actually get rid of any?

Karath's chattering, usually about things that interested her only vaguely, like hawking and the recent exploits of his friends, tended to pass through her head at the best of times like an express coach, without stopping to unload any information. This morning, as preoccupied as she was with keeping her scant breakfast down, she almost missed what he was saying entirely. Except that one word caught her distracted attention, forcing her to bring her mind back to the breakfast table, and she blinked and finally *looked* at him.

"Forgive me—I was woolgathering for a moment," she said apologetically. "What was it you just said?"

He pouted a little. He pouted, as he did everything, beautifully. It was distinctly unfair. If she'd been able to pout that prettily, she would never have to fight her Council.

"Sometimes I wonder if you ever hear anything I say in

the morning," he complained. "You always seem distracted at breakfast. I *said*, I think I'd like to have that handsome black stallion that just came into the Royal Stables as our wedding gift from Lord Ashkevron for my coronation mount."

Coronation mount? Hadn't he been paying attention at all?

"I thought that was what you said," she replied, choosing her words with great care. "You can certainly have the stallion all to yourself since *I* have no use for him, but Karath, I thought it had been explained that there won't be a coronation for you. You can't be crowned King of Valdemar."

"Why not?" he asked, pouting even more, though his eyes were getting stormy. "Don't you Valdemarans crown your Kings in a public ceremony?"

"We do." She felt a cold nausea that had nothing to do with pregnancy as she realized that they were about to have their first fight. Good gods—she *knew* all this had been explained to him! It had been in the marriage contract! Hadn't he even read it? "But you can't be King."

His mouth suddenly went from a pout to a hard, angry line. "Why not?" he asked tightly. "You are the ruler here. Your Council doesn't have any power except to advise you. I've seen what you can do when you want to. You've handed out properties and titles to anyone you choose without even *telling* them. You can make me King if you wanted to. You can tell your Council, just like you told them that you were going to marry me."

"No, I can't," she said, the nausea rising into her throat. "And it has nothing to do with the Council. It's the law that's keeping you from it, and not even the Queen is above the law. You *can't* be King, because you aren't a Herald. Only a Herald can be a King or a Queen in Valdemar."

He snorted with exasperation, as if he suspected she was prevaricating. "Then make me a Herald!" he exclaimed angrily. "If that is all that it takes, just make me a Herald and get it over with! I don't know why you haven't bothered to do it already!"

"I can't *make* you a Herald!" she replied, now getting a little angry herself. Hadn't he listened to anything anyone had told him since he had arrived here? Or did he only listen when what he heard was what he wanted to hear? "Heralds aren't made, they're Chosen."

"Then *Choose*—" he began, but she interrupted him.

"They aren't Chosen by a person, they're Chosen by their Companion," she told him flatly, a chill over her words that he seemed oblivious to. "So you can't be a Herald because none of them have Chosen you." She didn't bother to add that he would then have to go through the Collegium like anyone else before he became a full Herald and could be crowned co-Consort and King. If he really had ignored something so fundamental as needing to be a Herald before becoming a King, he would never grasp having to be schooled for four or more years first.

"You're telling me," he said, slowly and incredulously, "that the reason I can't be King is because I don't have a white horse?"

"They aren't horses," she began, but he was already pushing away from the table.

"There must be fifty or a hundred of those beasts in that field next to the Palace," he said, a dangerous edge to his voice. "They can't all belong to somebody. We'll see about this nonsense."

He stalked out, and she *might* have tried to stop him—except at that moment she lost her battle with her stomach, and with that, her will to try to break him of his delusions gently evaporated.

Let him stand around in Companion's Field with a carrot in his hand for the rest of the day, if he elected to. He'd only look silly, and maybe when he was tired, hot, and ready to come back to the Palace he'd be more reasonable.

:Chosen—: Kantor said, just as Alberich was correcting one of the younger Trainees' aim with his bow, nudging his feet into a better stance, showing him how to aim along the shaft, then elevate to allow for the arrow dropping in flight. *:I don't want to interrupt you, but there is about to be something of a crisis. And we are the closest—we, and Keren and Dantris, of course—to the situation.:*

Calmly, Alberich stepped back and let the Trainee shoot, not changing his expression by a hair. *:What crisis? What situation?:*

:Prince Karathanelan is coming to Companion's Field; he has three friends, they are all mounted, and they all have ropes. He thinks he's going to catch and break a Companion so he can be made co-Ruler. Evidently when Selenay convinced him just now that he couldn't be crowned unless he was a Herald, he put his own interpretation on being Chosen.:

Hardly surprising, if he was the sort of Prince that Alberich thought he was.

The arrow hit the target this time, at least, which was an improvement over the Trainee's last several shots. *:I fail to see the crisis. Surely you aren't going to try to tell me that he can catch one of you if you don't want to be caught?:* It wasn't as if the Prince could pin a Companion in a corner; the fence around the Field was mostly to keep people out, not Companions in. In fact, Alberich would not have put it past a Companion to leap the wall around the Complex, at need.

And besides, that, any Companion in danger of being caught against his will would be instantly rescued by the entire herd. No horse would stand there and face a charging Companion herd, no matter what his rider wanted.

:Of course not,: Kantor replied, now coming into view through the trees, trotting toward him. *:But I believe Caryo intends to be caught, so she can kick the fewmets out of him.*

And other than you and I and Keren and Dantris, I think the rest are inclined to let her have her way. She has put up with a great deal since he arrived here, and done without much of the company and attention of her Chosen.:

:*Ah.:* That put an entirely different complexion on things. At the least, if the Prince was damaged, Selenay would be distressed. If he was embarrassed, he'd make her miserable. And even if Caryo was not the sort to have murder on her mind, accidents could happen. He didn't bother to ask if the other Companions had tried to reason with her; Caryo was as stubborn as any Companion born, and as Kantor had pointed out, she'd had to put up with a lot of aggravation since Selenay met the Prince. This was one insult too many. "Students!" he said aloud, as Kantor reached him. "Some small trouble there is that I must attend. Trainee Telbren, you are in charge." And as he finished the sentence, Kantor stood steady and he vaulted onto Kantor's bare back. As soon as he had his balance, the Companion whirled on his rear legs and broke into a gallop. Which *looked* like more of an impressive feat of horsemanship than it actually was; Companions were legendary for their ability to keep their Chosen in the seat.

They were also legendary for their speed, but as they came out of the trees, bearing down on four strangers mounted on mere horses, he saw it was already too late. There was Caryo, neatly "caught," standing meekly with four ropes and a saddle and bridle on her—

His heart sank. *Oh, no. They used a horse-bridle.* If there had been *any* chance that the Prince might be forgiven his *faux pas* by the other Companions, given that Caryo was burning to teach him a lesson, it had just flown swiftly away. No Companion would ever forgive the insult of having a bit stuffed into his or her mouth, nor forgive the insult to a fellow Companion.

—and there was the Prince, down off his horse and approaching her with a swagger, grabbing the reins and preparing to mount.

"Highness!" he shouted, as a second white streak that could only be Keren and Dantris came into sight from the direction of the riding arena. "Highness, *look out—*"

But it was far, far, too late.

If he had blinked, he would have missed it. As it was, in one way, he was glad he had not, though in another, he *wished* he had.

From meek, docile, and trussed up, Caryo turned into a whirling, spinning—and quite deadly, if she chose—fury. In that brief moment, the merest breath, she expertly yanked three of the four ropes out of the hands of their holders and freed herself from their control, probably leaving the palms of those hands bloody and torn in the process, though they were in too much shock to register the pain immediately. The fourth rope was in the Prince's hands, and instead of ripping it out of his hands, she wound it around herself as she whirled and used it to pull him in closer, he being not bright enough to *let go*—

—and as soon as he was in range, both hind feet lashed out in a precisely calculated kick—

—which landed right in the Prince's midsection. He went flying backward through the air, most spectacularly.

Caryo rid herself of all four ropes, though he could not make out how she did it. She simply seemed to give a kind of shrug, and they loosened and fell off, and she stepped out of the loops lying on the ground. She spit out the bit, shrugged off the bridle as easily as she had the ropes, then she bucked off the saddle and kicked it after the Prince, and went galloping away, head high, tail flagged. Evidently, with the probable intervention of two Heralds and their Companions at hand, she considered that the single kick was enough.

Behind her, three young courtiers were bent over their hands and their saddle-bows, cursing and gasping. The Prince was on the ground, also gasping; not a surprise, given that the hammer blow of hooves to his gut must have driven every bit of air that had been in his lungs out of them. But he could have had broken ribs—

:He doesn't,: Kantor said. *:Though he'll have black-and-blue hoofprints on his belly for days. Caryo didn't actually kick him; it was more like a calculated and very powerful shove.:*

Keren got to the Prince first; rolled him on his side, then slammed him across the back until he could breathe again, then helped him to his feet, talking the whole time. Alberich reached them just in time to hear her finish.

"—terrible insult. Like putting a slave collar around *your* neck, Highness," she said. Alberich could tell, though, that the Prince wasn't listening. He was red-faced now, and it was with anger.

"I will hunt that beast down this moment, and I don't care who it belongs to," he said between clenched teeth. "And I will *destroy* it."

Enough was enough. Alberich seized both his shoulders, turned him so that he was looking right into Alberich's eyes, and shook him twice. Hard. Like a wolf with a snake. "Then on trial for *murder* and *treason* you will be, and pay for both with your life!" he rasped harshly. "To kill a Companion is *murder* by Valdemaran law. To kill the Queen's Companion, *treason.* Do not force your bride to hang you, Prince, for she will."

Evidently Alberich's words penetrated, for the Prince gaped at him in shock.

"For a *horse?*"

"For a *Companion.*" Blessed Sunlord, just how stupid was this fool? "They—are—not—horses," he continued, emphasizing each word with a hard shake. "No matter what your eyes tell you. Your eyes lie." He had done some reading since the Prince arrived, on Myste's insistence, and now he was glad that he had. "Have you broken ribs? A broken pelvis? No. Because it was a Companion that kicked you—shoved you with her hooves, rather—and not a horse. Think! Had it been a *horse* that had done this, would you not in blood and broken bones be lying? In your own land, lives the Shin'a'in Tarma—so I know that you know of this. The Companion is like to her *kyree* Warrl. Be grateful she did no more than kick you for your insults."

He saw the Prince's eyes widen, then narrow again, at the comparison. He heard also heard Kantor's snort of disgust at being compared to a *kyree*. But Kantor knew better than to object, since at least now the Prince had some basis for comparison that he *might* believe.

"So—" Karathanelan got out around clenched teeth, "How do I get one of them to let me ride it?"

"Choose you, you mean?" Alberich replied, letting go of the young man's shoulders. "After this?" He shook his head, and wondered at the monumental hubris that would permit the Prince to even think of such a thing. He considered trying to explain that it *might* happen—if the Prince were to have such a complete change of character as to be a different person. He opted for the simpler choice, for Karathanelan would never believe that he needed to change his character. "After such an insult to all Companions as this—never. Not even if the Queen was to come here and beg them upon her knees."

And satisfied at least that the fool was in no condition to try any more foolishness, he gave the merest sketch of a bow, and turned on his heel. Two steps took him to Kantor, and he mounted and rode off. There were more important matters to tend to than the petulant Prince.

At least for now.

Myste was laughing so hard that there were actually tears coming from the corners of her eyes, and her lenses fogged. "Oh, gods," she gasped. "Oh, *gods*. I wish I'd seen it!" She mimed the Prince's ungraceful arc through the air with one hand. *"Eeeeeeeeee—thump!* Oh, I wish I'd seen it!"

"No, you don't," Alberich contradicted her sourly. "The Prince has a good memory, and although he probably will not dare to touch another Companion, he is *going* to find a target for his anger. More than one, I suspect; anyone who actually witnessed his disgrace is going to find themselves on his short list of people he'll mark for punishment and revenge. With his reputation and manliness so utterly refuted, he will want to make someone pay."

"And what could he do to a Herald?" Myste scoffed.

"I don't know," he replied. "And that is what concerns me. He has already tried to have me dismissed from my post as Weaponsmaster today—for 'putting violent hands on a Prince of the Blood,' if you please. It was only the reaction of the Council to that statement that persuaded him that I am out of his reach for now." He shook his head. "Kyril stood up and said that he was lucky I had not finished the task Caryo started. And that for laying violent hands on a Companion, *he* could have found himself in the Palace dungeons."

"The Palace doesn't have dungeons," Myste said without thinking.

"I know that, and you do, but the Prince apparently does not." Alberich shrugged. "That is not relevant. The point is, he has already sent his three 'friends' packing. He tried to disgrace me. Keren has been warned, and is going to try to stay out of his sight." He grimaced. "Poor Selenay."

"Why 'poor Selenay?'" Myste asked, surprised.

"Caryo is *her* Companion," he reminded her. "I do not think that he will harm her physically, but there are other ways he can make her unhappy." Many other ways, actually. He wondered how Caryo had broken the news to Selenay, for surely she would not have waited for the Prince to tell his version of the tale first.

She shrugged. "I suspect that after he hears the news, he won't be inclined to take any of his pique out on her. If he wants a validation for his masculinity, he'll surely have it."

"The news?" He looked at her blankly. "What news?"

"She's going to have a baby, of course." Myste *tsk*ed. "Men. I suppose you think it isn't important."

But her words made his blood run cold, as he remembered that overheard conversation with Norris. "On the contrary," he said. "It is very important. If what we suspect about the Prince is, in fact, true—"

Myste lost her sarcastic smugness, and went a little pale. "I'd forgotten about that. Once the baby's born, if he can't be King—"

"—there is nothing in the laws of Valdemar that say that a Regent must be a Herald," Alberich finished grimly for her. "And even now you would find it difficult to persuade most of the members of the Council that he should not be Regent for his own child should something happen to Selenay."

Selenay had thought she was prepared for an unpleasant time with her husband—insofar as it was possible to be prepared, after getting a shock like that from Caryo. Bless her heart, Caryo had *not* said, "I told you so," she had only given the bald facts of the matter, and all she said in her own defense was, :*I was afraid if he managed to catch one of the youngsters, someone would have gotten seriously injured before it was over. And I admit, I wanted to put him in his place. I didn't exactly kick him, though, Selenay. There's nothing broken but his pride.*:

She could scarcely countenance, not only that he had tried to force a Companion to his will, but that he had done so in the mistaken belief that he would then be a Herald and could be crowned King and co-Ruler. It was as if every lesson in Valdemaran law that he had been given had soared over his head. Hadn't he even bothered to listen a little?

Apparently, it was only to what he wanted to hear.

When Caryo first told her, she was so furious she could not even see, and had to sit down as her knees went weak. Rage and an empty stomach do not combine well.

She raged inwardly at him, nevertheless. How *dared* he lay violent hands on a Companion? How *dared* he think that such a despicable act would actually gain him the Crown? If he had come to her at that moment, she might have snatched up some old sword hanging on the wall and beaten him with the flat of it.

But as a little time passed, she regained control over her temper. Though she was still going to give him a lashing, it would be with her tongue and not a whip or a sword blade. And she had the first phrase ready on the tip of her tongue when he finally appeared.

She had thought that after such a monumental act of stupidity, Karath would have come to her contrite and looking for forgiveness. In fact, she could not imagine any other scenario.

Instead, he burst in through the door, slammed it behind him, and proceeded to shout at her, quite as if she were somehow to blame for all this, and as if this business of not being made her co-Ruler was somehow her fault, something she had concocted to keep him from his rightful place, and as if the debacle with Caryo had been something that she had planned to humiliate him.

And that made her furious all over again.

His ranting was like a spark in dry grass; she pounced on the first available pause for breath, and *then* she made her riposte.

"If you think I'm going to take your side in this, you are very much mistaken, Karath. *I* told you—and if I told you once about how things are here, I told you a dozen times!" Selenay shouted at the angry face of her husband. "The *Council* told you! Your own *Ambassador* told you! For the gods' sake, Karath, it was *in the marriage contract* that you signed! In *both* languages! Just how *stupid* are you to have missed it that many times?"

She knew the moment that the words left her mouth that they were the wrong thing to say, but she couldn't help it. Just how stupid *was* he? Or did he live in some fantasy world where because he wanted something, it would simply be given to him?

Well, maybe that was the way things had been back in Rethwellan, but that wasn't the way it was in Valdemar.

"Stupid enough to have wedded *you!*" he shouted back, "Such a fine bargain I have made for myself! I have wedded no power, no responsibility, and no rank but that which I was born with! And for this, I have what? A wife with neither the face nor the form to stand out in a crowd—with common tastes and common, petty morals, a little girl who thinks more of her horse than of her husband! For this bargain, I take a cold, naive, ignorant *virgin* who grasps her little power as a miser does gold, who does not even know how to properly pleasure a man!" And before she could retort, he stormed out, and before the astonished eyes of her Guards, who had no doubt heard it all, he slammed the door behind him, leaving her feeling as if he had dealt her a blow.

She was left staring at the door he slammed behind him, torn between wanting to throw herself to the ground, weeping, and wanting to strangle him.

The latter won out, but not by much, and as she paced back and forth across her sitting room, there were tears streaking her cheeks as well as anger making her clench her jaw until it ached.

Her heart ached, too; ached bitterly, for every insult he had thrown at her felt like a blow.

She managed to get some control over herself in order to put herself into the hands of her maids; tonight she took extra care with her appearance, for surely he who was so conscious of the trappings of status would not absent himself from din-

ner where he sat at her right hand. Common, was she? She
would show him. She would make him mad to take her in his
arms again, and she would, by the gods, make him *beg* for the
privilege. And apologize, not only to her, but to Caryo.

But the chair at her right remained empty all evening.

She put on a good face, of course, replying lightly to Talamir's query that he was probably passing the time with the
friends who had come up from Rethwellan, to whom she had
given titles and property. "They are probably celebrating, now
that it is official," she said, with a false lightness. "And after
all, Talamir, you can hardly expect a young man to hover over
his wife every moment of the day! At some point every young
man *I* have ever known, be he never so devoted, has longed
for the company of his old friends!" Her laugh sounded hollow
to her own ears, but Talamir made no sign that he had noticed
her unhappiness. "Just because we are wedded, this does not
mean that we are joined at the hip!"

"No, of course not," Talamir agreed, and nothing more was
said on the subject in her hearing.

But as the dinner wore on, she was able to think less and
less clearly. By the time the sweetmeats were served, *she*
would almost have been ready to ask forgiveness of *him* if it
would put things back the way they had been yesterday. She
kept listening, dreading that she would hear something about
the debacle in Companion's Field, but evidently no one was
going to talk about it where she could overhear.

Maybe that was why he wasn't here! He didn't want to
have to answer any questions about what he'd done; he didn't
want to have to explain himself. . . .

She felt a great surge of relief, then, and was able to talk
normally, able to think of something besides wondering where
he was. She was still angry at him, especially for the cruel
things he had said to her, but she was ready to forgive him, so
long as he asked for forgiveness.

Except that he did not appear in their quarters after dinner.

Tonight she had retired to her suite as soon as dinner was over, letting her Court amuse itself for a change.

And he did not appear as the hour grew later and later; she filled the time with attending to her private correspondence, something she had neglected badly over the past fortnight or two. But her heart was not in it, and time after time, she had to throw out a letter that was ruined by tears falling on it.

He had not come when her maids arrived to help her prepare for bed, and he still had not arrived when they blew out the candles, leaving her alone in the dark in that great bed.

And when she realized that he wasn't *going* to come, the anger ran out of her.

What was wrong? How could he not understand, at least by now, how she was powerless in the face of the law? How could he not realize by now the enormity of the insult he had given Caryo? Of course he had been angry, but how could he have flung those horrible insults at her? She thought he had *understood* her, as no one had ever understood her before. Hadn't they shared all those long conversations about how miserable it was to be a child of royal birth? Hadn't he commiserated with her about it as no one else had ever done before? Hadn't he told her how he had dreamed of finding someone he could care for as well as merely marry for the sake of an alliance, and had given it up as an idle dream until he met her? How many times had he sworn that to her? How many times had he shared his dreams with her, and how many times had she discovered to her joy that they were the same as hers?

What had gone wrong? How could he have changed so? What had she done to make him turn away from her?

She had no answers for any of this, and she waited, fruitlessly, in her cold, lonely bed, until at last she cried herself to sleep.

Alberich contemplated the glass image of the Sunlord—defined at the moment by the lines of leading rather than the colors of the glass—and tried to think of all of the possible paths that the Prince might take after this afternoon.

The most obvious, of course, was the most direct; wait until the baby was born, and engineer an "accident" that would kill or incapacitate Selenay. There was no law in Valdemar that the Regent had to be a Herald; as Regent, it was even possible that he would have the same power as the Monarch, just without the title.

But that was only one of a number of courses he could take—

:Chosen, the Royal Guard Kimel is coming down the path,: Kantor warned, breaking into his train of thought. :I can't imagine he'd be coming to see anyone but you at this time of night.:

Forewarned, Alberich got up to meet the young man as soon as he entered the salle, greeting him at the door. But it wasn't until he got to Alberich's private quarters that the Herald could see his expression, and it was both grim and troubled.

"Master Alberich," the young man said, when he'd taken the proffered seat and been offered, and refused, any refreshment. "I overheard a conversation this evening that—that I do not much like."

"Did you?" Alberich replied noncommittally.

The Guard nodded. "It was during the hour of dinner for the Court. I was on duty when I heard two voices raised in argument on the other side of the wall where I was standing—I happened to be in the gardens, and there was an open window right above my head."

"Assume, I must, that you overheard something that might of importance be?" Alberich prompted.

"Two men arguing," Kimel replied. "And one of them was the Prince." He coughed. "I knew about what happened this afternoon, and I guess he'd gone to someone to complain about it." He frowned as he concentrated on what he was going to say. "I didn't recognize the voice, but he got not much sympathy. In fact, the person he was talking to gave him a regular dressing-down about it. The man said that the Prince was on the verge of 'spoiling it all,' though he didn't say what 'it' was."

"Go on," Alberich told him. Surely there was more to this story!

"Well, then the Prince said something about the unfairness of it all, and the other man told him to be patient, and that Selenay was—" here Kimel blushed, "—well, anyway, what he went on to say was 'once the child is born, there is no law preventing you from becoming Regent, when something happens to Selenay. All you have to do is to be patient.' And the Prince muttered something, and the man laughed, and they all went out of the room."

So. There it was. "You may have done Her Majesty a great service, Kimel," Alberich said gravely.

"I am in a position to do more," the young Guard replied, to Alberich's surprise. "So long as I wear my uniform, and look as if I am guarding *something,* no one ever notices me. I could make sure that if I am not on duty elsewhere, I can follow the Prince all over the grounds of the Palace. Perhaps I might discover who he was speaking with."

"If you did, invaluable, it would be," Alberich said, hardly able to believe the luck.

"Then I will." That seemed to be all that Kimel felt urged to say on the matter; he remained a little longer, but not much, and excused himself.

:Well?: he said to Kantor when the young man was gone.

:I think we've gotten an ally, who will at least be watching out for Selenay. I don't know how useful what he learns or overhears will be.:

:It's better than nothing, which was all we had,: Alberich pointed out.

:Yes, Chosen. It is at that.:

EVERYONE knew the obvious that night—that the Prince had not attended the Queen at dinner. By morning, though, there was a better bit of gossip to take its place—that the Prince had not spent the night with the Queen, nor even (it was said) in the Palace.

By breakfast, that gossip had inflated further, with the addition that the Prince had returned at last, from somewhere outside the Palace walls. And he had gone to his own suite, not the Queen's.

Valdemaran royal marriages, like most royal marriages, were not always for love. Hence, the Consort always had his (or her) own suite of rooms within the larger Royal Suite. It had its own entrance; the one who occupied it could come and go without disturbing the Monarch. It would not be the first time that the Monarch's spouse had elected to take up residence in his own private space. The trouble was, this defection of the Prince would have gone unnoticed except that this was supposed to have been a love match. Selenay herself had virtually bullied the marriage through the Council. And now, it seemed, it was already falling apart.

So tongues were wagging from the first, and Alberich did not think it possible that Selenay was unaware of the gossip. She'd have to be blind and deaf, and she was neither. It made him sick inside to think how unhappy she must be, but there was little he could do about it.

She was paying a heavy price for her infatuation; this was going to be a very expensive lesson in thinking things through. However unhappy the Prince was with his wife and his situation, Alberich doubted that Karathanelan was going to relinquish what he *did* have willingly, once he realized the alternatives. Even if Selenay became *so* unhappy as to wish to dissolve the marriage, such a move could not be made without the agreement of the other party—and the Prince would never agree.

No, unless the Prince actually committed an overt act of treason, Selenay was stuck with her bad bargain. And if she was unhappy now, when the last of the infatuation wore off, she was going to be even less happy.

Alberich wished there was something he could do, but he knew that, in this case, there really was nothing. He was entirely the wrong person for her to confide in on two counts. First, the task required someone who was a close friend, which he was not—someone, perhaps, that was Selenay's yearmate at the Collegium. Second, his sex was against him; he knew instinctively that to become a confidant and adviser in this situation, a man just would not do.

Which, unfortunately, left Talamir out of the running as well. Perhaps she was confiding in her Companion; perhaps at this point Caryo was about the only one she could confide in. He hoped that Caryo was wise enough to know not to criticize the Prince herself at this point—because Selenay would feel impelled to defend him, and that would only prolong the agony, so to speak.

The Prince continued to shun the company of his Queen; one or two days stretched into a week with no sign of him in or around the Palace from the time he rose until the time— which was usually very late—he returned from wherever he had just spent his day. Alberich grew increasingly weary of the words, "They say—" as the days passed. But not weary enough not to listen, for there were several nuggets of information to be mined from the dross.

One of them sent him out in disguise one evening, to an establishment known as "The Silver Horn," which catered to "the discriminating tastes of gentlemen." Or at least, it catered to those with money who cared to call themselves gentlemen; certainly you could find both the highborn and the monied lowborn there, although there were special places within the establishment to which money alone did not guarantee entrance. Alberich already had a persona established here, that of an elderly, semideaf gentleman with a substantial fortune— elderly, because that way he would not be looked on askance for not making use of the opulent rooms up the parlor stair and the ladies who inhabited those rooms, as jewels graced a setting. Alberich would, every now and then, dodder in, partake of a splendid meal, and sit enjoying the entertainments on offer in the more public rooms—generally scantily clad young ladies singing or dancing, though it was said that they performed far more interesting maneuvers elsewhere in the establishment—until he apparently nodded off. Then, if he had overheard nothing of importance, he would "wake," and dodder off again. He found the place far more useful than the Court for obtaining information about the goings-on of the highborn.

The Horn provided something of an educational tradition with the aristocracy. Young men were often brought here by brothers or even fathers for their first (so far as the parent knew) sexual experiences. Then, as they grew older, they would come here by themselves or with friends to make a night of it—fine meals, gambling, entertainment, and then a romp. It wasn't cheap—but Alberich wasn't paying for this out of his own pocket. And there were times when he felt as if, given the number of candlemarks he had spent in the Broken Arms and other, even fouler dens, lurking on street corners in the freezing dark, getting soaked with rain or baking in the hot sun, that he had earned an occasional evening in the Horn. Even if all he did was have a meal and lurk.

He had heard that friends of the Prince were going to introduce him to the pleasures of the Horn, and as a consequence both of that, and of an internal prodding too vague to really be called ForeSight, after the third night in which the Prince did not appear, Alberich began haunting the Horn nightly. He was a forgettable enough character that no one really noticed. And the Prince did, indeed, appear that first night, and every night subsequent.

Unfortunately, to Alberich's vast disappointment, the Prince kept himself to the "exclusive" areas for the most part, and Alberich never saw more of him than his back as he swaggered through the public rooms and into the private areas.

It seemed, after three nights, that Alberich was wasting his time, that all the Prince was doing was roistering. Fine, he *could* bring this to Selenay, but what good would it do?

Yet that vague prodding only strengthened as the nights went on, and although he never got a glimpse of ForeSight, after the fourth night he *knew*, with absolute certainty, that if he kept up his watch, something significant would happen.

And then, on the seventh night, it was not the Prince who became the center of attention when he walked in the door.

It was the actor, Norris. And with him was young Devlin.

Alberich was in a shadowy corner, slumped in one of the Horn's supremely comfortable chairs, fingers interlaced over his "paunch," chin on his chest, seeming to doze. This time he had chosen a seat *because* of the feeling that this was where he needed to be—again, it was a feeling and not a vision, nothing concrete, but he was certain that it was linked to his ForeSight, and he acted on it. One of the young ladies had made certain to tuck a cushion on either side of him so that he wouldn't put a crick in his neck; he had muttered vague and sleepy thanks, and she had giggled and left him alone. Now everyone seemed to have forgotten he was there, which gave him ample opportunity to watch the room from mostly-closed eyes.

When Myste had made absented herself from the theater, Alberich had continued to keep an eye on the actor at a distance, through other contacts, but there did not seem to be any sign of further chicanery. In fact, Norris was so busy, Alberich couldn't see how he managed to find the time to sleep, much less write letters and find ways to pass them to anyone. In addition to rehearsing and performing, he spent every waking moment at the site of his new theater, obsessing over details and virtually flogging the workers into going faster.

But here he was, and as soon as they saw him, those young ladies who were not otherwise occupied left what they were doing and clustered around him with exclamations and coos of delight.

The odd thing was, although he put on a very good show of being pleased, and it was clear that young Devlin was nervously gratified to have him here, Alberich got the distinct impression that he very much would rather not be there.

Then again, as busy as the man was, Alberich wondered where he had found the time to come here in the first place.

The only possible corner of the room that could have been considered secluded was the one in which Alberich had ensconced himself. Norris accepted refreshments, teased and flirted with the ladies, but took none of them up the stairs, which was so entirely out of keeping with everything that Alberich knew about the man that he was immediately on alert. Devlin did not move from his side either, and it seemed to

Alberich that the young noble was keeping a sharp watch on the door.

And perhaps three-quarters of a candlemark later, the Prince strolled in, with an escort of young sycophants.

Except that one of them apparently was not as much of a sycophant as the Prince had thought, because before Karathanelan could vanish, as usual, into one of the private parlors, that young man steered him over to Norris' chair. Devlin and the other young man exchanged a glance; Devlin nodded, and within moments, the newcomer gathered up the Prince's escort and hustled them into the private parlors.

"Highness," Devlin said with a bow to the Prince. "Our patron wishes you to have a discussion with my friend." And at that, he took himself off, going, not into the back like the others, but back out the front door.

Alberich was torn between following—for surely he was going to report to someone!—and staying to listen. But his own internal urging said *stay,* so stay he did.

And Norris, looking up indolently at the Prince, indicated with a nod that Karathanelan should take a seat beside him. "Run away, my beauties," the actor said, in an amused tone of voice. "We gentlemen need to discuss things too delicate for your tender ears."

With giggles and pretty pouts, as the Prince glared his outrage, the ladies did as they were told. "Sit down," Norris said, and then, when the Prince did not move, repeated, with force, *"Sit down.* Now."

"I shall do nothing of the sort!" the Prince said tightly. "I *will* have you horsewhipped and thrown into the street for your insolence!"

"You won't if you know what's good for you," Norris said, without turning a hair. "I am here at the behest of, and doing a *very great favor* for, our mutual sponsor, and if you *don't* sit down, I am going to walk out of here and tell him why I did so. You can see what will happen to you without his protection then, but I don't recommend it."

The Prince sat down.

"That's better," Norris said pleasantly.

"What about *him?*" the Prince growled, nodding at Alberich.

"Nothing to worry about." Norris dismissed Alberich with a shrug. "He's older than dirt, half senile, mostly deaf. I tested him—" Norris grinned then. "If he'd been conscious when I tipped little Kassie's skirts up, he'd have at least twitched."

Yes, and you aren't quite as clever as you think, Alberich told him mentally. *Because a real agent wouldn't have reacted even if you'd taken the girl on the spot.* He wasn't sure *he* would have had the ability to remain "asleep," but then again—he'd yawned through worse, down in the Broken Arms.

"Now," Norris continued, losing the grin. "Before we begin, I'll trouble you to remember that I have no loyalty to you, or to anyone else who has not paid my fee. Once bought, however, I stay bought; this is good business, and it is why our patron brought me here, but remember that I do not give a damn what happens to *you.* My part of your education should have been over moons ago, and it would have been, if you hadn't been such an idiot a week ago."

"Idiot?" the Prince hissed. "I think not—"

"Exactly," Norris interrupted. "You *don't* think. If you did, you would realize that you are expendable, fellow-my-lad."

The Prince started, and looked at Norris as if he thought the actor had run mad.

Norris wagged a finger at him. "Turnabout is fair play. Sauce for the goose will serve for the gander. If your bride has done her dynastic duty by getting with child so quickly, *you* have done your work at stud, and she doesn't *need* you anymore. Didn't that ever occur to you over the past few days, while you've been doing your best to make her hate you?"

Alberich couldn't see the Prince's face, but he sounded smug. "She cannot be rid of me. I would not agree to the dissolution of the marriage."

"Which just shows how much of a fool you are," Norris countered flatly. "Certainly, a marriage can't be dissolved without the consent of both parties—*if you were an ordinary couple.* But you aren't, you are in a foreign land, and the law can be whatever she gets the Council to agree to. And if you should be so indiscreet as to do something treasonable, she wouldn't even have to dissolve the marriage. She could simply arrange for the Council to make her a widow." Norris examined his nails critically. "They hang traitors to the Crown in Valdemar, you know."

"She—couldn't!" the Prince gasped, as if it hadn't occurred to him.

"She could," Norris replied matter-of-factly. "And you're skirting perilous close to it, let me tell you; if your lovely bride had chosen, your little folly in the matter of a mount would have had you facing a High Court already. In fact, the only reasons you haven't been charged with treason already are because our patron is protecting you, and because our patron is fairly certain that your wife is still weeping over your misbehaving and hasn't yet gone from tears to anger. Which is why our patron brought me here. Because you mean nothing to me, I owe you nothing, you can *do* nothing to me, and I can and will tell you what no one else around you would dare." He leaned forward and shoved his index finger at the Prince. "Now, you listen to this; you'd better believe it, and you'd better act on it. Our patron's patience is not inexhaustible, and he won't continue to support and protect you while you run about like a tomcat. You're wasting those very expensive lessons of mine; you can be replaced, and you *will* be, once your wife decides that she's going to stop crying herself to sleep in an empty bed and start doing something about the situation. You might survive the experience, but I'd bet not; our patron has enemies of his own, and they'd be perfectly happy to bring you down and replace you with one of their own choices. And he won't go down to save *your* worthless hide."

Alberich "snored" gently, and wondered just who the "mutual patron" was. More than that, what did this mysterious entity expect to get out of his patronage of Karathanelan? If he could "protect" the Prince, surely he could get whatever he wanted for himself.

The Prince was silent for a long moment. "I don't like this. How do I know that this is true?" he said at last.

"I don't care what you think about it," Norris replied impatiently. "And I don't have to prove anything to you. I already have what I wanted out of the bargain, and I don't particularly care whether or not you believe me. *You* are wasting *my* time, not the other way around. Time to wake up and deal with the mess you've made, lad, before you find yourself neck-deep and no way to get out."

Norris' very indifference seemed to work as a powerful argument with the Prince. "What do I do?" he asked at last, grudgingly.

Norris snorted. "Do I have to draw you a map?" But when the Prince looked at him blankly, he sighed. "Apparently I do. All right then, the first thing you do is go apologize to your wife for whatever you said to her and everything you've done since you quarreled with her. Groveling to her, if need be, until you get her forgiveness."

"I will never—" the Prince began hotly.

"You will if you want to keep your head on your neck," Norris hissed. "And once you've groveled enough, you tell her that now that you've come to your senses and have looked back on your unspeakable conduct these past several days, you realized tonight how unsatisfactory all these other women you've been bedding are, compared to her."

The Prince sniggered. Norris shrugged. "Of course that's ridiculous, but that's what she wants to hear, and believe me, it is the *only* thing you could say that will make her forgive you for sleeping with anyone else. Then you will have to go *right* back to your first lesson with her, and woo her all over again. Only it will be a little easier this time, because she knows what you can do in bed, and you won't be handicapped by having to hold back with her to save her virtue. Remember what I taught you, and everything our patron managed to find out. *Use* that. Make her feel that you are the only person in the whole world who could possibly understand her. I wrote you the scripts; drag them out again."

The Prince seemed to think it over, and finally said, grudgingly. "If this is what our patron wants. . . ."

"Hang our patron. This is the only thing that will keep you out of a dungeon cell," Norris said bluntly, as Alberich mentally cursed. If only he could have counted on the Prince's arrogance to push things and keep pushing them, until Selenay was ready to be rid of him!

Well, it looked as if that was a vain hope.

"Very well." The Prince got up, but did not offer his hand to Norris. "You and our patron have been right in the past. I must assume that you are right, now. Fare you well."

"Right," Norris replied, waving him away indolently. "Just see that you remember what I've told you, the next time you're tempted to assert yourself."

Alberich continued to "doze" until the Prince was inside the door to one of the private parlors, and Norris was surrounded again by his bevy of beauties. Then, with a "start," he "woke," surveyed the room indulgently, then levered himself up out of his chair to totter away.

Part of him wanted to string up Norris as soon as the Prince had been dealt with. But part of him, which had been listening to the conversation with keen interest, had a better idea.

:*I think we should hire him when this is over,*: he said, knowing that Kantor had been following everything that had transpired.

:You what?*:* Kantor asked, incredulously. Kantor had no need to ask who "he" was.

:I think we should hire him as our agent,: Alberich amended. *:Mind, I wouldn't tell him just who is hiring him, but he could be damned useful to us.:*

:But he said himself he could be bought!: Kantor protested—then stopped. *:And he said that once he was bought, he stayed bought. Didn't he.:*

:That was exactly what he said,: Alberich replied. *:I think he could be a valuable agent. More valuable alive and working for us, than in prison. If we could even find something to charge him with. Which I doubt.:*

:Emotionally, I don't like it,: Kantor replied unhappily. *:But logically—you're right. He's an amoral beast, but better he's been bought by us. At least then we can control him.:*

:As much as such a one is ever controlled,: Alberich finished. And sighed. *:And this assumes that his patron—whoever that is—loses interest in him. If he's the sort who stays bought, we'll never get him otherwise.:*

:Good,: Kantor said firmly. *:I'd rather we didn't. I'd rather we could have him thrown in jail.:*

:Which we can't, because he hasn't done anything wrong,: Alberich pointed out. *:All he's done that we know of is to give the Prince lessons on how to woo and win the Queen. Which is hardly illegal. And we can't even prove that he did that much, really, not to satisfy a law court. But oh, how I wish he hadn't been here tonight!:*

:I know exactly what you mean,: Kantor said glumly.

Karathanelan might have been an arrogant, self-centered beast, but apparently he was bright enough to know when he was getting good advice.

He was also phenomenally lucky.

Because the next day, the *very* next day, word came from Rethwellan that his father, the King, was dead.

Now, that might not have been thought of as luck, except that word also came from Rethwellan that the King had *already* been buried, that Karath's presence was not required at home, and that, in fact, his brother the new King, Faramentha, suggested strongly that he should remain in Valdemar at the side of his new bride and do his mourning in private.

Even while the Rethwellan Embassy was being swathed in black, Karath hurried to the Palace, and in full view of everyone as Selenay herself was hearing the news, and flung himself weeping at her feet.

Selenay canceled the rest of her audiences that day, and took him with her back to her chambers. Alberich could not know, of course, *what* the Prince told her, aside from the "script" that Norris had provided for him, but he could guess. What would appeal to Selenay more, than to have her beloved husband suddenly bereft of his own father?

Certainly he went about after that in heavy mourning, and certainly Selenay was as unshakably attentive to him as he was to her. To Alberich's disgust, he was more firmly in Selenay's good graces than he had been before, always by her side, and playing the devoted husband. Selenay spent a disturbing amount of time gazing at him or into his eyes with every sign of being firmly under his spell.

And in public, at least, he was as devoted as she could ever have wished.

In public, he was also playing the tragic figure of the mourning son and rejected brother. When a new Ambassador came from Rethwellan to replace the old one, he showed a very chilly face to the man, who was, in his turn, no better than icily polite.

Which meant nothing to Alberich, until Talamir enlightened him, one late summer evening.

"Oh, do *think* about this for a moment," Talamir told him,

with unusual impatience. "The Prince was not told of his father's death until Faramentha was firmly on the throne. And he was not recalled. What does that tell you?"

"Ah." Alberich shook his head. "I was thinking too much of our own side of this, and not beyond our Borders. Faramentha does not trust his brother. And the Prince holds Faramentha in enmity."

"So—?"

"So—whether or not the old King was privy to Karathanelan's plans, the new one is not, probably."

Talamir nodded. "And unless I miss my guess," he added shrewdly, "the Prince's grief is not all sham. Not that he is brokenhearted over being rejected by his brother, nor mourning terribly for his father—"

"If he is," Alberich was moved to point out, "The ladies of the Horn have not noticed."

"Precisely. But if there is one thing the Prince cares about, it's his own well-being. And with his father dead and his brother, who despises him, on the throne?"

"He has nowhere to go if he fails here—" Alberich felt cold. "I do not like this."

"Neither," Talamir said delicately, "do I."

But there was not much either of them could do about it. Karath had too many good cards in his hand, and Selenay's own condition was aiding him; by summer's end, as the first leaves began to turn, Selenay was deep in work, and when she wasn't working, she was generally asleep, or at least, resting. Her pregnancy was hard on her, not so much that it was difficult, but that she was finding it exhausting, according to Crathach, who made no secret that he disapproved of her getting with child so quickly. This left ample opportunity for the Prince to comport himself as if he was a bachelor.

But he went about it so discreetly that most of the Court had no idea.

Unfortunately, one of the things that was wearing Selenay

out was that he still had not given up the notion of being crowned. Even though he was not fighting with her about it, using less aggressive means to get his point across, roughly once a fortnight, he would find some other reason to bring the tired old plaint back up, or some new scheme to get around the law. This, Alberich heard from Talamir, usually when Alberich came up to the Collegium to report on whatever new information he might have gathered on his prowls in Haven. The city was quiet of late, as the season passed from summer into autumn; even the criminal element was up to no more than the usual trouble. There seemed nothing that required Alberich's intervention. Stalking Devlin to try and find the identity of the "patron" was proving to be fruitless; where Devlin went, none of Alberich's personae was welcome. As for Norris, the actor was so busy with his new theater that even *he* was beginning to look a little frayed about the edges.

"He's come up with another one today," Talamir said, lowering himself wearily down into a chair by the hearth. He looked ancient tonight, and very transparent; Alberich wondered what he had been doing to wear himself so thin.

He wants to be gone, came the unbidden thought. *He's faced with things he can't do anything about, and he just wants to be gone—from problems, from life. And he wants it with all of his heart.*

He might want it—but he wasn't pursuing it, at least. Duty held him here at Selenay's side, however poorly suited he thought himself to the task.

At that moment, Alberich pitied the Queen's Own.

"This time, what?" Alberich asked, knowing that the "he" could only be the Prince, and that the "another one" was yet another ploy to pressure Selenay into somehow getting him a crown.

"That she's shaming him in front of his family—or so he says," Talamir said wearily. "According to him, that she hasn't made him King means that she thinks he is unworthy of a crown, and now he says that this is why his own brother has rejected him and kept him from his father's side when the King was dying."

"Ah. So now he attempts guilt?" Alberich replied.

"I would guess," said Talamir, and shook his head. "At least she came to me with this, looking for reassurance. And I planted another seed."

"Perhaps you can use the papers soon?" Alberich hazarded. They finally had a translation of them; it took long enough to break the code. When they had, as Alberich had suspected, they proved to be instructions on what to do and say to Selenay to win her, with some very intimate details. Some were things that Alberich blinked at; things that one would have thought were the sort of confession that Selenay would not have given to anyone—girlish daydreams, actually, about the sort of man she was looking for, and the loneliness of being who she was, the despair that she would never have the kind of marriage her father had enjoyed.

Where had all of that come from? Even Talamir had been surprised at the bitterness and anguish of some of it.

But maybe Selenay had been pouring her woes into the ears of one of her servants. Alberich would have *thought* they were trustworthy, and probably they were, but he supposed there was no reason why they shouldn't tell others what Selenay had told *them.*

Some of what had been written were intimate glimpses into Selenay personally, and what to say to her to play to her sympathies, but others—well, Alberich had found himself blushing at the step-by-step instructions for seduction; they did not merely border on the pornographic, they *were* pornographic. And Alberich was no longer surprised that Norris was so popular with the ladies, nor that Selenay was so deeply infatuated with the Prince. How could she not be, if the Prince was following these instructions, meant to make Selenay believe that here, past all her hopes, was not only her soulmate but a lover who could guarantee the satisfaction of a female partner, closely and with all his attention? Part of him wanted to burn the wretched papers, but they were useful, very useful. If ever Selenay's attachment began to fade, at the right moment, showing her these things could turn her fading infatuation to distaste. Only she could know how closely the Prince followed his "scripts"—but the more closely he had, the more obvious it would be that he *was* following a script, and that there never had been any real feeling behind his act.

"Not until after the child is born," Talamir sighed. "Crathach says that he doesn't want any more stress on her right now; between matters of state and the Prince's continuous pressure, she's got more than enough on her. He's playing the 'bereft orphan' very convincingly, and of all of the acts he could contrive, that's the one that will make her excuse him nearly anything."

Alberich counted up the months in his mind. "Spring, then," he said with a sigh. "But the Prince himself will, perhaps, overstep before then?"

But Talamir shook his head. "No, I think that this 'patron,' whoever he is, has found a way to clamp controls down over the Prince. More than just Norris, I mean, or even young Devlin. Devlin can't be more than a messenger. It astonishes me. And I wish I knew how real the threat to Selenay is."

Alberich nodded. There was the real question, truth be told. There were actually a number of interpretations that could be placed on what Norris had said to his control.

First, it could be all bluster. It was one thing to say that the Queen was dispensable; it was quite another to actually *act* on those words. Norris was, when it all came down to cases, a commoner. Whatever he knew about life at Court he could only learn from brief glimpses and the rather unrealistic views of life among the highborn that he got from his plays, or just perhaps by whatever his patron told him—assuming the patron told him anything at all about life at Court. Selenay was surrounded night and day by Guards that Alberich himself had trained and could vouch for, and by the Heralds as well. To actually assassinate her, someone would have to get past them *and* Selenay's own impressive self-defense abilities, and it was guaranteed that whoever tried would not survive the attempt. So the enemy would have to find someone highly skilled, clever, and suicidal—not an easy task. Poison was out of the question; Healers checked everything that she ate and drank, and even if someone managed to slip poison past them, there were no "instantaneous" poisons other than some rare snakebites; Healers would almost certainly be able to save her. Norris (and, presumably, his "patron") might simply be counting on the hazards of childbearing to remove Selenay. To Alberich's mind, that was as foolish a hope as finding an assassin; Selenay was in excellent health and by no means delicate. Women gave birth without complications every day *without* the small army of Healers to attend them that Selenay had.

"I wish I could hazard a guess," Talamir replied. "It seems a preposterous idea on the face of it. The ForeSeers are no real help either."

Alberich knew what *that* meant. Too many future possibilities to sort out. That, or so he had been told, was why *he* never got any visions inspired by ForeSight that extended into the future by more than a candlemark. His Gift evidently operated in the same fashion as he did—if there were too many choices, his Gift elected not to show any of them, so that he could concentrate without distractions pulling him in a dozen directions at once. It only showed him things he could actually act on.

"It is that I think, sometimes, our Gifts are more hindrance than help," he said sourly.

"Some of them, at any rate," Talamir agreed. He looked broodingly off over Alberich's left shoulder for a long moment, staring at nothing, but doing it in a way that tended to raise the hackles on the back of Alberich's neck. What was he looking at, so intently, with that expression of focused detachment? Alberich was used to that "listening" look that Heralds got when they were conversing with their Companions, and this wasn't *that* expression. It also wasn't the absentminded look most people got when they were engrossed in their own thoughts. The closest analogy that Alberich could come to was that odd look that cats sometimes got, when they stared intently at something that apparently wasn't there. It was a Karsite tradition that when they did that, they were looking at spirits. Talamir's look was very like that.

But if the Queen's Own was seeing ghosts, he hadn't said anything about it to anyone.

Alberich repressed a shiver and coughed quietly to bring Talamir's attention back to the present.

Talamir blinked, and picked up the conversation where it had left off.

"I have to think at this point that your actor's conversation was a deliberate attempt on his part to remind his control and his patron that *he* knows where all the skeletons are," Talamir said. "I think he was trying to extract more money from them to buy his silence in case anything *did* happen to the Queen."

Alberich thought that over. It was plausible. More plausible than any of his own theories. Norris might stay bought, but when you did that, there was less incentive for your "employers" to try to keep you in their pocket once they had what they initially wanted.

And theaters were more expensive to maintain than a stable full of racehorses.

"A dangerous ploy, that one," Alberich observed. "He could be removed before a danger he becomes."

"Perhaps, perhaps," Talamir admitted. "But that is the best fit for what you overheard."

Alberich nodded his agreement, but not without a sense of relief. If *that* was all it was . . . !

They finished their business, and Alberich made his way back to the salle through the dark. Not alone, of course; the moment he crossed over the fence into Companion's Field, Kantor joined him.

:You're still troubled,: his Companion observed.

:I don't like it, for some reason,: Alberich admitted. *:Unfortunately, I don't know why.:*

:Well, what can you do about it?:

He pondered that for a moment, trying to think of all of the times Selenay *could* be vulnerable. Not when holding Court, not at Council meetings. Probably not in the gardens or in her own quarters, or at meals or entertainments—unless the harpists suddenly produced arrows and used their instruments as bows.

Not very likely.

But before the arrival of the Prince, Selenay had occasionally donned the working Whites of a common Herald, and gone off for a long ride, down to the Home Farms, outside the walls of Haven, usually accompanied only by Talamir and sometimes not even him. And then, if ever—

:You know, I believe I am going to start attending the Hurlee practices,: he said slowly. *:I believe I will begin working with the Hurlee players. She might object to an escort; she won't object to a crowd of cheerful youngsters nattering about sport. In fact, she might even enjoy their company. But it will not take much to turn them from gamesmen to melee-experts.:*

:Hurlee is cursed like a melee already,: Kantor observed.

:And that is the point,: Alberich replied. *:Furthermore, unless she is really craving privacy, Selenay won't think anything of a Hurlee team riding along with her. They're only Trainees, not Guards.:*

:So she won't object,:

He smiled. *:I believe she will welcome them.:* Then he sobered. *:The hard part will be in training them to be weapons at her side, without any of them realizing that is what I am doing.:*

:If anyone can,: Kantor said firmly, *:you can.:*

He sighed, and hoped his Companion was right.

A HARSH, cold wind blew across the Hurlee ground, rattling the last of the sere, brown leaves still clinging to the trees. A helm and neck-brace weren't much help in protecting from the cold; the wind ripped gleefully down the Weaponsmaster's collar and the sudden chill brought back memories of long patrols in the lonely hills of Karse in weather worse than this, when he would wake cold, patrol until he and his men were warm only where their bodies were in contact with their horses' hides, then gather around smoking fires where you warmed little bits of yourself, while the rest stayed achingly cold. Now—well, he had come from a warm salle, and he would be going back to it; this was just minor discomfort, inconsequential.

Alberich gravely surveyed the twelve best Hurlee players in the Collegium now gathered before him; in their turn they gazed fearlessly back at him. They were all superior athletes, all either in their last or next-to-last years, and all were old enough to give Alberich respect untempered with fear. They

were past that half-fearful, half-awestruck stage, past thinking him an unreasonable taskmaster. They knew him now,
knew what he was about, knew why he did what he did with
them. There were those that were this lot's yearmates that still
had not grasped those truths; that was why he had picked his
candidates so carefully.

And if they suspected what he was about with them now
was going to be something more than turning them into vicious Hurlee players—well, he reckoned *they* only thought to
the moment when they were to get their Whites, and assumed
that he was fitting them better to be Heralds in some of the
more dangerous sectors. And it was true enough that this
training would serve that end, so they were not entirely wrong.

The real purpose was a secret held by him, Talamir, Kantor
and Rolan—and the Companions of these dozen young Grays.
After careful consultation with Kantor, he and Talamir had
elected to include the Companions, but not the Trainees, because of the risk that someone would let something slip. No
secret was ever safer, and he and Kantor felt that to get the
best result, he needed the informed cooperation of the Companions. Other than that, no one else had been told. Not even
Myste knew, though of course, he would tell her eventually for
the sake of the Chronicles. Just not now; later when the danger
was past, and his fears were proved false—or true.

The twelve sat shivering in their saddles, waiting for him
to speak. They wore more than the usual Hurlee protections;
shin, knee, and calf-guards, kidney-belts, elbow-guards, arm-
guards, neck-braces. And they were finding, as he already
knew, that none of these protections helped against the teeth
of the wind.

There were no observers today. No one wanted to sit in the
cold, in the open, with no shelter on a day like this. Not even
to watch the best Hurlee players in Haven. It seemed an espe-
cial irony that rather than being overcast, the sun shone down

among swiftly-moving scuds of cloud in a mostly-blue sky. It gave no help against the cold.

"Two teams of six for now," he said, and pointed. "Harrow. You sit out, throw in the ball, referee. I will play this third and the next."

When Hurlee had first been turned into a game and not a form of exercise, it had started with as many players as could be crowded onto the field, but now the official tally was twenty-four on the field, twelve to each side. Two of the twelve were goaltenders, two played close to the goals, and another two were "rovers" outside the scrum, on the alert for a miss-hit ball or a pass from one of their own side. Alberich was paring the teams down again to two goaltenders and four others; four roaming players, one on the home goal, one on the shared goal.

"A new rule," he continued. "The Companion a fair target is." He was counting on any ambushers being armed with swords rather than any other exotic weapons—it would be easy enough to incapacitate Companions by thrusting the shafts of spears among their legs in a melee—a broken leg would send a Companion down as easily as a horse. But it was still possible, more than possible, for a Companion to be killed by a sword thrust. He would have to teach them to avoid the possibility.

And as for the stroke that had killed the King and his Companion, and killed Rolan's predecessor—well, that would be coming in later lessons.

"Yes," he repeated, with a little more force. "The Companion a legal target is." *That* startled them, though the Companions all nodded or snorted and pawed the ground to indicate willingness. Well, *they* knew, and knew why; this only surprised their Chosen. Startled, and shocked them, as if he had suggested that they should practice assassination techniques on infants. Still, they were all intelligent, and in a moment, they nodded too. And this probably confirmed their suspicions;

that he was fitting them for dangerous missions, missions in which their Companions would *most definitely* be targets, the targets of people who were out to kill them, not incapacitate them.

Well, he was. *If* he needed them, it would be facing people who would probably strike at their Companions first. The Prince might be willfully ignorant when it came to the Companions, but his comrades weren't. And they would know what the Tedrels had known; kill the Companion, and the Herald is lost as well.

"And Companions—you are to target opposing riders," he continued, and he thought he caught a wicked glint in one or two blue eyes. "Pull them down, out of the saddle; knock them over. Chase them to the boundaries." The Companions would be quicker to adapt than their Chosen; at least at first. The Companions of this lot were all full adults, more experienced than their riders.

"So—" he held up his stick; the "traditional" beginning to a Hurlee game was for all players to raise their sticks and crack them together. Belatedly, the rest of them cracked theirs against his. "Harrow—throw in the ball and referee. Signal no fouls, only danger or hurt. We play."

Harrow had a whistle, but under these rules, he wasn't to blow it except to start game play unless someone was injured. These were real no-holds-barred conditions, with the Hurlee stick becoming a weapon—club, spear, staff, whatever suited. As the two teams lined up against each other, staring at each other, waiting, it occurred to him to be amused at himself. Who ever would have thought that his impulse to give a set of overexcited youngsters something to burn off some energy with would have turned into this?

Harrow's whistle cut through the cold air, and the "game" began.

As he had expected, the Trainees promptly forgot the new rule about targeting Companions. *He* hadn't, though, and Kantor charged straight into the Companion of the opposing team's captain, using his greater bulk and muscle to literally knock the other off his feet. The others scattered before that charge; Kantor in a full charge was a terrifying sight. Kantor angled sideways at the last moment, ramming the other with his chest, as Alberich thrashed at the rider with his stick, and missed, the rider ducking under the blow. The shock of the meeting jolted through him. The Companion went over, knocked right off-balance, his rider remembering his equitation classes and jumping free at the last minute, and as Alberich charged down on him, he brought up his stick defensively in time to deflect the blow Alberich was aiming at his head.

Alberich and Kantor galloped past and Kantor whirled with a hip-wrenching reversal of direction, charging for the opposing team's goalminder. Meanwhile, thinking just a little faster on his feet than the rest, Alberich's shared-goal minder followed the Weaponsmaster's example and slapped his counterpart's Companion over the rump with his stick. Trumpeting indignation, the offended Companion leaped out of the way, giving Alberich's team a clear shot at the goal.

Which they took.

Harrow whistled to stop play, and ran in to fetch the ball.

The first play was over, and the only "casualty" was one rider unhorsed, one Companion slapped. And the second would likely not happen again. Alberich felt his heart swell with pride. They were good. They were more than good. They were brilliant: adaptable and clever.

And before time to change came up, they were all playing by the new rules without having to think about it too much.

Not that any of them had *much* of a chance against Alberich, because he was not holding back for their benefit. He wanted them to feel what it was really like, fighting against an adult, and an experienced and cunning one as well. *He* had tested the Prince's skills himself, and he was not going to assume that the Prince's chosen accomplices, should he try this thing, were going to be any less skilled. But unless the Prince somehow recruited people from the Tedrel Wars, none of *them* would have had anything like real combat experience, nor anything like what he and these Trainees were practicing.

When change-up came and Harrow signaled them, for the sake of making it a bit fairer as far as scoring was concerned, he switched sides; Harrow came in, and a player from the other team came out. And the game began again, except that this time, they all were playing like they meant it.

And at the third change-up, Alberich sat out altogether, and ran a critique from the sidelines. By this time, they were playing by the new rules *without* having to concentrate on them, and the riders suddenly found themselves confronted by something that had never happened to them before.

Their Companions were no longer entirely mindful of their Chosen. Not when they were busy avoiding dangerous blows themselves. That meant that there were moments out there when they were no better off than if they'd been riding a superbly trained horse. Those were the moments of greatest danger, just as they had been in real combat. Those were the moments when, if they thought about it at all, these young Trainees got their first taste of real, bone-chilling fear.

When he brought the game to an end, they were all—himself included—absolutely exhausted, bruised, and battered. And there was a light of grim, ready-to-drop satisfaction in their eyes.

:*And you're warm,*: Kantor observed, with weary humor. :*Though you won't stay that way if you start making a speech.*:

Alberich ignored him. "Good," he said, and their eyes lit up. "Very good. Look, you. This a special class will be. Every day, this time, until I say. For now, we Hurlee a-saddle, but the next step will be—unhorsed, and you Hurlee aground until you can get mounted again. And those mounted will try to separate you from your Companion. And *you* will be trying to take the Companion down from the ground. So be thinking on this."

"Yes, Weaponsmaster," they said in a ragged chorus.

Harrow, quicker than the others, looked pale, but asked, "You mean, we're trying to repeat what killed the King and the Monarch's Own Companion?"

"You are striving to *prevent* that," Alberich corrected gently. "And it will take time. So here you will be, every day, for two candlemarks or a full game, whichever arrives first."

"But what if we've got a class or work scheduled?" one of them piped up, voice trembling only a little.

"See Talamir; he will tend to it," Alberich ordered. "This class, precedence has." And several of them exchanged meaningful glances. Sober ones, too, he was proud to see. So, they knew; somehow in this first round of mock-combat, they had learned that deadly lesson, that fighting was dirty, foul, and ugly—that combat meant hurt. That *they* could be hurt, which was a difficult lesson for any young person to grasp.

He did not think that they had yet come to grips with the other lesson—that they could *die.* But at least they knew that there was no glory to be found in this, and there *was* a great deal of danger.

He hoped.

:*Oh, they know. And they're thinking furiously, trying to come up with the reason for all of this,*: Kantor told him. :*Don't worry; we'll encourage the "right answer."*:

Good. He needed them to concentrate on that "answer." Because by the time the snow was falling, he'd have them practicing in full armor.

And by the time it melted, he would have them practicing in sets of custom-made armor that would not show under Trainee Grays. When that armor arrived, he wanted them to be firmly fixated on their own answer, and not his.

He raised his stick; automatically, they raised theirs, and

they all clashed together overhead. "Good game," he said with satisfaction. "Same time tomorrow."

Fat, fluffy flakes of snow fell thickly from a sky that was a uniform, featureless gray from horizon to horizon. The damp, still air seemed oddly warm, but perhaps it was only because there was no wind blowing at the moment. Already the new snow was a thumb's-breadth deep everywhere, covering the old, crusty, knee-deep stuff, softening the harsh, bare bushes and skeletal tree limbs.

It covered everywhere, except the Hurlee field, which was a churned-up mess of dirty snow, clods of earth, and grass. There was not a single spot on the field that wasn't pounded down with hoofmarks.

Despite the muffling effect of the falling snow, the game was loud enough. Not because of the shouting of spectators (there weren't any), nor the shouts of the players themselves (mostly they just grunted). No, it was the clash of stick on armor.

Every one of the players wore armor, including Alberich; thigh-, shin-, and foot-guards, breast- and back-plates, shoulder-, neck-, and arm-guards, and, of course, the helm. It wasn't articulated plate of the sort that a knight might wear; the Trainees wore protective plates riveted onto leather. Much lighter and easier to move in—relatively.

Easier to fit under or over other garments, anyway. Under the armor, they wore padded gambesons, and over it, padded surcoats. The Companions were armored, too, at least for these practice sessions—a face-plate to protect their heads, articulated plate along their necks, and leg-guards. Alberich didn't want any of them injured either—

He was on home-goal guard this session, which gave him more opportunity to watch the rest as they skirmished. And they had made amazing progress in the past few moons.

I should have expected it, I suppose, looking back on how all those young Trainees drove themselves before the last Tedrel War. He felt a warmth toward them that was almost paternal; challenge them, and they rose to the challenge. Let them but *think* that there was a challenge in the offing, and they rose to it. And they'd go through fire to meet it.

Most of the noise was coming from sticks connecting with the Companions' armor, since *they* weren't wearing any padding over it, and he wondered if perhaps he shouldn't order the armor off. When the day came that they began riding guardian on Selenay, there was no way to disguise what was essentially horse-armor, so the Companions would have to do without. If it was making the Companions dependent, possibly careless—

:It's not; they just aren't ready yet to have us dodging underneath them. Not with all that extra weight.:

Kantor's assurance was all he needed; he stopped worrying about it. This was only the third session under armor, and they still weren't used to it. Fortunately, the custom-made and fitted armor he had ordered up for them was going to be lighter than this stuff. Not as strong or protective, but it should easily be good enough against the kinds of light court-blades that the Prince and his friends sported, if Alberich's worst fears came true.

And if the Prince and his friends elected to attempt to hire professionals rather than doing the dirty work themselves, Alberich would hear about it. There was no job involving dirty work in Haven that at least one of his personae didn't hear about, either via the rumor vine, or directly.

If the Prince decides to hire out his evil work, wouldn't it be a great irony if he approached me directly?

Just as he thought that, the melee surged toward his goal; he judged his moment, and as soon as they drew near enough to be a threat to the goal, Kantor charged the rider nearest him. The Companion's powerful muscles surged under him.

Kantor's unusual weight and size—quite as large as any war-horse—was next to impossible for another Companion to stand up to. The best they could do was to try and turn aside at the last moment so that he slid along a flank—or to dodge out of the way.

But there was nowhere for this Companion to dodge to, and no room to turn. Kantor hit him hard, and the shock of the meeting jarred both his body and Alberich's. *They* bounced back; Kantor anticipated the shock and caught himself without a slip. The other Companion's hooves scrabbled desperately in the snow as he tried to stay upright; the rider dropped his stick, grabbed the hold on the pommel, and hung on grimly.

And Kantor charged again, while Alberich swung at the rider.

It was a short charge, more of a push, but the other Companion's hind feet slid right out from under him, at the same time that Alberich's stick connected with the rider's helm with a solid *clang* that vibrated up the stick and into Alberich's arm.

Down they both went, the Companion sliding over sideways with a squeal of pain, the rider just—falling. Not jumping free, not even trying. And Alberich knew as soon as they started to fall that they were both hurt.

Blessed Sunlord. . . .

So did Shanda, who was refereeing; she gave a blast to her whistle as the two hit the slushy ground, and the scrum instantly *stopped.*

What have we done?

The rider groaned, and tried to rise as Alberich leaped off Kantor's back and ran for him. The Companion got to his feet, with a lurch and a scramble, whining under his breath with pain, but when he stood, it was on only three legs.

:Not broken,: Kantor relayed instantly, *:but it's a bad sprain.:*

Alberich unfastened Harrow's helm strap and lifted the helmet from Harrow's head. "Look at me," he commanded, and it didn't take a genius to see from the unequal size of the boy's pupils that he'd been concussed. And it didn't take a genius to see why either; the padding had come loose and slid down the back of the helm to bunch up against the neck protector.

Shanda was on the case already; she and her Companion were dragging up the two-horse stretcher they kept at the side of the field. Alberich didn't have to give them a single order.

They worked as if they had rehearsed for this disaster; half of them lifted Harrow straight up off the ground without moving his back or neck, and placed him on the stretcher. Within a moment, they were heading toward Healer's Collegium with Harrow held securely by the straps around the stretcher.

Meanwhile the other half of the Trainees left behind were buckling Harrow's Companion onto the saddles of two more Companions so they could take some of his weight and he wouldn't have to put that injured leg to the ground. In another moment they, too, were on their way to the Healers, picking their way through the uneven snow.

Alberich was left to pick up the helm and stare numbly after them. He felt sick, but what could he do? There were injuries like this even in normal practice, much less the risky stuff he was asking them to do now. And if he didn't push them—if they didn't push themselves—if it came to a real fight, they might not live through it. He wasn't going to apologize—

But what were they thinking?

"Find us a substitute, Weaponsmaster," called Brion over his shoulder as the second lot limped toward the Collegium with Harrow's Companion. "We're not good enough yet, and this just proves it. Get us a substitute, or get us just a referee and *you* substitute, and we'll pick this up tomorrow."

The words both startled and gratified him, and for a moment, he actually felt his eyes burn. "I will!" he called after them, hoping that they didn't notice the slightly choked quality caused by the lump in his throat. "But session is ended for today, I think."

:*Tell the others with Harrow, will you?*: he asked Kantor.

:*Certainly,*: There was a pause. :*Harrow says to tell you he apologizes for not checking his helm better, and that this is all his fault.*:

That called for an apology. :*Tell him that he is right—but that it is also my fault for not checking the equipment first myself, and that I also beg his pardon for my carelessness.*:

:*That ought to scare him out of his bed,*: Kantor chuckled. :*You, apologizing!*:

But as Alberich hung the faulty helm on the pommel of his saddle, and turned to mount Kantor's saddle and head for the salle, he caught sight of movement out of the corner of his eye.

For one horrible moment, he thought it was someone from the Court. Perhaps one of the Prince's people—

Which could be a disaster.

Then he saw the color of the mount and the rider's clothing and had another sickening feeling. This was another Trainee and Companion, and they'd seen the accident. If he thought he was being portrayed as a monster before—

:*No Companion thinks you're a monster.*:

He hadn't seen them there; he'd thought there had been no one watching. In a moment, he recognized them, with something of a start. The Trainee was young Mical, his Companion Eloran—two of the unholy trio whose antics had broken that mirror in the salle and had inadvertently sent him down the road to discovering what the actor Norris had been up to.

What were *they* doing here?

But Mical's punishment was long since over; what could he possibly have been doing out here? It wasn't for pleasure; he looked practically blue with cold, and he must have been here the entire time they'd been playing.

"Weaponsmaster Alberich?" the boy called, as soon as he

was within easy conversational distance. "Can we volunteer to be that substitute?"

Alberich raised an eyebrow, making certain that none of his considerable surprise showed on his face, although his jaw ached with the effort of keeping it from dropping. He knew very well that young Mical had a reputation as a demon Hurlee player, despite the late start that he and Eloran had on it because of the punishment work he'd been doing. But that was regular Hurlee, not this—this combat version. Surely no one sane would volunteer for this, not after today, not seeing that the *Weaponsmaster* would injure one of the Trainees and apparently not think twice about it. And Mical had at least three more years to go in his training, not one or less than one.

"How long have you watching been?" he asked, keeping his tone flat. He expected to hear a slightly cocky "Long enough," but once again he got a surprise.

"A little more than two moons," Mical replied. "It took me a while to get my chores scheduled so I had the candlemark free. I heard about it, and I started watching. At first it was— well, because it was *Hurlee*." He emphasized the game as if invoking the name alone would explain everything. "Then I stayed."

Kantor snorted. *:Well, well. This is interesting.:*

"This no kind of game is," Alberich told him, harshly. "Not anymore. Not *this* group. There is this, serious injury today. More, there are likely to be."

"I *know* that, Weaponsmaster," Mical replied, head up, eyes blazing. "But I'm good, *really* good at regular Hurlee, and I want to help." His Companion moved forward until he was nearly nose-to-nose with Alberich, and the rest of his speech was made in a whisper. "I know why you're doing this," he continued, and if his hands and voice trembled a little, his gaze was firm. "That is, I think I know *what* you're doing. You're training up a bunch of people who are always at the Collegium until they graduate into Whites, and who nobody is going to even consider as adequate protection. Not even the Queen, so we could go anywhere. You think that if the Queen ever leaves the Palace grounds, someone is going to try to kidnap her. Maybe even the Prince's friends, to try and get the Queen and the Council to agree to make him a King."

Since that was very near to what Alberich *was* afraid of, he actually started, and stared at the boy, and this time he didn't even try to keep his jaw from dropping. "But—how—" he began.

Mical shrugged. "Healer Crathach is my second cousin, and my uncle knows people who know the Prince's set. I'm good at putting things together, and my Gift is Touchreading." At Alberich's puzzled look, he explained. "If I pick up something barehanded, and I want to know, sometimes I can tell where it's been and what it's been doing going back to when it was first made." He gulped. "I haven't had it working for long, not so I could trust it. Otherwise I'd have told you."

Alberich blinked again. So did Kantor. *:I was under the impression that Mical's Gift was fairly unreliable.:*

"My Gift-teacher still thinks it's unreliable," Mical continued. "But in the last moon it's been getting a bit more under control, and that was when I noticed something. If someone has been handling what I pick up very recently, and feeling strongly about something, it's pretty dead-accurate. I can pick up bits of what they've been thinking about. When I realized there was something strange about this Hurlee team, I—" He flushed. "I started snooping on you. You've been awfully worried lately, and you've been doing a lot of repairs on the practice equipment." His chin firmed. "I know this *is* dangerous; you just cracked Harrow's skull for him, and that was just in practice! But I still want to help."

Alberich thought about it for a long, long moment, as the snow fell all about them, sealing them off from the rest of the world inside a wall of white curtains.

"All right," he said at last. "Come down to the salle with

me. I will need to measure you, and get you armor. And your gods be with you."

Mical went off with his measurements taken, a set of armor of the approximate size ready for him, and an admonishment to say nothing of his speculations, not even to his fellows on the team. "Tell them that you are the substitute, you may," Alberich told him. "If you care to."

Mical just shook his head. "They aren't my yearmates, and it'll be better coming from you," he replied, showing a maturity that Alberich hadn't expected. "If *you* say it, they'll just figure you picked the best you could think of. If I do, it'll sound like I'm boasting."

It sounded as if young Mical had learned a lot more in that glassworks than how to make mirrors.

And there had not been one single attempt on Mical's part to suggest some of the stage-fighting techniques he had been so enamored with a year ago. He'd done a great deal of physical growing in the past year, too; he'd gone from weedy adolescent to a young powerhouse with muscles as hard as rocks. It was no wonder that he was reputed to be such a demon Hurlee player. Evidently pumping those bellows had been very good for him.

But as Alberich brooded over his solitary supper, he was still worried. The boy might be big and strong, but he was still a boy, still three years younger than the rest of the team. He'd volunteered, but did Alberich have the right to accept him? He thought of poor Harrow, even now being taken care of by the Healers. He would be throwing young Mical into the middle of a team that was already playing a deadly game; *they'd* had moons of practice at it, and Mical and Eloran didn't.

:But he's been watching,: Kantor reminded him.

:Watching isn't the same as playing.: Would Mical just end up in a bed next to Harrow in the next day or two?

:Eloran is getting some special coaching, this minute,: Kantor told him. *:This business is half the Companion's job, remember. And Eloran is a lot faster than Harrow's Companion.:*

Another shock; this was a day full of them. *:I thought all of you were fairly equal—:*

:Oh, no. Not that any of us is the Companion equivalent of Myste—: There was a snicker in that, and Alberich could hardly blame him. Poor Myste! By now she was so notorious that Selenay just had a page assigned to her to follow around behind her, picking up the things she dropped and gathering up the things she put down and forgot. Well, she might forget where she left her spare pair of lenses; she *never* forgot a fact, a law, or a precedent.

:Some of us have different priorities,: he replied truthfully.

:As do we. At any rate, Eloran is a little nimbler than Lekaron, with slightly better reactions. That should make up for lack of experience.: But he detected a hint of doubt in Kantor's mind-voice, and oddly enough, that comforted him. If Kantor was having feelings of guilt, at least it meant that Alberich wasn't being overly nice about this situation.

:They're terribly young,: he said gloomily.

:Lavan Firestorm and his Companion weren't any older.:

:And Lavan never got the opportunity to grow any older.:

Kantor was silent for a moment. *:Lavan never really got the opportunity to volunteer. Mical did.:*

There was that. But could someone that young have any real idea of what he was volunteering for? Bad enough to take the Trainees he *had*—all adolescents to one extent or another thought they were immortal, that death was something that happened to someone else; the older lot at least were well aware that they could be horribly hurt. But fifteen-year-olds *truly* thought that they were immortal, yes, and invulnerable, that even injuries would nod and pass on by. And in spite of what he'd seen, was this truly informed consent?

:When do you trust someone?: Kantor asked, seemingly out of the blue.

:Excuse me?:

:When do you trust someone? Is it by age, or maturity? What is the magic number? When do Trainees start to think like adults?:

He understood what Kantor was saying, of course, and his head agreed with it. Mical had been there on *the* worst day the team had experienced. He'd watched them for two moons at least. And he'd evidently learned some sobering lessons in the glassworks.

He'd shown every sign of acting in a measured and mature fashion this afternoon. So when did Alberich stop doubting and start trusting?

:When my gut decides to go along with my head, I suppose,: he replied glumly. *:And my gut is going to be screaming, "but he's only a child!" for a little while longer at least.:*

He might have said something more, but at just that moment, a bell rang out, cutting across the winter night.

And for one, horrible moment, he thought it was the Death Bell, and his thoughts fastened on Harrow—

But no, it wasn't. It was the Great Bell at the Palace—not the Collegium Bell, that sounded the candlemarks and the meals, but the huge, deep-toned Bell that sounded only for major occasions. So what—

A moment later, his question was answered.

:It's time! It's Selenay!: said Kantor, and given the gravid condition of the Queen, that was all Kantor needed to say.

Selenay had gone into labor. By dawn, Valdemar would have an Heir-Presumptive.

And from that moment on, the Queen would be standing between Prince Karathanelan and his ambitions.

Alberich shivered. It had begun.

21

"I'M sorry, Weaponsmaster," Mical sighed. He pushed the papers away from him, and reluctantly, Alberich took them and folded them up, tightly. "All I get from them is—" he screwed up his face, "—the writer was in a hurry, really annoyed with something, and wanted to get this over with. I *think* he was that actor fellow—the one we all thought was so—interesting." He paused again, then smiled wanly. "And about the only thing that I can tell you besides that is that he thought the person he was writing to was very, very thick."

Alberich sighed. It had been a long shot, of course. He'd hoped that somehow the secret instructions from Norris to the Prince would have some link to the unknown patron. But—no luck, it seemed. Whoever the patron was, Norris had not been thinking of *him* when he'd been writing the Prince's "scripts."

"My thanks, regardless, Mical," he said. He saw Mical glancing with longing at the door, and he found a bit of sympathy for the boy. It was the first fine day in—well, since autumn. And Mical, no longer under punishment-duty, was probably afire to be out in it. "Go along—"

He hadn't so much as gotten the words out when Mical was out the door like a shot.

"Frustrating," said Myste redundantly. "We've got one end of the path—Norris to Karath. We have the other, Devlin to Norris. But we still don't have the so-called 'patron' who links it all into a neat circle."

"Nor will we," Alberich said with grim certainty. "I believe it was the same person who was paying for unrest against the Queen earlier. I even believe it was the same person who was selling information out of the Council during the Wars. And I have my suspicions who that person is. Unfortunately, I do not have a shred of proof. He is too clever at covering his tracks and hiding his identity. He is *probably* in disguise most of the time when he deals with underlings."

This "certainty" was not true ForeSight, but it came with the scent of ForeSight on it. He would have liked to confide his suspicions to someone who had some other Gift that might be used to spy upon this person, but unfortunately, the suspicion was so wild that he knew that even the Heralds would have stared at him with incredulity.

Yes, even Talamir. Even Myste.

Even, perhaps, most of the Companions.

:*But not me,*: said Kantor, with equal certainty. :*So you and I will watch and wait and bide our time—quietly. We'll catch him eventually.*:

"So all we can do is keep a guard on Selenay?" Myste asked mournfully.

"It seems so," he replied. She sighed.

:*I wish I could tell her,*: he said to his Companion.

:*You can when it's over,*: Kantor replied. :*You're used to keeping secrets.*:

And that, alas, was only too true.

It was just too bad that Selenay had not realized that little fact before all of this had begun, and had confided in *him* rather than—well—whoever she had, who had been so *poor* at keeping them.

Selenay tried to concentrate on the reports in front of her, but her eyes kept drifting to the window, and her thoughts drifting off into nothingness. It was only two moons since the baby's birth. Two moons. Spring was just beginning outside those windows, and she was stuck inside. And when she managed to wrench her eyes and her thoughts back to the job at hand, an angry wail from the next room cut across her concentration and she winced, and shoved down the surge of angry irritation that made her want to go into the nursery and put a pillow over baby Elspeth's face—

And immediately, she felt sick with guilt.

—horrible thought. She was a horrible mother. How could she think such things about the baby? She should have been all moony-eyed and willing to bear with *anything.* She should be longing to hold Elspeth, to cradle her for hours and hours, she should be spending every waking moment hovering over the cradle, gazing down at the little mite with adoration.

Instead, she had thoughts of wanting to smother the poor thing. She was unfit to be a mother. She should never have had a child. . . .

:That's not a child,: Caryo said testily. *:It's a stomach with a warhorn attached to one end, and a mechanism that produces more excrement than a full-grown cow attached to the other.:*

Selenay was glad that there wasn't anyone in the room to see her as she choked on a laugh. There was some truth to that, though Selenay herself seldom had to attend to the latter. Still. The former—

Elspeth's wails scaled up a notch. Selenay's own nurse, old

Melidy, was in charge of the nursery, but she seemed to have her hands full with Elspeth, who had an awfully robust set of lungs for something so small, and the need to demand attention *constantly.*

Do all babies cry so much?

At least baby Elspeth's demands were reasonable; milk, comfort, a clean napkin. Unlike her father. . . .

Selenay's irritation increased, as did her headache.

He'd been pouting again this morning. He didn't even have to *say* anything anymore, just pout and look aggrieved and put-upon. His pouts didn't seem quite so attractive anymore either, and his bereft-orphan pose was beginning to look a great deal more like a pose than like her own, real grief. She knew what true mourning looked like, from the inside, and—well, all his protestations to the contrary, it had begun to look to her as if his father's death and brother's estrangement were things he really didn't feel deeply about.

If at all.

Oh, come now! said her conscience. *You can't blame him for* wanting *to be a King, now that his brother is King of Rethwellan. And he's been thoroughly agreeable since Elspeth was born. Didn't he say he had sent for* his *old nurse for her, so that old Melidy wouldn't have to do all the looking-after by herself? And with two Chief Nursery Attendants on the job, there shouldn't be any more of this howling while you're trying to get some work done.*

Agreeable he might be, but she couldn't help the feeling that it was all on the surface. He certainly wasn't about whenever something needed doing. When they retired for the evening and she wanted to tell him about the annoyances of the day, just to get them off her chest, *he* would launch off into some hunting story or other, ignoring her hints that another topic—*any* other topic—would be welcome. And what had happened to Karath the lover? All very well to speak tenderly of wanting to give her plenty of time to recover from Elspeth's birth, but just how long did he think she needed?

Besides, it wouldn't hurt her to be held and comforted, now and again. She could do with more of the commiseration about the burdens of the Crown that he used to give her, and less complaining that he wanted the crown himself.

He's the father of your child, she reminded herself. Though as Elspeth's wails turned into distinctly angry howls, that was seeming less and less of a good thing.

Finally, just when she thought that her head was going to split, she heard the sound of feet running into the nursery and the howls cut off—and lest she worry that someone *else* had put a pillow over the baby's face, she heard suckling and cooing noises. The wet nurse had been found, it seemed. Her Highness was now satisfied.

If only *His* Highness could be satisfied so easily.

She sighed, and pinched the bridge of her nose to try and ease the pain in her head. Demands for attention, demands for service, wanting everything *now,* this moment, totally self-centered. . . .

Perfectly reasonable in an infant.

Not so attractive in her father. And unfortunately, at this late date he was unlikely to grow out of it. Things seemed dreadfully clear, all of a sudden—when she wasn't looking into those beautiful eyes, and listening to that honey-sweet voice whispering in her ear. When she had been sleeping alone for far too long. When she realized that the demands were never, ever going to stop, and she began to understand Caryo's antipathy to him—and wonder which Karath was the real one.

What was I thinking? she thought with despair. *What have I done?*

She dropped her head into her hands, and for a moment, gave way to the despair.

She who had been afraid of being trapped had trapped herself. She was trapped within the hard shell of the Crown, trapped with an infant she had not really planned for, trapped with a husband who was—

Face it, Selenay—who is beginning to look like someone who put on a show for you.

She wanted, suddenly, to get away, away from the Palace, away from the Crown. Not forever, just for a few candlemarks, where she could be just Selenay, not the Queen, not a mother, just herself. She needed to be able to think clearly, and she couldn't even think at all with the baby fussing in the next room. Something had changed between her and Karath; she needed to figure out what it was, and somehow get things back to the way they had been before that terrible quarrel.

If she could. She had to think about that, too. She had to be able to step back from the whole situation and try to look at it objectively, as if this was Selenay sitting in judgment in the City Courts.

If only she could go somewhere that held no memories of the Prince, where she could be herself entirely again, the Selenay she used to be.

I'll do it. To the seven hells with these reports. They can wait a few candlemarks more. She pushed away from her desk and stood up. *:Caryo? Would you be amenable to a ride to the Home Farms? Just the two of us?:*

This was the best day for practice that they had gotten in a long time. Spring rains hadn't yet begun, the ground was good and dry, and although the air was chill, it was not cold enough to be uncomfortable even if you weren't moving.

Alberich watched his teams as they writhed in a knot of flying sticks and flailing bodies; the view was excellent from the sidelines, and he allowed himself a moment of grim satisfaction. They were good. And they were ready. He had believed in them, and they had repaid that belief in full.

Even young Mical, that most unlikely of prodigals.

The boy had flung himself into his self-appointed niche with the controlled energy of a tightly-wound spring, and a concentration Alberich suspected he never would have had if he had not spent those moons in the glassworks. You dared not lose your concentration around hot glass, for if you did, the best you could expect was the total ruin of all your work. And the worst—the worst could cost a limb, or a life, or worse than just your life, if you were a glassblower. He didn't know if the Collegium Healers could do anything about scorched lungs before the patient died of the injury. He did know that it was one of the nastier and more painful ways to die.

Although no such disaster had occurred at the glassworks while the two Trainees had been serving their time there, Mical had probably been witness to several minor accidents, and certainly had been told all of the horror stories. It was amazing to see the level of steadiness and concentration he had attained—

It was nevertheless true that steadiness and concentration couldn't make up for a difference of three years of age and growth. The boy was *not* the most skilled of the skirmishers. Although in the normal Hurlee games Mical was a star player, in these practices he was merely at the level of all the others. Still, given that they were three years older than he, and had several moons of learning and practice that he *hadn't* had, that was absolutely astonishing.

Part of it, Alberich was sure, was a natural ability in combat, or exercises that were combatlike. Alberich had taught a few youngsters who possessed that near-magical combination of reflexes, strength, coordination, cleverness, and the instinct for combat; Mical was definitely one of that number. Take, for instance, the way that he and Eloran worked together, moving through the pack, smooth as an otter in a fast-flowing stream. Never a wasted moment, often managing to anticipate the next blow and thwart it by the simple expedient of not being there when it fell—

—the next blow—

Flash of blue.

Alberich clung to his pommel as the ForeSight Vision slammed him between the eyes.

Selenay—

But it wasn't a long one.

It didn't need to be, actually. He had spent the last several moons anticipating exactly what it showed him; all it needed to give him was the *where* and the *when.*

Where—

Outside the city walls, on the Home Farms. He recognized that spot, along the riverbank, beyond the point where he and Selenay had fished for eels. It was secluded there, quiet, and out of sight of any of the farmworkers.

When—

Soon—

Too soon. Moments at most. Terror rose in him.

:Not for us!: Kantor said fiercely, before he could even begin to panic, as the players suddenly froze in place, their Companions relaying to them what Alberich and Kantor already knew. "Weapons!" cried Harrow. "No time!" shouted someone else, and suddenly they were all in motion, Alberich and Kantor in the lead, flying across the grass, leaping obstacles, scattering Trainees and courtiers out of their way, and out of the main Palace Gate before Alberich even had time to *think* about what they were doing.

They knew! How did they know?

No—no they didn't know—or hadn't known *consciously* before this moment. But the peak of readiness they had attained was such that at this point they had been ready for *anything.*

:Warn Caryo!: he told Kantor urgently—and needlessly, of course—

:I—the trap's sprung. Don't panic. We can get there in time—: And with grim satisfaction, *:They weren't expecting her to fight.:*

Alberich had his sword, for even in the Hurlee practices he never left the salle without putting it in a saddle sheath. The teams, however, had no weapons. But they *did* have their modified Hurlee sticks, special sticks sheathed in metal, of a wood so hard they called it "ironwood," so dense and tough that even without the metal sheath it dulled blades that tried to cut it. And they were all in their fitted armor, which Alberich had insisted they wear as soon as it was available.

And the *Companions* were armored.

In all the time that Alberich had been a Herald, he had not understood what it was like to be in the saddle when Kantor was at full gallop. He had *heard* about the extraordinary speed of a Companion, but he had never fully experienced it for himself. When Kantor had rescued him from the burning shed and carried him out of Kärse, he had been drifting in and out of awareness.

It was exhilarating and terrifying.

Already the troop was down in the crowded streets of Haven, and the houses and shops blurred past as the hapless bystanders pressed themselves against the walls in an effort to get as far out of the way as possible. Somehow the crowds were parting before them like a school of minnows in front of a pike.

Thank the Sunlord! Being in the lead as he was, he could *see* them making way, as if something invisible was shoving them to either side of the street ahead, just in time to avoid being trampled. But if someone *didn't* get out of the way in time—

:They will. You leave that to us.:

Somewhere behind them, the Palace and Collegia were a-boil; of course, only he and his teams had been *instantly* ready to respond, but the rest, every man and woman who was in

Whites and no few in Grays were scrambling to join the rescue, getting weapons, saddling up—some, like Keren, probably not even bothering with a saddle.

How did that bastard know? The vision had shown him the Prince and a mob of his hangers-on; how had he *known* that Selenay would be there, and alone, when even *he* hadn't known she'd left the Palace?

He must have had a small army of watchers on the Palace, waiting for her to leave under *exactly* the right circumstances, following her to see where she went, sending back the message he had been waiting for. This was not spur-of-the-moment or something conceived in passion. This had been long in the planning, probably from the moment he came into Valdemar.

Or else someone else had planned it all for him.

No time to think about that now. He had to try and remember what the vision had shown him—

Swiftly, as swiftly as Kantor was running, he worked out a rough plan. They'd have to be fools not to expect rescue coming from the Heralds. But they wouldn't be looking for it so soon.

Alarm bells were sounding all over the city; if the Prince had thought he was going to be able to carry this off quietly, he was going to get more than one rude surprise. At least the alarms had the effect of clearing the streets entirely; Kantor somehow redoubled his speed, and they shot through the gates going at such a rate that even Alberich was dizzy. And he was *not* going to think about what would happen if any of them tripped and fell—

There was no finesse in this. Down the road, in at the gates of the Home Farms, riders clutching their weapons in grim silence, hooves pounding like thunder—so loud they couldn't hear the fighting ahead of them—

—so loud that the ambushers surely thought it *was* thunder—

And they didn't even pause as they sighted their target. Just as the team had been taught, just as they had practiced for moons and moons, they crashed in among the milling ambushers, exactly as if it was a Hurlee skirmish. They broke into the mob around Selenay, and their sticks went to work.

In that first and last glimpse, Alberich got the sudden, heart-sinking realization that there were more of them than he had thought there would be, or than he had Seen. A lot more. The odds were roughly two-to-one, in fact.

Hard on the heels of that realization was another—he hadn't *heard* about this down in the rough parts of Haven because the Prince hadn't needed to recruit anyone for this plan. He'd brought them with him, in the guise of servants, of hangers-on, of sycophants.

And last of all—even as he raised his stick and Kantor ran straight into the horse of one of these pseudo-servants, he looked up and saw Selenay lose her sword—

—to Norris. Norris, who had regarded women as mere objects of convenience, and would no more hesitate to kill her than he would hesitate to kill a fly.

There was a bulwark of fighters three deep between him and her. There was no way he could fight his way to her in time.

And that was when he saw the incredible, the miraculous, the totally insane.

Eloran, coming in at full gallop from the *side,* where there was no one in the way; crashing into Norris' horse.

Just as Mical rose in his stirrups, pushed off, and with the momentum of Eloran's charge behind him, flung himself out of his saddle at Norris. *Somehow* he wrapped his arms around the actor when he hit, pinning Norris' sword to his side as they tumbled out of the saddle to the ground. *Somehow* he managed to stay uppermost. They went over the side of the horse and out of sight.

Selenay took advantage of the moment of confusion that

followed to get Caryo a little farther into the open, where the Companion's hooves came into play. That cleared a little more space for her to fight, and as Alberich's stick connected with the man in front of him, Kantor shoved through to her side.

"Here!" he shouted, and tossed his sword, hilt-first, at her.

"Here! Alberich!" he heard from somewhere below, and as Kantor pirouetted on his hindlegs, Mical thrust a sword up at him from the ground, hilt first, doing so left-handed, holding his right tight to his belly. Norris wasn't moving, so the blade was presumably the actor's. Alberich snatched it, and Mical scrambled out of the way. Eloran rammed his way in beside his Chosen, and, even one-handed, Mical was able to haul himself back up into the saddle.

From the way he was holding that arm, however, he wasn't going to be a further factor in the fighting.

Then it all stopped having anything to do with thought, as the mob closed in around them again, and he and Selenay fought side-by-side against the tightening circle. Kantor kept himself interposed as much as he could between the fighters and Caryo. *He* was armored; Caryo was not.

Norris' sword wasn't much better than a Hurlee stick, but at least it had a pointed end and not a blunt one.

And that was just about all that Alberich had time to think about.

Then, for what seemed like forever, it was all shouting, blow and counterblow, screams and blood and last-minute parries, and far too many people trying to kill his Queen.

Until suddenly the fighting melted away from in front of him, and those who were not on the ground groaning (or dead) were in full retreat, as the reinforcements came pounding up on their Companions with swords in their hands and rage on their faces.

And it was at that moment that he looked down and realized that the last man he had bludgeoned to death with that pathetic excuse for a sword was the Prince.

He had not even known who it was he was fighting.

Mical had a broken wrist; there were some slices and cuts to the others, but his was probably the most serious injury. Alberich could have wept with relief; his gamble of putting them into armor had worked, for the Prince's ambushers had foolishly worn none at all.

Mical had done the impossible, and Norris' phenomenal luck had run out just before the Prince's had, for when Mical had hit him and taken him down to the ground, he had not been able to compensate for his attacker's weight. All of his agility and training had, after all, counted for naught. He'd broken his neck as they hit the ground together.

Alberich limped over to where Crathach was tending to the boy, who looked up at him, too weary and full of pain to care about much of anything. "That, one of your fool play-acting moves was," Alberich growled. "Yes?"

The boy nodded.

"And practiced it, you have been?"

Mical hesitated. "Um. *Sort* of. With a straw-man. Eloran and I didn't think it was really going to work, so we'd kind of given up on it, but when we came up on the ambush and saw Norris with Selenay. . . ." He shrugged and hissed with pain. "I *knew* I couldn't fight him; it's not just stage-fighting he knows and he's better than me. The important thing was to immobilize him long enough for you to get to her."

He would have said more, but Alberich held up his hand. "Enough. Good reasoning. Right action. *Never* do it again. Your neck broken, it could have been, not his."

Mical turned a bit green, and not from the pain. Alberich

didn't blame him. This was his first kill, and it had literally been with his bare hands; not an easy thing for a boy of fifteen to cope with. Alberich turned on his heel and left him with Crathach, who was better suited to helping him deal with the emotional ramifications than the Weaponsmaster himself was. Alberich went to find the rest of his team, make sure *they* were all right, and if not, see that they were under someone's wing before he went looking for the Queen.

He found Harrow last of all; the boy was staring down at one of the ambushers' bodies, running his hands reflexively up and down the Hurlee stick. Just as Alberich came up to him, he looked at his hands and realized what he was doing. With an expression of repulsion, he threw the thing away.

"I am *never* playing again!" he said to Alberich, who nodded, understanding all that the youngster could not put into words. That it wasn't a game anymore; that it would be forever tainted for him. That he could never even think of Hurlee without knowing that he had killed at least one man with his stick.

"Go to see Crathach," was all he said, and then made sure that he did so.

:*Why do I think that Hurlee is now going to fade away into the mists that hold all old fads?*: Kantor asked, rhetorically.

:*Oh, someone might revive it again, when this lot has gone on into Whites. Not until then. And that's not a bad thing; it won't be such an obsession when it comes around for the second time.*: He, personally, wouldn't be sorry to see it go. The business of the Collegia was learning, after all, not gamesmanship. And there were other ways to teach teamwork.

Selenay was sitting a little way away, under a tree; when Alberich came up to her, Talamir was speaking earnestly to her in a low voice. Alberich caught the name "Norris" and the word "script" before they both looked up at him.

She had been crying quietly, and she rubbed the tears from her face with the back of her hand. "So it was an act from beginning to end," she said bitterly. "Every bit of it."

"Tailored precisely to you, Majesty," Alberich agreed, since she seemed to be waiting for a reply. "Sorry, I am."

"I don't want your pity!" she snapped, then wilted. "Damn. I apologize. It's not your fault. And I probably wouldn't have listened to you before—" The tears started again; she seemed unaware of them. "It's not fair. I'm glad you killed him."

"Majesty, I am not," Alberich replied, and she looked up at him, startled. "In death, he has escaped the consequences of his actions. And left you to deal with them. I am not glad. And what His Majesty of Rethwellan will say and do, I know not."

"Leave that to me," Talamir said instantly. "Although, given not only what Karath claimed but what my agents have verified for me, there was definitely no love lost between the King of Rethwellan and his brother." He brooded a moment. "No. No love lost at all. He seems to have been—more welcome in his absence than his presence, and it was not by *his* doing that he was not told of his own father's death until it was long past the moment when he could have been recalled for the funeral."

Alberich nodded; that wasn't much of a surprise. "So, King Faramentha, not so displeased to hear of this will be?"

Talamir shrugged. "I believe that if we are discreet, or as discreet as we may be, having roused all of Haven, this will probably be no more than a matter of some delicate maneuvering. In fact, I suspect it will be of more import that it is clear that we do not hold His Majesty responsible for his brother's actions than that we—were forced to eliminate a Prince of Rethwellan."

Alberich caught a little movement from the corner of his eye. Selenay was staring at him. "And when I think of what you've been doing so quietly all this time, Alberich—and to think that at one point I thought you were just jealous because he was as good a swordsman as you and that was why you weren't up at the Palace anymore—you're—"

She was about to say it. He cut her off.

"Selenay, no hero am I," he told her firmly but gently. "For heroes, look to young Mical, who I think was certain he would be killed when the actor he attacked. Or Myste, who is no great dissembler, and could not have herself defended, had Norris discovered her intent."

"If you are no hero, then what are you?" she demanded.

He managed a smile—the first genuine smile he had felt on his face since she'd married. "Your Weaponsmaster. Your Herald." And he held out his hand. "I hope, your friend and brother. Nothing more."

She took it, and looked long and hard at him, and he knew then that at one point she herself must have had something of a crush on him, now long past—but that she was afraid that *he* might now be the one with secret feelings for *her*.

It wouldn't have been the first time such a thing had happened. He was just as glad that the whole notion was so absurd. "I always wanted a brother, growing up," she said aloud, and let go of his hand.

"Good." He smiled again. "Then if my advice you will take, you will make of Myste and Mical great heroes, and let your Shadow Herald stay where best he is suited."

"And I will second that," Talamir agreed, and gave Alberich a look that the Weaponsmaster had no trouble interpreting. *You can go now.*

:Hmph. We know when we aren't welcome.:

:Don't be absurd,: he chided Kantor. *:Do you really want her weeping and raging at us? Then do you want to be embroiled in the political maneuvering this is going to cause?:*

:Well—: Kantor admitted. *:No.:*

:Good.: He scratched his head, encountered a patch of someone else's dried blood in his hair, and grimaced. *:I want a bath. Let's go home.:*

"I may never forgive you," Myste said, her head on his shoulder. It was the first time she'd been in his quarters since the rescue, and he was mortally glad to have her there.

He would be even gladder to have her in his bed—but not quite yet. For now, it was enough to have her in his arms.

"For telling Selenay to make you a hero?" he asked, amused, and shifted a little on the couch so that his position was a little more comfortable. "Someone has to be."

"But why *me?*" she demanded.

"Because you earned it," he replied, staring into the stained-glass face of Vkandis Sunlord. "Because people need heroes. But primarily because you are the *least* likely hero I can think of."

"Well, there I agree with you, but wouldn't that—"

"Hear me out," he interrupted. "People need heroes, and Heralds are that. But Heralds aren't very *ordinary.*"

"Hmm." She did think about it. "I see your point. Most of them are athletic, and even if they aren't handsome, the Whites at least make them look distinguished."

"But you, my dear Chronicler, represent someone who is just like them, or like people they know. And *you* went and did something very dangerous, something that your Whites would not protect you from, something that not even your Companion could have protected you from."

"Hmm." She pushed her lenses up on her nose. "I see your point. And Mical?"

"Everyone likes to have heroes who are young, handsome, and a touch reckless." He laughed. "It won't spoil him. He knows if he gets too much above himself it's back to the glassworks for another couple of moons."

She chuckled. "To think all this began over a broken mirror! Isn't that supposed to mean bad luck?"

"It was bad luck," he pointed out. "For Norris and Karathanelan. Because if it hadn't been for Norris, the mirror would never have gotten broken in the first place."

She fell silent then, leaving him alone with his thoughts. Comforting as it was to think that they had closed the circle, he knew that this was not in the least the case. *Someone* had been Karathanelan's patron, and Norris'; someone who was high in Court circles and privy to some very personal information about Selenay. And they still didn't know who that was.

No, the game wasn't over yet. And if or when *that* person was uncovered, there would, without a doubt, be more troubles on the way.

But at least for a little while, there would be some breathing space. And in the end, that was all anyone, Herald or Queen or ordinary citizen, could ask for.

"Now," he breathed into her hair, "would you like to find out how a hero is rewarded?"

Her response was everything he could have wished for— and he knew that for a few marks, at least, the world would be completely all right for both of them. It would not remain that way for long—

—but it was enough that it remain that way for now.